Memories

to Die For

John V. Kriesfeld

iUniverse, Inc.
Bloomington

Memories to Die For

iUniverse books may be ordered through booksellers or by contacting:

iUniverse
1663 Liberty Drive
Bloomington, IN 47403
www.iuniverse.com
1-800-Authors (1-800-288-4677)

Because of the dynamic nature of the Internet, any web addresses or links contained in this book may have changed since publication and may no longer be valid. The views expressed in this work are solely those of the author and do not necessarily reflect the views of the publisher, and the publisher hereby disclaims any responsibility for them.

Any people depicted in stock imagery provided by Thinkstock are models, and such images are being used for illustrative purposes only.

Certain stock imagery © Thinkstock.

ISBN: 978-1-4697-7322-3 (sc)
ISBN: 978-1-4697-7321-6 (hc)
ISBN: 978-1-4697-7320-9 (e)

Library of Congress Control Number: 2012902215

Printed in the United States of America

iUniverse rev. date: 3/21/2012

Chapter 1

Long days and hours I've toiled with plaguey care,
Still nagging questions asks How? When? and Where?
Old Master Death is feeble grown and slow,
And even loses grip on Whether or No;
On rigid limbs I'd often feast my eyes,
And all was sham, for they would stir and rise.

Goethe, Faust II

Doctor Richard Rathbone watched as a nurse checked the vitals of the patient in room 224. A sign above the bed identified the man as James Chandler. Heavy sounds of mechanical breathing filled the ward as the life-support systems battled to support the patient's vital functions. Rathbone studied Chandler's bloated white face and then reviewed the machine's displays near his bed.

A prime candidate, he thought dispassionately. *Without the machine, he'd be dead in minutes.*

'Let me know immediately when the family arrives,' he instructed the nurse before resuming his tour of the wards.

The call came shortly after 2 p.m. The mother and daughter were hunched nervously around the bed as Rathbone hurried in.

'How are you both today?' he asked sympathetically. They smiled bravely, and he assumed a grave look. 'Would you mind stepping into my office? I have a serious matter to discuss.'

They followed apprehensively, and Rathbone waited until they were comfortably seated.

'I'm sorry to inform you that according to our tests Mr Chandler's brain has degenerated beyond the point of recovery.' Both women gasped, and he turned to address Chandler's wife. 'I know it's distressing, but I need to explain a few things about your husband's situation. Is that all right with you?'

Mrs Chandler nodded weakly, her hands fluttering helplessly on her lap as she struggled to control her emotions. 'Thank you, I'd like to know,' she said finally.

Rathbone inclined his head, acknowledging her spirit. 'Medically speaking, a person is considered to be brain-dead when a critical mass of neurons known as the brainstem is destroyed.'

'Excuse me, doctor,' interrupted the daughter, her voice sounding harsh as she battled to control it. 'Can't the body regenerate these brain cells? Isn't that why people lapse into comas, so the body can rest while it repairs itself?'

'No, I'm sorry, but once a neuron is destroyed it cannot be replaced. Unfortunately, your father lost the supply of oxygen to his brain during his stroke. Although he was resuscitated, critical damage had already occurred.'

Mrs Chandler looked up, her eyes anxious. 'Are you saying he hasn't got much time, Dr Rathbone? He doesn't seem any different to how he's been for the past few days. His breathing even seems a little stronger. Surely that's a good sign, isn't it?'

Rathbone shrugged. 'He's on a respirator, Mrs Chandler. The machine does the breathing for him. Because you want him to improve, you look for little signs to reinforce your belief. I'm sorry, but if you have any last words to say to Mr Chandler, now would be an appropriate time.'

The daughter folded her arms defiantly. 'So you're just going to let him die.'

Rathbone chided her gently. 'Letting him die is only meaningful if we could prolong his life and not do it. In this case, we're allowing your father to die with dignity.'

Mrs Chandler looked wearily at her daughter. 'We've already talked about this, dear. If the machines are of no further use to your father, they should go to somebody who could benefit from them. Your father was never selfish.'

'I'm glad you understand,' murmured Rathbone sympathetically. 'Disconnecting the respirator should be seen as no different to pulling a sheet over the recently dead. These actions symbolize death; they certainly don't contribute to it.' Mrs Chandler was still an attractive woman, and he put a consoling hand on her shoulder. 'I'll tell the ward nurse to give you some privacy.'

Rathbone let his hand linger on her shoulder and then walked briskly from the room and hurried down the corridor into 224. He took a syringe from the thin, metal case in his pocket, filled it with insulin, and injected the liquid into the patient's IV line. Then he slipped into the adjoining ward and waited.

An alarm abruptly sounded, and Rathbone rushed back as several nurses hurried in to attend to the patient.

The Chandler women were by the side of the bed, silently clutching each other; they stared at the monitoring machine as it emitted one long, steady beep. Rathbone pushed his way through to the bedside and quietly asked one of the nurses to take the family members outside. He always enjoyed this piece of theatre. He flicked on a torch and peered under the patient's left eyelid.

'Come on, damn you, be there,' he muttered loudly as he shone the torch directly into the patient's eye, looking for a response. He finally straightened up with a sigh, reached out for the monitor, and turned it off.

'He's gone,' he decreed gravely. 'Send his body to pathology immediately. I will carry out the post-mortem.'

Mother and daughter looked at him fearfully as he joined them in the passage, and he dramatically shook his head. 'I'm sorry; it happened even quicker than I thought.'

The daughter wiped away her tears with the back of her hand. 'Are you sure? You didn't even try to resuscitate him.' Her tone was accusing. 'I mean, I've read about supposedly dead people waking up in morgues and at funerals, and I just wondered ...' Her voice trailed off as she stared at him.

'No, no,' he said patiently. 'The machines were keeping his body functioning, but his consciousness, his core being, was no longer there. If it will help, we do have grief counsellors available.'

'No, that won't be necessary,' said the mother, pulling herself up to her full height, the strength in her quite apparent. 'It's probably for the best. It's time he was left in peace, but I would like to be alone with him for a moment.'

'I understand,' said Rathbone as he glanced at the nurse busily detaching the machines from Chandler's body. 'You can have a couple of minutes once the nurse has finished.' He spoke briefly to the nurse, nodded to the family, and quietly left the room. Within seconds, his solemn demeanour disappeared and he whistled happily as he strolled back to his office. When seated at his desk, he put through a call to his business associate.

A soft, sibilant voice answered. 'Borkov speaking.'

'Isaac, it's Richard. I have another package for delivery.'

'Excellent work, Richard. Your usual fee will be deposited into your account upon receipt. You may be interested to know we are about to launch Prototype One once the software is installed. If Prototype One is successful, we will start placing advance orders with you. Your business is going to pick up.'

'I'm not sure I follow you. I'm already supplying your needs now.'

'Yes, but the haphazard nature of your current delivery program will not be suitable once we move to our next operational phase. We will place an order for a certain date, and you will fill it.'

Rathbone frowned. 'You have to understand, Isaac, that a suitable package may not be available when your order comes through.'

Borkov laughed carelessly. 'No, my friend, you have to understand that the package will be available when ordered. The success of our enterprise depends upon it. You're a resourceful person and have a wonderful supply of raw materials. I have full faith in you.'

Rathbone shook his head in annoyance. 'I don't think so, Isaac, it's too dangerous. This is beyond our agreement. You don't know what you're asking for.'

'My dear Richard, I know exactly what I'm asking for, and believe me, it will be far more dangerous if you don't do as I ask. Too many powerful people have a vested interest in this project to allow your misplaced ethics to get in the way.'

'Are you threatening me, Isaac?'

'Of course,' replied Borkov as he ended the call.

Rathbone stared at the phone in consternation, knowing he was trapped. If he went to the authorities, he would be charged with murder. Borkov was right about one thing: he was resourceful, and he slowly relaxed as he considered his options. If he handled things carefully, everything should be okay. He could certainly do with the extra money. Maybe it wouldn't be so bad after all.

Chandler's body was delivered to pathology shortly after 3 p.m. Rathbone had fewer than twenty minutes to complete his task, as degeneration to the brain after that point would make it unusable. He adeptly cut around the scalp just into the hairline and peeled the skin back from the skull. Then he cut the top off the cranium with a surgical saw.

The flow of blood was minimal, which allowed him to perform the operation by himself. Using a slender pair of shears, he began snipping around the extremities of the brain. His instructions had specifically stated that he protect the lobes of the left hemisphere.

The final section was the hardest. He gently lifted the brain from the rear, inserted the shears underneath until he reached the spinal cortex, and began the awkward task of detaching the brain. It came away quickly. He placed the brain in a metal ice chest, carefully packing shaved ice around it.

Returning his attention to the body, he cleaned the edges of the skull, glued the top of the cranium into place, carefully folded the peeled skin around the skull, and stepped back to admire his handiwork.

'Not bad, if I do say so myself,' he muttered softly. Many families insisted upon 'viewing' funerals, and it wouldn't do to have a body with the top of its skull missing. He tugged off his surgical gloves and hurried to meet the courier outside the Pathology entrance.

～

A man of medium height alighted from a taxi as it stopped outside a spacious house set neatly among aging elm trees. He tugged a coat around his shoulders and hurried through the rain, only stopping when he reached the shelter of the veranda. He glanced curiously at the sombre funeral wreath fastened to the front door, absently touching the leaves as he pondered its significance. He then keyed in the security code and entered the house.

An observer, parked in the shadows across the road, captured his actions on a digital camera.

Once inside, the man draped his wet coat over a chair and ambled towards the kitchen, pausing in the doorway to admire the trim figure of his wife as she busied herself peeling potatoes. He had always liked her in black, although she usually softened the effect with a colourful scarf or blouse.

His wife had aged elegantly and, while well into her fifties, she looked ten years younger. He smiled as he crept up behind her and covered her eyes. 'Guess who, my little chicken?'

The blonde woman stiffened in shock. She tugged free and whirled around, her eyes wide. She screamed and pressed back against the bench.

'Who are you?' she gasped, her hand fluttering to her throat, and the potato peeler dropping to the floor. 'What are you doing in my house?' Her breathing was laboured.

'Honey, what's the matter? It's me,' he said softly as he stepped towards her.

She inched away from him until she found herself trapped in the corner. 'Don't come any closer,' she warned weakly as she grabbed a large soup ladle and held it defensively in front of her.

'Come on, Annie, this is ridiculous. What's gotten into you?' he asked, puzzled by her behaviour. He sensed movement behind him and turned to face an angry young woman brandishing a golf club.

'Tracey ...' he began, but her savage words cut him off.

'Get away from my mother, you bastard. Who the hell do you think you are, creeping in here and scaring the daylights out of her? Get out now, or I'm calling the police.' She held the club higher and took a step towards him.

'Now, just hold on a minute, Tracey,' he said in a mixture of anger and bewilderment. 'What's going on? Why are you behaving like this?' He turned and sat on a chair, folding his arms as he did so. 'If you're playing a joke, it's in very poor taste. I've had a hard day, and I don't expect to come home and be treated as if I've stepped into another dimension.'

'Your home? Are you insane?' The young woman brandished the club menacingly.

He waved a hand at her. 'Take it easy with that club, Tracey. It was a present from your mother, and I wouldn't like to see it damaged.'

The blond woman gave a small gasp. 'How did you know that? Who are you?'

The man stared at her with genuine concern. 'What's the matter with you? Have you both been drinking? It's me, James,' he said with a frown. 'Your husband.'

'You low-life scum,' the young lady screamed as she rushed towards him. 'My father died of a heart attack five days ago. We buried him this afternoon, you sick bastard.' She swung the golf club at him, and he only avoided serious injury by tumbling backwards off the chair.

'Jesus Christ!' he shouted indignantly. 'What's gotten into you both?' He rolled away from the outstretched golf club and quickly moved to the other side of the table.

Tracey brandished the golf club in his face from across the table. 'You've had your chance. Leave now or I'm calling the police.'

'That's fine with me. Let's get this sorted out.' His neck felt stiff and bruised, and he gave it a quick rub as he struggled to make sense of the situation; when he looked up, nothing had changed.

'Go on,' he repeated, 'call the police.' He turned back to the woman who had been his wife for the past thirty-four years. 'Listen, honey, I don't understand how you can stand there and tell me you don't know who I am. I'm your husband for God's sake.' He spread his arms beseechingly. 'Look at me? Do I look dead to you? Ask me anything you like.' He thought for a moment. 'What about that small scar on the inside of your thigh? You told me you got that falling off your bike when you were a young girl.'

The older woman stared at him in horror and began sinking slowly to the floor. 'How could you know that?' she whispered despairingly. 'Please don't say anything more. Just go away.'

Tracey hung up the phone and hurried over to her mother. 'The police are on their way.' She turned and snarled at the man. 'I hope they lock you away forever. How do you know about us? Have you been spying on my mother?'

The man sat down and slumped miserably against the table. 'I don't understand any of this.' He suddenly straightened and looked at the two women. 'Annie, your favourite colour is light blue, you have a handicap of 18 at golf, you were born in May, your best friend is Mary, and the first dog we owned was called Dusty. I know you hate pumpkin, and I know Tracey had her appendix out when she was seven. Ask me anything you like. Go on, ask me.'

The two women huddled closer together as they watched him in mute horror. A police siren sounded faintly in the distance.

'Please, I beg you,' said the older woman, 'don't do this. Please.' Her voice trailed off, and she hid her face in her daughter's shoulder, small sobs racking her body.

The three of them waited in heavy silence as the siren grew closer. A loud knock at the door caused the man to jump nervously. Tracey backed slowly to the doorway, and a buzzer sounded as she pressed a button in the panel by the door. 'We're in the kitchen!' she yelled, her voice tinged with relief. 'The door's open.'

A burly police sergeant holding a collapsible baton moved cautiously into the kitchen followed by his female partner.

'You won't need that, officer.' The man sighed. 'This is just a bad dream. It'll be okay once I wake up.'

'Sure, mister,' replied the policeman pleasantly. 'In the meantime, please place your hands on the table where I can see them. And you can put down that golf club, young lady; your grip's all wrong to start with.' He paused while he replaced the baton in his belt. 'Now, who can explain the problem?' He nodded towards Mrs Chandler. 'Why don't you go first, madam?'

The older woman looked up at him with tear-filled eyes. 'I'm Anne Chandler, and this man says he's …' She turned to look at her daughter and began sobbing again.

'I'll tell you,' said Tracey bitterly. 'This has been a terrible week for us, and now this scumbag has made it worse by breaking into our house and terrorizing my mother.'

'Terrorizing in what way?'

Tracey snorted. 'I know it's ridiculous, but he claims to be her husband, my father, for God's sake. I think he's a bit, you know.' She tapped the side of her head.

'Is that right, sir?' asked the sergeant. 'Do you claim to be this lady's husband?'

'Of course I'm her husband,' spluttered the dark-haired man in exasperation. 'How can I not be?'

Tracey glanced meaningfully at the officer and rolled her eyes.

'Do you have any identification on you, sir?' asked the sergeant, firmly but politely.

The man patted his pockets. 'No, I'm sorry. I don't appear to have my wallet with me.'

'Never mind,' said the sergeant amiably. 'It shouldn't be too hard to get to the bottom of this.' He thought for a moment before turning to the daughter. 'Would you fetch a recent photo of your father? Oh … and a mirror.'

'Sure,' replied Tracey with sudden understanding. She returned almost immediately and handed the photograph and mirror to the sergeant.

'Now, sir,' said the policeman patiently. 'Please look at this photograph and tell me who it is. Take your time, please.'

The dark-haired man grabbed the photo and glanced at it. 'That's a picture of me taken at my niece's wedding last year. Remember,' he said turning towards the woman, 'you made me buy a new suit.'

The blond woman continued sobbing into her daughter's shoulder.

'Now, sir,' continued the policeman calmly. 'Look into this mirror, and tell me who you see.'

'You've got to be kidding,' spluttered the man. 'Who do you think I'm going to see, the man in the moon? Jesus! Now I know I'm dreaming.'

'Sir,' repeated the policeman stubbornly as he held out the mirror.

The man gave an exasperated sigh and snatched the mirror from the officer's outstretched hand. 'Okay, if it'll make you happy.' He looked at the mirror and jerked his head back as if he'd been struck, his eyes growing large. 'That's me as well,' he finally whispered as he continued to stare at his image. 'How could I have forgotten that?'

'Sir?' prompted the sergeant. 'Do you have a statement to make?'

'I ... that is ...' He dropped the mirror on the table and put his head in his hands. 'What the hell is happening to me?' The room had gone very quiet.

'My name', he said finally, 'is Stephen Kimpton. I remember that now. But'—he hesitated—'it's also James Chandler. How can that be?' His voice rose to a higher pitch. 'I've never met Mrs Chandler before in my life, and yet I've been married to Annie for more than thirty years.'

'Take it easy, sir,' said the sergeant gently. 'Are you currently on any medication?'

Kimpton looked at him blankly. 'No, I'm not on any drugs if that's what you mean, but I have been taking pills for high blood pressure. Well, that is ... if I'm James, I have.' He lapsed into silence.

'How old are you, Stephen?' asked the policewoman.

'Nineteen.'

'Then how can you be this lady's father?' she said, pointing to Tracey.

The thin man's face took on a very unhealthy pallor. 'I know I can't be, and I also know that I always have been,' he stammered. He started to rise and staggered, his eyes rolling up into his head as he crashed to the floor with a sickening thud.

'Maybe that'll knock a bit of sense into him,' muttered the sergeant dryly. 'Get on the blower, and call an ambulance,' he directed his colleague. He turned to the two women who were staring wide-eyed at the body on the floor. 'He obviously has an unhealthy fixation on the two of you. Have you seen him following you around?'

The two women looked at each other and shook their heads.

'He knows so many intimate details about us,' said Mrs Chandler, almost to herself. 'Do you think he's dangerous?' The officer shrugged absently. 'That's for the psychiatrists to determine. However, I recommend you change the security number for your alarm. How he got hold of that is a worry in itself.'

'Sarge?' said the young policewoman as she returned to the room. 'I ran a check, and a Stephen Kimpton was reported missing two days ago.'

∼

Laura Munroe snuggled closer to the warm body lying next to her. She had been sharing an apartment with Daniel Jordan for three years and was as much in love with him now as she'd been when they moved in together. She detected the faint smell of apples as her face brushed lightly against his hair. *He's been using my shampoo again*, she thought, and gave him a playful slap on the bottom.

A muffled, 'What?' rewarded her effort.

'You're snoring again,' she said accusingly.

'Huh,' he mumbled only half-awake. 'I don't snore. You probably woke yourself up.'

'Are you accusing me of snoring?' she said indignantly as she gave his bottom another slap.

'Do fish swim?' He scrunched himself into a protective ball as she rained ineffective blows on his bare skin.

'Well, that's my morning exercise taken care of,' Laura said as she flung the blankets to one side.

'There are other exercise options, you know,' suggested Jordan hopefully.

'You never miss an opportunity do you?' Laura laughed as she threw her pillow at him. It struck a marble statuette on the bedside table, causing it to topple over. As it executed a reverse somersault, Jordan reached out and plucked it to safety. Laura smiled gratefully as she climbed slowly out of bed.

Jordan watched her as she pulled on a satin robe. 'Marry me,' he said quietly.

She half-turned to face him, and he noticed the sadness in her eyes. 'We've been through this before, Dan. I need security. It's fine while I'm working, but what happens when I become pregnant? I have no intention of ditching my baby in a day care centre because I need to go back to work.'

'I'll have a regular job by then,' he argued. 'I'm only one good story away from getting a job with a major paper. '

'You've been one good story away for the past two years.'

Jordan looked at her in surprise. 'That's not fair. Everybody in the business knows you have to do your apprenticeship as a freelance journalist if you want to make it into the big league.'

'Yes, but what about Frank Johnson and Sam what's-his-name? They're still working freelance and are as poor as church mice. Why don't you face it: most freelance journalists never make it into the big league.'

'Both Sam and Frank work that way because they enjoy the lifestyle.'

'Why don't you ask their wives if they "enjoy the lifestyle"? Look, Dan, you're a trained electrical engineer. Get a proper job, and I'll happily discuss marriage with you. Now, if you'll excuse me, I must have my shower or I'll be late.'

'Bitch,' he muttered as she left the room.

'I heard that,' she called sweetly.

'You were supposed to,' he yelled. He thumped the statuette noisily back onto the bedside table.

The Memtech board members clapped respectfully as their CEO, Jean-Paul Toulemonde, entered the room. Toulemonde was tall, angular, and almost bald. His cheeks were slightly sunken in his half-moon face, and although his eyes twinkled cordially, the benevolence was false. When he spoke, everybody listened.

Toulemonde smiled at the applause and then waved the directors into congenial silence. 'It is my proud duty to declare that Project Brain Drain is an unqualified success. I offer my sincere thanks to all of you for helping make this dream a reality. We have now moved beyond the dream and are finally in a position to take advantage of the reality. The next phase, however, is critical. Our London facility can service our initial requirements, but we must expand once the orders start rolling in. Our French facility is almost operational, but we will need further capital to develop new facilities in Japan and the United States. I agree that opening this venture to outside investors is risky, but time is not on our side. Today we must decide whether we're going to be a global force with the will and the passion to dominate world affairs or a local concern whose members are nothing more than a closet secret society.' He laughed sharply. 'I think you know my views.'

'Indeed we do, Jean-Paul.' An elderly man with finely chiselled features and oily grey hair raised a common concern. His name was Dermot Jarvis, a senior government public servant who covertly channelled government funds in Memtech's direction. 'Global dominance is an excellent motivator, but it's difficult to enjoy power and wealth if we're languishing behind bars. It is too early to go public on this.'

Toulemonde glanced around the room in quiet amusement. 'I'm sure we will eventually achieve our goals if we remain small scale, but none of us will be alive to see it, and I personally have an issue with that.' There were a few quiet chuckles. 'There has never been a greater prize in history, and the risks therefore must be commensurate. We have the opportunity to establish a vast, global dynasty, and it is imperative that we gain the necessary funding by making our services available to the people who can afford them.'

He looked around the room, gauging the level of support by the faces of his audience. 'We have spent the past six months identifying like-minded people in the broader community who we believe, given the opportunity to share the benefits, would gladly invest. We have checked their bank accounts, backgrounds, and beliefs, and we're confident that if approached correctly, they will become enthusiastic devotees to our cause.'

'It's still a risk,' repeated Jarvis. 'I have made government funds available in the past and plan to do so in the future, so there is no reason why we cannot continue to grow. Although the growth will be more circumspect, it will certainly be 100 per cent safer. The more people involved, the greater the chance of exposure.'

Toulemonde looked scornful. 'A business venture such as this requires some risks, so while we appreciate your financial assistance, your public service mentality is a hindrance to us.' He stared slowly around the table. 'Is there anybody else who shares Dermot's reservations?' The other members remained silent, although several of them chose to stare at the table.

'Excellent,' beamed Toulemonde. 'I applaud your courage. Our world will never be the same.'

Jarvis left the meeting in a concerned frame of mind. As his car hurried through the traffic, he rang ahead and arranged a meeting with his boss, Sir Rupert Northfield. Sir Rupert's department officially existed as an arm of the Department of Trade but was actually a shadowy extension of MI6. The department secretly funded the development of new, risky technology. Most politicians weren't even aware of its existence.

'How's our investment paying off?' asked Northfield as he lounged back in his chair.

'They're making solid progress. Surprisingly, they've actually downloaded memory from one individual to another.'

Northfield frowned as he leant forward. 'You're certain it's not a con job? How do you know they're not lining their pockets and covering up with spurious data?'

Jarvis hesitated. 'It's a possibility, but I seriously doubt it. They regard me as one of their own, so if I'm being conned, so is the rest of the board.'

'Well, I'm pleased they're making progress. Was that the reason for this meeting?'

'In part, but my main concern is that they want to inject further funds by organizing a cartel of investors.'

Northfield's voice hardened. 'That's just too damned risky. Tell them they can't do it.'

Jarvis massaged his eyes wearily. 'I tried, but they refused to listen, and I didn't like to push too hard in case I alienated myself.'

'They'd be finished if news leaked out. If we got our hands on their procedure, could our people replicate the results?'

'Yes, if they were given enough time.'

'Hmm,' mused Northfield as he sank back into his chair. 'Imagine what the foreign office could do with such a technology. Keep me informed, but if they slip up, we'll need to move in immediately and secure their premises. We cannot risk this information becoming common knowledge; otherwise we'd never be able to use it ourselves.'

Chapter 2

Lord! In your name, even evil spirits are under our control!
And He said to them: 'I saw Satan falling
like lightning from Heaven.
You know: I gave you power …
over all the strength of Satan …
Nevertheless, don't take pride in the fact
that spirits are subject to your control,
but, rather, because you belong to God …
The Father has given Me all power.
Luke 10:17–22

Laura sighed as she mulled over Stephen Kimpton's file. It just didn't make sense. She had interviewed his mother, his sister, and three university colleagues to help her understand the case but found nothing.

One interesting aspect was that nobody had seen him for nearly a week prior to the incident. His disappearance had caused his mother to notify the police.

Stephen's medical history was normal with no family history of mental disorder. He was a bright student who worked several part-time jobs to support himself. His friends confirmed that Stephen was not into drugs, although even if he were, that wouldn't explain his intimate knowledge of the Chandler family.

She leafed through the statements made by the Chandlers, searching for a clue she overlooked. Stephen had known the security code and had drawn an accurate layout of the house, and yet the Chandlers were adamant that they didn't know him. Laura had reviewed her textbooks on multiple personality disorders without success, hoping to discover something.

There was a knock on the door, and she smiled as an orderly ushered Kimpton into the room. 'Stephen, it's good to see you again. Please sit down,' she said brightly. Stephen looked at her in hopeful expectation. His pallid complexion and the dark smudges under his eyes were more pronounced. 'How have you been?' she asked. 'Have you been eating well?'

He shrugged listlessly. 'Not really. The food's okay, but I don't have an appetite.'

'You must keep your strength up.'

'Yeah, right, healthy body and healthy mind—that's a joke,' he said bitterly.

'Have you been getting much sleep?'

He looked at her defensively. 'It's the dreams,' he finally muttered.

'What about the dreams, Stephen?'

'I know I'm not really this Chandler character, and if I concentrate I can remember my life before he came along. But when I go to sleep, my dreams become confused, and I wake up feeling quite nauseated.'

'Can you explain why you thought you were James Chandler before? Why you went to his house?'

He stared at her, his eyes slightly glazed. 'You still don't understand, do you? I am Stephen Kimpton, and I am also James Chandler. It's as though there are two people sharing my brain. I only have to think *I'm James Chandler* and I can tell you everything about myself. About James, that is,' he added hurriedly.

'So, you're aware that you are James Chandler and Stephen Kimpton—both at the same time?' she asked kindly, hoping that a gentle probe might uncover the answer.

'Yes,' he exclaimed in exasperation. 'Didn't I just say that?'

'Then why didn't you know you were Stephen Kimpton when you went to the Chandlers' house last week?'

'I don't know. I'd forgotten who I really was. I can't explain it,' he said miserably.

'So who are you at this very moment?'

'Who would you like me to be?' He sounded distant.

'Have you remembered how you got the bruise on your neck?' she asked, changing the subject.

He grimaced. 'No, that's another mystery. I don't know how that happened.'

'It's probably not important. What about your memory of the week prior to your arrest? Has anything come back?'

He snorted derisively. 'I have two memories, and both of them are blank. What are the odds on that?'

'Indeed,' murmured Laura as she made a note. 'Neither your mother nor your friends have heard of James Chandler until last week. What does that suggest to you?'

His tone hardened. 'I have no idea. I can only tell you what I remember.'

She turned several pages in his file. 'I have a statement by the Chandlers concerning your visit. Do you remember that Tracey said her father died of a heart attack?'

Kimpton shook his head slowly. 'I know I'm not James, but I remember everything that he knew. It's like we're both sharing the same body, but I'm the one driving.'

'Does James ever take over?'

'No, and I don't know why I thought I was James before. I was just confused. I'm sorry I upset his family.'

'I only asked about James because I wondered how self-aware you are.'

'I'm aware, all right. I'm aware I'm losing my friggin' mind.'

'Stephen,' Laura said finally. 'You mustn't give up hope. We're doing everything possible to help you. Something happened during the week prior to your arrest, and once we understand what it was, we'll have an idea of what we're dealing with.'

Kimpton looked at her with sudden desperation. 'I'm bloody possessed, I know it. I've read about it, but I've never believed it.'

'You're not possessed,' Laura said firmly. 'Stephen, I need your permission to search your apartment to try to find some clue as to your whereabouts during that period.'

'Sure, why not. Feed my goldfish while you're there,' he added listlessly.

'I'm sure your mother's been feeding your goldfish.'

'My mother's been dead for nearly twenty years ... no hang on a moment ... wrong memory.' He laughed nervously. 'The thing that worries me is the fact that I haven't fully come to grips with what's happened. I think once I do, I'll just go insane, instantly, at that very point of understanding. My greatest defence is denial, and that's wearing thin.'

Laura looked at him momentarily and then pressed the buzzer for the orderly.

Kimpton was her last case for the afternoon. After he left, she locked her office and walked thoughtfully down the corridor, waving absently to several people who called good night to her. Dr Colin Tweddle walked out of his office and fell into step beside her.

'Fancy a quick drink before you go home?' he asked as he placed his hand on her arm.

Tweddle specialised in marriage guidance counselling amid persistent rumours that he took advantage of the vulnerable women who came to see him.

Laura shook her head. 'Some other time, Colin. I'm in the middle of a difficult case and plan to spend the evening doing research.'

'Know what your problem is? You get too involved in your cases. You need to get out and relax more. If you're not careful you'll end up being somebody else's case study.' They caught the lift to the underground parking lot, and Tweddle stood back, allowing her to leave first.

'Thanks for the invite, Colin. I'll keep your advice in mind.'

'Any time,' he called, admiring the sensuous sway of her hips as she walked briskly to her car.

~

Paul Frampton lounged comfortably in his executive chair as he read his mail. He had inherited his newspaper empire, and although sales were slowly declining, it was still a force to be reckoned with. Frampton's opinions became those of his paper and regularly shaped the thoughts of 19.7 per cent of the population.

He picked up an embossed envelope marked 'Private and Confidential'. He extracted the carefully folded note and straightened in his chair as he noted the signature. 'Jean-Paul Toulemonde,' he murmured. He had met Toulemonde at a dinner party several years ago but had seen nothing of him since.

'What the hell does he want?' he muttered as he began reading.

Dear Paul,

Do you dream of true immortality?
This power is now attainable—for a price.
Do you thirst for the knowledge others want kept hidden?
This ability is now attainable—for a price.
An intimate gathering of your peers has been arranged to enlighten you on the information presented above.
You are an astute man. Ignore this unparalleled opportunity to invest in your own future at your peril.
Full details are attached. I look forward to the pleasure of your company.

Sincerely yours,
Jean-Paul Toulemonde
CEO, Memtech Industries.

'Toulemonde's gone senile,' he muttered, although he thought it might be amusing to see who else had received an invitation.

∼

Laura Munroe pushed a chunk of fried chicken listlessly across her plate, decided against eating it, and took another sip of Chardonnay.

Daniel Jordan chided her gently. 'I think your chicken has travelled more miles dead than when it was alive.'

'I'm sorry,' she said ruefully. 'I have something on my mind.'

He feigned surprise. 'Really? I had no idea.'

'That's the whole problem. I have no idea either, and it's driving me crazy.'

'Care to share? Talking through a problem often helps.'

'Thank you, doctor; I must remember that next time I meet with a patient.'

'I know your work is confidential, but if you want to talk about it in general terms, I'm happy to act as a sounding board. I'm serious. If you continue to bottle up these problems, you'll end up in therapy yourself.'

Laura gave a wry smile. 'You're the second person to say that to me today.'

'There you are then; it must be true. Who was the other person?'

She pulled a face. 'Colin Tweddle. He asked me out for a drink. Said I needed to unwind.'

Jordan frowned. 'Wasn't he the one at your Christmas party who couldn't keep his hands off you? I think it's more than drinks he's after.'

Laura laughed pleasantly. 'Colin's harmless. Now if you really want to help, come with me while I look through the apartment of one of my patients.'

Jordan raised his eyebrows. 'That's a little unusual, isn't it?'

'It's an unusual case. Will you do it?'

'Okay, but only if you share this unusual problem with me.'

Laura hesitated. 'All right, but you know I can't go into specifics.'

Once she finished her summary, Jordan sat looking at her with a bemused expression. 'The guy's right; he's possessed. What else can it be? For nineteen years he's normal, and then this other fellow dies and moves in with him. It sounds like possession to me.'

Laura looked at him. 'You're an expert on possession, are you?'

'No, but I'll do some research and get back to you. Until we understand more it can't be ruled out.'

～

Jordan parked outside a block of run-down apartments the following morning. It was a typical low-rent building, ideal for struggling students, and it took only a moment to locate Kimpton's apartment. The small rooms and limited furniture made their search a simple task, and it didn't take long for Laura to discover Stephen's diary stacked away neatly on a computer table in his bedroom.

She flipped through the pages until she came to Tuesday, 28 February, the day of his arrest. He had a physics paper due on Monday and had a relatively quiet weekend planned prior to that.

Jordan walked up behind her and peered over her shoulder. 'What have you discovered?'

'Nothing yet.' She continued reading. Thursday the twenty-third was the day James Chandler had been officially pronounced dead, but the only entry for that day referred to an appointment with the notation 'Memtech'. 'This could be something,' she said expectantly, pointing to the entry.

'Memtech? Never heard of it. Let me check the telephone directory.' Jordan grabbed the book from underneath the telephone but was unable to find a listing.

'I'll talk to Stephen about it this afternoon,' said Laura. 'He may be able to shed some light on the subject.'

However, the session with Stephen proved unproductive, and Laura left for home feeling increasingly frustrated. He had never heard of Memtech and had no idea why he had written the note in his diary. He was sinking deeper into depression, and Laura was concerned about his well-being.

It was her turn to cook dinner, but the meal was below her usual standard. 'I'm sorry,' she apologised as she handed Jordan his plate. 'I'm just not in the mood for cooking.'

'That's okay, I'm sure you'll find a way to make it up to me.'

'I'm not in the mood for that either.'

'Anything I can do to help?'

'If you can track down Memtech, I might have a mood swing,' she said sweetly.

Jordan brightened. 'What if I enrolled in an evening class at Kimpton's university? I could discretely enquire about Memtech.'

She raised one eyebrow. 'What class would you do?'

'What about pottery?'

'Pottery! What made you think of that?'

'Oh, I don't know really,' he replied casually. 'I just have this sudden urge to pot. I need to let my artistic juices flow.'

'Well, I'm sure if you put your hand to it, you'll manage beautifully,' she answered pleasantly.

'Yeah, right,' he muttered.

~

Laura Monroe received an excited call from Jordan the following morning.

'Laura,' he bellowed over the phone. 'I've found something.'

'I'm not deaf,' she replied as she held the phone away from her ear. 'What did you find?'

'I found a note on the student notice board. Memtech Industries wants volunteers for research into past-life memory. They're paying twenty pounds an hour, and there's a phone number.'

'That's an attractive offer for a struggling student. I'll give them a call and see if they have any information on Stephen. What are your plans for this afternoon?'

'I've arranged a meeting with a priest called Father O'Brien to discuss demonic possession. He does exorcisms, and I'm hoping he'll allow me to watch him in action. I already have expressions of interest from two magazines and a Sunday paper. I should have become involved in your work sooner.'

'My work does not involve demonic possession,' she said icily.

'I'll allow my readers to interpret the facts for themselves.'

Laura rang the Memtech Industries number immediately after lunch and was transferred to Moira Ridgeway, the memory-research department head. She explained her official involvement and then asked to know what sort of testing Stephen Kimpton had undergone.

Ridgeway hesitated. 'The name isn't familiar. Let me check the files.'

When she returned several minutes later, Laura thought she detected a nervous edge to her voice. 'Stephen Kimpton was a test subject here, but we weren't able to use him.'

'Why not? What was the problem?'

'Unfortunately, he wasn't suitable. Are you familiar with our activities?'

'Not really.'

'We're a private corporation. Most of our funding is derived from private sources, although we do receive a small research grant. As a psychologist, I'm sure you're familiar with past-life memory.'

'I have read about it,' confirmed Laura, 'although I prefer to suspend judgement upon its authenticity.'

'I was sceptical myself before I joined Memtech. However, we have hundreds of files filled with recordings of people speaking foreign languages they normally have no knowledge of or speaking English with idioms and grammatical constructions consistent with sixteenth- or seventeenth-century society. None of this can be explained logically.'

'It is interesting,' agreed Laura a little impatiently.

'It's only possible to fully examine this phenomenon under hypnosis,' continued Ridgeway. 'Our research has discovered many subjects whose memories correlate with documented happenings of individuals who lived and died many years ago.'

'So Stephen was one of those people?' prompted Laura.

'Unfortunately, no,' answered Ridgeway quickly. 'Our testing indicated that he wouldn't make a productive subject.'

'Why not?'

Ridgeway explained cautiously, 'Approximately 20 per cent of the population have an innate resistance to hypnosis and therefore make poor test subjects. Stephen fell into this category.'

'So he was tested and deemed not suitable,' confirmed Laura. 'What usually happens then?'

'Nothing. We pay them for their time and then show them the door. Can I ask what this is all about?'

'Stephen is suffering short-term memory loss from around the time he visited your centre. In fact, he has no memory of having been to Memtech at all. Could his memory loss be a reaction to the hypnosis treatment he received?'

'Stephen was only given a suitability trial to test his susceptibility to hypnosis. He wasn't actually hypnotized, so it's not possible that we're responsible for his memory loss. It could have occurred as a result of many things. A knock to the head while playing a sport for example.'

'You could be right. He did have a nasty bruise on his neck when he was brought to me.'

'There you are,' said Ridgeway triumphantly. 'However, I assume there is more to this than what you've told me. The Department of Corrective Services isn't usually involved with matters of simple memory loss.'

'Indeed,' confirmed Laura pleasantly. 'However, in this case it's more personal curiosity than anything else. Thank you for your help.'

After hanging up, Ridgeway immediately sought out Borkov in his office. 'We have a problem, Dr Borkov.'

'Yes?' replied Borkov, raising his right eyebrow fractionally.

'I just received a call from the Department of Corrective Services concerning Stephen Kimpton.'

'How did they know to call here? You assured me that all knowledge of Memtech had been erased from Kimpton's memory.'

'Blocked, not erased,' corrected Ridgeway stiffly.

His dark eyes met hers. 'I'm not interested in semantics. Just answer the damn question.'

Her lips had suddenly become very dry, and she licked them nervously. 'I don't know how they knew.'

'For God's sake, didn't you ask?' he roared.

'I was surprised by the call. I didn't think to ask.'

Borkov took a deep breath. 'All right, tell me what they wanted to know.'

Ridgeway repeated the conversation. Borkov turned and stared out the window as he sifted through the implications. A beady-eyed dove stared back at him from the window ledge. 'I don't believe any damage has been done, but we cannot afford to take chances. Inform your staff that any further calls concerning Project Lazarus must be directed to me.'

'Yes, Dr Borkov,' she answered heavily.

'Leave the Kimpton file on my desk on your way out.' He waved his hand dismissively, and she fled gratefully from his office. He took a small black book from his inside pocket and flicked through it until he found the number he wanted. The phone rang twice before a terse voice answered.

'Michael Madison.'

'Borkov here. I have a job for you. We need to eradicate an experiment that has passed its use-by date. I'll fax you the details.'

'Clean or messy?' asked Madison clinically.

'Totally clean, we're not using this as a warning, and I don't want to arouse any suspicions.'

'Okay, it'll take me forty-eight hours to set up. I'll expect my usual bonus once it's done.'

'Fine. Call me when it's accomplished.'

Borkov sighed as he sat down heavily on his leather couch and picked up the newspaper. The front-page headlines screamed, 'Crucifix Rapist Murders Fifth Victim.' He shook his head wearily.

'Fucking animals are everywhere,' he muttered.

～

Jordan stood on the worn steps of St Pauls and watched as two solidly built ladies laboured towards the imposing church doors. The steps were coated with a thin layer of ice, and the ladies walked gingerly, taking care not to fall.

Jordan hadn't been to church in years. He stepped through the open doors and ventured slowly towards the front of the church. A thin priest with aquiline features was talking quietly with a distraught woman, and Jordan waited until they had finished.

'Excuse me,' said Jordan, 'I'm looking for Father O'Brien.'

'Well, then you've found him. I'm Father Michael O'Brien.' His voice carried a hint of an Irish accent, and his eyes possessed a softness that belied his rough-set face. 'You must be the journalist come to talk about the devil.'

'Daniel Jordan,' prompted Jordan as he stuck out his hand. The priest had a strong grip, and Jordan tried not to wince. 'Thank you for seeing me, Father. I was told you're an authority on demonic possession, and I want my article to be as factual as possible.'

'Factual, is it?' repeated O'Brien. 'So do you believe in the devil?'

'Um, probably not.'

'I appreciate your honesty, but why should you care about reporting facts if you believe the whole thing is religious mumbo-jumbo?'

Jordan smiled. 'I didn't say it was mumbo-jumbo, and I would never scoff at another person's faith.'

'But you think it is, don't you?' persisted the priest.

Jordan studied O'Brien before answering. 'I'm sorry, but I've always believed the devil was something created by religious authorities to keep the oppressed under control. What better way to keep the masses in their place than to convince them there was a better life waiting if they suffered passively? Anybody who spoke up was clearly influenced by the devil and dealt with accordingly.'

The priest looked at him ominously. 'Go on.'

Jordan thought for a moment. 'It's a clever concept, isn't it? You can't disprove the devil's existence to a true believer. If you believe, then your faith is strong, but if you harbour doubts, then you've already succumbed to the devil's guile. You won't be on guard, therefore making his job a hell of a lot easier.' Jordan grimaced. 'Sorry, Father, that was unintentional.'

'A pity,' said O'Brien. 'A good pun is a sign of an active intelligence. Now I'm sure you didn't seek me out just to air your views on the devil's role in perpetuating social injustice.'

'Yes, you're quite right. Something happened recently to spark my curiosity.' Jordan briefly explained the Kimpton case and then waited for the priest to comment.

'An interesting situation,' said O'Brien finally, 'but it doesn't fit any of the classical possession patterns I'm aware of. Contrary to what you believe, the devil is indeed real, and his influence is all around us. He is the master of smoke and mirrors, and as you correctly pointed out, it suits his purpose for the modern world to believe he is a myth. This allows him to operate with more freedom than at any time in the past. People need to be aware of this. As a journalist, you can help raise this awareness.'

'I'd be happy to do that,' confirmed Jordan. 'I just want to get to the bottom of this case, and if Stephen is possessed, I want to know all about it.'

O'Brien scratched the back of his head thoughtfully. 'Would you like to see an exorcism? I've been working on a case involving a young lady, and it is now reaching its final phase. One of my assistants pulled his hamstring playing football, and I need another pair of strong hands. Yours are as good as any.'

'If it's not too much trouble,' replied Jordan casually as he tried to hide his excitement.

'Oh, it'll be a lot of trouble; I can guarantee that,' said O'Brien forcefully. 'You have no idea how much trouble. Meet me in front of the church tonight at 8.30 p.m. I need to go through the rules with you, and it's essential that you obey them to the letter. Is that all right with you?'

'Tonight? Sure,' said Jordan enthusiastically. 'I really appreciate this opportunity.'

The priest stared at him through hooded eyes. 'We'll see if you still appreciate my generosity when the nightmares begin. Wear the oldest clothes you own, have a light dinner, and be prepared to stay up all night. I won't blame you if you change your mind.' The priest gave him one last look and then turned to greet a gnarled parishioner.

Jordan returned to the church later that evening and joined several shadowy figures sheltering in an alcove out of the icy wind.

O'Brien gave him a brief smile and introduced him to two burly gentlemen, whose roles were to restrain the sufferer, and to another priest who was there to assist O'Brien. 'If I get into difficulties during the exorcism, it is Father Ryan's task to bludgeon me and take over. He assures me he's quite happy to perform this task, although the necessity has yet to arise. Come on, I'll explain the rest on the way.'

They walked briskly down the steps and stopped beside an old black Bentley. As he clambered into the back seat next to O'Brien, Jordan received a strong whiff of garlic, and he wrinkled his nose in distaste.

'We have been working with this girl for nearly twelve months,' continued O'Brien, once they were comfortably seated. 'We don't conduct an exorcism without making a thorough assessment, and we have reached the conclusion that she is a genuine case of evil-spirit possession.' He paused to scratch his nose. 'I must warn you that you will see, hear, and smell things that will shock you. Your senses will be battered unmercifully, and I guarantee you will never be the same again. We have two simple rules you must follow implicitly. Say nothing, and do only as I instruct you. Is that clear?'

'Yes,' replied Jordan as he leant back from O'Brien. The strong smell of garlic seemed to be coming from him.

O'Brien arched his eyebrows, his demeanour gravely serious. 'You think you understand, but you have no concept against which to measure your understanding. The evil spirit is the master of deception. If it focuses its attention on you, then you will feel compelled to answer. You must resist mightily. It will search for any weakness and exploit it with honeyed words and flawed logic. A person can only be possessed if they invite the spirit in. Say nothing.'

'I understand,' confirmed Jordan, a little huskily.

'Take these.' The priest thrust a small envelope in Jordan's hands. 'Ear plugs and cotton wool. You'll still be able to hear, but the ear plugs will deaden the worst of the noise.'

'And the cotton wool?'

'It's for your nose. They've been soaked in a strong herbal solution.' The priest didn't elaborate.

'How many of these cases have you done?' asked Jordan nervously. He had an urge to keep talking, but it was obvious that the priest had other things on his mind.

'I've done a couple,' O'Brien replied grimly. 'Now, if you'll excuse me, I must concentrate on the task ahead.' He opened a thin leather-bound book and began reciting Latin phrases under his breath.

Jordan settled back apprehensively in his seat. Strong waves of garlic assaulted him each time O'Brien moved. He wound down the window a fraction to lessen the smell, but O'Brien glared at him as a blast of icy wind swirled through the car, so he hastily wound it up again.

They arrived at the apartment just after 9 p.m., and Jordan was relieved to step out of the car into the fresh air. However, the reprieve was short-lived. He was hit by a fetid, stale stench the moment he entered the building, and as they climbed the stairs, the pungent odour became stronger. The other members of the group paused to stuff the small wads of cotton wool in their nostrils, and Jordan hurriedly did the same, but the smell still seeped in.

The same distraught woman Jordan had seen talking to Father O'Brien earlier in the day greeted them at the door. She took their coats and scarves, and they waited silently in the hallway while the priests adjusted their clerical attire. Two other helpers holding candlesticks and a tape recorder hovered restlessly nearby waiting for direction. The newcomers were introduced, and Jordan discovered that the elder of the two was the girl's father.

'Right,' commanded O'Brien, 'let's do it. Remember my instructions and no harm will come to you.' He made the sign of the cross and held out his hands as if to encompass them all. 'May the Lord hear our prayers and be with us tonight.'

He ushered them down the hallway and into a small bedroom, and Jordan sensed that the rest of the group shared his unease. The room had been stripped of all furniture apart from a bed, a small bedside table, and a wooden chest of drawers. The candlesticks and tape recorder were placed upon these.

A young woman lay quietly on the narrow bed, watching the activity around her with a nonchalant superiority. She wore a flimsy nightdress, and Jordan noticed that the usual bed linen had been replaced with a single plastic sheet. The floor around the bed had been covered with old newspapers that rustled faintly as he walked on them.

'I'm sorry, Father,' said the girl's father apologetically. 'I tried to get her to wear something more respectable but ...' His voice trailed off.

'It's of no consequence, but, please, nobody is to speak again,' said O'Brien sharply. 'Now hold her down firmly. Do not be deceived by her appearance. She possesses immense strength, and if she struggles free she may hurt herself.'

Father Ryan lit the candles while the men took hold of her arms and legs. Jordan grabbed hold of her ankle but it had a slimy feel, and he wiped his hands on his clothing before taking a stronger grip.

Father O'Brien stood at the foot of the bed and held up his crucifix while he sprinkled the girl with holy water. 'Maria, creature of God who created you and of Jesus who saved you, I command you to hear my voice as the voice of the Holy Church and to obey my commands.'

The girl had been lying quietly, but now she thrashed around suddenly and violently. She broke free long enough to sit up and emit an ear-piercing screech that completely filled the room. Jordan cringed at the noise and was thankful his earplugs had deflected the worst of it.

She was quickly forced down by two of the assistants, and the scream changed to a wailing moan that went on for an impossibly long time and still seemed to linger even when she eventually paused to take a long breath.

The two priests continued with their formal ritual, ending with the Lord's Prayer. As their final words died away, the girl suddenly spoke in a surprisingly deep voice.

'Who dares to disturb me? Do you not know that I am protected by the kingdom? The kingdom and I are one. I have made my choice as you have made yours so leave me in peace,' she whispered softly. 'I'm happy in the kingdom. You have no right to disturb my tranquillity. No right at all.' Her voice faded away, and she lay absolutely still.

'Maria,' commanded O'Brien.

'Yes,' she answered lazily. She opened her eyes and the group gasped aloud. Her eyes had turned entirely upward revealing only an opaque white nothingness. 'I see you for who you really are, all of you,' she continued in that same deep, lazy voice. 'None of you are fit to come here and judge me.'

'Maria,' repeated O'Brien forcefully. 'I command you to answer.'

'Are those earplugs making you deaf, you hatchet-faced faggot? I am Maria. I answer for myself. I make my own decisions. I am not a puppet to be played with—unless that is one of your fantasies.'

'Unclean spirit, and all your companions who possess this servant of God,' intoned Father O'Brien solemnly. 'By the mysteries of the incarnation, the sufferings, and—'

'Shut the fuck up!' screamed the girl savagely as she ripped her left arm free and began tearing the flimsy clothing from her body. A dazed helper finally forced her arm back to her side, but her nightdress now hung in shreds from her naked body.

She lifted her head and looked at Jordan. 'I know you, don't I?' she whispered hoarsely. 'I've seen that look before. You want me so badly; I can feel your hunger. You all want to fuck me. Even the faggot priest wants to have a piece of me.'

The girl slowly raised her left arm despite the best efforts of the burly helper assigned to restrain it. The veins in his neck stood out like cords as he struggled to force her arm back to the bed. She gestured slightly towards the wall and several strange words appeared as if branded into the woodwork.

'The writing's on the wall and can no longer be denied. Which one of you has the balls to dip their pen in my forbidden ink?' She arched her body as best she could in simulated sex. 'Who's man enough to pump me first?'

Jordan felt overwhelmed by the combined assault on his senses and closed his eyes in an effort to recover his mental balance. However, this only seemed to magnify the intensity and clarity of her voice, and he forced his eyes open in a moment of sudden panic. She was looking directly at him with her sightless gaze and slowly ran her tongue around her lips in a grotesque parody of sexual desire.

Her father started weeping silently as O'Brien continued with his incantation. A distant sound intruded into their consciousness, softly at first and then louder and louder. A single voice of despair echoed hauntingly around the room and was rapidly joined by another and another until it became a moaning, tortured chorus, growing ever louder. The desolate clamour seemed to come from nowhere and yet everywhere and filled the group with such a sense of loneliness and black depression that several of them cried out in horror.

Jordan had been feeling increasingly queasy. He finally lost the battle with his stomach and turned his head to the side as he vomited noisily over the newspapers lining the floor under his feet. Nobody seemed to notice, and the ritual continued unabated.

O'Brien pointed a long, lean finger at the girl. 'Most unclean, invading spirit, in the name of Our Lord Jesus Christ, be uprooted and expelled from this creature of God.'

The girl groaned loudly as a grey-green foam began dribbling from the corner of her mouth. 'Enough,' she gasped painfully, forming her words with difficulty. 'This farce is over. Take your insipid handmaidens and get the hell out of my world. Only I was invited in, not you.'

'You were not invited, you invaded, and in the name of Jesus, I command you to desist at once and leave her.' O'Brien made the sign of the cross while Father Ryan sprinkled her with holy water.

'We exorcise you, unclean spirit, power of Satan, infestation of the enemy from hell. Be uprooted and put to flight from the church of God, from the souls made in the image of God and redeemed with blood of the divine lamb. God the Father, the Son, and the Holy Spirit command you.' Father O'Brien held out his crucifix and approached the head of the bed, and as the girl screamed and struggled in protest, he laid it lovingly upon her heart. She threw her head back and let out a howl of anguished distress that started deep within the bowels of her body and grew impossibly louder and more sorrowful as it continued to fill the room many minutes after it first began.

Jordan held his breath in involuntary empathy but was forced to continue breathing as the howling continued to build until it gradually became a gut-wrenching shriek. The girl abruptly jerked forward and whispered several harsh words in a language Jordan didn't understand and then collapsed lifelessly back onto the bed. Jordan now understood why the bed was covered in plastic sheets as the ordeal left her without any control of her bodily functions.

'It's over,' whispered O'Brien. 'Please, get her cleaned up and into some fresh clothes before she recovers. It will help diminish her memory of tonight and speed up the recovery process.' He walked slowly over to the girl's father and put a hand on his head. 'I'll come by tomorrow and see how she is. The strength of your faith has been an inspiration to us all. Don't stumble now that we're in sight of the finishing line.'

As they walked down the stairs to the car, the priest paused and looked at Jordan. 'Still believe your friend is possessed?'

'No,' replied Jordan tiredly as he rubbed his hands together in a forlorn effort to ward off the cold. He could still taste the stale vomit in his mouth, and he ran his tongue around his teeth and spat into the darkness.

The priest's dark eyes shone brightly in the poor light. 'Still think possession is a figment of deluded minds?'

Jordan grimaced. 'To be honest, I don't know what to think. I couldn't answer the simplest question let alone one like that.'

The priest gave a forlorn chuckle. 'I know exactly how you feel, my boy—exactly. However, if it will help, I'll have a look at your friend tomorrow after I've had a good rest.'

Jordan nodded silently. He could still smell the awful stench and hear the inhuman screams. It was obvious that Stephen didn't fit into the same category as the girl, but what category did he fit into?

Jordan stumbled through the front door of his apartment at three in the morning and stopped to strip off his clothes. He propped the front door open, dashed nervously outside and threw them in the garbage bin. He finally fell into bed after spending half an hour in the shower fruitlessly trying to scrub the stench out of his skin.

'My God,' mumbled Laura as she moved away from him. 'Have you been rolling in manure?'

'I've been working on the Kimpton case, for your information,' he replied tartly, 'and I'm in no mood to take any shit from anybody.'

'It's too late for that if my nose is any judge. Why didn't you have a shower before you came to bed?'

'Yeah, yeah,' he replied despondently. 'I'll tell you all about it in the morning.'

When he woke up later, Laura had already left for work. There was a distinct smell of air freshener throughout the house, and he had a vague memory of being liberally sprayed as he lay in bed.

He rang Laura and explained briefly about Father O'Brien and the incident with the girl. "I can assure you that whatever it is that's wrong with Stephen Kimpton, it's not possession. Despite that, I thought it can't do any harm for Father O'Brien to have a look at Kimpton. I hope you don't mind.'

'I'm not sure what value he can add to the case but I have a spare half hour around three this afternoon,' she said finally. 'I'll meet you at the clinic. Don't be late.'

He called the church and arranged to meet the priest at the Gillespie Rehabilitation Centre, and then he treated himself to another long, hot shower.

Chapter 3

Wisdom is the principle thing; therefore get wisdom;
and with all thy getting, get understanding.

Proverbs 4:7

S tephen was in a cheerful mood when they were admitted to his room. Laura introduced him to Father O'Brien and Jordan, and he gave them a polite nod before turning excitedly back to Laura.

'I was in bed last night wondering why this bizarre thing had happened to me and what I had done to deserve such rotten luck, and it dawned on me that I've been focusing solely on the downside of this disorder. I realised there's also a positive side.'

'You definitely sound a lot happier, Stephen,' agreed Laura as she settled herself on the edge of his bed. 'I'd like to hear more about it.'

'I'm finally learning to sort all the memories. It's still damn confusing, and half the time I don't know whether I'm Arthur or Martha, or should that be James or Stephen,' he laughed awkwardly, 'but I'm starting to transfer memories between myself.' He held up a hand in response to their blank expressions. 'I'll give you an example: I was being taken for my morning walk today, and as we went through the sitting room there was an old lady playing "As Time Goes By" rather badly on the piano. I recognised the tune because James knew it, and what's more, he knew how to play it. They allowed me to give it a try and I played it beautifully, but, and here's the interesting thing, I played it as Stephen. It was James's memory, but I was able to transfer it to my knowledge. If you were to wipe James completely from my mind this instant, I would still be able to play that piece of music.'

Jordan and O'Brien exchanged glances. 'Did you play the piano before James appeared on the scene?' asked O'Brien.

'I used to do a bit of jamming with my friends, Father, but I couldn't play nearly as well as I can now. I know my mind's a mess, but if I can work through this, I have a feeling I'll be much better off. James has more than sixty years of experience and knowledge that I can use to enrich my own life. If I could tuck him away in my mind and just pick out the pieces I wanted, the advantage I would have over people my own age would be tremendous.'

'That sounds great,' acknowledged Jordan. 'I'm envious just thinking of the possibilities.'

'The problem is that my mind is flooded with two sets of memories that just clutter and confuse me.' Stephen beamed suddenly, surprisingly. 'There is one bonus I've discovered; James has a few secrets he kept from everybody, including his wife. However, surprise, surprise, he can't keep them from me. I'm not going to tell you all the juicy details because a secret is still a secret, but I discovered he has a private bank account under an assumed name. James is an intelligent person and very security conscious, or should that be *was*?' He looked momentarily confused before continuing. 'Anyway, he has a code for the account that I would never have worked out if I hadn't already known it.' He borrowed Jordan's pen and wrote the code on a tattered envelope. 'See if you can decipher that.'

'You appear to be talking about James in the third person more and more. Is this something you're aware of?' asked Laura.

'Well, I am Stephen after all, aren't I? It's just that I seem to have James's memories superimposed over my own. If memories are the essence of who we are, then part of me is also James, although I'm sure he has no awareness of this. As I said before, it's very confusing, but I am starting to sort things out.'

Father O'Brien interrupted gently. 'How did you know that James had secrets? How did you know where to look?'

'It's very simple, Father. Let me use the example of the bank account. I was thinking about money because I'll need some when they let me out of here, and I remembered that I had a substantial amount hidden away in my secret account. Now that was one of James's memories that I accessed without even realising it. It was the thought concerning money that triggered it.'

'So there could be lots of other information you're still unaware of,' said Jordan.

'Sure. You don't keep all your knowledge in your immediate memory. If I were to ask you about the first pet you owned, you'd think about it and then remember. It's the same with this. Unless I think about it, the memories stay hidden. The point is that I possess knowledge which up until a week ago was locked up inside somebody else's head.'

'I'm really pleased to see you doing so well, Stephen,' announced Laura as she checked her watch and got to her feet. 'Unfortunately our time is up, but it's great to see you making significant progress.'

An orderly locked the door behind them as they left, and Laura gave Jordan a quick peck on the cheek before hurrying off to her next appointment.

'What do you think?' asked Jordan as he and Father O'Brien ambled back through the clinic grounds.

'Whatever is ailing that young man is beyond my expertise.'

'Hmm.' Jordan nodded in vague agreement. 'He's nothing like the girl we saw yesterday so I think we can rule out possession.'

'Indeed,' continued the priest. 'Now I'm no expert in this particular field, but he appears to be under the influence of a post-hypnotic suggestion. I've seen it before, and the signs are occasionally in his eyes.'

'Hypnosis?' Jordan hadn't considered that possibility. 'You think he's been hypnotized to believe he's somebody else?'

'It's unlikely, but it may pay to have him checked out. Any lead is better than none.'

'Thank you, Father,' acknowledged Jordan graciously. 'You've been most helpful.'

O'Brien held out a plain brown paper parcel he'd been carrying tied loosely with a piece of string. "I'm usually a pretty good judge of character so I don't mind lending you this if it will help with your research.'

Jordan undid the heavy parcel and took out a thick, leather-bound book before holding it out appraisingly. The cover and spine had been inlaid with delicate metal patterns and the page edges were gilded a dull golden colour. 'This book must be worth a fortune, Father. What is it?'

'It's an in-depth study of possession and exorcism and was translated from the original Latin in the early eighteenth century. It's one of my most prized possessions.'

Jordan shook his head and attempted to hand it back to the priest. 'I can't take this, Father. It's too valuable.'

'It's only for a lend," replied O'Brien grumpily. 'I expect you to return it once your article is finished. Anyway, a book is of no value if it spends its life collecting dust on some forgotten bookshelf. Books are made to be read.'

'I really appreciate this Father,' replied Jordan as he carefully wrapped the brown paper around the book.

O'Brien glanced appraisingly at Jordan's blotchy skin. 'There's something else I should have mentioned last night: don't scrub yourself away. It's a common reaction, but some people scrub themselves so raw we end up having to forcibly restrain them. Scrubbing fever we call it.'

'But the smell …'

'The smell will leave your skin in about four to five days, although it will take far longer to leave your mind. A good wash each day is helpful, but go easy on the scrubbing brush.'

Jordan stifled a grimace. 'I don't know how you put up with it, Father, time after time. It's bad enough just once.'

O'Brien stopped and placed a gentle hand on Jordan's shoulder. 'I have learned to protect myself with a little trick that my mentor passed onto me. You probably didn't notice it last night, but I wear a full body stocking rubbed liberally with raw garlic. It keeps me warm on a cold night and prevents the stink of the devil from invading my body.' He chuckled lightly. 'It can be expensive though as I can only wear them once.'

Jordan held out his hand. 'Thanks for your help, Father. It's been a pleasure meeting you, but in some ways, I wish I never had.'

'I know exactly what you mean, my boy. Take care, and may God go with you.'

After the priest had gone, Jordan pulled the tattered envelope from his pocket. Stephen had written 'A dozen eggs'.

It was early in the morning when Vincent Dawson and Carlos DeLuca parked their van outside the Gillespie Rehabilitation Centre and unloaded their cleaning equipment. All cleaning was handled by subcontractors, and nobody gave them a second glance. Dawson was a large man whose body had seen better days, although he still moved with the casual grace of a ballet dancer. His nose had been broken on more than one occasion, and his light blue eyes had a strangely hypnotic look. His partner was the complete opposite. He was also a strongly built man but the absence of excess body fat made him appear slimmer than he actually was. His long black hair was covered in gel and was slicked back, and his narrow face, combined with intense dark eyes gave him a dangerous, feral look.

The patients being treated at Gillespie ranged from maximum-security mental patients to voluntarily committed drug addicts who were guarded by security only for their own protection.

Kimpton's room was located in the maximum-security section, and the two men set up their cleaning signs outside his room and then glanced carefully around. The corridor remained deserted. Dawson took out a set of lock picks and unlocked Kimpton's door.

They slipped inside and stood silently in the shadows while they assessed their surroundings. The room was faintly illuminated by a red light glowing softly from the ceiling. Kimpton's bed was against the far wall. DeLuca pulled a grey tube from his pocket and held it securely while he gave the end a firm twist. A thin, steel needle slid out with a muted clunk. Soft footsteps sounded in the passage, and the two men instinctively pressed back into the shadows until they were certain it was safe to proceed.

Dawson gently shook the sleeping form. 'Stephen?' he whispered as he watched Kimpton stir from his sleep. 'Stephen Kimpton?' he repeated softly, making certain the sleeping figure was their intended target.

'Yes, what is it?' replied Kimpton thickly.

'We've been told to give you something to help you sleep, Stephen. I'm sure the doctor told you about it.'

'Why do you want to help me sleep?' mumbled Stephen. 'It's the dreams that are the problem.'

'This will cure your dreams as well,' murmured Dawson. He stood back to make room for DeLuca, who stepped forward and placed the tube against Kimpton's ear and then punched the needlepoint deep into his brain. He felt his victim stiffen momentarily before going completely limp.

DeLuca wiped the trickle of escaping blood with a piece of cotton wool and then placed it in a plastic bag and quietly followed Dawson out of the room.

'Now we wait,' said Dawson as they moved their cleaning signs further down the corridor.

An orderly appeared shortly after and unlocked the cell next to Kimpton's. 'Time to pack up,' said Dawson as he stopped and stretched. The orderly approached Kimpton's room and peered through the peephole before unlocking the door. Dawson took out his phone and his call was answered after one ring.

'Go ahead,' said Madison tersely.

'Termination completed,' replied Dawson. 'It's time to collect the package.'

They picked up their equipment and strolled down the corridor as orderlies and nurses burst into a flurry of activity behind them. It had rained during the night, and although the clouds had since passed, dark puddles of water still lay in the sunken crevices of the concrete path. Dawson dropped the small plastic bag into a storm water drain and watched as it was swept away by the sluggish flow. 'Sometimes this job is just plain boring,' he muttered.

Isaac Borkov calmly surveyed the crowded Memtech boardroom with a sense of satisfaction. His orders had been clear and precise: find twenty individuals who were ruthlessly ambitious, had more wealth than they know what to do with, and were openly receptive to new and challenging concepts.

Borkov held up his hand to stem the flow of conversation. 'Benjamin Franklin said that nothing is certain except death and taxes. He was wrong about taxes, and you are about to learn that he was also wrong about death. We are about to unveil an astounding technology to you, and while we still have some way to go in its development, it is important to understand that the end cannot be realised until the original concept has been discovered. The first aeroplane bears little resemblance to the space shuttle, but it had to be designed and built before we could conquer space.'

He glanced around the room judging their mood. 'Imagine your power if you could gain access to any knowledge you desired. Now I'm not talking about finding the lost treasure of the Incas,' he said with a chuckle. 'This knowledge must reside in somebody's head. There has always been a natural learning curve as each generation slowly pushes the boundaries beyond that of their predecessors. Now, imagine the acceleration if we could extract the relevant knowledge from the brain of somebody such as Einstein and load it directly into a bright, young mind. Overnight he would reach a point that would normally take decades of hard work. The application of this technology is only limited by your imagination. How is this done, I can hear you asking. Professor Hauser will now explain this to you.'

Professor Hauser began his lecture by holding up a small jar. 'Ladies and gentlemen, I would like you to meet the creatures responsible for my discovery. These little fellows are flatworms and are special due to their carnivorous nature. McConnell first began experimenting with them in 1962. He divided the flatworms into a control group and an experimental group and then put each group into a box with a light at one end and a dark area at the other. Flatworms dislike light so each group moved to the dark end of their respective boxes. The experimental group was then subjected to a series of electric shocks, forcing them to worm their way to the other end of their box, which was shock free. So we now had the control worms in the dark and the experimental worms in the light. McConnell then did something brilliant. He took the experimental worms, minced them up, and fed them to the control group. Something very interesting happened.'

Hauser lowered his voice for effect. 'The control group began moving towards the light. These worms now knew that the dark section of the box was a place to be feared. How did this happen? What change had taken place in the control group as a result of eating the experimental group? This experiment raised the possibility that memory was a chemical substance and could be transferred from one being to another. This was, of course, a very basic experiment with the control group being fed entire bodies rather than just brains, but they were still able to absorb enough chemicals to effect a change.

'It's interesting to note that according to folklore, the headhunters of Borneo were said to inherit the wisdom of their victims. Given that the victims' memory residue had to first pass through the stomach of the tribesman, it is no surprise that the references to knowledge transfer in these cases are vague. Obviously, this is an antiquated experiment, and we would not expect anybody to invest capital solely on the basis of this information, but it does provide a broad platform for our *pièce de résistance*.'

He pressed a button and waited as the lights dimmed. 'Please observe a recent experiment of ours. The young man on the screen, Mr X, was a volunteer in our program. He had a memory solution injected into his neck, which then fed directly into his brain. The solution was extracted from an elderly patient called Mr P, who had recently died of a heart attack. Memory transfer is most effective up until thirty minutes from the moment of death, and then there is an increasing rate of dissipation lasting another thirty minutes. After that, the exercise becomes pointless. The entire procedure takes several days, as the imported memory requires time to correctly align itself within the brain. Once we deemed that Mr X was sufficiently recovered, he was given a post-hypnotic suggestion blocking all memory of his real self, and he was put into a taxi.

'The pictures on the screen were taken of Mr X arriving at the home of Mr P. In this photograph, Mr X is entering the code for the building's security system, information he could not have ordinarily known. For all intents and purposes, he was Mr P, which was something of a shock to the newly bereaved Mrs P. This was not our first transfer experiment, but it was the first one we road tested, and Mr X heralded the successful completion of the stage we termed Prototype One. This was always going to be a messy experiment as we dumped the entire contents of Mr P's memory into Mr X. Although still in its infancy, this particular aspect of the technology will eventually allow you to retrieve the memories of your loved ones—or anybody else for that matter. The deceased person's memory can be loaded into the brain of the recipient and, *voila*, back from the dead.'

Paul Frampton could contain himself no longer. 'What a load of bullshit! That would never work. The person receiving the memory would be become a schizophrenic. They'd be in the same boat as this Mr X.'

Professor Hauser eyed him sadly. 'A valid point, Mr Frampton. In my enthusiasm, I appear to have gone too quickly. Let me explain by putting forward a hypothetical case. Imagine you are married to somebody whose best years are past but who you still love very much. There are many beautiful women from Eastern Europe, Asia, you name it, who are looking for a husband. Imagine if you could shop around for the woman of your dreams and then load your wife's memory into her. We are the sum total of our memories and experiences, and this woman would truly believe she was your wife; in fact she would be your wife but merely in a different body. You could even consider the option of cloning.

'As for her original memories, we are on the verge of solving that problem. The issue of extinguishing memory is crucial to the success of this program. We have discovered a way to change the chemical component of existing memory so the brain no longer recognises it and therefore no longer draws upon it. The memories are still there but effectively irretrievable. To put it briefly, you would select the woman, and we would expunge her existing memory, load in the new memory, and plant a powerful hypnotic suggestion so that she recognised herself physically as your wife. You could arrange a second wedding to satisfy everybody else and the job would be complete.'

'And what about my old wife?' sneered Frampton. 'I don't think she'd be very understanding.'

Dr Borkov stood up and spoke before Professor Hauser could reply. 'It's important that we are perfectly clear about this so I will be blunt. The donor of the memory will be dead. D-E-A-D, dead. Your previous wife will therefore be in no position to cause any difficulties with her lack of understanding. The extraction process involves removing her brain and selectively distilling the memory chemicals from it. It is not possible to survive this process. Our corporation, as part of the total service, will discretely dispose of her body. We would neither condemn nor condone your decision, but we would ensure that your risks are effectively minimised.'

'So to give my wife a new lease of life, I must first murder her,' said Frampton.

'Murder is such an ugly word. We prefer to use the term "re-vitalise". As they are fond of saying in royal circles, "your wife is dead, long live your wife."'

'What about the sense of self?' asked a well-dressed woman on Borkov's right. 'Merely transferring my memories into somebody else doesn't make them me. She might sound like me, but my self-awareness would have been extinguished when I died. You make it sound as though I'd wake up in a new body, but the fact is, I just wouldn't wake up. I would be D-E-A-D, dead.'

'You have made a valid point, Miss Astbury, and I shall address it shortly.' He gestured for Hauser to continue.

Hauser resumed his place on the platform. 'Now I'd like to discuss the next stage called Prototype Two. The brain stores information according to its own unique filing system. We have painstakingly mapped the biological path underpinning the brain's storage and retrieval system, and we can now isolate specific item classes of memory. After all, it's hardly helpful if we are trying to download Einstein's knowledge of physics into an eager young mind, and all he ends up with is the memory of the professor's holiday in Paris. Entertaining maybe, but hardly worth the price the professor would have paid. Compartmentalising knowledge is our next frontier. Until now, we have been restricted by the limited number of donors and test subjects, but extra investment capital will mean the program can be accelerated considerably.'

Hauser continued for another twenty minutes, discussing the general benefits of chemical memory transfer, before asking for further questions.

Jane Astbury's interest had been growing, although she still harboured doubts. She raised her hand to attract Hauser's attention. 'What would happen if a female was the recipient of male memory and vice versa?'

'Oh, that would be impossible,' exclaimed Hauser, with a shake of his head. 'The structure of the female brain is significantly different to that of the male. The memory would become lost in transit and would be of no value to anyone.'

'Thank you, professor, but I was thinking more of the resulting gender confusion if a male were to receive female memory.'

Hauser nodded in appreciation. 'I understand, but my original answer still stands. Gender confusion would only occur if the transferred memory was locked into place, and our research has shown this cannot happen.'

Hauser glanced quickly around the room for any further questions and then handed the floor back to Borkov.

'You have been exposed to radically new information this afternoon,' began Borkov, 'and I wouldn't blame you for experiencing technological shock. Miss Astbury asked a question concerning self-awareness, which I will now address by posing the following question. What is the sense of self, the soul if you like, and how does it develop? Professor Hauser has just demonstrated that our memory is chemically based, and we believe the sense of self is similar. We don't know where or what, but we do know that it's only a matter of when before we discover it. Then I will be able to offer each and every one of you'—Borkov paused before emphasising the final word—'immortality! Throughout history, as science has broken through existing frontiers, social order has always been reluctant to change and follow. You have an opportunity to be pioneers of a new class of society, the Eternals.'

He stopped and glared at the audience. 'The world is full of bleeding hearts who will stop at nothing to destroy our dreams, to paint us as criminals, and trap us in their mundane terminal world. We may eventually operate in advance of legalised social change, but this doesn't mean that what we are doing is immoral. Laws are based on past events, and it is inevitable that our laws and current realities will occasionally be out of synchronisation. The future will belong to us, but only if we can continue undisturbed. I cannot emphasise this point enough.' He lowered his voice. 'Do not talk to anybody outside this room about anything you have heard today. The Memtech Corporation is deadly serious about protecting this technology—deadly serious.'

He paused to allow the audience time to digest his words, and then, unexpectedly, he smiled. 'Finally, I am authorised to offer each of you one share of Memtech stock for ten million pounds. Our financial analysts are forecasting a conservative return between 25 and 30 per cent over the first twelve months. I understand the information is scant, but you're all risk takers, so weigh up the odds and make your decision.'

Paul Frampton shook his head and grumbled sourly to the elderly man next to him, 'I've heard some wild stories in my time but immortality? He must think we're imbeciles.'

His colleague smiled thinly. 'I think you're wrong but of course time will tell.' Frampton shrugged and, still muttering, left the way he had come in.

Chapter 4

Accidents will occur in the best-regulated families.
Charles Dickens

Laura was told the following morning that Stephen Kimpton had passed away overnight. The cause of death was unknown, and a full autopsy was being carried out. She immediately contacted Jordan.

'Something isn't right here,' announced Jordan angrily. 'He was fit and healthy when we saw him yesterday. Somebody that young just doesn't suddenly die overnight.'

'Until we get the coroner's report we're only guessing,' said Laura soothingly.

He shook his head, unconvinced. 'I have a journalist's instinct, and this smells bad.'

'You're overreacting, Daniel, although it no longer matters. Without Stephen, this case is as good as closed.'

'Exactly. Stephen disappears for five days, and a dead man's memory suddenly appears in his head, but before we can delve too deeply into how and why, he conveniently dies. The whole thing reeks of a cover-up. We owe it to Stephen to discover the truth. Incidentally, Father O'Brien thought Stephen may have been under some sort of post-hypnotic influence, although he admitted he's no expert.'

'Hmm,' muttered Laura thoughtfully, 'I'll call Memtech Industries and ask them to check their records again. Perhaps he was hypnotised after all.'

'What, into thinking he was James Chandler?' scoffed Jordan. 'You can hypnotise me into believing I'm Napoleon, but I still won't know any personal details about Josephine.'

Laura frowned. 'I know it's damned thin, but it's the only clue we have.'

'Do you want me to poke around at the clinic?' asked Jordan. 'I might discover something useful.'

'There's not really any point is there?' replied Laura.

'I don't mind. I have another appointment I'm dreading, so the longer I delay it, the better.'

'And what appointment would that be?'

'I'd rather not say.'

'Humph … well, have fun and I'll see you tonight.'

Jordan arrived at the Gillespie Clinic shortly after ten and asked the receptionist if he could see Stephen Kimpton about an urgent issue. The receptionist consulted her computer and then asked him to wait while she called a staff member to deal with his request.

A woman appeared and introduced herself. 'I'm Anne Ramsey. I've been told you want to see Stephen Kimpton.' Her smile looked as if it had been painted on.

'Yes, it's quite urgent.'

'May I ask what your relationship is with Mr Kimpton?'

Jordan smiled disarmingly. 'I'm Daniel Jordan, a close family friend.'

'Hmm, I see. Come over here, Mr Jordan, and sit down.' She guided him in a motherly fashion towards a couple of secluded chairs. 'I'm afraid I have some bad news for you.' Jordan discovered that Anne Ramsey was a grief counsellor, well versed in the art of disclosing death to unsuspecting friends and relatives of the recently departed.

'But he was so healthy the last time I saw him,' protested Jordan. 'Don't you find it suspicious that he should die so suddenly?'

'Suspicious?' prompted Ramsey sharply.

'Sorry, I meant unusual.'

'Daniel, anybody dying so young is unusual,' acknowledged Ramsey consolingly.

'He was very depressed the last time I saw him. Perhaps he decided it was all too much.'

'Suicide?' said Ramsey quickly. 'No, that's not possible. He was in a suicide-proof room, and his medication was carefully monitored. No, he was discovered lying peacefully in bed.'

'So none of the other inmates could have ...?' He left the question hovering in the air, and she deftly smacked it into the outfield.

'Mr Jordan, this is a reputable hospital. We do not have dangerous patients wandering the hallways getting up to mischief.' Her voice hardened. 'Mr Kimpton's room was kept locked at all times and was still locked when his body was discovered this morning. There is not the slightest possibility that a third party was responsible for his death. It is simply out of the question.'

'So there was nothing unusual about his death,' repeated Jordan obstinately.

'Nothing at all. Apart from two ambulances turning up to collect poor Mr Kimpton, it's been an extremely normal morning. Now, if you'll excuse me, I have a great deal of work to get through today.' She stood up dismissively.

'Pardon me,' said Jordan as he rose slowly to his feet. 'Two ambulances?'

'Yes.' She laughed. 'Most days we struggle to get one, and today we got two. It never rains but it pours.'

'Were they both from the same hospital?'

'I wouldn't know, dear, I'm not with dispatch, and now I really must be going.' She walked briskly away.

Jordan watched Ramsay disappear down the passage and then walked back to the receptionist and asked for directions to the dispatch department.

'Turn left down that passage,' she replied with a smile, pointing to her right. 'It's the third door on your right marked Communications Room. The dispatch officer is Don Sanders.'

Jordan pulled out his notepad and pen as he entered the communications room. A squat, bald man was slouched behind a computer, and Jordan noticed he was playing a card game on his PC.

'Mr Sanders,' bellowed Jordan.

The squat man jumped visibly and flicked off the card game. 'Yes,' he replied nervously. 'I'm Sanders. What can I do for you?'

'My name is Daniel Jordan. I'm investigating the alleged misdirection of municipal ambulance facilities by this clinic.'

'I don't know anything about that,' stammered Sanders.

'Is that so? I understand two ambulances were called to transport one body. As one ambulance is usually sufficient, the second ambulance must have been misdirected. How do you explain this?' demanded Jordan officiously.

'We don't coordinate the ambulances so there's nothing to explain,' growled Sanders. All requests go through central dispatch and they organise the pick-up. In this case they stuffed up and sent two ambulances.'

'Were they both from the same hospital?'

Sanderson scowled and flipped through a couple of documents on his table. 'The first came from Mercy West, which is unusual because they're right across town. The other one came from Sacred Heart General, which is only a couple of blocks away.'

'So the ambulance from across town arrived before the one from around the corner,' mused Jordan as he wrote down the names of the hospitals.

'Didn't I just say that?' grunted Sanders. 'Where'd you say you were from again?'

'I didn't. Thanks for your help, it's much appreciated.' He turned on his heel and hurried from the building.

He reflected on the issue of the two ambulances as he drove through the city, wondering if it meant anything. He found a parking spot close to his destination and walked the remaining two blocks until he stood in the shadow of an old and weathered, grey stone building. The sign above the entrance read 'Bureau of Employment'. The cold wind snatched at his coat as he gave a deep sigh and dragged himself inside.

～

Borkov leaned back in his well-worn chair and propped his feet on his desk. His heels made dirty scuff marks, but he didn't care. He relaxed, enjoying the mellow feeling of achievement. His indulgent reverie was shattered by the shrill tone of his phone. He leaned forward, saw it was Moira Ridgeway's number, and pressed the hands-free button.

'Yes?'

'Dr Borkov,' said Ridgeway nervously. 'I have Laura Monroe on the other line. Do you want to talk to her?'

'Who?'

'Laura Monroe. She rang last week asking about Stephen Kimpton.'

Borkov scowled. 'I thought you answered all her questions.'

'Apparently she has more. Will I put her through?'

Borkov grunted his assent and then growled into the mouthpiece. 'Dr Borkov speaking, how can I help you?'

'Dr Borkov, my name is Dr Monroe, and I am a psychologist with the Department of Corrective Service.'

'I know who you are, Miss Monroe,' he interrupted gruffly. 'Please get to the point.'

Laura maintained her calm manner. 'One of my patients, Stephen Kimpton, was a subject at your centre. When Stephen was brought to me, he appeared to be suffering from abnormal memory displacement. Unfortunately, he died recently, and I am now tying up the loose ends so I can close his file.'

'How sad,' replied Borkov with careless sympathy, 'but I don't understand how I can help you. My assistant has given you all the relevant information.'

'Yes, she was very helpful, but I'd like to run a few ideas past you before I close his file. I want to be satisfied that all possible avenues have been explored.'

'I'm sorry, Dr Monroe, I'm sure your theories are fascinating but I should have been in a meeting five minutes ago.'

'What about lunch? I have an interesting theory on memory displacement, and I'd really appreciate your thoughts,' said Laura obstinately.

Borkov hesitated. 'All right, I'll give you half an hour. I'm having lunch at Valentino's on Albany Street at one o'clock. Now I really must go.'

The phone clicked loudly in Laura's ear, and she smiled triumphantly. She was convinced that the five unaccounted days held the key to Kimpton's condition and found it increasingly difficult to believe that Memtech was blameless. Something must have happened there.

An elderly waiter took her coat when she arrived at the restaurant and showed her to Borkov's table. He was a large, corpulent man with the shoulders of a weightlifter, and she felt a moment of fear when he glanced up from his menu to study her. His eyes were a dull black, and she could feel them probing her features. He made no attempt to rise, so she introduced herself and sat down opposite.

He smiled unexpectedly and held out a large hand in greeting. When he spoke, his voice resonated with a rich purr. 'A pleasure to meet you, Dr Monroe.' He handed her his business card, and she glanced at the motto: 'Your Past Is Our Future.'

'Please call me Laura.' She felt slightly flustered as she slipped the card into her purse. 'Thank you for seeing me. I know how busy you are.'

'Do you?' he replied diffidently. He drained the remaining contents of his glass and signalled for a refill. 'I hope you don't mind, but I've ordered seafood for us.'

'No, seafood's fine,' she answered neutrally.

'Now, Laura, what makes this case of yours so special? I'm sure there's more to this than just short-term memory loss.'

'Stephen's case has me baffled, but I'm sure his memory loss is connected to the answer in some way.' Their food arrived as she gave Borkov a brief description of her patient's condition. He stared at her thoughtfully once she finished.

'It seems a fascinating case,' he said finally. 'What a pity he chose to die. Was it suicide?'

Laura looked doubtful. 'I don't think so. I'll know more when I receive the coroner's report this afternoon.' She took a mouthful of food and waved her fork at Borkov. 'The thing that puzzles me is how a dead man's memory can reappear in another person. I know it happened, so there must be an answer. What if memory is composed of a series of electrical impulses that are stored in the brain and then accessed upon demand? Under the right conditions, these electrical waves might then have the ability to travel from one brain to another. I'm sure you've heard of psychic connection.'

Borkov held up his claret and studied it briefly before replying. 'Ah yes, the interesting phenomenon where a soldier dies in a foreign war, and his mother starts screaming that her boy is dead. It's been well documented but is hardly cutting edge.'

Laura blotted her lips with a napkin. 'How many times have you been with somebody, and you've both said precisely the same thing at the same time or somebody else says exactly what you're thinking? Our normal response is to assume that both parties picked up common clues from what is happening around them, but what if it's more? What if some people are natural broadcasters and others are natural receivers? Get these people together, and there's a good chance that unconscious thoughts will pass between them.'

'An amusing thought, Miss Monroe, but hardly scientific.'

'Yes, but what if somebody had found a way to amplify these messages and transfer them from one person to another? Wouldn't that account for what happened to my patient?'

Borkov burst into buoyant laughter. 'My dear lady, I'm afraid you've been watching too many science fiction movies. Transferring memory through amplified electrical impulses indeed. I must say, you've brightened my day, but I now fear I'll pay the price with indigestion.' He patted his stomach and signalled imperiously to the waiter. 'Unfortunately, I must depart, but please stay and finish your meal. The bill has been taken care of.'

'I'm sorry that my fanciful ideas have upset your lunch, Dr Borkov, but I'm convinced that my patient was tampered with, and I intend to get to the bottom of it. Look at the time line. James Chandler dies, Stephen Kimpton disappears for five days, and when he resurfaces he has James Chandler's memories tucked away inside his head.' She fixed him with her strong brown eyes. 'And do you know the interesting thing? His last point of call before he disappeared was your institute, where he underwent an examination for memory testing. Merely coincidental? Somehow I think not.'

'I'm afraid that's all it is, an interesting coincidence.' He chuckled pleasantly. 'I wish you luck in your quest. I'm sure it will make a very provocative article in the medical journal.' Borkov gave her a small bow as he left. Once outside the restaurant his demeanour changed, and he reached for his phone.

It rang twice before a male voice answered. 'Dawson,' it said simply.

'I want to see you and your partner at our usual meeting place at 6 p.m. Don't be late.'

Dawson and DeLuca arrived at the Regent theatre shortly before six. Borkov handed Dawson a thick envelope. 'The subject's name is Laura Monroe. I have included several newspaper cuttings of a serial murderer currently terrorizing

London, along with a report on his methodology; this is from my contact at Scotland Yard. I want a copycat murder.'

'What's the completion date on this one, Boss?' asked Dawson as he watched a tall blond woman in a tight, red dress walk behind Borkov and disappear into the theatre.

'It's fairly urgent,' replied Borkov. 'The stupid bitch is starting to meddle where she shouldn't. How soon can you get everything in place?'

'We should wrap up that other job tonight, and then we'll be free to concentrate on this one. Three days at the most.'

'That will have to do. You should be paying me for this one.'

~

Jordan scratched the top of his ear. 'A dozen eggs,' he mumbled. 'It's a six-digit PIN number; so how the hell do you convert twelve eggs into six-digits?' He crumpled the paper and lobbed it off the wall and into the dustbin. The doorbell interrupted his thoughts. He heaved himself off the couch with a sigh and opened the door. Matt Kilpatrick, his old university buddy, greeted him with a smile and thrust out a six-pack.

'Busy?'

'Not really, Killa, I'm trying to solve a problem for Laura. Come and have a look at it.'

Half an hour later, Jordan tossed yet another crumpled wad of paper over his left shoulder and into the bin.

'Nice shot,' said Kilpatrick admiringly. He tapped the piece of paper in front of him with his pen. 'Do you know something? I don't think it's a code.'

'Of course it's a code. What do you think it is? A strategy for greeting politicians?'

'I notice you only trot out your sarcasm after you've drunk my beer. Now pay attention, you dullard. It's obviously a cryptic reminder for the owner of the PIN, but it's not an alphabetical code.'

'I see,' said Jordan heavily. 'It says a dozen eggs, but it's not alphabetical.'

Kilpatrick waved the paper under Jordan's nose. 'You want six digits, you've got six digits. Change the dozen into numerals and you have twelve eggs. Six digits.'

'Yes, but what does it mean?' exclaimed Jordan in frustration.

'I don't know,' answered Kilpatrick in a matching tone, 'but I'm sure somebody does.'

'Somebody did, but they're both dead,' replied Jordan tiredly.

'Excuse me?'

'Maybe his family knows,' mused Jordan, 'although Stephen did say it was a secret.'

'Whose family? Stephen who?'

Jordan looked at his friend. 'Would you like to hear an interesting story?'

'Are the dozen eggs connected to hot chicks?'

'No.'

'Oh well, tell me anyway.'

Laura arrived home shortly before Jordan reached the conclusion and sat cross-legged on the floor with her back to the gas fire as he told Kilpatrick about the second ambulance.

'I find the whole thing a little difficult to believe,' said Kilpatrick dubiously. 'It sounds like something out of the *X-Files*.'

'Believe what you like,' said Laura wearily. 'I had a meeting with Dr Borkov today, and I got the feeling he knows more than he's telling.'

Jordan raised a questioning eyebrow. 'What makes you say that?'

'Nothing I can put my finger on.'

'I see, women's intuition,' said Jordan teasingly.

'Nothing of the sort,' replied Laura tartly. 'Somebody in his line of business should have been intrigued by the whole affair, but he simply dismissed my theories and didn't bother to offer any of his own.' She suddenly shuddered. 'He actually gave me the creeps.'

After Kilpatrick left, Laura gave Jordan a hand to prepare dinner. 'I received the autopsy report on Stephen today,' she said. 'The cause of death was an aneurism.'

'Isn't that unusual for somebody his age?'

'Unusual, yes, but not unheard of. If only we knew what happened to Stephen during those five missing days.'

Jordan shook his head in annoyance. 'It's damned frustrating, but I can't think of anything further to investigate. Our leads have dried up.' He sprinkled a few herbs over the meat. 'Now that we're in the mood, do you want to hear my totally depressing news?'

'Love to.'

'Tomorrow, I start work for Tellink as a systems engineer,' he said morosely.

'That's terrific.' She gave him a hug. 'I'm very proud of you.' She picked up the scrap of paper and stared at the code. 'I wonder if this means anything.'

'I doubt it, but who's to know?'

'Maybe his family can help us.'

'I don't think so. Stephen said they didn't know about it.'

'What if we've been going about this backwards? What if Chandler holds the key?'

Jordan shook his head. 'He's as much a dead end as Stephen is. Sorry, no pun intended. He was in a coma when Stephen disappeared.'

Laura sighed. 'That's it then. I can't think of anything else to do.'

She looked so dejected that Jordan stepped across and took her in his arms. 'Tell you what I'll do. I'll pick up Killa and see the Chandler family after work tomorrow. They should be told about the secret account anyway.' She gave him a hug in return as she settled her head on his shoulder.

～

The icy wind blew gusts of misery around the group of men huddled together beneath Putney Bridge. A smouldering fire set in a rusted drum radiated a small amount of heat, and the men passed around a cheap bottle of wine for additional comfort. One of the men stirred from beneath his covering of rags and threw a piece of wood onto the dying embers. A passenger boat slipped out of the swirling mist and glided by, the inhabitants celebrating cheerfully as the beat of their music washed over the group of silent watchers.

Distant footsteps echoed dully from the damp paving stones, and the men turned to watch a dark form approaching along the path. Strangers at this time of night were not good news. Another dark form appeared from the opposite side of the bridge, and they struggled to their feet in anticipation of trouble. A powerful light suddenly transfixed the ragged group, and they raised their arms in a futile effort to shield their eyes from the painful glare.

'Police! Stay where you!' commanded an authoritative voice. The dark shape moved closer, holding the group of men in place with the beam of his torch.

'What do want with us?' one of the men asked tentatively. 'We ain't done nothing wrong. Shouldn't you be out catching criminals?'

The officer stopped several metres from the small group. 'This is your lucky night, boys. We have orders to take you to a shelter. The city council is tired of finding frozen bodies cluttering their walkways.'

'We like it here,' mumbled the most adventurous of the group. 'Besides, there ain't no shelters around here for the likes of us.'

'That's where you're wrong, mate,' said the officer cheerfully. 'The Sisters of Mercy are offering hot food and a warm bed. Now move along before I get angry.'

The men muttered rebelliously but followed the officer back to a waiting police van. They were bundled into the back and then driven to an old refurbished warehouse. The officers ushered them inside, and a nun immediately hurried from behind a walnut desk to greet them.

'Who do we have here?' she asked as she stopped in front of them. 'My, you do look famished. Come with me, and we'll get a nice hot meal into you. I'm sure you'll all enjoy that.' She continued to prattle happily as the men followed her down the hallway.

Another nun approached the two policemen and handed over an envelope.

'How many more do you want, Sister?' asked the senior officer softly.

'Just keep bringing them in, and we'll let you know when we're full,' she replied, equally as softly. 'At fifty pounds a head, I'm sure you won't have a problem with that.'

He patted his coat pocket. 'You don't hear us complaining.'

The homeless men weren't complaining either. They were fed a nourishing meal and then given a hot shower. When they emerged feeling warm and relaxed, they were presented with a new set of clothing.

The men accepted each offering with an air of suspicion. When they were finally ushered into a long room already alive with the sounds of other men they looked at each other in mild bewilderment and then gratefully climbed into the narrow bunk beds that promised a comfortable night's rest.

Paul Frampton accelerated away from the following traffic on the motorway. The blonde woman next to him laughed and put her hand on his thigh. He pushed the Porsche to 150 kph and grinned as the woman's grip tightened on his leg. Frampton loved driving at this time of night. He checked his rear-view mirror and was surprised to see a pair of headlights keeping pace behind him. He slowed instinctively, causing his girlfriend to glance at him questioningly.

'I might have picked up a couple of cops,' he said with a grin. The car behind abruptly turned its lights onto high beam.

'Fucking hell,' swore Frampton as he moved his head to avoid the reflection from his mirrors. 'What's that bastard playing at?' He angrily floored the accelerator and sped up to 180 kph, passing a succession of slower vehicles, but the other car remained glued behind him.

The pursuing car finally drew level, and Frampton glanced over in annoyance. It was a black Mercedes coupe. Instead of racing past, the Mercedes veered closer, and Frampton cursed under his breath and moved into the left lane. He decided to slow down and let this maniac get clear of him.

His girlfriend suddenly screamed as she pointed at the Mercedes. The man in the passenger seat was aiming a gun directly at him. He instinctively swerved further to the left, but the other car moved with him. A safety barrier loomed out of the darkness. Frampton corrected to avoid it, but the heavier Mercedes smashed into his front wing and sent him careening directly towards the barrier's edge. He desperately swung the wheel, but the barrier was too close. The passenger side smashed sickeningly into it, flipping the car into the air. It landed back on the road and swerved wildly for several seconds before turning sideways, rolling twice, and then smashing back into the barrier.

DeLuca brought the Mercedes to a swift stop and reversed to the smashed vehicle. Dawson was out of the car and moving towards the Porsche in an instant. Broken glass from the shattered windscreen crunched beneath his feet as he quickly inspected the wreckage.

One glance at the girl confirmed she was dead, the top of her skull taken off with surgical precision. The car was a wreck, but Dawson opened the driver's door effortlessly. 'God bless German machinery,' he murmured. The air bag had saved Frampton's life but had broken his nose as it exploded into his face. A trickle of blood bubbled from the corner of his mouth. Dawson took a small syringe from his coat and injected 25 ml of pure alcohol into a vein in Frampton's arm.

'Never drink and drive,' he scolded as he leant across and checked Frampton's pulse. 'Touch and go,' he whispered to Frampton, 'but you might live.' A shout from DeLuca alerted him to a car pulling up behind them. Dawson grabbed Frampton's neck and gave it a powerful twist. There was an audible crack as it broke. 'Then again, maybe not.'

He straightened up and moved towards the newly arrived car. 'Stay back,' he shouted to its two horrified occupants. 'There's petrol leaking everywhere, so it's best not to use a cell phone. We're going down the road to phone for an ambulance.'

'I thought the paintwork was a perfect match,' said DeLuca as he drove away.

'I dunno,' said Dawson. 'I thought his black was a bit darker than ours, but then it's so hard to tell at night.'

'Black is black,' said DeLuca firmly.

'I can't argue with that,' replied Dawson with a laugh.

Jordan rang Tracey Chandler the following morning and explained that he was a journalist investigating the strange circumstances involving Stephen Kimpton and her father. Although her attitude was cold, she reluctantly agreed to meet him that evening.

He spent an uneventful day at work and then picked up Kilpatrick and drove to the Chandler residence. The sky was threatening further rain as they hurried along the path towards the house.

Tracey Chandler opened the door with a frosty stare when they rang the bell. 'Yes?'

'I'm Daniel Jordan,' he announced pleasantly. 'I rang this morning about the ... er.'

She continued to stare coldly at him, and he quickly introduced Kilpatrick.

'I suppose you'd better come in,' she said in a surly tone. 'I'll give you five minutes.'

A large Labrador clambered from a rug by the fire and lazily inspected them as they followed her into the lounge room. Jordan gave Tracey a wry smile. 'We know you've been through a lot lately, and we appreciate your seeing us.'

She stared at him without blinking. 'You've got three minutes left, so you'd better get to the point.'

'Of course,' said Jordan hurriedly. 'We're investigating Stephen Kimpton's movements during the week prior to his appearance in your kitchen. We were wondering if it was possible for him to have met your father during that time.'

Tracey snorted in disgust, and the dog stirred behind her. 'You're kidding, right? My father was either in a coma or dead during that week. The only person he could have met was his maker.' She stood up. 'Are you finished?'

'Not quite.' Jordan held out a piece of paper. 'Apparently your father had a secret bank account which can be accessed with this code. Unfortunately, it's cryptic.'

'A secret account? How could you possibly know that?'

Jordan glanced at Kilpatrick before answering. 'Stephen Kimpton told us before he died.'

'He's dead?'

'An aneurism. We believe Stephen and your father were part of an experiment involving memory transfer.'

'I don't have time for this rubbish,' scowled Tracey. 'Your five minutes are up.'

'Okay, but would you mind looking at the code before we leave?'

Tracey snatched the paper from Jordan's outstretched hand and glanced at it. 'It's meaningless.'

'That's it then,' sighed Jordan as he walked towards the door. 'Thanks for your time.'

Kilpatrick stood his ground. 'Apart from Stephen Kimpton, has anything else unusual happened recently?'

'Not a thing,' she replied gruffly.

'Not even a minor incident?' persisted Kilpatrick.

'My father did have somebody else's bank card in his belongings, but that was just a mix up at the hospital. I was going to post it back tomorrow.'

'Can I see it?' asked Kilpatrick cautiously.

'Only if you promise to leave once you've seen it.' She picked up a card from the table and thrust it at Kilpatrick.

'Charles Jedamn.' Kilpatrick looked questioningly at Jordan, who merely shook his head.

'Nice knowing you,' said Tracey as she retrieved the card and ushered them towards the door.

'I've got it!' exclaimed Kilpatrick suddenly. 'Charles Jedamn, James Chandler. It's an anagram. This must be the card to his secret account.'

'There is no secret account,' snapped Tracey. 'I want you to leave now.'

'It could contain a lot of money,' replied Kilpatrick quietly. 'All we have to do is work out the code.'

'Yes, but the code doesn't make any sense,' muttered Tracey. 'In fact, none of this makes any sense.'

'It must have made sense to your father,' insisted Kilpatrick. 'Why else would he have used a dozen eggs to remind him of his PIN? Is there anything in your father's past involving hens or chickens?'

'I told you, it means nothing to me. The only person who knows is dead, so we can't really ask him now, can we?' She blinked back several tears.

'I'm sorry,' apologised Jordan. 'We didn't mean to upset you. We thought you might know.'

'Well, I'm sorry, but I don't,' she said tearfully. Her dog roused itself from the warmth of the fire and gently pushed its nose between her knees. 'My father was very keen on puzzles and mind teasers,' she continued as she pushed the dog away. 'He loved solving the chess problems in the paper, white to mate in four, that sort of thing.' She suddenly snapped her fingers. 'I remember he was fascinated with calculators when they first became popular. Yes,' she murmured, 'I bet that's it.' She hurried out the room, her dog in close pursuit. 'I'll be right back,' she called as she disappeared down the hallway.

'Calculators?' echoed Kilpatrick.

'Just be patient,' said Jordan softly. 'With a little luck, all will be revealed.'

Tracey returned with a calculator and quickly punched in a series of numbers. 'There you are,' she said triumphantly. 'Mystery solved.'

'Let me see,' demanded Kilpatrick. 'I've spent a sleepless night over this.' He studied the display and then glanced quizzically at Tracey.

She reached out and turned the calculator upside down. 'You see now?'

'So simple,' he groaned. 'a dozen eggs: 566321. I wonder how much is in the account.'

'I can check that over the phone,' replied Tracey. They waited while she called the bank and gave them the account PIN. She wrote a figure down and hung up, a stunned look on her face.

'How much?' asked Kilpatrick.

She glanced at the paper. 'There's 257,894 pounds.'

Jordan whistled appreciatively. 'That's a lot of money. What did your father do for a living?'

'He was a stockbroker. Knowing my father, I'm sure this was all earned legitimately.' She looked at Jordan thoughtfully. 'How could Stephen have known about this account?'

Jordan shrugged. 'As I said before, we believe it was an experiment in memory transfer.'

'But who are these people, and how did my father become involved?'

Jordan smiled apologetically. 'All we have are a few random facts and odd situations, nothing concrete. We're stumbling around in the dark trying to make sense of it all.'

'Perhaps Tracey can help,' said Kilpatrick excitedly. 'Her father is the pivotal link. We need to understand his movements during the period Stephen went missing.'

Jordan coughed politely. 'Tracey's already told us he was in hospital when Stephen disappeared, and then he … er …'

'Oh, of course,' mumbled Kilpatrick awkwardly. 'Then we need to look at the people who had access to him. Something or somebody connected to Mr Chandler will provide the thread that will lead us to Stephen.'

'It sounds logical,' said Jordan slowly as he glanced at Tracey. 'What do you think?'

'If you think it will help, I'll do what I can.'

'Great,' said Kilpatrick. 'Tomorrow's Saturday, so why don't I come around in the morning, and we can make a list.'

'Me and my big mouth,' muttered Tracey. She was brusque but pleased. 'All right, but not too early, and don't go talking about this in front of my mother. It will only upset her.'

Jordan had been feeling increasingly unsettled for some time and abruptly stood up to leave. 'Listen, Killa, would you mind taking the tube? I can't explain it, but I have to go straight home.'

'Forgotten something important? Somebody's birthday perhaps?'

Jordan shook his head. 'No, it's nothing like that.' He grabbed his coat and dashed out to his car. The engine reluctantly kicked into life, and he slammed it into first gear and cut out into the peak hour traffic.

Chapter 5

She takes just like a woman, yes, she does
She makes love just like a woman, yes, she does,
And she aches just like a woman,
But she breaks just like a little girl.

Bob Dylan

Laura parked her BMW and walked briskly to her front door. Dead leaves, unswept since late autumn, blew across the lawn and light drizzle spotted her fawn overcoat with small beads of water. She gave it a quick brush before closing the door behind her. The house was uncharacteristically cold and dark and there was a faint smell of dampness in the air as she turned on the gas heater and hung her coat next to it.

Jordan was usually home before her, and she had grown accustomed to stepping into a warm, well-lit house. She felt momentarily guilty that she had driven him down a career path he clearly disliked.

Dawson and DeLuca watched the house lights blink on from the warmth of their car. Dawson hated rushed jobs. A successful job resulted from thorough preparation, and understanding the victim's movements was a key requirement. A hurried kill was known in the industry as a 'Murphy' because that was when things usually went wrong. However, on Dawson's scale of difficulty, this one barely registered. He had pulled rank and declared that he would carry out the rape. 'It looks as though she's alone, so let's get this over with. The last thing I need is another late night.' His breath hung in small white clouds as he spoke.

'I'll swap if you're not feeling up to it,' suggested DeLuca hopefully.

'I'll manage.' Dawson pulled on a pair of surgical gloves and rang the bell. There was a metallic scraping sound before the door opened, constrained by a heavy security chain.

Laura peered through the gap. 'Yes? Can I help you?'

'Laura Monroe?' asked Dawson.

'Yes,' she replied, slightly puzzled.

'We've come to check out your plumbing,' said Dawson in a matter-of-fact voice. Behind him, DeLuca, DeLuca struggled to suppress a grin.

'I think you've got the wrong address,' Laura replied pleasantly.

'Is that so?' queried Dawson. He took a step back, swivelled lightly, and delivered a powerful kick just above the door handle. The screws securing the chain exploded from the woodwork and the door cannoned into Laura's shoulder, knocking her to the floor. The two men quickly stepped inside and shut the door.

'Find the bedroom; then check the rest of the house,' ordered Dawson. DeLuca gave a brief nod and disappeared down the hallway.

Laura was lying in shock on the floor. Dawson dragged her to her feet and pulled her into the lounge room. Her eyes were wide with fright. As she opened her mouth to scream, Dawson punched her cruelly in the abdomen, driving the breath from her body. She collapsed to her knees, gagging and gasping desperately for air. He grabbed a handful of hair and brutally jerked her upright, holding a thin, ivory-handled knife in front of her terrified eyes. 'Don't even think about screaming,' he snarled as he pushed the blade against her cheek and drew a small bead of blood. 'Understand?'

Laura was still gasping for breath and tears of distress ran freely down her face smudging her carefully applied makeup. She tried to speak but the effort was too much, and she finally nodded with a stiff movement of her head.

Dawson smiled wolfishly. 'That's a good girl. I'd hate to cut up someone as pretty as you.' He changed his grip on the knife and slashed swiftly through the buttons on her blouse. She jerked back involuntarily but he pulled her to him in a show of effortless strength. His skin had a sour smell, and she wrinkled her nose in disapproval. Her blouse hung open at the front, exposing her lace-trimmed bra, and there was a thin line of blood where the knife had nicked her skin. He placed the knife between his teeth, reached behind her, and ripped off her blouse. She struggled for a moment, and he gave her a savage backhanded blow that sent her reeling over the coffee table. He was onto her again in two quick strides.

'Behave.'

'Please, don't hurt me,' she pleaded hoarsely, her voice breaking as she spoke.

'Then do as you're told.'

She stood silently for a moment, feeling completely powerless, a trickle of blood escaping from a cut on her lip. 'What do you want from me?' she finally whispered.

He laughed. 'I would have thought that was obvious. Here, I'll give you another clue.' She felt the cold steel of the blade touch her back momentarily, and there was a slight tug as the elastic on her bra briefly resisted the knife's keen edge. His pale eyes held her transfixed, and he leaned forward and kissed her left nipple. Dawson grinned as she shuddered at his touch. 'That's right. Be afraid, be very afraid,' he mimicked, his pale eyes glittering menacingly. 'If you do as I want, I might let you live.'

DeLuca returned to the room and glanced casually at her naked breasts. 'Very nice,' he muttered. 'Couldn't we both ...?'

'No, we couldn't,' snapped Dawson. 'It would ruin the MO. Which room is it?'

'Second on the left. The rest of the house is clear.'

'All right, give me the candles, and no peeking.'

'As if I'd want to watch your hairy backside pumping up and down,' retorted DeLuca as he dug two squat candles from his pocket.

Laura had gone increasingly pale as reality washed over, but before she could protest, Dawson took a firm grip on her hair and dragged her towards the bedroom. She whimpered in fear as he flicked on the bedroom light and kicked the door shut.

'Why are you doing this?' she gasped as he pushed her onto the bed. She knew that establishing a bond sometimes saved the victim from the worst of the attack. 'I'm not a bad person. I don't deserve this.'

'It's all part of the big picture,' he said as his shoes clattered to the floor. 'Too bad you can't see it, but this is your destiny.'

She heard the sound of a cigarette lighter before the lights were turned off. 'Quite romantic, don't you think,' he said as he admired her body in the candlelight. She lay there unmoving as he tugged off her shoes and stockings and then expertly removed her skirt and panties.

'Oh, Daniel,' she whispered. 'Where are you?' She was dismayed to find herself waiting submissively for this creature to coldly rape her. She had always imagined that she would fight, bite, scream, and claw if she found herself in such a predicament, but all she had done was become numb.

'Nature's been kind to me, Laura,' he said as he forced her legs apart, 'so I suggest you relax and enjoy yourself.'

Her eyes widened slightly at his use of her name. They had also used her name when she opened the door. She had been singled out for this, but why? 'You're going to kill me,' she said in a flat voice as she turned her head and looked him squarely in the face.

His pale, hypnotic eyes never blinked. 'We'll see,' he answered simply.

God, she thought, *this isn't happening. Surely, it's just a bad dream.*

He felt her shudder beneath him and moved his body slightly in order to force his way inside but then suddenly stopped. 'Damn, I forgot something,' he muttered harshly. He pushed himself to his knees and reached behind him. Laura toyed for an instant with the idea of drawing up her legs and kicking him in the testicles, but then he turned back, and she noted with horror that he was holding the ivory-handled knife.

'This isn't my idea,' he said softly as his hand moved. She was unable to stifle a sharp scream as she felt a searing pain above her left breast.

～

DeLuca wandered aimlessly around the lounge room looking at the pictures and ornaments that defined the life of the girl they were about to murder. His surgical gloves prevented any careless fingerprints being left behind, but he was still careful not to touch anything. He wandered up the passage and listened at the bedroom door but was unable to hear anything, and now that the initial excitement had waned, he was becoming bored.

He badly needed to go to the toilet. He had been cooped up in the car for the past few hours, and the spicy chicken he'd eaten for lunch was beginning to disagree with him. He could probably wait another half hour, but he was still angry with his partner for not sharing the woman. 'If he can't protect himself from a bloody woman while I take a crap, then fuck him,' he muttered angrily as he made his way to the upstairs bathroom.

Jordan parked his car in the street and hastily locked it before walking briskly towards the house. He had made excellent time by taking several risks he would normally have avoided. The nagging feeling that something was wrong had grown stronger as he drove home. The bathroom light suddenly blinked on, and he smiled at his unwarranted fears. 'I'm getting worse than my mother,' he chided himself as he fumbled through his keys. His stomach abruptly lurched as the splintered wood surrounding the safety chain grabbed his attention. The whispered fear that had driven him home suddenly burst into full voice. He slowly pushed open the door and stepped into the lounge room.

Laura's bra was lying crumpled on the floor, the strap cut cleanly in two. Jordan's initial reaction was to scream her name, but he calmed himself and moved cautiously into the hallway. He had become proficient at Zen Do Kai karate at university, and although he had subsequently let his training lapse, the skill he had achieved gave him tthe confidence to move farther into the house.

Laura's sudden scream galvanised him into action. He sprinted down the hallway and yanked the door open. The sight of a large semi-naked man kneeling on the bed holding a bloodstained knife froze him in his tracks. Laura was lying naked beneath him.

'I told you not to come in here,' the man on the bed growled.

Jordan stepped forward and snatched the statue of Chloe from the bedside table. Dawson noticed the movement and instantly raised the knife in a fluid defensive movement as he realized it wasn't DeLuca who had entered the room. Jordan ignored the knife and swung the heavy marble base at the man's head.

Dawson saw the blow coming but his position on the bed prevented him from effectively blocking it. The corner of the marble base crashed into his temple with all the brutal force Jordan could muster. The knife dropped instantly from his nerveless fingers, and he toppled sideways onto the far side of the bed. 'Fucking Murphy,' he said quite clearly, and then he was still.

'Thank God,' sobbed Laura.

Jordan stood motionless for a moment, staring at the stranger. 'I think I killed him,' he said as he slowly sat down next to Laura. He looked at the blood covering her left breast. 'Are you all right?'

'Not really.' She sat up and pulled him to her in a fierce embrace. 'God, I'm shaking all over.'

'So am I,' shuddered Jordan. 'Who the hell is he? What was he doing here?'

She turned and looked at Dawson, who stared back at her from sightless eyes, their hypnotic appeal gone. 'He was going to rape me,' she said, her voice tinged with disbelief.

Jordan turned to her, their faces almost touching. 'He didn't ...' He was unable to finish the sentence.

She shook her head. 'All he did was touch me, but I still feel utterly violated. It was so close. Another minute ...' She buried her face in her hands.

'The bathroom light,' exclaimed Jordan, springing to his feet. 'I saw the light turn on and thought it was you.'

'There were two of them. What if the other one comes in?' whispered Laura in a horrified voice. 'God, this is a nightmare.'

'Come on.' Jordan pulled Laura to her feet and propelled her into the en suite bathroom. He wrapped a towel around her and handed her his cell phone. 'Lock yourself in and call the police while I barricade the bedroom door. Promise me you'll stay in here until the police arrive no matter what happens.'

'What about you?' she asked frantically. 'These men are killers.'

'Don't worry, I'll be all right,' he said as he wrapped a wet cloth around his wrist, where he had suffered a cut from Dawson's knife.

Laura locked the door behind him as he hurried back into the bedroom. Jordan decided on the solid chest of drawers as a suitable barricade and gave it a heave to push it into place against the door. A framed picture toppled to the floor, and Laura called his name in alarm. As he reassured her, he heard soft footsteps in the hallway, and he frantically pushed the chest against the door. Somebody rattled the doorknob, and Jordan added his weight to the barricade.

A voice cried out. 'Dawson, what's happening in there? What's going on? Speak to me.'

Jordan remained silent. There was a sudden jolt as the assailant threw his body against the door. The impact caused a small gap to open. The assailant thrust his foot into the opening and began to slowly push. Jordan strained to keep him out, but the gap steadily widened.

DeLuca pushed his hips into the narrow space and then shoved with his knees and arms to widen it. The bottom of the door slowly buckled under the pressure, and DeLuca forced his lower leg into the gap, heaved again, and was suddenly through.

Jordan moved farther around the bed keeping his eyes on the swarthy young man who had burst into the room. He wasn't as powerfully built as the dead man was but still had a distinctly evil look about him.

DeLuca glanced at Dawson's body and then turned back to Jordan. 'Where's the girl?'

'She's gone to ring the police.' Jordan tried to sound confident. 'They'll be here at any moment, so you should leave while you can.'

'No, I don't think so. You'd have gone with her, so I think she's hiding in the bathroom.' He moved across and tried the door but it was locked. He stepped back to give it a hefty kick but Jordan picked up the broken figurine from the bed and threw it. DeLuca swayed out of the way, and the statue sailed harmlessly by and crashed into the wall.

'Okay, tough guy,' sneered DeLuca as he walked around the bed full of casual confidence. 'How about I cut off your cock and feed it to your girlfriend while I'm raping her. Let's see how she likes that.'

Jordan shook his head. 'Laura's not *really interested* in ménage-a-trois.' He slowly moved back until he was trapped in the far corner. DeLuca dropped into a tight fighting stance, reminding Jordan of a leopard closing in for the kill. He realised his only chance was to lull his attacker into believing he posed no threat and then catch him unawares. DeLuca suddenly swivelled and delivered a powerful roundhouse kick to Jordan's head.

Jordan moved to block the kick, but DeLuca's foot still smacked heavily into his face. The impact stunned him, and he felt a trickle of warm blood run into his mouth. DeLuca grinned and swivelled to deliver another roundhouse kick. As Jordan moved to block it with his arm, DeLuca pulled the kick short and sent Jordan crashing into the wall with a forceful kick to the sternum.

'Not so tough now, are you?' jeered DeLuca as he moved in to deliver a brutal right-handed blow to the head. Jordan effectively blocked the punch and then, sensing his opportunity, leant back and delivered a sharp upward kick to his assailant's groin. He had practised the move many times during sparring sessions and knew an effective execution would cripple any opponent. The kick only had to travel three feet. To Jordan's dismay, DeLuca caught his leg in an iron grip, turned him around, kicked his other leg from beneath him, and threw him on top of Dawson.

'Stacks on the mill.' laughed DeLuca derisively.

Jordan glimpsed the ivory-handled knife as he hurriedly rolled off the dead body and away from his attacker. He discretely grabbed it as he stood up. 'Did your mommy teach you to bitch-slap like that? It would take a man to rape Laura, and you're not a man, are you? You're a mommy's boy,' he taunted scathingly.

DeLuca screamed furiously as he launched a flying kick that sent Jordan staggering back against the bathroom door and caused Laura to scream. DeLuca's left leg buckled painfully beneath him as he landed, and he looked down in surprise. Dawson's knife was buried in his calf muscle. Jordan took the opportunity to kick him brutally in the face. The blow sent DeLuca sprawling on his back, and as he struggled to regain his feet, Jordan noticed he had pulled the knife from his leg.

DeLuca took a lurching step towards Jordan, snarling menacingly. 'I'm going to cut you into little strips,' he growled menacingly. The sound of a siren wailing in the distance halted him in mid-step, and he looked round uncertainly before glaring at Jordan. 'This isn't over, fuckhead. This is personal now; do you hear me? Personal. No matter where you go or what you do, I'll be watching and waiting. One dark night and *urk*.' He drew his finger across his throat. 'And the same goes for your fucking bitch.'

He looked at the chest of drawers blocking the door and then hobbled over to the window and wrenched it open. As he climbed painfully over the windowsill, he turned and jabbed a threatening finger at Jordan. 'Personal,' he repeated, dropping into the darkness to stagger away to his car.

DeLuca drove for several minutes and then stopped and reported in to Madison, informing him that Dawson was dead.

'Dawson's dead?' queried Madison in surprise. 'I thought he was indestructible. How'd that happen?'

'The boyfriend came home unexpectedly and caught him off guard.'

'I see,' replied Madison slowly. 'Where's Dawson now?'

'I had to leave him at the scene. The police were called, and there was no time to tidy up.'

'There's nothing to trace Dawson to us is there?'

'No, we both travel clean.'

There was a whispered conversation at the other end of the phone, and Borkov came on the line. 'What about the girl? Is she dead?'

DeLuca grimaced before answering. 'No, there wasn't time, but Dawson roughed her up rather badly.'

'A simple hit and the best you could do was "rough her up rather badly,"' replied Borkov, mimicking DeLuca's voice. 'All right, make yourself scarce. We'll handle it from here.'

Borkov called Rathbone and ordered him to dispatch an ambulance to Laura's address. 'Unfortunate accidents happen in hospitals. I'll double your usual fee if this woman is one of them. Don't let me down,' he growled.

≈

Jordan sat painfully on the bed and wiped the blood from his face. 'You can come out now,' he shouted hoarsely. 'The bastard's gone.'

Laura opened the door and peered out. 'Are you okay?'

'I'll live.' He felt like vomiting and took a deep breath to steady his nerves. Several cars screeched to a halt in front of the house as waves of red and blue light bathed the room in an eerie glow. Jordan helped Laura slip into a dressing gown, and they met the police as they warily entered through the front door.

'He escaped through the bedroom window,' declared Jordan. 'If you're quick you might still catch him. He's wounded in the leg and bleeding quite badly.'

'Is that so?' replied the officer in charge as he drew himself up to his full height and looked down his nose at Jordan. 'And who might you be, sir?'

'Daniel Jordan. Look, there's a chance you could catch him if you're quick.'

The officer gave him a bemused look. 'All in good time, sir. I think you'll find we know what we're doing.' He glanced at Laura. 'Are you the person who phoned about the attempted murder and rape?'

Laura gave a brief nod as she pulled the gown tighter around her body. Jordan started to repeat his plea, but the policeman brusquely cut him off. 'Please remain silent unless I ask you a question.'

Jordan failed to hide his annoyance and glanced around the room in mute appeal, but the other officers stared back with stone-faced detachment.

The officer took Jordan's silence for compliance and turned to Laura. 'Madam, I'm Senior Detective Kent. You're quite safe now so you have nothing to fear by telling us the truth.' He paused for effect and then pointed accusingly at Jordan. 'Is this the man that attacked you?'

Jordan protested indignantly. 'Me? I'm not the one who did this.'

The officer gave him a warning look before turning back to Laura. 'Madam?'

Laura shook her head. 'No, of course not.'

'Are you sure, madam? He can't hurt you now.'

'Daniel would never hurt me,' she replied in a stronger voice. Jordan continued to splutter indignantly, his frustration increasing by the second. Before the officer could say anything further, one of his colleagues hurried into the room to report the discovery of a naked male Caucasian, deceased, in one of the bedrooms, who appeared to have been bludgeoned to death.

Kent turned to face Laura and Jordan. 'I think you have some explaining to do, don't you?'

The sound of voices attracted his attention, and he glared angrily as two burly men and a female officer walked through the front door. 'Banks!' he scowled. 'What the hell are you doing here? Have you come and see some real detectives at work?' He grinned at his colleagues.

'You're violating my turf, Kent. Anything to do with the Crucifix Killer falls under my jurisdiction,' replied Banks tartly.

'Who said anything about the Crucifix Killer? This is an open-and-shut domestic murder case.'

'Open-and-shut?' repeated Jordan in astonishment.

'Oh, yes, Sonny Jim. You've been clever, but not clever enough,' sneered Kent.

'Me?' replied Jordan. 'You think I did this?'

'Do you deny killing that man in the bedroom?'

Jordan looked startled. 'Well, no, of course not. He was attacking Laura.'

The officer standing next to Kent quickly interjected. 'Sir, he hasn't had his rights read to him yet.'

'It's of no consequence,' replied Kent nonchalantly. 'I understand precisely what happened here.'

Banks turned to his partner. 'I've had enough of this. Get the boss on the blower before I say something I'll regret.'

Kent smiled laconically. 'Fine. Call Fenwick. This has nothing to do with the Crucifix Killer.'

'I don't believe this,' muttered Jordan in disgust. 'You're standing here squabbling while the real culprit is getting away.'

'I'd desist if I were you,' admonished Kent sharply. 'All you're doing is making yourself look foolish. Let me tell you what really happened here.'

'Please do,' replied Jordan sarcastically.

Kent gave him a superior smile. 'It's not that uncommon really. You came home from work, unexpectedly I'd say, and found your girlfriend in bed with another man. You bludgeoned her lover to death in a fit of jealousy and then cut her up to teach her a lesson. As I said before, open-and-shut case.'

Banks was clearly angry but was prevented from saying anything by his partner, who handed him a phone. He spoke into it briefly before passing it on to Kent, who smiled in return.

His smile gradually faded as he listened intently before handing the phone back to Banks. 'Unfortunately, I've been called away on a more important case. I'm sure you can manage the final wrap-up on your own.' He gestured imperiously to his team as he strode from the room.

Banks turned to his partner, who was waiting expectantly at his side. 'Right, Evans, get the team in here pronto.' He shook his head apologetically. 'Sorry about that. I'm Senior Inspector Robert Banks, and this is my partner Detective Inspector Roger Evans.'

He signalled to a policewoman, who stepped forward and took several pictures of Laura's injuries before placing a cloth over the cut. 'I've called for an ambulance,' she said. 'They should be here in about fifteen minutes.'

Jordan glared angrily at Banks. 'If this is an example of the modern police force at work, then heaven help us.'

Banks gave him an understanding look. 'You shouldn't pay too much attention to Inspector Kent. Most domestic incidents start and finish in the home, and that's his way of sorting the chaff from the grain. You'd be surprised how effective that approach can be.'

'In the meantime, the real culprit gets away,' retorted Jordan angrily.

'I didn't say I agreed with it,' said Banks with an air of finality. He took out a stubby pencil and flipped open his notebook. 'I'd like to get a brief statement before the ambulance arrives.'

'Er … there really is a dead man in our bedroom,' said Jordan apologetically. 'Shouldn't you check that first?'

'My men will look after that. Now, who's first?'

Laura wiped her eyes with the back of her hand and started to speak but suddenly gave a low moan and grabbed hold of Jordan. 'I'm sorry,' she whispered, 'I can't do this.'

Jordan looked at her helplessly. 'Don't you think she's been through enough?'

I'm sorry, sir,' said Banks apologetically. 'I know it's difficult, but the sooner we start our investigation, the sooner we can catch the assailant and maybe prevent some other poor souls from having to go through this.'

'If you lot had acted quickly when you arrived, you might already have caught him.'

'I understand your anger, sir, but we want to catch him as much as you do. In order to do that we'll need your full cooperation,' said Banks soothingly.

'They knew who I was,' Laura said suddenly.

Banks stared at her. 'This wasn't a random attack?'

She shook her head. 'They knew my name.'

'That doesn't sound like the Crucifix Killer,' said Evans.

Banks nodded. 'Can you think of anybody who would want to do this to you?'

Laura stared back at him helplessly, unable to speak.

Jordan let out a sigh as he reached for Laura's hand. 'Laura's been investigating a company called Memtech. Perhaps they've got something to do with this.'

'And why they would want to murder Laura?'

'I don't know,' replied Jordan. 'It's only a thought.' Evans made a note of Jordan's concerns and promised to run a check on the company.

Jordan then briefly outlined the events of the evening and gave Banks a detailed description of his assailant. He promised to come down to police headquarters the following day and help with an identikit picture.

They watched absently as the two detectives examined the discarded items of Laura's clothing. They trailed behind as the detectives walked into the bedroom, drawn almost against their will by the sounds of activity. Several men were taking photographs of the body from different angles and dusting for fingerprints.

'What have we got?' asked Banks.

'Caucasian male about thirty-five years old,' replied a thin man in a tan overcoat. 'Dead about half an hour. Preliminary examinations indicate the cause of death was a blow to the left temple.'

'Found the weapon yet?'

'Ah, yes.' He held up a plastic bag containing a broken figurine. 'Venus de Milo.'

'Chloe,' corrected Laura absently.

'I beg your pardon?' said Banks.

'Her name is Chloe,' explained Jordan. 'She used to have arms before this happened.'

Banks noticed the young policewoman poke her head around the door. 'Yes, Saunders?'

'The ambulance is here, sir,' she replied briskly.

'Right,' said Banks. 'We've got what we need for now. We'll finish this tomorrow when you've been patched up. Do you have somewhere you can spend the next few days, with your parents perhaps or a friend? This house is a crime scene, and it's important that the evidence remains uncontaminated.'

'Sure, I understand,' said Jordan.

'Good,' replied Banks briskly. He escorted them out of the house to the waiting ambulance and watched silently as it sped away.

Constable Saunders stood next to Banks as they watched the departing vehicle. 'That's unusual, sir,' said Saunders.

'Hmm?'

'There's another ambulance just come around the far corner.'

'It must be here to pick up the body.'

'Maybe,' said Saunders, 'but I haven't requested one yet.'

'Then somebody else must have,' replied Banks sharply. 'Really, Saunders, it's been a long day, and it's far from over. Please concentrate on the task at hand, and maybe we'll get finished a little bit earlier.'

'Yes, sir,' answered Saunders as she hurried back into the house.

The ambulance carrying Laura and Jordan arrived at Mercy West hospital twenty minutes later. Jordan was taken to a small outpatient cubicle to have the deep cut in his forearm stitched, and then he was cheerfully informed that he was free to go. Jordan asked about Laura's condition, but the duty nurse shrugged and told him to ask at reception.

The receptionist was engrossed in a telephone conversation when he arrived, and she barely glanced at him before half turning in her chair and continuing her conversation. He was in a sour mood and pounded the round bell sitting on the counter.

The woman looked at him in annoyance. 'Yes,' she said wearily.

'Could you please tell me which ward Laura Monroe is in? She was admitted this evening.'

'Visiting time is over.'

'We were involved in an accident, and I want to see how she is,' Jordan persisted.

'Are you family?'

'She's my fiancée,' growled Jordan, starting to seethe inside.

The woman glared at him. 'There are valid reasons for hospital rules you know. Routine is very important to our patients' welfare. What was her name again?'

Jordan spoke through clenched teeth. 'Laura Monroe.'

The woman briefly consulted her computer and then rang a number. 'Is Miss Monroe in 327 fit to receive a visitor? Yes, that's what I thought.' She hung up and looked at Jordan. 'She's asleep. Come back in the morning during visiting hours.'

Jordan didn't feel like spending the night alone in a hotel. He called Kilpatrick, who immediately offered his friend a couch to sleep on. Jordan took a taxi back to his unit to pick up his car but the engine stubbornly refused to turn over, so he took Laura's BMW. Kilpatrick greeted him at the door and steered him towards his couch, which had been hastily made into a bed.

'It's not the Hilton,' apologised Kilpatrick as he attempted to wipe a stain off the pillow.

'It looks fine to me.'

'Good. Now, young man, I'm sure you know the rules. No pets, no loud music, no female company after nine o'clock unless you've brought a spare, and definitely no snoring!'

Jordan gave his friend a tired grin. 'You're just hanging around because you want to watch me undress. I've heard all about you.'

'Why would I want to give myself nightmares? Now I'm serious about the snoring. If you wake me up, I won't be responsible for the consequences.'

'I'm undoing my zipper,' taunted Jordan. 'I wonder if I remembered to put on any underwear.'

'Night,' called Kilpatrick as he hurried from the room.

～

The treatment of the homeless men at the Sisters of Mercy gave them no reason for concern. Every newcomer was given a set of house rules and told that they were free to leave whenever they wished. Those who committed to stay were subjected to a battery of tests for which they were paid a minimal fee. They were informed that their skills were being evaluated to assist with their re-entry into the workforce. Several corporations had generously committed a percentage of low-skilled jobs as part of their social responsibility.

The homeless men happily participated in the program as it was an easy billet, but none of them had any intention of accepting employment. It was a surprise, therefore, when they were occasionally informed that one their brethren had accepted employment and left to start a new life. They failed to associate the puffs of black smoke issuing from the crematorium next door with the recent departure of their colleague.

Chapter 6

And hast thou slain the Jabberwock?
Come to my arms, my beamish boy!
O frabjous day, Callooh! Callay!
He chortled in his joy.

Lewis Carroll

Kilpatrick rang Tracey the next morning to postpone their meeting. Once she knew the full story, she insisted on accompanying them to the hospital.

Kilpatrick greeted her warmly as she climbed into the back seat, but she ignored him and spoke to Jordan. 'Which hospital is your girlfriend in?'

'Mercy West.'

'Mercy West!' That's a coincidence.'

'In what way?' asked Kilpatrick.

'It's the hospital my father was in.'

'And it's the same hospital Stephen Kimpton was taken to after he suffered his aneurism,' added Jordan

Kilpatrick whistled softly. 'What are the chances of that happening?'

'It certainly makes you wonder.'

They entered the hospital and caught the elevator to the third floor and then hurried down the corridor, checking the room numbers until they found Laura's room. Jordan pushed through the curtains covering the doorway and almost collided with a nurse carrying a large bowl of soapy water.

'Can I help you?' she asked primly.

'Good morning,' said Jordan pleasantly. 'We've come to see Laura Monroe.' He peered over the nurse's shoulder but could only make out a dim shape lying in the bed.

'I'm sorry,' said the nurse as she attempted to steer them back into the corridor. 'Miss Monroe is not permitted to have visitors. Doctor's orders.'

'No visitors? Why not? What's happened?' asked Jordan anxiously.

'You'll need to talk to the doctor,' replied the nurse firmly.

Jordan held his ground. 'Listen, I'm her fiancé. I want to know what's wrong with her.'

The nurse hesitated, and Jordan pressed his attack, gesturing at the stitches above his eye. 'I was with her last night when she was assaulted. I've been worried sick, so at least tell me what's wrong.'

The nurse smiled gently. 'Laura is suffering from post-traumatic shock and has been heavily sedated.'

'She was fine last night,' protested Jordan.

'You shouldn't be too concerned. It's just delayed shock. She'll be fine after a good rest.'

'Can I see her for a second?'

The nurse reluctantly agreed, and Jordan walked apprehensively to the bed. Laura's breathing was slow and steady, and she had that air of innocent vulnerability all sleepers possess. Jordan bent and kissed her lightly on the cheek, being careful not to interfere with the plastic tube running into her arm. 'I won't let anything happen to you,' he whispered softly, and then walked out into the corridor, stopping to lean against the wall while he thought about the situation.

'Are you all right?' asked Kilpatrick.

'I don't know. It seems to be one thing after another. I can't take much more of this.'

'Do you want to know another coincidence?' asked Tracey.

'What?' grunted Jordan warily as he pushed himself away from the wall.

'Guess who Laura's doctor is?' Her face looked grim.

'How should I know?' exclaimed Jordan wearily.

'I saw it on the card above her bed. It's Dr Rathbone; the same doctor who treated my father. He's called my mother a couple of times to see how she's coping.'

'Yet another coincidence,' observed Kilpatrick quietly.

Jordan turned and clutched Kilpatrick by the arm. 'We've got to get her out of here.'

'What?' spluttered Kilpatrick. 'She's been sedated in case you hadn't noticed. She's in the best possible place she could be.'

He shook his head. 'You don't understand. They failed to kill her last night, and now they're going to try it again right under our noses. People die in hospitals all the time with no questions asked. I'm getting her out of here, with or without your help.'

Kilpatrick shook his arm free and stepped back from Jordan. 'You're becoming dangerously paranoid and jumping to illogical conclusions. Doctors are allowed to have more than one patient.'

'What do you mean somebody's trying to kill her?' interrupted Tracey.

'It's the same people who murdered Stephen Kimpton,' Jordan replied, the tiredness in his voice evident.

Kilpatrick looked at Jordan with a worried frown. 'There's no evidence Stephen was murdered.'

'Are you going to help me or not?' Jordan demanded. 'I don't have the energy to stand here arguing.'

'I'll help you,' replied Tracey as she gave Kilpatrick a meaningful look. 'I always thought there was something strange about Rathbone.'

'All right,' Kilpatrick said with a sigh, 'I'll help, but it's under sufferance. Remember to tell that to the court when they're determining the length of my sentence.'

'Thanks.' He thought for a moment. 'Okay, I've got a plan. Fetch one of those wheelchairs from the hospital entrance, and meet me back here in ten minutes.'

'What do you want me to do?' asked Tracey.

'Stay here and watch her room. If they move her, follow and find out where they take her. Okay?' Tracey nodded, and the two men hurried off to carry out their instructions. They met by the elevator ten minutes later. Jordan was wearing a green uniform and held out a similar one to Kilpatrick. 'Put this on over the top of your clothes.'

Kilpatrick held the clothing up. 'Very natty, I must say. Where'd you get this?'

'From the laundry hangers near the back entrance. I just walked up and took them. Nobody said a word. Now hurry up and get dressed.'

Tracey joined them as they walked back along the corridor. 'Nobody's been into her room since you left,' she said in a conspiratorial whisper.

'Well done,' said Jordan encouragingly. 'This will work, but only if we look as if we belong.'

They waited while a cleaner walked past, and then they marched into Laura's room. Jordan noticed that she hadn't moved, and he wondered anxiously if he was doing the right thing. He gently removed the drip from her arm, and they lifted her off the bed and placed her carefully in the wheelchair.

'See if you can find a spare blanket in one of the cupboards,' he whispered.

Kilpatrick pulled out a pale pink blanket. 'Is this what you're after?'

'Perfect,' replied Jordan. He wrapped it around Laura so that her face was almost covered and tucked the loose ends in behind her. They pushed Laura down the corridor at a leisurely pace, resisting the urge to break into a trot, and parked her outside the elevator.

Tracey jabbed the elevator button, and after what seemed like an eternity, the light above the elevator blinked on and the door slowly opened. An elderly doctor walked out without glancing at the group.

Jordan pressed the button for the ground floor, and as the doors began closing, an intern suddenly darted into the lift with them. He looked at the two men and smiled. They nodded briefly in response. To Jordan's relief the intern stepped out and hurried away when the elevator arrived on the ground floor.

They wheeled Laura out through the main entrance and pushed her quickly towards the car park. As they neared Laura's BMW, a well-dressed man walking in the opposite direction suddenly stopped and peered at the figure in the wheelchair.

'Laura? Is that you?' He reached out to pull away the blanket, but Jordan grabbed his wrist.

'What the hell do you think you're doing?' Jordan demanded as he pushed the man's arm away.

The man shook off Jordan's grip and continued to peer at the inert figure. 'That's Laura Monroe, isn't it? What's she doing out here in the car park? Is she asleep?' He peered closely at Laura again. 'She's unconscious,' he abruptly declared. 'What's going on? What are you doing with her?'

'Keep your voice down,' said Jordan angrily. 'Laura's in grave danger. We have to get her into her car.'

'I don't think so, chum,' replied the man indignantly as he planted himself in front of the wheelchair. 'Laura's not going anywhere.'

Jordan glanced anxiously towards the hospital entrance and then lowered his voice soothingly. 'I'll happily explain everything once Laura's safe. Just who are you anyway?'

The man put his hand on Laura's shoulder in a gesture of familiarity. 'Colin Tweddle, one of Laura's close colleagues. When I heard her sadistic boyfriend had beaten her up, I had to come and comfort her.' His voice rose slightly. 'I expected to find her relaxing in a warm hospital bed, not slumped unconscious in a wheelchair doing laps of the car park, and you have the nerve to tell me to keep my voice down because she's in grave danger.' His voice continued to rise as he took a step closer to Jordan.

'Of course she's in bloody grave danger, you stupid buffoon, so either take her back to the hospital, or I will summon the authorities.'

Several people were giving them curious stares, and Tracey stepped in front of Jordan and smiled placatingly.

'Listen, Mr Tweddle, we really do have Laura's best interests at heart. Help us get her into the car, and we'll tell you all about it once she's safe.'

'It's obvious Laura's in no fit state to travel, so this can't be in her best interest,' Tweddle said with a frown. He suddenly puffed out his chest. 'It's probably fate that I turned up when I did so I can end this stupidity.'

Jordan grabbed Tweddle's arm in frustration and pointed to the BMW. 'That's Laura's car. Why would we have her car if we weren't trying to help her?'

Tweddle looked confused. 'What's that got to do with it?' His eyes suddenly widened. 'You're the boyfriend, aren't you?' He shook his arm free from Jordan's grip. 'You're the bastard who put her into hospital.' His voice took on a sanctimonious tone. 'Oh, it's clear to me now. No wonder you want me to keep quiet. You're trying to sneak her away to cover up your crime. Well, guess what? That's not going to happen.'

'For God's sake, I didn't do this to her,' Jordan protested fiercely.

Tweddle was no longer listening. He had become the white knight, riding to Laura's rescue, and he turned to shout for assistance.

Kilpatrick stepped around the wheelchair and hit Tweddle with a short right cross to the jaw and then caught him before he hit the ground.

'I've always wanted to do that,' he said laconically as he sucked his knuckles.

'You didn't have to hit him,' admonished Tracey. 'He was trying to help Laura, for God's sake.'

'He was becoming a problem, so I fixed it,' replied Kilpatrick simply.

He lowered Tweddle to the ground and turned to Jordan. 'Okay, what's next?'

'Hmm. We can't just leave him here. You bring him, and I'll push Laura. Luckily the car's not far away.' Several people had stopped to watch, although they appeared loath to interfere. Jordan turned and smiled at a Japanese couple standing nearby. 'Poor chap's fainted,' he said loudly. 'We're just going to take him home.'

Kilpatrick bent down and grabbed Tweddle under the arms and then stopped and smiled into the distance.

'What the hell are you doing?' muttered Jordan angrily.

'That Japanese fellow's taking our picture.'

'I don't believe this. Just get him to the car, and let's get going. We haven't got all bloody day.'

Tweddle began to groan feebly and tried to sit up.

'You fainted,' said Kilpatrick in a comforting tone. 'The shock of seeing Laura in a wheelchair was too much for your delicate constitution. Here, let me help you up.'

Tweddle staggered awkwardly to his feet, and Kilpatrick propelled him quickly towards Laura's car. 'I didn't faint,' he mumbled thickly as he tried to dig his heels in. He suddenly stopped as they reached the car, understanding flooding back. 'You're kidnapping Laura,' he said loudly in a high-pitched voice. He half turned to shout for help.

'Watch your head,' warned Kilpatrick as he grabbed a handful of Tweddle's thinning hair and thrust his forehead against the side of the car.

Jordan swung around anxiously as he heard the thump, looking questioningly at Kilpatrick. 'I'm afraid he banged his head,' explained Kilpatrick. 'I did warn him.'

'You're enjoying this too much. Shove him onto the floor, and help me get Laura out of the wheelchair. We're starting to gather a crowd.'

'He should have just kept quiet,' muttered Kilpatrick as he pushed Tweddle through the back door and onto the floor. 'I can't stand these bloody self-righteous prigs always butting in where they're not wanted.'

They bundled Laura clumsily onto the back seat. Tracey clambered in and placed Laura's head on her lap and tried to keep her feet clear of the groaning figure on the floor. 'I hope you know what you're doing,' she said primly as Jordan started the car.

'If she hasn't woken up by tomorrow morning, I'll take her to another hospital. I don't trust this place. Apart from the cuts and bruises, she was fine last night and now look at her.'

'You heard what that nurse said. This sort of shock is common.'

'It's not for somebody as tough as Laura,' said Jordan as they drove out of the hospital grounds.

'Where are we going?' asked Kilpatrick as he waved to the small crowd still standing in the car park.

'Your place, of course. We obviously can't take her back to my apartment.'

'Sure, why not,' said Kilpatrick with a sigh. 'What are we going to do about Tweddle?'

'I don't know. He was trying to help Laura, so it's not really his fault. We can't just dump him on the side of the road, so I suppose we'll have to take him with us. It'll give us a chance to explain things.'

The chill wind whipped up a flurry of whitecaps across the width of the bay, causing the sailing craft anchored offshore to tug insistently at their moorings. Tony Lindhurst dropped his tracksuit on the damp sand and slapped himself vigorously around the chest to stimulate his circulation. The early morning swim had been a part of his routine for the past forty-two years, and he attributed his good health to his Spartan lifestyle. A small boat battled through the choppy swell several hundred metres offshore despite the unsuitable conditions for fishing. Lindhurst took a rough sighting on a red channel buoy and ventured purposefully down to the water's edge. He occasionally swam with one or two companions, but today he was alone. He had never been the type to run impetuously down the beach and dive headfirst into the sea, much preferring to acclimatise himself to the freezing conditions by moving back and forth with the motion of the waves as he gradually progressed deeper into the water. One of his companions had nicknamed him 'Dances with Waves'.

He reached a comfortable depth, dived gently over an incoming wave, and swam strongly towards the buoy. The cold water cleared his head, and his thoughts wandered back to the Memtech presentation. He wondered if he had been too hasty in turning them down.

As he rounded the buoy, his ankles were suddenly seized, and he was abruptly jerked beneath the water. He took an involuntary breath as he went under and immediately began choking. He frantically tried to kick free from the strong grip, but his unknown attacker continued to drag him down deeper. Lindhurst's vision began filling with red swirls, and he felt a strange lethargy come over him as his strength faded. As his brain shut down his last thought was, *Why is this happening?*

The figure in the black diving suit held on to his victim's ankles for another minute before swimming back to the small motor boat drifting near the channel buoy. Tony Pollock and Rod Harrison were former SAS soldiers currently on loan to Memtech via the generosity of their department head, Sir Rupert Northfield. As Pollock flopped aboard, Harrison turned and kicked the engine into life.

The incoming tide and relentless motion of the waves caused Lindhurst's body to inch towards shore until it finally floated back and forth amid the small shore break in a sad parody of his nickname.

~

'Well done, gentlemen,' beamed Chief Inspector Fenwick as he ushered Banks and Evans into his office. 'The serial killer finally brought to justice. A veritable feather in all of our caps.'

'Is the Jabberwock really dead?' murmured Banks under his breath.

'What was that, Banks?' demanded Fenwick suspiciously.

'Don't you think it may be premature to celebrate? We haven't got the tests back from the lab yet, sir.'

'Of course we've got our man.' The department had been under increasing pressure to catch the killer, and Fenwick smiled with satisfaction as he ticked off his fingers. 'One, the killer used a knife to cut the clothing from his victim. Two, he used two red candles as part of the ritual. And three, he carved a fucking great cross just above the poor girl's left breast. As none of these details are public knowledge, it would be bloody impossible for anybody else to perform a copycat rape and murder. Case closed,' he said emphatically.

'Yes, sir,' said Banks stoically, 'but there were two of them involved, and the previous evidence indicated we were dealing with a lone psychopath. Until we receive the DNA results, we won't know if we have a match with the other murders or not.'

Fenwick thrust his face close to Banks. 'Think logically. There is no evidence to suggest that two men were not involved in the previous murders, and as for DNA samples, it doesn't matter either way. If they match up, then there's your final proof; and if they don't, well, who's to say it wasn't the other fellow who committed those rapes?'

'But we have DNA samples from both of them,' persisted Banks, staring at a point directly between Fenwick's eyebrows. 'One of them has to match up otherwise we're worse off than before.'

'Worse off?' yelled Fenwick, spraying a light shower of spittle over over Banks's face.

'Yes, sir,' replied Banks, ignoring the urge to wipe his sleeve across his face. 'One,' he mimicked less than subtly, 'our resources are now deployed elsewhere with the killer still free, and two, we have a group of unknown people using confidential information to disguise their motives for the attack on Laura Monroe.'

'Poppycock! What's your opinion, Evans?' Fenwick scowled.

'Inspector Banks has a valid point, sir,' replied Evans cautiously, 'but the evidence is too strong to be ignored. The candles, the crucifix carved in her chest, it's all there, sir.'

'Precisely.' Fenwick took a deep breath and stepped away from Banks. 'I want to make this absolutely clear. You are both heroes in the eyes of the public, the media, and the department, so I do not want to see the vaguest hint in any of your reports suggesting that the "Crucifix Killer" is still at large. Is that clear?'

The two men answered in unison. 'Yes, sir.'

'Very good. Have your final report on my desk by this time tomorrow.'

'We haven't finished interviewing the witnesses yet, sir,' said Banks.

'In heaven's name, why not?'

'The girl was badly cut up, sir,' explained Evans. 'She was taken to the hospital last night.'

'Well, you'd better get moving then.'

As the two detectives left the office, Evans turned to his partner. 'What happens if you're correct, and the Crucifix Killer is still at large? Won't Fenwick look incompetent when he strikes again?'

Banks gave a mirthless chuckle. 'Hardly. Any crimes committed by the original killer will be dubbed copycat crimes. I can see it now, SOCK, "Son of Crucifix Killer".' He gave his partner a pat on the shoulder and wandered back to his office. He poured himself another cup of coffee and put through a call to the laboratory. The assistant informed him that there were no details yet on the DNA samples, but the request for fingerprint identification had been denied due to the classification level of their owner.

'Classified by whom?' asked Banks.

There was a pause. 'I'm sorry, that's also classified.'

'Is there any information on the report that's not classified?'

'Yes, sir.'

'Well, that's something. What is it?'

'The request was initiated by Senior Inspector Robert Banks.' He could almost see the assistant smirking on the other end of the line.

He hung up and then rang Detective Saunders and instructed her to arrange an interview with Laura Monroe.

Saunders rang back almost immediately. 'The hospital reported Monroe missing half an hour ago, sir.'

'Missing?'

'The circumstances are still unclear. The hospital believes she may have checked herself out without going through due process.'

'Who's been assigned to the case?'

'Ah, nobody, sir,' replied Saunders apprehensively. 'It's been assessed as low priority.'

'Bloody bureaucrats!' swore Banks vehemently. 'What's the name of the hospital?'

'Mercy West, sir.'

'Okay. Tell Evans to meet me at my car. Now!' He slammed the phone down and stalked angrily out of his office.

Jane Astbury had astutely built *Pert* magazine into a thriving business. Her fortune had doubled and then doubled again when she branched into cosmetics and fashion accessories. She had recently purchased a music company and was exploring the possibility of buying into pharmaceuticals.

Her assistant had laid out the morning newspaper along with a cup of strong black tea, and she flipped casually through the paper, searching for the fashion and social pages.

'Media Mogul Killed In Tragic Accident.' The headline above a graphic photograph leapt out at her. She quickly read the article. Eyewitnesses had reported seeing Frampton in a high-speed race with an unknown car, and the police believed alcohol might have been a factor.

Jane had met Frampton at various media events, and she remembered seeing him at the Memtech presentation. It was strange that he should end up dead only days after the meeting.

Jane had accepted the invitation to Toulemonde's presentation out of curiosity. The possibility of a breakthrough in the quest for immortality combined with a healthy return on her investment had seduced her into buying a share, and she had paid scant attention to the ethical questions raised at the meeting. Her business philosophy had always been to look after herself and not to worry about the motives or deeds of the opposition. She was used to inflated egos at business meetings as there was no point being powerful if nobody noticed. The discussions concerning murder and premature death were just the usual grandstanding by the usual people. She had placed Borkov in this category but now wasn't so sure.

What if Frampton's death hadn't been an accident?

Chapter 7

If you prick us, do we not bleed?
If you tickle us, do we not laugh?
If you poison us, do we not die?
And if you wrong us, shall we not revenge?
William Shakespeare, *The Merchant of Venice*

Banks arrived at the hospital as visiting hours were drawing to a close. The receptionist was on the telephone, her eyes flicking disdainfully over Banks as he approached the counter. He hammered the bell to attract her attention, and the woman flapped a disparaging hand at him. 'Be with you in a moment, sir.'

Banks pulled out his identification and held it at arm's length. 'Police!' he barked as he leaned forward and fixed the woman with a fierce stare. 'Now!'

'I have to go,' she mumbled and rose ponderously from her chair. 'Yes?' she asked in a quavering voice. 'How can I help you?'

'I want the room number for Laura Monroe and the name of her doctor.'

The receptionist hurriedly checked her computer. 'It's Room 327 but she's no longer there.'

Banks wrote down the number. 'And the doctor's name?'

'Er ... Dr Rathbone.'

'Thank you, you've been most helpful.'

After interviewing the ward nurse, it quickly became apparent that Laura's boyfriend had spirited her away. Dr Rathbone was adamant that she be immediately returned to his care once she was located. Evans made separate inquiries and discovered there had been an altercation in the car park, and the description of one of the men involved matched Daniel Jordan.

'What do you think he's playing at?' asked Banks as they returned to their car.

'I have no idea sir. Maybe the attack on his girlfriend unhinged his mind.'

'Possibly, but he seemed all right last night.' He threaded his way through the congested traffic to the apartment Jordan shared with Laura, but a quick check showed that it was deserted.

'We'll wait for a while and see if they turn up,' sighed Banks as he pulled out a tattered magazine.

∾

Tweddle had recovered sufficiently to help Jordan and Kilpatrick move Laura into the unit and make her comfortable in Kilpatrick's bed.

'You could have at least changed the sheets,' complained Jordan. 'These look like they haven't been washed in a month.'

'It wasn't my idea to bring her here,' retorted Kilpatrick indignantly.

Tracey scowled as she picked up Kilpatrick's crumpled clothing from the floor. 'I don't know how you can live like this.'

'I wasn't expecting company.'

Tracey watched as Jordan tucked the sheets firmly around Laura and then returned to the lounge room with the men.

'I have to go. I'll bring some clean sheets back tomorrow.'

Tweddle waited apprehensively as Kilpatrick left with Tracey to phone for a cab and then confronted Jordan. 'I have a right to know why you've kidnapped Laura, and why I'm being held prisoner.'

Jordan shook his head. 'We didn't kidnap Laura, and you're not being held prisoner. We brought you with us so we could offer you an explanation. It was important to get Laura away from the hospital as quickly as possible. Unfortunately, you were in the way.'

'Was Laura in your way when you hit her?' persisted Tweddle as he gingerly touched the side of his jaw, where a puffy swelling was beginning to show.

'For the last time, I didn't hit Laura,' snapped Jordan. 'I know we got off on the wrong foot, but hopefully you'll understand once you've heard our story.'

Jordan gave Tweddle a summary of events, beginning with the day Stephen Kimpton came into his life. Tweddle listened intently at first, but as the story gathered pace, he began to look incredulous, making small shaking movements with his head and muttering under his breath. He was finally unable to contain his emotions and leapt to his feet in an explosive movement, knocking over a cup of tea Kilpatrick had placed on the table next to him.

'You expect me to believe such cockeyed garbage?' he shouted in disgust. 'Spiritual possession? Murder? Simulated rape? You need psychiatric help.'

'How can you be such a fucking ass?'

Kilpatrick suddenly stepped between the two protagonists and bellowed for quiet. 'If you listen carefully, you might discover that Laura's awake.'

A faint croaking sound drifted fitfully down the hallway. Tweddle and Jordan immediately pushed past Kilpatrick and pounded into her room. They found her struggling to sit up, her face pale, and her eyes clouded with pain and confusion.

'Where am I?' she asked faintly. 'What's going on? What's all the shouting about?'

Both Jordan and Tweddle started talking at once. Laura subsided into her pillow with a groan and held up a hand for silence. 'I have the most fearful headache, and I'm totally confused. I don't know where I am, and I don't know why you're shouting at me.' She motioned to Kilpatrick, who was standing placidly in the doorway. 'Matt, please tell me what's going on.' She scowled at Jordan and Tweddle, who then glared at each other.

Kilpatrick smiled reassuringly and gave her a brief account of the situation. Both Jordan and Tweddle attempted to interrupt on several occasions, but Laura quelled them with a fierce glare.

'Thank you,' she said once Kilpatrick had finished. 'What do you propose to do now?'

'We need to get you back to the hospital immediately,' insisted Tweddle doggedly.

'Come on, Laura,' said Jordan earnestly. 'There's more to this than either of us understands. For some reason you've become a target, and the sooner you're safely tucked away, the better off you'll be.'

Tweddle scoffed. 'Your concern is laughable. Either return Laura to the hospital, or I'm going to the police and insist they charge you with grievous bodily harm and kidnapping. Do you understand me?' He folded his arms defiantly.

'That's not very helpful, Colin,' chided Laura. 'Daniel is concerned about my safety.'

'I'm concerned about you, too,' said Tweddle hurriedly. 'It's distressing to see you like this.' He reached over and patted her hand. 'I just want you to know that I'm here for you, and I'll do whatever you think is right.'

'I know,' whispered Laura. She began coughing uncontrollably, and the three men looked on helplessly as she struggled to breathe once the fit passed. She motioned weakly with her hand. 'Can somebody please get me a bowl? I think I'm going to be sick.' Kilpatrick rushed out of the room and returned moments later with a small plastic bucket and a towel.

'Look at her,' said Tweddle indignantly. 'Who's going to help her if she needs medical attention?' He suddenly suppressed a sly grin. 'If Laura's really in danger, then it won't take a genius to come looking for her here. If she needs to be hidden away, then it should be with somebody who hasn't been mixed up in this. Do you agree?' Jordan cautiously nodded, and Tweddle quickly continued. 'The obvious solution is for me to take her to my country house and hire a private nurse. I'll have the doctor drop by on a daily basis so she'll be safe as well as properly cared for. I can organise it now.'

'I'm not sure,' muttered Jordan gloomily. 'I don't even know you.'

'Colin's okay,' whispered Laura. 'This concerns me, and I think it's a terrific idea.' She held up the edge of a stained sheet and then let it flutter back onto the bed.

Tweddle gave a satisfied smirk. 'That's settled then.'

Laura smiled weakly. 'Thank you, Colin. You have a very charitable spirit.'

Jordan looked dubiously at Laura. 'If that's what you want …'

'That's what I want,' she replied as firmly as her aching head would allow.

Tweddle was jubilant. 'Splendid. Now that's settled, I need a lift back to the hospital to retrieve my car.'

Kilpatrick took one look at Jordan's glowering face and quickly offered, returning without incident forty minutes later. After settling Laura into Tweddle's Lexus, Jordan gave her a quick kiss and a hug, and she gave him a listless smile in return. 'Would you mind packing a bag with some clothes and such?'

'Do you want me to bring them to you?'

Tweddle interjected before Laura could reply. 'That won't be necessary. I can pick them up on my way home from work tomorrow.'

She reached up and patted Jordan's cheek. 'You take care of yourself.' She closed her eyes as she slumped back onto the seat, drained of all energy.

Jordan watched unhappily as Tweddle drove away. 'Come on,' he muttered testily. 'Let's get Laura's things before I forget.

The last thing I want is that smarmy bastard telling her I couldn't be bothered.'

They drove to the unit and only noticed the police car parked in the shadows once they had left their vehicle. 'Shit,' cursed Jordan softly. 'Cops.'

'Act naturally. We've done nothing wrong.'

'Kidnapping, abduction, assault,' muttered Jordan under his breath. He could feel his heart racing as the two policemen walked across the road.

'Yeah, but they don't know that,' replied Kilpatrick as he smiled guilelessly at the officers.

'Good afternoon, gentlemen,' said Banks. He held out his hand towards Jordan. 'I'm sure you remember my partner and me from last night.'

'Of course,' mumbled Jordan. 'This is Matt Kilpatrick,' he said as he gave his friend a gentle punch on the arm. 'He was kind enough to offer me a bed for the night.'

'Fine,' said Banks. 'It helps to have supportive friends. How is Miss Monroe by the way? We'd like to complete the interview we began last night. She's not in the house is she? You do realise, it's still a crime scene.'

'Er, no, she's not,' replied Jordan. 'After she rang and asked us to pick her up from the hospital, she left with a friend to rest in the countryside.'

'Miss Monroe rang and asked you to pick her up?' asked Banks pleasantly.

'That's right.'

Banks referred to his notebook. 'The hospital reported that Miss Monroe was heavily sedated, yet she was still able to make a phone call. Don't you find that strange?'

Jordan shrugged. 'She didn't look very well when we arrived at the hospital, but she insisted on leaving. We didn't care to argue with her.'

'Why didn't you check her out? The hospital reported her missing, and your actions have tied up valuable police resources.

I'm sure you realise the courts frown upon such irresponsible behaviour.'

'I'm sorry, but we did try,' explained Jordan. 'We took her to reception, but the lady behind the desk ignored us. Laura said she was going to throw up, so we took her outside into the fresh air.'

'That's right,' agreed Kilpatrick. 'That's when Laura's friend turned up.'

'All right,' grunted Banks resignedly. 'That story's as good as any I suppose. If the department wants me to take it further, then I'll be in touch.'

'Is it okay if we collect a few of Laura's things while we're here?' asked Jordan.

'I'm sorry,' replied Banks. 'Nothing can be removed from a crime scene under investigation. I'm sure you understand.'

'These are just some clothes and books,' protested Jordan. 'Surely the rules don't apply to items like that.'

'I'm afraid there are no exceptions.'

'Fine,' replied Kilpatrick as he took his friend by the arm. 'Come on, Daniel, it's time we let these gentlemen get back to work.'

'Laura was depending on me,' mumbled Jordan as Kilpatrick steered him towards the car.

'I'm sure she'll understand,' replied Kilpatrick soothingly.

Jane placed the latest edition of *Pert* between two rival magazines and shook her head in annoyance. 'Peas in a pod,' she muttered. How was she going to generate growth if the leading magazines were indistinguishable?

Her personal assistant knocked softly, placed a cup of tea on the table, and then hovered uncertainly until Jane looked up. 'Yes, Kylie, was there something else?'

'I was just wondering if you've finished with the paper.'

Jane had cut out an article detailing the tragic death of Tony Lindhurst, and scraps of paper still littered her desk. 'Yes, thank you. Sorry about the mess.' Kylie made no comment as she gathered the pieces of paper and retreated from the office.

Jane's phone rang as she picked up her cup of tea, and she took a hasty sip before answering.

'It's Melinda,' said an excited voice. 'Have you heard about Andrew Lawrence?'

Jane felt herself going cold. 'No, what about Andrew?' Lawrence had walked out of the Memtech meeting with Frampton and Lindhurst.

'The police found him wandering around Hyde Park at two o'clock in the morning.'

'So he's all right then?' prompted Jane anxiously.

'Not really. He appears to have total amnesia. He didn't even recognise his wife. Isn't it awful?'

'Extremely,' agreed Jane. 'Was he in an accident?'

'That's just the thing,' continued Melinda. 'He doesn't have a mark on him, and he still had a large sum of money in his wallet when he was found, so he wasn't robbed. Nobody knows what to think.'

'It certainly is strange, Melinda. Would you mind giving me a call if his condition changes? Thanks.'

She disconnected the call and sat back in her chair. Melinda was wrong; he had been robbed. Somebody had deliberately robbed him of his memory. Frampton, Lindhurst, and Lawrence had rejected the Memtech offer, and all three had been eliminated. Borkov's closing comments were definitely a veiled threat, and with the disposal of the three men, the warning was clear. It you talked or stepped out of line, you would be erased, physically or mentally.

Jane was under no illusions about her own safety if she talked. The three men were very influential, but that hadn't stopped Borkov from using them as an example. But she knew she would be guilty of moral cowardice if she did nothing. She finally decided to explain the situation to somebody who could act on it. If her identity was kept secret, she would be safe. She dialed Scotland Yard and asked to be put through to a senior officer.

'Certainly, madam,' said the calm voice. 'Please state your name, address, and the reason for calling.'

'I'm calling about the deaths of Paul Frampton and Tony Lindhurst, but I prefer to remain anonymous. Just call me Nikki.'

'I understand, Nikki,' replied the operator. He typed in the number she was calling from, bringing up the name and address of her magazine company. 'I'll check our database and cross-reference the investigating officers.' There was a pause. 'Okay, Paul Frampton died in a car accident, and Tony Lindhurst drowned recently following a suspected heart attack. The coroner's report in both cases stated that there were no suspicious circumstances.'

'Both of those men were murdered,' said Jane emphatically.

The officer paused. 'I'm afraid you're mistaken, Nikki. The coroner's report is very clear.'

'I have to talk to somebody,' replied Jane. A thought occurred to her. 'Can you check if anybody is investigating a company called Memtech?'

'Memtech?' asked the officer, surprised. 'I don't understand.'

'Please, there could be a link.'

He muttered incoherently as he typed in the name. 'The only mention of Memtech is related to a violent assault. One of the victims believed Memtech was implicated.'

'Is it possible to talk to the officer in charge?' asked Jane in some desperation.

'The investigating officer is Inspector Banks. I'll transfer you now.'

The call was answered promptly. 'Banks, how can I help you?'

'Er, I have some information you might be interested in. Have you heard of a company called Memtech Industries?'

Banks paused. The couple last night had mentioned Memtech Industries, and Banks didn't believe in coincidences. 'Yes,' he said at last. 'I've heard of them.'

'I have information that links Memtech Industries to the deaths of Paul Frampton and Tony Lindhurst,' she said with a rush.

'I'm sorry, but I'm not investigating the deaths of either of those gentlemen.'

'Their deaths were supposedly accidental, but I believe they were murdered, and that Memtech Industries was heavily involved.'

'These are serious allegations you're making Miss ... er?'

'Call me Nikki. Look, I'm a bundle of nerves. The sooner this is resolved, the better I'll feel.'

'I understand,' Banks said encouragingly as he glanced at his watch. 'Unfortunately, I'm already late for another meeting. Why don't you make an appointment to see me tomorrow?'

'No,' she said, coming to a sudden decision. 'I need to pass on this information as soon as possible. Is it possible for you to drop in and see me after your meeting?'

'Yes, if you're comfortable with that.'

'Good, I live near Walham Green, just off Fulham Road.' She gave him her street name and number. 'Is that far out of your way?'

'No, not really,' he said, fudging the truth. 'Expect me around seven.'

She stared out the window after she'd hung up, wondering if she'd done the right thing.

～

Carlos DeLuca had been given a routine office job while he recovered from his injuries. He was still seething from Madison's tongue lashing. The security team was a small clandestine affair consisting of ex-SAS operatives provided by Dermott Jarvis; with Dawson's death, they were stretched to the limit.

Consumed with the desire for revenge, DeLuca spent most of his rehabilitation constructing a powerful car bomb. Allowing Dawson's killer to remain alive had damaged his standing. The only way to erase that humiliation was with a display of unmistakable strength. He smiled grimly as he carefully soldered a thin wire to a container holding the Semtex. The blast would kill anybody standing within a twenty-metre radius of the explosion. It would be a very messy execution.

His computer signalled the arrival of a new email. He read it briefly and then phoned Madison, informing him that they had a problem.

'What sort of problem?' demanded Madison.

'One of the guests at the funding presentation has gone to the police.'

'Damn! I warned Borkov, but do you think he'd listen? Do you have any details?'

'Her name's Jane Astbury. She owns *Pert* magazine, one of those soppy rags for repressed women. I've got her address and the name of the officer she contacted.'

'How do we know her call was related to us?'

She said she had information relating to the deaths of Frampton and Lindhurst and mentioned a link to Memtech.'

'Bloody hell!' fumed Madison. 'Now the shit's really going to hit the fan.'

'It's not all bad news. The cop didn't have time to interview her, so she's probably going to see him tomorrow.'

'Fucking Borkov and his mind games,' cursed Madison. 'Well, we've got to do this quickly. Are Pollock and Harrison available?'

'No, they're away on assignment.' DeLuca cleared his throat nervously. 'Let me handle this for you.'

'No,' said Madison sharply. 'I need you here. I hate doing it, but we'll have to outsource this one. We've got two cops on our payroll helping with those homeless people. Get in touch and tell them to fix it today. There'll be a bonus for them if there's no inquiry. Got that?'

'Yes, sir,' replied DeLuca. He slammed the receiver down in frustration.

The officers hired to silence Jane parked their cruiser in a side street close to her Tudor-style mansion. Thick, ivy-covered walls protected Jane's privacy, and the main gate was monitored with surveillance cameras. The electronic system was wired into a company who promised to have a team at her front door within ten minutes of a security breach.

Jane was emotionally drained by the time she arrived home. It was already ten past six, so she decided to have a wash and change into something more presentable. She grabbed a container of yoghurt from the fridge and was heading for the bathroom when the speaker on the gate was activated.

'Perfect timing,' Jane muttered as she picked up the handset. 'Astbury residence, please identify yourself.'

'It's the police,' replied a muffled voice.

'You're early.' She glanced at the video screen and then activated the gate.

The two policemen looked at each other, confused. 'Early?' said the driver. 'What is she, psychic?'

His partner, the more senior of the two, frowned thoughtfully. 'She's obviously expecting someone, so we can't afford to waste any time.'

'That could be a problem. The pills take a while to work. What if they get her to a hospital in time?'

The older cop shook his head. 'There'll be nobody to let them in. By the time she's discovered, it'll be too late.'

Jane was waiting for them on the front porch and smiled nervously as the two men walked towards her.

'Inspector Banks?' she asked cautiously.

The older man smiled in response. 'Yeah, that's me. Can we come in?'

Jane turned to lead the way into the house. 'Your voice sounded different over the telephone, Inspector.'

'Really, Jane? Yours sounds exactly the same.'

Jane froze. 'I told you my name was Nikki.'

The younger policeman kicked the door shut with the side of his boot and brought out the bottle of scotch he'd been hiding behind his back. 'Time to cut the bullshit, lady. You've annoyed some powerful people, and they've asked us to teach you a lesson.' They pushed her into a nearby chair and quickly forced the bottle into her mouth, cutting her bottom lip as they did so. 'It's party time, lady, so drink up, and all will be forgiven.' He laughed loudly as he tipped the bottle higher, forcing her to gulp the liquid being poured down her throat. The scotch made her cough and splutter, and they quickly stepped back in case she vomited.

Jane took several deep breaths and wiped the tears from her eyes with the back of her hand. She tried to talk but her voice had disappeared, and before she could gather her thoughts, the older man emptied a bottle of pills into his hand, grabbed her roughly by the hair and forced them into her mouth. The other policeman immediately rammed the bottle back into her mouth so that it clicked against her teeth. His partner held her nose, giving Jane no choice but to swallow the pills. She was starting to feel nauseous and when they shoved another handful of pills into her mouth, she only put up token resistance.

'That's better,' said the older man soothingly. 'Soon this will just be a bad dream.'

Banks had escaped from his meeting earlier than expected and arrived at Jane's front gate at 6:15. He glanced at the house as he stopped in the driveway and noticed the police car parked behind the trees. He reached out to press the intercom button but then hesitated, his instincts warning him that something wasn't right. He decided to find an alternate way in.

The ivy covering the wall looked the best option. Several pedestrians watched him with studied indifference as he scrambled to the top. A line of staked roses ran along the inside of the wall. He grabbed hold of a slender branch from a nearby elm tree, swung clear of the roses, and dropped lightly to the ground. He stayed in a crouch for a moment and then ran cautiously towards the police car.

Banks didn't believe in coincidences. He drew his weapon and walked silently to the front door. He listened intently, but the traffic noise, muted by the wall, prevented him from hearing anything. He slowly turned the handle and gently pushed the door open.

'I think she's had enough,' said a deep, gruff voice.

'Shouldn't we finish off the bottle, just to be certain?' The speaker sounded as though he was standing several metres from Banks.

'There isn't time. She's already got enough pills in her to knock out an elephant. The sooner we're out of here ...' He stopped in mid-sentence as Banks stepped inside the room.

Banks quickly surveyed the room, noting the girl slumped in the chair with the two men leaning over her. He took a step closer, the eyes of the two men glued to the gun he was holding. 'What's going on? What have you done to that girl?'

The older man was standing behind the chair holding the girl's head. 'It's not what you think, sir.' He slowly straightened as he watched Banks advance towards him. Using the back of the chair to mask his movements, he drew his gun and fired.

Banks reacted immediately, throwing himself to one side. The bullet plucked at his sleeve before slamming into the plaster wall behind him. Banks turned the sprawling dive into a roll and hurriedly crawled behind a brown leather chair. The second policeman, who was still in full view, hastily threw the scotch bottle at Banks and then frantically clawed his own weapon free. Banks shot him twice in the chest. He stumbled backwards and crashed against the wall before slumping to the floor.

'Drop your weapon,' Banks called to the other policeman. 'It's over.'

'Not bloody likely.' There was a faint shuffling noise as the girl moved slowly into view. She could barely stand, and her head lolled from side to side as she was sluggishly propelled towards the door. The gunman shuffled behind her, supporting her with one arm, his weapon pointed at the chair Banks was hiding behind.

As they inched towards the door, the girl abruptly collapsed, slithering gracefully through his arms and onto the floor. The gunman stared at the girl in horror and then fired two quick shots at Banks. Banks flinched as the shots buried themselves in the chair, and then he returned fire. His first bullet took the man in the upper thigh, and the second hit him in the throat, killing him instantly.

As if in a trance, Banks rose from behind the chair and checked the officer's pulse, but he was dead. The other officer slumped against the far wall was still alive, but bubbles of blood dribbled from the corner of his mouth, and his eyes were largely unfocused. As the dying man became aware of Banks kneeling beside him he made a determined effort to speak but was unable to form any last words. He gave a convulsive shudder and died.

Banks holstered his gun and turned his attention to the woman who lay on the floor, groaning softly and unable to move. It was obvious she'd been force-fed a deadly cocktail of drugs and alcohol. Banks dragged her awkwardly to her feet and carried her to the bathroom. Several toothbrushes hung from an ornate holder near the sink. He grabbed one, grimacing in anticipation, and then seized a handful of the girl's hair and pulled her head back. He gently slid the toothbrush handle down her throat and she immediately gagged and began retching copious amounts of brownish white bile into the bath. Banks turned his head as he struggled to control his own stomach. He repeated the process until he was certain she had nothing more to bring up and then left her dribbling uncontrollably into the bath.

He called in the emergency to police headquarters and instructed them to arrange for an ambulance. He knew there would be an enquiry and the wisest choice was to stay and defend his actions, but his first priority was to get medical attention for the girl. After flushing the bath, he lifted her over his shoulder and jogged back to his car. The exertion caused her to cough up another mouthful of vomit, and he felt it ooze sloppily through the back of his coat.

Banks bundled her onto the back seat, turning her onto her side so she wouldn't choke, and then roared off towards Sacred Heart Hospital, his siren blaring. He screeched to a halt at the emergency entrance and added the blast of his horn to his siren. Two orderlies burst through the double doors and ran towards the car, expertly controlling a padded hospital trolley. Banks opened the rear door, and the orderlies loaded Jane onto the trolley and raced her into the hospital.

'She's had a drug overdose.' Banks panted as he ran to keep up. 'Mainly pills and alcohol from what I could see. I've managed to get rid of most of it but she needs to have her stomach pumped to get the rest.'

'Anything else we need to know?' questioned the orderly as they steered the trolley through the busy corridor traffic.

Banks shook his head. 'No, I don't think so.' They arrived at another set of doors, and Banks glanced at the girl as the trolley stopped. She was unconscious, and the colour had drained from her cheeks.

'Dr Faraday will be here shortly,' explained the orderly as the trolley was wheeled into the room. 'You can stay and watch although I don't recommend it. It's not a pleasant sight.'

Banks closed his eyes while he fought a wave of nausea. 'I'll wait outside if it's all the same to you.'

'Splendid.' The orderly smiled. 'In that case you can help me fill out the paperwork.'

'I don't really know the young lady that well,' protested Banks, who loathed paperwork.

'It's nothing too hard. Name, address, that sort of thing,' cajoled the orderly. 'Come along, and I'll make you a cup of tea. You look as though you can use one.' He set off down the corridor as Banks followed reluctantly behind.

Dr Faraday cleared the remaining contents of Jane's stomach followed by a routine check-up. He assured Banks that no lasting damage had been done, and all she required was twenty-four hours of rest.

Banks bundled her back into his car, and she sat slumped in the passenger seat as he drove cautiously through the misty rain. She was still deeply affected by the alcohol and barbiturates in her bloodstream, and Banks knew she would have the mother of all hangovers in the morning. He parked outside a seedy hotel in Stepney and helped the girl inside.

The proprietor of the White Stag was an old acquaintance. He allowed Banks to use the hotel as a safe house and in return, Banks turned a blind eye to the girls working out of the hotel. Banks pushed his way through the heavy glass door and sat the girl in one of the old chairs sprinkled around the small lobby.

'If it isn't Inspector Plod,' said an unkempt old man propped behind the lobby desk, reading a form guide. He was lean and thin faced with short, dark, receding hair.

'Harry. You're looking as good as ever,' replied Banks with a half grin.

Harry stared approvingly at the girl. 'Nice-looking woman. All primed for a night of passion by the look of her.'

'Afraid not, Harry, this is business.'

'You should reconsider. She won't remember a thing in the morning.' He gave Banks a knowing wink.

Banks laughed. 'You're incorrigible, Harry. Now, I need a room with two beds for a few nights. I need to keep her safe until I sort out a few problems.'

Harry shrugged his shoulders laconically. 'Easily fixed, boss.'

Banks dropped his voice. 'She's in extreme danger. Nobody must know she's here, including the police.'

'Dear me,' chided Harry as he pulled out a cigarette and tapped it against the side of the packet. 'This is a turn-up for the books. Not on the run, is she?'

'The less you know, the better. If anybody comes nosing around, just play ignorant.'

'Sure, Inspector, that's my specialty.' He tossed a key at Banks. 'Second floor, and the room's at the end of the corridor. The fire escape outside your window leads into an alley.' He tapped the side of his nose as he blew a smoke ring towards the ceiling. 'You never know when you might need it.'

Although the room was small by modern standards, it had its own bathroom and toilet. The beds were well sprung and looked reasonably comfortable despite the thin mattresses. He helped the girl onto the nearest bed and removed her jacket and shoes, tucking her in as comfortably as he could. She was shivering slightly, and he leaned over and patted her head. 'You're safe now. Get some sleep, and I'll be back shortly.'

She mumbled something unintelligible, and he switched off the light and locked the door behind him. He arranged for Harry to supply her with meals plus anything else she required and handed him a roll of notes. Harry stubbornly refused. 'Please, Inspector, we go back a long way, you and me. I help you and you help me; that's how it works.'

Banks gave Harry an apologetic smile. 'Sure thing, Harry, I understand. There's something else you can help me with. I need a gun.'

'One gun isn't enough for Rambo?'

'Something like that. If it's too hard, then forget it.' He thanked Harry again and walked back to his car, checking his watch as he slid behind the steering wheel. It was going to be a long night.

Fenwick was in a foul mood when Banks finally scooted into his office. A panel of senior officers had been hurriedly assembled, and Banks noted that the Commissioner himself was in charge of proceedings. Kent leered at him from the rear of the group, clearly happy with the situation.

Fenwick was furious at the delay. 'Where the hell have you been? Where's Jane Astbury?'

'Who?'

'Don't play games with me,' Fenwick said angrily. 'The girl you rescued, Jane Astbury.'

'Oh, I'm sorry. She told me her name was Nikki.'

'Nikki, Jane, whatever,' snapped Fenwick. 'Where is she?'

'Safe,' Banks replied calmly.

The Commissioner interrupted Fenwick. 'We'll get to that in a moment, Chief Inspector.' He turned to Banks. 'We've convened this preliminary inquiry to determine our next steps. This is normal policy. Two police officers are dead at the hands of one of our own, so we'd like to hear your version of the incident before we go any further.'

He could feel everybody's eyes upon him as he methodically took them through the days' events. They were curious about why he'd been distrustful of the police car parked in the driveway. He told them he didn't have a definitive answer; he'd simply relied upon his instincts, and several officers nodded in understanding. Banks described the gun battle and then outlined his handling of the woman to minimize the effect of the drugs and alcohol. He finished by stating that the victim was now resting in a safe house and should make a full recovery.

'Which safe house?' demanded Fenwick.

'I refuse to tell you,' replied Banks as he lowered his eyes.

Fenwick seemed caught off balance. 'I'm afraid that won't do,' he protested. 'This woman is a prime witness in the deaths of two policemen. It's imperative we bring her in for questioning. If you're telling the truth, then you've got nothing to worry about.'

Banks looked up at his chief. 'If I'm telling the truth, then two police officers attempted to murder my informant before she could pass on vital information. How many other officers are involved in this conspiracy? I can't guarantee her safety, so I won't bring her.'

'Banks!' Fenwick sprang to his feet and thumped his fist on the table. 'This girl must be brought before this board of inquiry immediately so the matter can be cleared up. Tell us where she is, and I will personally guarantee her safety.'

Banks looked grim. 'I can't do that, I'm sorry. The woman was assaulted by two men from this division, and the question must be asked as to whose orders they were acting upon.'

The Commissioner intervened. 'Okay, it's a fair point. She will have to be interviewed, but for now, I'll allow the status quo to stand. When do you propose to bring her in?'

'Give me twenty-four hours to think about it, sir. Once I've heard the girl's information, I'll have a clearer picture of what to do next, and the need for her to be silenced will have diminished.'

'This is highly unethical,' protested Fenwick as he sank back onto his chair. 'You could simply be covering your tracks.'

Banks refused to be deterred. 'I understand the girl is your only witness, but she's also the victim, and her safety is paramount.'

The Commissioner held up a placating hand. 'All right, you have twenty-four hours. Circumstantial evidence agrees with your version of events, so I have faith that you're acting in the girl's best interests. However, until you have been fully exonerated, I'm afraid I will have to place certain restrictions on you. I'm sure you understand why.'

Banks massaged his eye. 'Am I being suspended?'

The Commissioner gave a curt shake of his head. 'Not at this stage. All we need are your weapon and passport. We'll discuss the situation and let you know our next steps tomorrow.'

'Yes, sir.' Banks wearily placed his gun on the table in front of Fenwick. 'I'll bring in my passport in the morning if that's okay.'

Fenwick grunted his assent. Once Banks had left the room, the Commissioner turned to him. 'Do you think we should have suspended Banks on full pay?'

Fenwick smiled artfully. 'If we allow Banks enough rope, he'll hang himself if he's guilty.'

The Commissioner patted him on the shoulder. 'Let's hope your instincts are correct.'

'Oh, I think you'll find they are, sir.'

~

Isaac Borkov was surprised by the summons to appear before the board of directors. The board members were already seated around the U-shaped table when Borkov arrived, and he was instructed to sit at the open end of the table. His chair looked firmly padded, but as Borkov disappeared into its depths, he realised that its appearance was deceptive. The directors now towered above him, reinforcing their image of superiority.

Toulemonde stared briefly at Borkov. 'Thank you for coming, Isaac. We have several issues that need clarifying.'

Borkov nodded vaguely in Toulemonde's direction. 'I'm always pleased to be of assistance, Mr Chairman.'

'The board is concerned about the high level of attention we're currently attracting,' continued Toulemonde. 'Maintaining a low profile is essential for the continued development of our company.'

'Of course, Mr Chairman. That goes without saying.'

'Please, Isaac,' said Toulemonde icily, 'do not interrupt until I've finished.' Borkov flushed at the rebuke and settled back into his chair, his arms folded defensively across his chest.

'The last thing we want is to attract attention,' continued Toulemonde, 'but recently we have witnessed a series of related incidents that can be traced directly to us. If this were to happen, our operations would be compromised, effectively destroying years of steady progress.' He slapped the table with the flat of his hand. 'These unnecessary actions must cease immediately.'

'I'm not sure what this has to do with me,' said Borkov stiffly.

Toulemonde pushed back his chair and rose to his feet. 'This has everything to do with you, Isaac.' He snatched a sheet of paper from the table and brandished it at Borkov. 'Stephen Kimpton, murdered on your orders. A connection has been made to Memtech.'

'That was sanctioned by this board,' protested Borkov. 'I don't understand how we can be linked with that, but it's unfair to single me out if we have.'

'I agree, and as an isolated incident it would not have attracted any attention.' Toulemonde began pacing around the table. 'Paul Frampton, murdered on your orders. Once again a connection has been made to Memtech.'

'What?' shouted Borkov incredulously. 'How?'

'Tony Lindhurst, murdered on your orders. A connection has been made to Memtech,' continued Toulemonde remorselessly. 'Laura Monroe, attempted murder on your orders. A connection has been made to Memtech.'

'The police have blamed the Crucifix Killer,' exploded Borkov as he struggled to his feet.

'Sit down, Borkov. What you read and what the police believe are two different things.'

'I've seen the official reports, Mr Chairman, and there is nothing in them to link Laura Monroe with Memtech.'

'Can a connection be made between Monroe and Memtech?' inquired Toulemonde softly.

'I don't see who would have that knowledge.'

'Is that a "yes", Isaac?'

Borkov scowled and returned to his chair.

'I will take your silence as an affirmative.' Toulemonde glanced at the paper. 'Jane Astbury, attempted murder resulting from your previous actions. Yet again a connection has been made to Memtech.'

'Jane Astbury?' repeated Borkov, looking puzzled. 'The name's familiar, but I didn't authorise any action in regard to her.'

'That's correct,' agreed Toulemonde, 'but as the attempt to silence her resulted from your previous bungling, the board feels you should still bear the responsibility.' He gestured towards Borkov. 'May I be so presumptuous as to ask why you felt it was necessary to eliminate Frampton and Lindhurst?'

Borkov looked incredulous. 'Surely it's obvious, Mr Chairman. Our core business must be protected at all costs. Everybody in this room knew we were exposing ourselves to a major risk by opening our business to new shareholders. Even though we screened everybody thoroughly, we were pragmatic enough to realise a few bleeding hearts might slip through the net. The best way to ensure their silence is through fear. Silencing the people who rejected our offer helped achieve this aim and eliminated them as a threat.'

'Astbury contacted the police as a direct result of the deaths of Frampton and Lindhurst. So much for your policy of control through fear.' Toulemonde spat the words angrily at Borkov. 'This woman actually held Memtech Industries responsible for their deaths. What do you have to say about that?'

'The principle is still correct,' replied Borkov stubbornly. 'What steps have been taken to neutralise this woman?'

'I've already told you, an attempt to silence her failed.' Toulemonde briefly outlined the details of Jane Astbury's escape.

'This Inspector Banks must be made to disclose her whereabouts,' exclaimed Borkov, 'then they must both be silenced.'

'The inspector no longer trusts his colleagues, and with good reason I might add. He's hidden her away, and despite pressure from his superiors, refuses to reveal her location. There have been too many unnecessary deaths already,' warned Jarvis, who didn't like the direction this conversation was taking. 'Killing a high-ranking policeman is asking for trouble.'

Toulemonde smiled. 'I agree, but there are many ways for Banks to die without raising suspicion. So, what is to be done? We have already attached a tracking device to his vehicle, and we have two operatives following him. It's only a matter of time before he leads us to the girl. If this fails, then we have an excellent contingency plan.'

'But I'm in charge of security,' protested Borkov. 'Why wasn't I consulted?'

Toulemonde frowned. 'You're no longer responsible for security, Isaac. The board believes this debacle is a direct result of stretching our resources too thinly. Prototype Two will be your sole focus. Incoming orders are outstripping our ability to supply, and it is vital we take the next step forward immediately. Security will now be my domain.'

'I'm still not happy with all these deaths,' murmured Jarvis as Borkov sat silently fuming. 'Questions are bound to be asked.'

Toulemonde smiled. 'I agree. Once we have the girl, we'll erase her memory and then load her brain with a selection of conflicting memories. After several days of schizophrenic trauma, assisted with a post-hypnotic suggestion, she will tragically end her life. That should send a clear message to anybody else thinking of contacting the authorities.'

Jarvis nodded in admiration and turned to Borkov. 'A much better solution, don't you think, Isaac?'

Borkov leaned forward in his chair, his confidence returning. 'You presume too much. This venture is only a success because of me. Hauser and Ridgeway are experts in their fields, but without my knowledge and ability, the program would quickly disintegrate. You will never complete Prototype Two, profits will dwindle, and your dreams of eternal life will disappear. Poof!' He clicked his fingers insolently.

Toulemonde gave Borkov a quizzical look. 'Just so I understand correctly, are you making a threat, Dr Borkov?'

The room became very quiet as Borkov smiled coldly in return. He knew how to play this game, especially when he had the upper hand. 'Of course.'

Toulemonde shook his head ruefully. 'You disappoint me, Isaac. Still, it's often the way with egocentric people—unable to see the forest for the trees.' He paused, letting the silence stretch. 'All knowledge can be transferred,' he said finally. 'Everybody is expendable. Nobody is immune, not even you, Isaac, so I would be very careful about making any further threats, very careful indeed. You may go. Your presence is no longer required.'

Borkov stared at Toulemonde in horror as he climbed ponderously to his feet and then pulled back his shoulders and strode from the room. His anger continued to build as he hurried back to the sanctuary of his office, slamming his door with such fury that the pigeons on the windowsill were scared into a brief flurry. They quickly returned and watched with beady eyes as Borkov threw himself angrily into his chair.

'If they think they can threaten me with impunity, they can think again,' he muttered.

Borkov pushed aside the papers on his desk and buried his head in his hands as he tapped his fingers lightly on his forehead. 'These imbeciles need to be put in their place, but how do I protect myself from their threat?'

Chapter 8

Damn with faint praise, assent with civil leer,
And without sneering, teach the rest to sneer;
Willing to wound, and yet afraid to strike,
Just hint a fault, and hesitate dislike.

Alexander Pope

Tweddle was feeling immensely pleased, enjoying Laura's reliance upon him. He had played the role of warm and caring gentleman to perfection, catering to Laura's needs with a cheerful smile and a genial manner. He believed he was building a genuine rapport with her but knew that one false move could destroy the fragile web he was slowly weaving.

'Softly, softly, catchee monkey,' he muttered before pouring himself a large brandy and settling back into his chair with a self-satisfied sigh.

He had returned to Kilpatrick's house to pick up Laura's belongings, but Kilpatrick had explained that the police wouldn't allow anything to be taken from the crime scene. Jordan arrived with Tracey as Tweddle was leaving, and they limited their exchange to angry glares.

Tweddle had sorrowfully explained to Laura that Jordan seemed too busy with other interests to pick up her clothing and books, describing the attractive girl with great relish. Laura had looked puzzled and a little disturbed but had made no further comment before retiring to her bed.

He had dreamt erotically of Laura the previous night, and the overpowering memories had stayed with him throughout the day. He jumped slightly as the telephone interrupted his thoughts. 'Colin Tweddle,' he answered smoothly.

'Good evening, Colin, it's Daniel. Could I please speak to Laura?'

'I'd rather not disturb her, if you don't mind. She's sleeping, and the doctor has insisted she gets as much rest as possible.' He sniffed and swirled his brandy gently. 'I can wake her if it's important.'

'Uh, no. I was just wondering how she was getting on.'

'Well, she's improving, but it's a slow process.'

'I understand. Can you ask her to return my call when she wakes up?'

'Certainly, Daniel. Good night.' He hung up and returned to his brandy.

Laura walked slowly into the room and stood with her back to the fire. 'I thought I heard the phone.'

'Sorry about that,' he said apologetically. 'I hope it didn't disturb you.'

'No, I was awake anyway. Was it anything important?'

'No,' he answered with a warm smile. 'My golfing partner wanted to know if I was free this weekend, but I told him I had other plans. I thought we could go for a picnic down by the river. It'll be good for you to get out into the fresh air.'

'Yes, that would be nice,' she answered vaguely. 'I was rather hoping it was Daniel calling. I'm surprised I haven't heard from him.'

'He's probably been too busy. Didn't you tell me he had a new job?'

'Too busy to call me?' Laura was unconvinced. 'No, Daniel isn't like that. Perhaps I should give him a call.'

'Are you sure it's wise?' Tweddle replied hastily. 'You don't want to tire yourself. The doctor made it very clear that you shouldn't overdo it.'

'I feel fine,' she laughed. 'It's only a telephone conversation. Really, you're starting to sound like my mother.'

'I don't think that's a compliment,' he said as he took a quick gulp of his brandy.

Laura dialled Daniel's number and listened until the answering machine politely asked her to leave a message. 'He's not in,' she said, glancing at Tweddle over her shoulder.

Tweddle had been inadvertently holding his breath, hoping the house was still considered a crime scene. 'He's probably out with the boys.'

'He could still find time to call,' she replied reproachfully.

'We all need companionship from time to time. I'm sure it's all very innocent.'

'Innocent?'

Tweddle looked earnest. 'He's been through a traumatic experience. I'm sure the girl he's with is just a good friend, some sort of therapy.'

Laura's eyes narrowed. 'Therapy?'

'He probably needs someone to talk to, so please don't upset yourself over nothing.'

She shook her head. 'I'm not upset, Colin, just worried. What if he's been attacked again?'

'That's unlikely. He's already bludgeoned one attacker to death and stabbed another, so he's quite capable of looking after himself.'

'You're being overly dramatic, Colin.'

'Am I?' persisted Tweddle. 'The facts speak for themselves. However, if it will make you feel better, I'll drop in tomorrow and tell him to give you a call.'

'Thanks, Colin, I don't know what I'd do without you. You're my safe harbour. Now I really am starting to feel tired. I'll see you in the morning. Good night.'

He blew her an unseen kiss as she walked out the room. 'I'll see you in my dreams,' he murmured.

~

Banks's eyes slid shut, and he blinked fiercely to stave off the sleep his body was demanding. The traffic was heavy despite the late hour, and he was relieved when he finally pulled into a vacant parking space outside a busy shopping complex. The cold air attacked his lungs as he strode briskly towards the entrance, and he hunched over to lessen the effect of the icy wind.

DeLuca followed behind, happy to be back on the streets. He'd been annoyed when he discovered his new partner was a woman, but she was reasonably attractive and respectful, so he accepted the change. He wore a headset attached to his cell phone and sent his partner whispered updates.

Banks inserted his card at an ATM and entered his PIN. The display flashed once and then returned to the original screen.

'What the hell?' he muttered as he gave the thick, protective plastic a sharp thump with the heel of his hand. He turned to the lady waiting behind him, a look of bewilderment on his face. 'The damn thing's eaten my card.'

She shook her head in sympathy. 'It's shocking the way they do that. No explanation, no nothing. It's there one minute and gone the next. It's probably expired.' She moved forward, and Banks reluctantly made way for her. He had sufficient cash to cover his immediate purchases, but without his card he'd be unable to buy anything further.

He spent a few minutes selecting an assortment of clothing, toiletries, and magazines as DeLuca trailed behind. There was one awkward moment when Banks suddenly stopped and retraced his steps and DeLuca had no option but to walk straight past him. After that incident, he drifted further behind so he wouldn't make the same mistake again. Banks abruptly picked up his pace, turned to his left, and hurried out an exit.

DeLuca immediately instructed his partner to bring the car around to the north entrance and then raced after him.

Two elderly ladies pushing a shopping trolley blocked DeLuca momentarily, and he pushed roughly past and dashed outside. Several taxis were parked across the road, and DeLuca glanced down the road as one drove away from the rank and stopped at the intersection leading to the highway. His partner was nowhere in sight.

'Where are you?' he demanded over the phone.

'I'm just coming to the north entrance now. I can't see you though.'

'I'm standing next to the taxi rank. Hurry, damn it, he's getting away.'

'I can't see any taxis.' She sounded frantic.

'Open your fucking eyes!' he yelled, causing several people to look at him.

'Jesus Christ,' he muttered. What he wouldn't do to have Dawson back with him. He sprinted to the cab at the front of the line, but it was empty. The driver climbed out of the third car in line and walked towards him.

'Are you wanting a cab, sir?' he asked pleasantly.

DeLuca looked back down the road to the empty intersection and swore again. The driver continued to wait patiently. DeLuca shook his head and stalked back to the pavement. A grey Renault roared around the corner and screeched to a halt in front of him. DeLuca climbed slowly into the car and looked at his partner reproachfully. 'We've bloody lost him thanks to you. Where the hell were you?'

His partner looked at him warily. 'Waiting by the north entrance as requested.'

'Bullshit. You just drove around the corner now.'

'Yes, but this is the eastern side of the building,' she explained, trying to keep the anger from her voice. 'When I couldn't find you on the northern side, I drove around here in case you were still following the target.'

'All right, what's happened has happened,' said DeLuca gruffly as he realised his mistake. 'It's your first time in the field so I won't mention this in my report. Just make sure it doesn't happen again.'

She held his gaze for several seconds before looking away. 'Yes, sir,' she replied stiffly.

~

Banks watched DeLuca disappear from view as the taxi turned the corner. The description matched the one given to him by Jordan, and the man still walked with a slight limp. Banks had suspected he might be followed, and his suspicions were confirmed when he noticed the grey Renault dogging his movements through the heavy traffic.

But suppose he did lead them to Jane? Did they then plan to kill them both? He was a senior police officer. The only way his death could be covered up was through complicity within the department itself. He felt a shiver of apprehension and glanced out the rear window, but the road was clear of pursuit.

He asked the driver to drop him at Waterloo Station and then walked down to Westminster Bridge and caught another cab. It was a tedious practice, but years of experience had taught him that shortcuts invariably led to failure; 90 per cent of criminals were caught because they were careless, complacent, or stupid. The other 10 per cent were just unlucky. The criminals that didn't match those categories were still free.

It was after midnight when he trudged up the stairs to Jane's room. She was sleeping soundly, and he gently shook her awake to make sure she really was sleeping rather than unconscious. She opened her eyes, looked at him blankly, gave a deep sigh, and slumped back against the pillow.

Banks stumbled wearily across the room to the spare bed and climbed in between the thin sheets. He lay there reviewing the case, trying to make some sense of it but to no avail.

He awoke early the next morning and opened the window to let in some fresh air. Muted noises from the waking city drifted in with the breeze, and he glanced across at Jane but she was oblivious to the faint disturbance. She'd had a restless night as her blankets were in complete disarray, scrunched around her body in a protective cocoon. Her colour was good, and she was breathing easily, so he had no qualms about leaving her.

He wrote a short note and stuck it firmly to the door before slipping quietly from the room. After retrieving his car from the shopping centre, he drove to work and was instructed to report to Fenwick's office. To his surprise, Fenwick greeted him warmly. 'I trust you slept well last night after your recent excitement.'

'Never slept better, sir,' replied Banks stoically.

'So, are you fit for restricted duties? Do you need time off to recover?'

'The best therapy is to remain active, sir.'

'Exactly,' agreed Fenwick. 'Don't give yourself time to brood.' A thickset man with huge shoulders and a florid face stood next to the desk watching Banks intently. Fenwick rose and put his hand on the man's shoulder. 'Inspector Evans rang in sick this morning. Apparently he sprained his ankle putting out the garbage. Sergeant Pollock will replace Evans until he returns. The sergeant recently transferred to homicide, so this will be an opportunity for him to learn from the best.'

Fenwick handed an envelope to Banks. 'I want you to investigate the allegations involving Memtech Industries. If they can be substantiated, your assertions about police corruption may be correct. Check out their facility, and see if there's any substance to the claims. They've been told you're investigating allegations of deceptive business practices. That's all.' He waved them away and turned his attention to the pile of papers in front of him.

Once they arrived at Memtech, Banks drove around the outside of the facility to get an overall feel for the place. The area had a look of decay and abandonment, and the listless people on the street reinforced the feeling. Struggling weeds grew sporadically through the cracks in the footpath, and old papers and rusty cans jockeyed for position in the shadowy recesses of the decaying brickwork.

A set of refurbished office blocks sat opposite the entrance to the main building, although many had vacancy signs. Memtech occupied the northern end of the block and abutted against several deserted warehouses filling the rest of the street. One of the warehouses had been renovated, and its façade of clean, unbroken windows contrasted starkly with those of its derelict neighbours. A simple white cross above the door identified the building as a house of God, and Banks read the small sign set in the brickwork as he drove past.

'Sisters of Mercy,' he muttered as he peered through the grimy windscreen.

'What was that?' asked Pollock, who was sitting slumped in the front seat with his eyes half shut.

'Nothing of interest. I'll drive around the block, and then we'll head into Memtech.' As Banks turned into a narrow street, a well-dressed man in a light grey suit and top hat stepped out from a gateway and held his hand up for Banks to stop before gesturing towards the gateway. An immaculately polished Mercedes backed silently into the roadway, and the man touched his hat deferentially to Banks before stepping gracefully into the car.

'Fucking hearses,' muttered Pollock as he straightened up. 'Give me creeps they do. Who'd want to work with dead people for a living?'

Banks edged forward and peered through the ornate gates at the squat bluestone chapel. Two large chimneys protruded from the top of a solidly built stone building at the rear of the chapel. 'Okay, that's enough sightseeing,' he said. 'Do you need to go through it once more?'

'Don't worry about me, pal,' replied Pollock laconically. 'I know exactly what I have to do.' He gave Banks a knowing grin and settled back in his seat.

Banks drove up to the Memtech gatehouse and gave their names; they were ushered through by an elderly guard.

Moira Ridgeway met them at reception and issued them nametags. She took them on an extensive tour of the facility, answering their questions as they wandered through the various departments. Banks noted that security was very tight, with every door requiring an access card. Even the lifts required a card.

'You have excellent security,' he commented as they sauntered down a long corridor lined with abstract pictures of interconnected circles and squares.

Ridgeway gave him a sideways look. 'Implying that we may have gone a touch overboard?' She gave a short laugh. 'Our research is at the cutting edge, and intellectual property is a difficult asset to safeguard. Our security probably isn't rigorous enough.'

Banks laughed in return. 'Point taken.' The tour ended in a room set up like a hospital operating theatre, and he asked Ridgeway its purpose.

'We have approval to carry out controlled experiments on cadavers in the same manner as a university,' replied Ridgeway. 'I'll give you an example. Our research is based upon past-life memory, so let's look at reincarnation. If we assume that life after death is a fact, our soul is liberated upon our demise. A significant part of our brain is dedicated to storing and retrieving information, and it's obviously a vital function. Although we require a vast organic support system to store and retrieve memory when we're alive, our soul has the same functionality but without the physical restrictions. If we believe the evidence of past-life experience, our soul is then reborn and is able to bring these memories from the past.'

Ridgeway looked at the two men intently. 'Now, this is the interesting part. Nobody knows where the soul resides within the human body. None of the spiritual books such as the Bible or the Koran mention this. However, with deep-resonance mind scanning, we are on the brink of discovering its location. We can study a patient's brain while the patient has regressed to a past-life identity, and it is only a matter of time before our equipment is sophisticated enough to identify the exact location of this stored memory. This will then pinpoint the exact location of the soul.'

'I don't follow you,' grunted Pollock, clearly puzzled. 'Surely memory is memory.'

Ridgeway shook her head. 'If regressed memory resided in the same location as normal memory, you'd remember your past-life memories just by thinking about them. Obviously we can't do that, so clearly they're different to our normal memories; hence, if we find them, then we find the soul.' She beamed unexpectedly. 'Can you imagine that? If we could determine the molecular structure of the soul, with our expanding knowledge of DNA, the future is almost incomprehensible. Can you imagine cloning a soul?'

'It's certainly an interesting concept,' agreed Banks noncommittally.

Ridgeway sighed. It was always difficult talking to people with limited vision. 'I trust I have been of some assistance with your investigation. Please wait here, and I'll notify our CEO that you're ready to meet with him.' She shook hands briefly and then left the room.

Banks turned to his partner. 'What do you think?'

'She's got a screw loose if you ask me. All of that stuff about cloning souls. A real fruitcake.'

'Apart from that,' prompted Banks. 'What about the allegations?'

'From what I've seen, this place is completely harmless.'

'Maybe, maybe not,' mused Banks. He wandered around the room while he waited for the CEO. He noticed the operating table had leather wrist and ankle straps attached to it and wondered why they would need them to operate on cadavers. As he turned to speak to his partner, Pollock hit him with a savage blow that slammed him against the table. He tried to rise, but Pollock punched him again, and he fell to the floor, unconscious.

Pollock lifted Banks onto the operating table and tightened the buckles around his victim's right wrist. Banks groaned softly, and Pollock quickly darted around the table and grabbed Banks's right ankle and dragged it across to the thick ankle strap.

As the fog began to clear from Banks's head, he thought for a moment that a rat was gnawing at his ankle. He opened his eyes in a convulsive response, saw Pollock running a leather strap through the metal buckle on the ankle restrainer, and jerked his leg free in a panicked reaction. His shin smashed heavily into Pollock's jaw, delivering a sickening blow that threw the man back across the room, where he sprawled semi-dazed on the floor.

Banks slid groggily off the table and started towards his opponent but was jerked to a halt by the strap securing his right wrist. He fumbled frantically with the buckle as Pollock rolled onto his stomach and began climbing to his feet. Banks fought his way free and looked around desperately for a weapon.

He grabbed a yellow gas cylinder from a nearby trolley and staggered towards Pollock. Pollock threw a disorientated punch at Banks, who swayed out of the way but then clouted Pollock over the side of the head with the cylinder. It made a dull, pinging noise as it made contact, and Pollock toppled sideways, his face smashing into the tiled floor with a wet smack. Banks stood over him for a moment and then slowly dragged him over to the table.

The effort exhausted him, and he realised that even fully fit he would struggle to lift Pollock onto the table. He heard footsteps in the corridor and quickly knelt down and removed Pollock's wallet. As a final thought, he hurriedly switched their nametags.

A burly man in a white coat pushed his way through the door and stopped when he saw Banks bending over Pollock's large form.

'Having some trouble?' he asked. His head was completely shaven, and his grim appearance was heightened by a purple tattoo that curled around his neck and onto his cheek.

Banks felt a trickle of sweat run down his back as he offered an apologetic grin. 'I was instructed to knock him out and strap him to the table, but as you can see ...' He shrugged his shoulders in defeat.

The tattooed orderly nodded sympathetically. 'He's a big one all right.' He helped Banks heave Pollock's dead weight onto the metal table and then buckled him into the straps.

A man in a green surgeon's uniform strode into the room and glanced at the patient before turning to Banks. 'I'm Dr Rathbone. Did he put up much of a struggle?'

'Not really. I got him while he wasn't looking, although he still managed to knock me around a little.'

'I dare say,' replied the surgeon absently. 'Are you going to stay and watch?'

'Are you going to interrogate him about the missing girl?'

'In a manner of speaking.'

'I wouldn't mind staying, but I need to get back and report the success of the mission.'

'Please yourself, but you'd better wait until he's confirmed dead.'

'Dead?'

'It's the only outcome,' replied Rathbone dispassionately. He pushed back one of Pollock's eyelids and shone a torch into his eye, watching the effect of the light on the pupil. 'Hmm, he'll be awake in a moment. Prepare the injection, please,' he instructed the orderly. 'It would be most distressing if he woke up and started pleading with me.'

As if in response, Pollock suddenly opened his eyes and attempted to sit up. Rathbone yelled frantically at the orderly. 'For God's sake, hurry up with that injection.'

'It's ready, Dr Rathbone,' replied the orderly as he passed the syringe over.

Rathbone plunged the contents into Pollock's neck. 'Goodbye, Mr Banks,' he grunted harshly.

'No, no,' shouted Pollock as he struggled desperately against the leather straps. 'You're making a mis ...' His words trailed off into nothing as his eyes glazed over, and he slumped back onto the table.

'That's better,' muttered Rathbone as he checked Pollock's vital signs before turning to Banks. 'All right, he's dead so you can go, but tell Borkov I'm charging triple for this one.'

Banks backed away in horror, desperately trying to hide his emotions. He turned and tugged at the door handle, but it refused to budge. 'I'm sorry but I wasn't issued with a security card,' he mumbled apologetically.

Rathbone absently pulled a card from his pocket. 'Take mine. I can soon get another one.'

Banks took a deep breath to calm his nerves as he grabbed the card. 'If you don't mind my asking, what are you going to do with him now?'

Rathbone studied him impatiently. 'He had information that you want, right?'

'Yes, so I believe.'

'Well now he's going to tell us everything you wanted to know.'

'Isn't that a bit difficult seeing that he's dead?'

Rathbone laughed. 'Dead men tell the best tales.'

When Jane finally struggled awake, she had no idea where she was or why she was there. She had the worst hangover of her life but couldn't recall having been to a party the previous night. She eventually realised she was in a shabby hotel room and crawled out of the bed, minimising her movements to diminish the pounding in her head and warily explored her surroundings. Clothing was laid out on an adjoining bed along with an array of toiletries and magazines. She seized a packet of headache tablets and hastily swallowed several. She longed to climb back into the bed and sleep for another twelve hours but needed to understand her circumstances first. An envelope stuck to the door attracted her attention. It was labelled, '*Urgent. Read me now!*' She ripped it open and forced her eyes to focus on the untidily written words:

Do not leave this room. Your life is in grave danger. Do not contact anybody—friends, family, the police, anybody! There has already been one unsuccessful attempt on your life. Arrangements have been made for your well-being. Do not open the door for anybody, no matter how harmless or official they seem. The only two people who require access to your room already have a key.

Inspector Robert Banks

Snatches of broken memory flitted through her mind. She remembered contacting Inspector Banks but when he arrived with his partner, they had forced whisky and pills down her throat and told her she was going to die. Jane shuddered as the memories flooded back. She could still taste the remnants of stale whiskey. Inexplicably, she was still alive, but she was now locked in a hotel room. She felt an overwhelming sense of panic building in her stomach, threatening to paralyse her, and knew she had to escape before Banks returned. She clutched at the knob and desperately rattled the door, but it refused to open, and she slumped back against the wall, the savage pounding in her head almost unbearable.

'Think!' she urged herself. 'You're an intelligent woman.' A thought struck her and she grabbed her bike jacket off the table and pulled out a thin cell phone. It was less than a quarter charged and she frantically punched in 999, fearfully watching the door as she waited for the operator to answer.

'Please state your name, address, and the nature of your emergency,' said a calm male voice.

She started to talk but could only make a soft croaking noise. 'My name is Jane Astbury, and I'm being held prisoner in a hotel room.' She felt her voice strengthening as she spoke. 'The man who drugged me is a policeman called Banks.'

'What is your location?'

She looked around the room. 'I don't know,' she wailed. 'Can't you trace this call? Please help me. I'm sure he'll be back at any moment.'

As if to confirm her statement, a key rattled in the lock, and she quickly ended the call and shoved the phone under the bed before fearfully facing the intruder standing in the doorway.

It was a gaunt, old man carrying a breakfast tray. 'Do you mind if I come in?'

'Who are you?' asked Jane tentatively as she pushed herself back against the wall.

'Call me Harry. I run this noble establishment. Mr Banks asked me to look after you while he's at work. Said he'd be back about six.'

'You work for Banks?' she asked nervously.

He laughed and set the tray down on the bed. 'No, Miss. He helped me when I was in trouble a few years ago so now I return the favour when he needs to keep somebody safe.'

'Safe?' she echoed.

'He said you were in trouble so that was good enough for me. No questions asked; you know what I mean?' He tapped the side of his nose.

'I'm not sure that I do.'

'Get this food into you, and you'll start feeling better. You look like shit, if you'll pardon my French.' He held out a key. 'This is for you, but keep the door locked. It wouldn't do your health any good if you were noticed.'

She snatched the key from his outstretched hand. 'So I can just leave?'

'Of course, but if you're in danger, the best thing you could do is stay put, you know what I mean?'

Jane sniffed unhappily and sat down next to the food. 'Thank you for breakfast,' she said finally. 'I'll think about what you said.'

She waited for him to leave and then picked up a piece of buttered toast and took a small nibble. She was suddenly ravenous and poured herself a cup of steaming tea as she stuffed the rest of the toast into her mouth. She didn't have a clue as to what to do next. Should she find out the hotel's location and call the police again or stay quiet as the note requested?

She listlessly tugged several items of clothing off the bed and put them on. The fit wasn't too bad but the fashion lacked taste. She finally unlocked the door and padded down the stairs and into the deserted lobby. She hesitated momentarily and then pushed her way through the glass-panelled doors and out into the street. Deciding that one direction was as good as another, she hurried towards the distant traffic lights.

～

DeLuca parked across the road from Jordan's car and patiently scanned the house. A sign on the van proclaimed 'Wilson's Mobile Auto Repair', and DeLuca wore an old pair of overalls to complete the picture.

The house looked deserted. He spoke briefly on his phone and then waited. Fifteen minutes later, a pizza delivery vehicle stopped in front of the house and a young girl carrying a padded pizza bag got out and walked up to the front door. She hesitated when she saw the police tape but after glancing around, ducked under it and rang the doorbell. DeLuca could tell by her body language that she knew she was on the receiving end of a hoax. She rang the doorbell once more and then stormed back to her car and roared off down the street.

DeLuca picked up the leather satchel containing his bomb and walked over to Jordan's car. It took him thirty seconds to undo the bonnet. He fitted the bomb snugly against the engine and then stripped the ignition wires and attached them to the bomb. It would only require a small spark from the ignition to complete the circuitry, and the ensuing explosion would hurl the driver to hell and beyond. He whistled tunelessly as he wound the wires together and covered them with electrical tape. It was a simple affair, but he double-checked it before stepping back to admire his handiwork. He gave the bonnet a cursory wipe and then strolled back to his van, certain that Dawson would approve.

Chapter 9

Be courteous to all, but intimate with few,
And let those few be well tried before you give them your confidence.
True friendship is a plant of slow growth,
And must undergo and withstand the shocks of adversity
before it is entitled to the appellation.
George Washington, Letter, 1783

Banks struggled to retain his composure as he hurried from the operating room. The man on the metal table was supposed to be him. Somebody wanted him dead. Was it Fenwick or somebody else? They obviously wanted the girl, but how could they find her if he was dead? He scribbled down the doctor's name as he rode the elevator to the ground floor and then hurried past reception, controlling the urge to sprint to his car.

He glanced in his rear-view mirror as he drove away and then swung the car into the midday traffic and headed towards the White Stag. As he drove along half-listening to the midday news, he was startled out of his reverie when the announcer mentioned Jane Astbury's name.

'The magazine publisher was kidnapped from her Walham Green residence last night. Details remain sketchy, but two policemen may have been killed trying to protect her. The motive for the kidnapping is not yet clear. Turning to overseas news, there has been a fresh outbreak of violence in ...'

Banks switched off the radio, turned left down the first side street, and parked behind a white van. Everything was happening too quickly. He needed time to think. The report had cast the killers in the role of protectors, and it was only a matter of time before Banks was named as the kidnapper. The men behind the scenes believed Banks was dead and would be closing in on the girl. Her unfortunate death would also be pinned on Banks. A statement would then be released announcing that Banks had been found dead in a seedy hotel room, driven to suicide by the enormity of his crimes. Case closed.

He had to find out what Jane knew. He roared back into the traffic, parked several blocks from the hotel, and then jogged the remaining distance.

He hurried through the deserted lobby and dashed up the stairs, deciding that the elevator would be too slow. He knocked softly on the door but there was no sound from within. 'She can't still be sleeping,' he muttered as he unlocked the door. 'Jane?' he called as he stepped into the room. A quick glance in the bathroom confirmed that the room was empty.

He picked his crumpled note and absently smoothed it out as he considered the situation. A sudden beeping noise startled him, and he glanced anxiously around the room but could see nothing. He shrugged stoically and then threw his belongings into a bag. The soft beep sounded again, almost at his feet. He peered under the bed and raked out a small phone from among the dust balls. The battery needed recharging, and he stared at it thoughtfully before pressing the redial button, recognising the emergency telephone number immediately.

He cursed softly. 'Bloody women, can't they do anything right?' He bounded down the stairs and pounded on the bell in the lobby. 'Harry!' he bellowed. 'Where the hell are you?'

Harry hurried through the dining room doorway. 'Can I help you, sir?' he asked with mock politeness. 'I do have other guests you know.'

'The girl's not in her room. Do you know where she's gone?'

'No, I don't. I'm not her damned keeper.' Harry glared at him.

'Sorry, Harry. I'm a bit irritable at the moment.'

'Who'd have known?' Harry held out an object. 'A Beretta. Small, but powerful.'

'That's for me?'

'Of course, who else?'

There was a brief rush of air as the front door opened. Harry quickly hid the gun as he turned around. Jane Astbury stood framed in the daylight.

'Jane!' Banks frowned. 'I told you to stay in the room. What the hell do you think you're doing?'

Jane looked suitably contrite. 'I'm sorry. I was confused when I woke up, but the fresh air helped me put things in perspective. I want to thank you for saving my life.' She walked towards Banks with her hand outstretched.

Banks grabbed her hand and pulled her protectively closer. 'We've got to get out of here,' he whispered urgently. 'Collect your things, and I'll meet you upstairs shortly.'

'I thought we were safe here.'

'Apparently somebody rang the police.'

'Oh, yes, that. I'll get going then.' She hurried over to the elevator.

'Use the stairs,' ordered Banks. He sighed in exasperation as he turned back to Harry. 'I assume you have bullets?'

Harry handed over the Beretta along with two yellow boxes. 'You're not dealing with an amateur, Inspector.'

Banks tucked the ammunition into his coat pockets. 'How much do I owe you?'

'Well, guns aren't easy to find at short notice. The overheads are naturally higher than normal.'

'I don't need the labour pains, just give me the baby,' groaned Banks. 'I really am in a hurry.'

'Three hundred pounds,' said Harry, running the words together quickly.

'Three hundred pounds? It's a lady's gun for God's sake.'

'Shh! Keep your voice down. As I said, it's not easy getting a quality weapon at short notice, and the overheads ...'

'Yeah, yeah, are higher than normal. I'll send you a cheque. I'm short of cash at the moment.'

'That's all right, Inspector. I know you're good for it.'

'Thanks,' replied Banks heavily. 'We'll be leaving by the outside staircase, so this is goodbye. The cops will soon be swarming all over this place, so it may pay to warn your other guests.'

'It's always a pleasure having you here, Inspector. You do wonders for my business.'

'The pleasure's mutual, Harry.'

Jane was waiting patiently outside the room. She followed him as he picked up their bags and clambered down the fire escape and into an alley. Pools of water lay among the old cobblestones, and they stepped carefully, mindful not to turn an ankle.

'Where are we going?' asked Jane.

'I'm not sure,' replied Banks. He dropped the bags on the ground at the end of the alley and held out the cell phone. 'Look familiar?'

She looked at him sheepishly. 'Where'd you find it?'

'Under the bed. The battery's very low so how much usage time is left?'

She held the phone on an angle away from the light. 'Not much, about three minutes if you're lucky.'

'Let's hope it's enough.' He pulled out his tattered notebook and then rang a number. 'Hello, Daniel,' he said. 'It's Inspector Robert Banks. I'm sorry but I don't have much time. Your fears about Memtech are well founded, and my investigations have landed me in trouble. On the news? I'm not surprised. Are you able to pick up my friend and me? I'll understand if you say no. You will? That's great.' He gave Jordan the address and disconnected the call. 'He'll be here shortly, so I suggest we wait back in the alley.'

'Who's your friend?' she asked as Banks handed her the phone.

'Somebody who's also interested Memtech.' His face hardened as he glared at Jane. 'Apparently my face is all over the evening news. I'm wanted for murder and kidnapping. Now why would they think that?'

Jane slumped down on the pile of bags and pulled out a handkerchief. 'You have every right to be angry,' she sniffed. 'I was frightened and confused when I woke up. I thought you'd kidnapped me. I'm sorry. I'm sure I can straighten this out with your superiors.' She glanced over the top of her handkerchief, but he was watching the road.

'I'm not blaming you,' replied Banks as he gave her a reassuring pat on the shoulder. 'Memtech has a mole in the force, and I don't know who to trust. The moment we surface, it will be a case of shoot now and apologise later. We both know too much.'

'They've tried to kill you too? When?'

'I'll tell you later. I need to find a safe refuge for a couple of days while I think about this. Memtech thinks I'm dead, so I can't afford to be seen.'

'Why would they think that?'

'They just do, but I'm not sure how long they're going to believe it.'

'You're rather secretive, aren't you?'

'Not really.'

'Yes, you are, but if we're going to be a team, you'll have to be more trusting.' A van pulled up at the end of the alley, and the driver peered anxiously out the window. 'Is that our ride?'

Banks jerked around and smiled. 'Yes it is.' They carried the bags out to the van, and Banks introduced Jordan to Jane. 'Where'd you get the Tellink van from?' he asked as they settled into the cabin.

'I just started work for them. Freelance journalism doesn't pay the bills, so it was strongly suggested that I find myself a real job. I'm supposed to be on the way to fix the phones at a textile factory, but I'm sure they won't mind waiting. So where to, Gov?'

'A good question. We need somewhere safe to stay, and I was hoping your friend had room for a few more guests.'

'Killa? He'll be happy to put you up.'

'Killer?' repeated Jane slowly.

'Matt Kilpatrick. Killa to his friends,' explained Jordan.

'There may be some danger,' continued Banks. 'They're going to comb the city for Jane.'

'There's nothing to connect Jane with Matt so fasten your seatbelts—next stop "Hotel Kilpatrick."' He eased the van out from the kerb and joined the steady flow of traffic.

Tweddle tossed his briefcase onto a chair as he strode through the house calling for Laura. He heard the back door open with its customary squeak and headed for the kitchen.

'There you are,' he said warmly as he met her by the kitchen door.

'What is it?' she asked curiously. 'What's all the fuss about?'

'I've got a wonderful surprise for you.'

'Well, come on, out with it.'

'You're not going to believe this, but Professor Bertwhistle McWilliams is speaking in the shire hall tonight, and I've been lucky enough to get two tickets.'

She furrowed her eyebrows. 'Bertwhistle McWilliams?'

'Yes, he's a world renowned authority upon the evolution of modern society. Surely you've heard of him?'

'It's not the sort of name one would easily forget, is it?' she replied, evading the question.

'Everybody of note is going to be there. It'll do you good to get out of the house and take your mind off Daniel. I'm sure there's a good reason why he hasn't called.'

A shadow passed over Laura's eyes. 'It is strange.'

Tweddle shrugged. 'I did remind him, but he seemed preoccupied with that girl I told you about.'

'Maybe it's time I went home.'

Tweddle smiled to himself. 'I understand your concern, but we need to keep you safe. So forget about the unpleasantness and spend a relaxing evening being wined, dined, and entertained? What do you say?'

'I suppose.'

'Good girl. It'll be a chance to meet my friends. I'm well thought of in high society you know. I'm forever being asked to stand for local politics, but honestly, who's got the time?'

Laura shrugged her shoulders, not sure what to say. 'What time does it start?' she finally asked.

'Dinner's at seven thirty, and Bertwhistle will start talking around nine. I've booked a cab, so we can both let our hair down and relax.'

Tweddle was unable to keep the satisfied smirk off his face as he ushered Laura into the crowded hall and strutted from group to group. Waiters circulated busily among the guests, and Tweddle happily handed Laura a sherry while he quaffed a glass of wine. 'This is my dear friend Laura Monroe,' he announced as he introduced her to the circle of socialites. 'She's an eminent psychologist in London and currently my house guest.' He winked suggestively at several of the men and they grinned in return.

Laura tired quickly and asked Tweddle to take her to their table. He smiled warmly and steered her towards the front of the room. 'Best table in the house,' he boasted as he signalled for another glass of wine. After an excellent dinner, Professor McWilliams delivered his oration to an enthralled audience.

As the applause died down after the presentation, Tweddle turned to Laura. 'A fascinating man, isn't he?'

'He certainly had some interesting things to say,' agreed Laura. She noticed that Tweddle was slurring his words and wished he wouldn't lean so close. 'We should think about going,' she said as a waitress placed a steaming pot of coffee on the table.

'What's your hurry?' replied Tweddle as he loosened his collar and slumped back in his chair. 'The night's still young, and there'll be all sorts of parties going on. Be a chance to let our hair down.'

'I know. You said that before. I'm not stopping you from having a good time, but I've developed a headache. All I want to do is go home to bed.'

'I wouldn't dream of letting you go home by yourself. Why don't we have some coffee and then find a taxi?'

'Fine,' agreed Laura. She poured them each a cup and listened as Tweddle discussed the lecture with other people at the table, interspersing his comments with several glasses of port. When he finally stood up Laura noticed him hurriedly clutch the table for support. 'Are you all right?' she asked softly.

'Nothing wrong with me, dear girl. I've had a wonderful evening, but now it's time to go,' he replied stridently. 'Come along, fair lady, our chariot awaits.' He waved airily to the table at large and then walked determinedly towards the exit. Laura hurried to catch up, and they walked out into the clear night air together.

Several taxis were parked nearby, and one of them immediately responded to Tweddle's raised finger. 'So what did you think of McWilliams?' he asked once they were settled comfortably in the back seat.

'I can't get over the fact that somebody called their son Bertwhistle,' said Laura.

'Well, they did, so stop evading the question.' Tweddle spoke slowly in an attempt to form his words correctly.

'To tell you the truth, it left me somewhat unfulfilled.'

Tweddle snuggled closer. 'I can fix that you know.'

'Don't be bothersome, Colin.' Laura frowned as she inched away. 'Are you interested in my opinion or not?'

'Course I'm interested,' muttered Tweddle as he ran his fingers up her arm and across her chest.

Laura slapped his hand. 'Don't do that, Colin.'

Tweddle ignored the rebuff. 'I think there's been enough talking for one night, don't you?' he suggested with a leer. 'It's time we got to know each other better.' He leaned over and attempted to nibble Laura's ear.

'Stop it, Colin!' warned Laura as she glared at him. 'Please don't spoil a pleasant evening.'

'I'm not trying to spoil it,' murmured Tweddle as his grin faded. 'I'm trying to make it more memorable.' He put his hand on her knee and then ran his fingers up her thigh as he whistled a little tune.

His drunken actions rekindled vivid memories of her attack, and she shoved his hand away with a grimace. 'Touch me again,' she muttered through clenched teeth, 'and you'll regret it.'

'Oh, I love it when women play hard to get,' he chuckled as he leaned forward and belched. Laura jerked her head away in disgust. Unabashed by her reaction, he put his hand on her shoulder and let it slide down to cover her breast. 'Wait until we get home, and I'll show you what happens to naughty girls who like to tease.'

She slapped him in the face, causing the driver to glance in his mirror. 'Don't touch me!' she snarled. 'I shall leave first thing in the morning.'

Tweddle slumped back in the seat. 'I was jus' having a little fun,' he mumbled sulkily. 'It's hardly my fault if you lead me on and then change your mind.'

'I beg your pardon. I was not leading you on,' she replied frostily.

'It's an honest mistake then,' he said earnestly. 'I thought you were. Really, there's no need to leave.'

'My mind is made up,' she said and turned to watch the passing streetlights.

~

After searching through his computer directory, Borkov downloaded a series of files, filling three disks. He stopped once he was satisfied he had enough evidence to carry out his plan. He made copies of the disks and placed them in a small resealable plastic bag along with a letter. He then made meticulous notes of everything he had done in the past twenty-four hours. His final entry was a note to himself about seeing Dr Ridgeway for an appointment in ten days' time.

'So it begins,' he muttered as he closed the book and pushed it across the desk.

~

Jordan organised a council of war once Banks and Jane had settled in. After introducing Tracey, he asked Banks to update them with his news. Banks demurred, suggesting Jane should tell her story first.

Jane felt a momentary attack of nerves as she studied their anxious faces. She often gave high-powered presentations, but this felt different. While boardroom discussions were often couched in terms of life and death, it was all window dressing to help deliver the bottom line. This was the real thing and the people listening to her story were relying upon her knowledge to save the day. It was a sobering thought.

She cleared her throat and then began. 'I first became involved with Memtech when I was invited to listen to their vision of the future, and I admit I was flattered at being asked. They demonstrated quite clearly that memory is a chemical substance, which makes sense when you think about it, and believe me, that's something I've done quite a lot of over the past few days.' She outlined the presentation describing how they uploaded a donor memory into the brain of an unwitting volunteer.

'Tracey's dad,' interrupted Kilpatrick. 'He was the donor.'

'The bastards,' muttered Tracey. 'It's awful just thinking about it.'

'In hindsight, it is awful,' agreed Jane almost apologetically, 'but at the time their proposals were very seductive, and I don't think any of us truly understood the ramifications.'

'What proposals?' asked Jordan.

'There were several, but the key for most of us was the prospect of immortality.' She gave a soft, derisive laugh. 'They called us the "Eternals". You simply select a suitable subject and take over their body. You could live forever jumping from one body to another. Of course, this is still hypothetical, but the first step has already been taken.'

'It sounds so futuristic,' observed Kilpatrick. 'Without any proof, nobody will believe a word of this. They'll just lock us up in padded cells.'

'It is a problem,' agreed Jane. 'However, there were other benefits. If the government was interested in another country's secrets, they'd simply abduct an official or scientist and extract their memory. There'd be no need for messy torture or truth drugs.'

Banks clicked his tongue. 'Every government in the world would be interested in the technology. Imagine the edge it would give you.'

Jane shook her head. 'I don't think it's got that far, otherwise they wouldn't be talking to the private sector about funding. If the government knew, they'd lock it up tightly and use it for their own ends. Imagine what unscrupulous politicians could do with it.'

'Is there any other type?' muttered Kilpatrick. 'How much did it cost to become an Eternal?'

'Ten million pounds.'

Kilpatrick whistled soundlessly. 'That's a lot of money. Does that mean you're a millionaire?'

'Several times over.' She smiled apologetically. 'The cost was prohibitive, but a small price to pay against the prospect of immortality.'

'What happens to people whose memory is extracted?' asked Jordan curiously. 'Do they become the equivalent of zombies?'

Jane gave a wintry smile. 'No. They become the equivalent of dead. The extraction process involves removing the brain from the skull.'

'The bastards,' repeated Tracey tonelessly. 'It just gets better and better, doesn't it?'

Jane finished by telling them about the three men who had been neutralized.

'That's quite some story,' said Jordan. 'Do you know how they expunge memory?'

'Apparently they can alter the chemical structure of existing memory so the brain no longer recognises it. I'm sure that's what they did to Andrew Lawrence.'

Jordan shook his head sadly. 'Why is it we always use new technology for the wrong things? Think of the people who could benefit from this discovery.'

'Like who?' said Tracey sharply.

Jordan's dark eyes were thoughtful. 'People whose lives have been destroyed by unpleasant incidents; victims of rape or sexual abuse who have never recovered from their ordeal.'

'I suppose,' admitted Tracey reluctantly.

'And why stop there?' continued Jordan. 'What about artificial memory? If memory is a chemical substance, it can certainly be mapped and copied.'

'You're right,' interjected Kilpatrick. 'If we could create artificial knowledge, you wouldn't need to study or learn anything. Schools would become obsolete. Kids could spend their time being kids until they turned eighteen and then simply choose their career path and have the knowledge injected into them. You could learn advanced mathematics in three easy injections. Changing your job or profession would be simple. We'd have designer injections for anything you wanted to know. Sport, music, history, physics, you name it.' He suddenly grinned. 'I could become a gynecologist.'

Tracey wasn't convinced. 'I don't think it's that simple.'

Kilpatrick ignored her. 'All of the teachers could be gainfully employed elsewhere, and the money spent on education could go to health and recreation. It would be the most significant single event in the history of mankind.'

'This is all very interesting,' interrupted Banks in his no-nonsense voice, 'but we're getting off the track.'

'Quite right,' conceded Jordan. 'So from what Jane says, we're up against a powerful and ruthless organization that will stop at nothing to achieve their goal.'

'Now I'm depressed again,' said Kilpatrick.

'Unfortunately, I've had first-hand experience of their influence,' replied Banks grimly. He briefly described his rescue of Jane and the events at the Memtech facility. 'Everybody believes I'm a cold-blooded killer. I know their influence reaches into the police force, and they could also have moles in the government. I can't clear my name until I know who to trust, and if I make myself known to the wrong people, then we're all dead.'

'So what do we do?' asked Kilpatrick.

Banks frowned thoughtfully. 'It comes down to whether we want to be hunters or collectors.'

'I don't understand,' said Tracey.

Banks looked around the room and his tone hardened. 'We have two options. We can run for cover and hope we remain undiscovered, or we can hunt the hunters.'

'We're not all in danger,' replied Jordan. 'Matt and Tracey don't have much to worry about.'

Jane smiled thinly. 'If you were caught, and Memtech extracted your memory, then Matt and Tracey would soon be added to their list of loose ends.'

Jordan suddenly stood up. 'There's only one option as far as I'm concerned. We know who the enemy is, so let's work out how to defeat them. I will not crawl off into a dark hole and live the rest of my life in fear.'

'I didn't say that,' replied Banks neutrally.

'I know what you said,' replied Jordan, 'but this isn't a pleasant debate over a nice cup of tea and then voting for the best option. I've made my choice. Those bastards are going to pay.'

'I agree with Daniel,' said Kilpatrick.

'And me,' replied Tracey. 'I owe it to my father to see this thing through.'

Banks gave Jordan a hard look. 'To be successful, we need to look at every alternative, but in this case I agree with you.' He glanced at Jane. 'What about you?'

'Running away has never been my strong suit,' she replied firmly.

Banks gave her a warm smile. 'Then it's agreed, but please remember, we're a team. We can't charge off like a bull at a gate every time we feel the urge for action.'

'I didn't say that,' replied Jordan irritably.

Banks gave him a tight grin. 'The first thing we need is an agreed plan. You were saying you had an idea, Matt; so let's hear it.'

'Sure. If we want to find some evidence, we need to get someone inside their facility. I thought I'd sign up for the memory testing program and follow the same path that Stephen did. Once I'm inside, I can snoop around and hopefully discover the proof we need.'

'Isn't that dangerous?' said Tracey. 'Look what happened to Stephen.'

Kilpatrick shrugged. 'From what Jane said, Stephen was simply in the wrong place at the wrong time. They needed a guinea pig, and he was it. If they were killing off people holus-bolus, the authorities would already be asking difficult questions.'

'They are killing off other people,' replied Tracey grimly.

'Only people they regard as a threat, and I'll be as unthreatening as possible.'

'I still think it's too dangerous,' repeated Tracey. 'What does everybody else think?'

Kilpatrick frowned. 'It doesn't matter what anybody else thinks. It's my plan and my decision. Besides, I thought you wanted to avenge your father? If you're afraid of being hurt, maybe you should have taken the other option.'

Tracey's cheeks coloured as she blazed back at him. 'Don't you talk to me like that. I'll do anything necessary to expose these vermin. If you want to play the hero and put yourself in the firing line, then fine, why should I care? Why don't you paint a giant target on your chest and ride into Memtech on a white charger while you're at it?' She folded her arms and pouted at the room in general. Kilpatrick subsided into a state of confused bewilderment.

'Right,' said Banks in a briskly cheerful voice. 'That's one plan put to bed. Who's next?'

The others looked thoughtful but remained silent. 'Okay,' he said, 'let me outline a few thoughts. I have several contacts in the department I can trust.'

'With your life?' asked Kilpatrick wryly.

'You need to respect my judgement on this. I have a couple of leads to follow, and a few phone calls to make, but to do this I need a car. Public transport's out of the question with my high profile.'

'You can use my car,' offered Jordan. 'I'm using Laura's car while she's away.'

'Thanks, but I can't use any vehicles that can be traced back to us. If I'm spotted, the number plates will lead them directly to you, and it'll be game over. So we either buy a used car with no questions asked, or we steal one every time we need to go somewhere.'

Jane raised her eyebrows. 'Steal one? Isn't that risky?'

'It's not my preferred option, but I don't have any funds. They were already one step ahead of me and confiscated my card when I used an ATM.'

'I'd like to help, but I've barely enough money to buy a bicycle,' said Jordan. He looked at Kilpatrick, who merely shook his head.

'I could lend you my credit card,' said Jane, 'although they've probably frozen my assets.'

'Thanks, but we'd have the same problem of traceability,' said Banks.

'Isn't fate a wonderful thing,' murmured Kilpatrick.

Banks glanced at him. 'Sorry, I didn't catch that.'

Kilpatrick gave Tracey a gentle nudge. 'I believe Tracey has the answer to your problem.'

Tracey scowled in annoyance. 'I suppose I do. My father left me an unexpected inheritance, which happens to sit in an untraceable account. You can use that.' Her voice was expressionless, and she subsided further into her chair once she'd made the offer.

'That's very generous,' said Banks as he looked around the room and smiled.

'I'll be happy to reimburse you once this is over,' added Jane helpfully.

Tracey smiled bleakly. 'There's no need for that. It makes strange sense that I use the money for this.' She turned back to Banks. 'So what are these leads you intend to follow now you've got my money?'

'It's not much but often the smallest lead can result in a case unravelling.' He pulled out his notebook and flipped through several pages. 'The orderly mentioned the doctor's name when I was in the operating room. It's Rath something. I was in a hurry when I wrote it down so my handwriting's a bit hard to read.'

'Rathbone,' said Tracey quietly.

Banks looked surprised. 'Yes, that's it, Rathbone. How did you know?'

'He was my father's doctor.' She turned to Jordan. 'And your girlfriend's doctor, if you remember.'

'Bloody hell!' exclaimed Jordan as he leapt to his feet. 'I was right, they were trying to kill Laura.'

'Dr Rathbone,' repeated Tracey thoughtfully. 'If we could get him to talk, he could be the thread you were talking about.'

'And how do you propose to do that?' asked Kilpatrick sarcastically. 'Invite him around for tea and cucumber sandwiches and appeal to the better side of his nature.'

'That might work,' she said slowly, 'but my idea is far more attractive. Let me talk to my mum, and I'll get back to you.' Her mood seemed to brighten. 'If somebody can direct me to an ATM, I'll get us some money.'

~

Banks parked near the entrance to the underground station and strode down the stairs. Jane had trimmed his hair and dyed it blonde the night before, and Jordan had bought him a pair of clear glasses from the local optometrist. Even Banks was surprised at the change in his appearance.

He chose the middle booth in a line of public phones and then glanced nervously at his watch as he waited for his partner to answer.

'Roger Evans.'

'Hello, Roger, it's Robert.'

There was a pause. 'Rob? This is a surprise.'

'Roger, I need your help.'

'You need help all right, chum. Let the girl go before anybody else gets hurt.'

'Roger, it's bad enough being trapped in a 007 movie without having to listen to gratuitous advice, so please don't interrupt my train of thought.'

'You realize I'll report this conversation.'

'It's a free country, Roger. My situation's nothing compared to those poor wretches in the Middle East.'

'Okay, what sort of help do you need?'

'Find out who we can trust. If I give myself up, I need to know we'll be safe. The true story about Memtech must come out.'

'I'll do what I can, but I can't promise anything. How will I contact you?'

'You won't,' said Banks. 'I'll contact you.' He glanced at his watch. He had another thirty seconds. 'Why didn't you come to work last Wednesday?'

Evans grimaced. 'Can you believe it? Some idiot whacked me on the knee with a baseball bat. Must have thought I was an ice skater.'

'You'd better explain that.'

'I'd just left the house to go to work, and next thing I know I'm rolling around on the ground in agony. My wife saw the whole thing from the front door. Said a large burly chap hit me. She got me inside and phoned for an ambulance. She reckons I was squealing like a girl, which is unfair. My knee's not too bad now. I still can't bend it much, but I'm mobile enough.'

'That'll teach you to stay away from your neighbours' wives. Banks glanced at his watch. 'I've got to run. I'm two hours late for a dental appointment. 'Bye.' He hung up, merged into the crowd and returned to his car, grinning as he pictured Roger standing by his telephone trying to decipher the message.

Five minutes later a worried inspector Kent delivered a recording of the message to Fenwick. 'Banks just contacted his partner.'

'Banks? That's not possible.'

'It's definitely him,' confirmed Kent. They listened to the recording together, jotting down the key words.

Fenwick glanced at Kent when it ended. 'Any idea what it means?'

'Not really, sir. He said he was thinking of giving himself up.'

'Yes, yes, that part is quite clear. Where did the call originate?'

'We traced it to a public phone in Blackfriars Station. We had a car there within minutes but found no sign of him.'

Fenwick paced slowly around the room. 'It's a very strange message. Has Evans reported this conversation?'

'Yes, sir. He rang here immediately and reported the conversation almost word for word. We don't need to worry about Evans, sir. He seems as anxious to catch Banks as we do.'

'I'm sure he does, but consider this. Would Banks and Evans assume the phone would be tapped?'

'It's a reasonable assumption.'

'So Evans's actions are entirely consistent with somebody whose words and deeds are under the microscope?'

'I suppose they are, yes.'

Fenwick continued. 'So if Banks wanted to give Evans a message without compromising him, he would need to be very circumspect. Somewhere in this message are the clues that will lead us to him. All we have to do is discover them. In the meantime, I want surveillance on Evans stepped up. If he has decided to help Banks, then he could lead us right to him.'

Kent nodded. 'I'll send the tape to our analysts and see if they can find any cryptic clues.'

Fenwick ran a hand through his thinning hair. 'I want you to take charge of field operations. When you bring Banks to me, I will personally guarantee your promotion.'

He waited until Kent left and rang Madison. 'It's Fenwick,' he said.

'My dear Chief Inspector, how are you today?' replied Madison smoothly.

'Cut the crap, Madison. What did you discover from that memory transfer conducted on Banks?'

'Our recipient hasn't given us anything yet, but it's still early, and the donated chemicals may not be fully aligned. I should have something within the next twelve hours.'

'Want to bet?'

'Is there something you're not telling me, Chief Inspector?' asked Madison cautiously.

'I don't know whose memory it was that you transferred, but it didn't belong to Banks.'

'What do you mean?'

'Banks is alive and well. He contacted his partner half an hour ago.' Fenwick suddenly clicked his fingers. 'Pollock! It was his memory you extracted, the poor bastard. Banks must have turned the tables on him.'

'So all we've got is rubbish.'

'Exactly. Where's the body? I'll send somebody down to identify it.'

'Not possible I'm afraid,' murmured Madison. 'We cremated it immediately. It doesn't pay to leave such damning evidence lying around.'

Fenwick swore and hung up. He was starting to run out of operatives.

Evans caught a taxi to the station and then made his way painfully into work and spent the day catching up on paperwork. He left early, citing pain in his knee, and cadged a lift to the station with a colleague in mobile patrol. Inspector Kent, accompanied by two plainclothes detectives, followed discretely. Kent suddenly nudged one of his accomplices and pointed to a timetable board. 'What's the betting he gets off at Bond Street Station?'

As a train pulled into the platform, Kent called in his hunch and ordered a team to cover the entrance to Bond Street Station and then followed Evans onto the train. He remained in the background while the other detectives split up, one of them managing to get a seat opposite Evans. Evans simply passed the time sorting through a file of papers on his knee. As the train stopped at Bond Street Station, he cautiously edged through the door and hobbled onto the platform. The detectives moved after him.

As Evans neared a soft drink machine he stumbled awkwardly into the path of a well-dressed young man carrying a thin black briefcase and was knocked to the ground with a sickening thump. The file of papers he was carrying landed in a scattered heap a short distance away. The young man apologized profusely and helped Evans climb shakily to his feet.

Jordan was standing next to the drink machine and watched as Evans tossed the papers in his direction. He dropped a brown envelope down the inside of his coat and onto the ground and then strolled away. Several helpful bystanders quickly gathered the papers and handed them to Evans, who smiled gratefully. The young man, satisfied that Evans was unhurt, apologized once more and continued on his way. A detective detached himself from the dispersing crowd and followed him. Two policemen quietly appeared out of the shadows near the exit and whisked the bewildered young man away for questioning.

As Jordan turned to leave, he noticed a familiar figure standing close to Evans. It was the same man who had accused him of assaulting Laura. Close to panic, he pushed further into the crowd, desperate to escape the detective's scrutiny, understanding that everything could end right here if he was spotted. He hurriedly boarded the nearest train, not caring where it was headed, and only looked up as it drew out of the station. Kent was still standing in the same position scanning the crowd but then, as if drawn by a sixth sense, turned and looked directly at Jordan. He immediately ducked his head and slid slowly down into his seat, allowing his breath to escape in a long soundless sigh. He wasn't sure if Kent had seen him but decided to change trains at the next station anyway.

Evans retrieved his walking stick from an elderly lady, who gave him a sympathetic smile, and then he walked the final couple of steps to the soft drink machine. He bought a can of lemonade and collapsed onto a nearby bench while he sorted through his papers. He immediately noticed the brown envelope and made sure it was secured safely in the file. He finished his drink as another train slid into the station, lobbed the empty can into a bin, and then followed the hurrying crowd onto the train, ignoring the strong urge to rip the envelope open.

Chapter 10

Heaven and Earth have no pity;
they regard all things as straw dogs.

Lao-tze, Tao Te Ching

Rathbone was flattered when Anne Chandler had asked him out to dinner as repayment for his kindness during her late husband's illness. She was an attractive woman, and he felt his blood stir at the thought of coaxing her into his bed. He poured himself a small, congratulatory drink and saluted himself in the mirror.

Anne Chandler had organised everything, insisting that the night was on her. He smiled as he recalled her words, as the night would indeed be on her. He checked the volume on his CD player, ensuring the right mood would be created when they returned after dinner. The doorbell rang as he turned down the lights, and he glanced at his watch. Five minutes early. She was obviously eager. *Eager beaver,* he joked to himself. What could be better?

He opened the door, still chuckling at his little joke, and then stood there, confused. The queen and Mick Jagger grinned garishly back at him. An excruciating pain shot through his eyes, and he staggered back into the hallway. The masked figure of Kilpatrick gave Rathbone another squirt of the ammonia and detergent solution and then followed him into his house. Jordan had been standing out of sight but now pushed past Kilpatrick and yanked a thick balaclava backwards over Rathbone's head. Rathbone was still pawing at his eyes and yelling incoherently as Jordan grabbed his arms and forced them behind his back. Kilpatrick snapped a pair of handcuffs on him as Tracey pulled off her Queen Elizabeth mask, flipped up the front of the balaclava, and shoved a gag in his mouth.

Kilpatrick held a cautionary finger to his lips. 'Remember, keep the talk to a minimum, and no names.'

Jordan gave him a conspiratory grin. 'I'll go out the front and whistle when the coast is clear.'

Tracey gave a nervous giggle. 'When the coast is clear,' she repeated. 'I feel like a spy.'

'No talking,' cautioned Kilpatrick.

Rathbone continued to moan loudly, and Kilpatrick cuffed him over the head. 'Shut the fuck up,' he growled.

'Do you think we put too much ammonia in the solution?' whispered Tracey.

'I don't know. It was just a guess. Fetch some water, and we'll wash his eyes out, but we'll need to make it quick.'

Tracey reappeared with a bucket of water, and they quickly replaced their masks.

'Hold your head back, so we can wash your eyes out,' Kilpatrick barked as he tugged the balaclava above Rathbone's eyes. They needn't have worried about hiding their identities as Rathbone's red rimmed eyes were tightly shut and weeping a steady stream of cleansing tears.

Tracey looked at the bucket. 'It'll make a bit of a mess.'

Kilpatrick shrugged. 'Who cares?' A soft whistle penetrated the hallway. 'Hurry up, it's time to go.'

Tracey emptied the bucket over Rathbone, and then Kilpatrick pulled the balaclava down and propelled Rathbone out the door. Tracey followed closely behind and climbed into the front seat next to Jordan.

'The mask?' prompted Jordan as he turned to face her.

'Sorry,' she said as she tugged it off. 'I'm still a bit nervous. This is my first kidnapping.'

Kilpatrick shoved Rathbone onto the back seat floor and sat with his feet resting on Rathbone's back. 'Not us. We're old hands. You'll find it gets easier with practice.'

Jordan cautioned. 'Weren't we keeping talk to a minimum?'

'Yeah, right. Mum's the word.' He poked Rathbone with his shoe. 'That goes for you too. We've bathed your eyes so quit your bellyaching.'

'You bathed his eyes?' questioned Jordan.

'We gently pampered him, but he's still not happy. You can't please some people.' He poked him again and then settled back comfortably.

Jordan parked the BMW in his driveway, and they manhandled Rathbone down the wooden steps leading into the cellar.

'This place is perfect,' muttered Kilpatrick as Jordan turned on the light. The air smelt slightly damp, and mildew lined several of the thick brick walls. He prodded Rathbone in the chest. 'You can scream all you like, chum, but nobody will hear you.' Rathbone made a muffled sound, and Kilpatrick laughed derisively. 'Can't understand a word you're saying.'

They dragged Rathbone over to a workbench and handcuffed him to the metal leg. 'Listen carefully,' growled Jordan. 'We'll be back later with a few questions, and we expect your full cooperation. Cross your legs if you need to go to the toilet.'

Jordan nodded to the others, and they walked silently up the stairs leading to the kitchen.

Tracey said, 'So now we leave him to stew for the night and then question him when his nerves are stretched nice and tight?'

'That's the plan.'

'And what do we do if he refuses to cooperate?' continued Tracey. 'How long can we keep him here?'

'We should have a couple of days before someone realises he's missing. After that we can dump him on the other side of the city.'

'Alive?' asked Kilpatrick.

'Jesus! What do you think?' snapped Jordan.

'I'm just making sure we have a clear understanding.'

'Oh, yes? And who was going to do the deed?'

'I was just making sure, all right?' repeated Kilpatrick loudly. 'Dead bodies are piling up everywhere, and it can be contagious, particularly if you're personally involved.'

Tracey interrupted. 'Accidents have been known to happen.'

'There are no accidents when you've kidnapped somebody,' said Jordan. 'If he dies, then it's murder.'

Kilpatrick could feel his temper rising. 'For the last time, I wasn't suggesting we murder anybody.'

'Okay, okay,' muttered Jordan, 'keep your voice down. The neighbours don't know I've moved back in, so we don't want them calling the police. It'll be a trying day tomorrow, so let's get some rest. I'll sleep on the couch, so I can hear if our guest gets up to any mischief.'

'Yeah, fine,' said Kilpatrick. 'I'll show Tracey where the spare room is.'

'I'm sure you will,' said Jordan, 'and remember, no lights. I'll let the neighbours know I've returned in the morning.'

Roger Evans slipped off to his local pub after dinner. He glanced around as he walked to the hotel but couldn't discern a tail. Once inside, he sat by the front door so he could watch everybody coming in. Several strangers entered after he arrived but left after a couple of drinks. He waited for an hour and then wandered over to the public telephone and called the number he found in the brown envelope. After several rings, an elderly female voice answered.

'Hello, can I help you?'

'Er ... I'm sorry. I was expecting somebody else.'

'Were you, dear, then why did you ring my number?'

'I'm sorry,' mumbled Evans as he hung up. He checked the number and tried again.

'Yes,' said the elderly voice. 'Can I help you?'

'Oh, it's you again,' said Evans feeling mildly embarrassed.

'You sound surprised, young man, but if you keep ringing me, I'll keep answering.'

'Can I check the number with you?' asked Evans.

'Yes, that's my number,' she confirmed as Evans read it out. 'What can I do for you?'

'I'm actually trying to get in contact with an old friend, and he gave me this number.'

'And your name would be ...?'

'Ah, Roger. Roger Evans.'

'Pleased to meet you, Roger. My name is Doris. Now I have another number for you. Do you have a pen?'

'Go ahead,' he said. He wrote down the number and then thanked her for her help.

Evans dialled the new number, and a familiar voice answered immediately. 'Robert speaking.'

'It's Roger. I got your message without too much trouble, if you don't count a couple of additional bruises. I'm afraid I didn't get the Middle East connection until I saw Daniel standing by the soft drink machine.'

Banks chuckled softly. 'And I see you worked out the time.'

'Do me a favour,' scoffed Evans. 'Two hours late for a dental appointment. Even Fenwick would have worked that out.'

'Oh, I don't know. I thought it was clever.'

'Who was that lady I spoke with?'

'My aunt. I gave her this number after you received the envelope. She's a good old stick and knows I'm innocent.'

'But what if the police had got hold of the envelope?'

'Old people can be so forgetful and besides, what could she have told them? She doesn't know where I am, and she didn't have this number. Now are you calling from a safe phone?'

'I'm in the local pub.'

'Okay. I need you to do a couple of jobs for me. Close the case on Daniel Jordan and his partner Laura. Tell Fenwick you're satisfied it was the Crucifix Killer. Their house is no longer a crime scene, and all pending charges against him are to be dropped.'

'Fenwick will happy about that. He's been putting pressure on me to wrap it up.'

'Right. Conduct a check on a Dr Rathbone at Mercy West hospital. Find out if there have been any unusual happenings or complaints.'

There was a pause as Evans wrote the information down. 'Okay, anything else?'

'I'm interested to hear more about your accident.'

'I got clobbered, what else is there to know?'

'Motive, for a start. Do you have any idea why you were targeted?'

'No, I'm sorry, I can't help you at all.'

'That's okay, I have my own theory. When did you ring to say you wouldn't be in for work?'

'I didn't tell them. I was in a lot of pain, remember? Sarah called them once the ambulance had taken me away. She told them about the attack and said I wouldn't be in for several days.'

'When did Sarah called the department?'

'Around ten, I think.'

'Can you find out the exact time?'

'Sure,' replied Evans. 'Is it important?'

'I don't know but Fenwick knew about your accident much earlier than ten o'clock.'

There was a momentary silence, and when Evans finally spoke there was a sharper edge to his voice. 'Are you saying I was attacked in order to get me out of the way, and Fenwick knew about it beforehand?'

'Something like that.'

Evans snarled menacingly. 'The bastards. So at least we know one person who can't be trusted.'

'Possibly, but we can't be sure until we get the timing sorted out.'

Evans snorted. 'I never did like him. Do I contact you on this number if I find anything?'

'No, I won't use this number again. Call Doris, and she'll give you another number.'

'Okay, I understand. Take care of yourself.' He hung up and walked slowly back to his table, wondering what it was he was getting mixed up in.

~

Tweddle jumped in fright as his alarm elbowed him awake. He squinted blearily at the time and then shuffled slowly to the kitchen. Laura was already dressed and having breakfast, and he sat down opposite and mumbled what he hoped sounded like a cheerful greeting.

She regarded him with distaste, maintaining a stony silence as she ate the last of her toast. 'I've tried to call a cab, but the number is engaged,' she said at last.

He frowned as he struggled to comprehend. 'I'm sorry,' he said finally. 'Are we going somewhere?'

'Not us, me. I'm not staying here another minute,' she proclaimed. 'Your behaviour last night was inexcusable.'

Tweddle was genuinely puzzled. 'Excuse me, my behaviour last night? We went out for dinner and had a good time. What's wrong with that?'

Laura snorted accusingly. 'You surely can't have forgotten your pathetic attempts to grope me during the ride home in the taxi?'

He cowered under her icy gaze. 'I don't remember that bit.' His severe hangover confirmed that he'd had too much to drink the previous night, and he cursed inwardly.

'Believe me, it happened,' continued Laura coldly. 'Once I get through to the taxi company I'm out of here.'

'So you're going to leave? Just like that?' spluttered Tweddle. 'Anything that happened last night was completely unintentional. You know I would never do anything to upset you.' His words tapered off into a soft whine.

'In your case, actions speak far louder than words,' she said simply. 'My mind is made up.'

Tweddle was desperate. 'But you can't just leave. I've done everything possible to make you feel welcome. I've fed you, nursed you, and bought you clothes and presents. You name it, and I've done it for you.' His frustration gradually turned to anger. 'I've even inconvenienced myself to make you comfortable, and now you're just going to walk out over a simple misunderstanding? How can you be so inconsiderate?'

Laura was seething. 'How dare you imply that I used you? I was in a fragile state when I came here, and I trusted you to look after me. I'm sorry if I caused you any inconvenience, but abusing my trust was not part of the deal. I thought we were friends for God's sake, but you obviously had other plans in mind. I feel dirty just sitting here.' She gave him a scornful look. 'There is no relationship between us, there never was and there never will be. I'll send you a cheque to cover your expenses. I don't want to owe you anything.'

She turned to storm angrily out of the room, but he quickly stood and blocked her way. 'Laura, I'm trying to apologise, not make things worse,' he said plaintively. 'If you've decided to leave because of my actions, the least I can do is drive you home.'

'Don't inconvenience yourself any further,' replied Laura icily. 'I'll take a cab.'

'I insist,' said Tweddle as he attempted an apologetic grin. 'It's my way of saying I'm sorry.'

'Suit yourself. I'll be leaving in five minutes.'

Tweddle attempted to lighten the mood during the journey but eventually succumbed to the bracing chill of Laura's scornful silence. His elegant fantasies slowly shrivelled into hopeless oblivion, and he played his final card as they neared their destination. 'What will you do if your house is still off limits?'

'I'm sure the police have already finished their investigation.'

'Not necessarily. These things can drag on for weeks,' replied Tweddle assertively. 'If that's the case, then you'd be wise to return with me.'

'I'm already wise to you,' replied Laura primly as Tweddle subsided into chastened silence.

Laura sighed in relief as they pulled up in front of the house. 'Our cars are there so he's obviously been allowed to return.'

'I'll help you carry your things into the house and check it out to make sure,' replied Tweddle gallantly.

'Please yourself,' she replied dismissively as she rang the doorbell. There was no response.

'There's nobody home,' said Tweddle triumphantly.

'The bell isn't very loud,' explained Laura. 'You can't hear it if you're down the back of the house.'

Tweddle pointed at another car parked in front of the building. 'Maybe he's got company and doesn't want to be disturbed. Do you have your key?'

Laura gritted her teeth. 'You know I haven't. Still, that's not a problem.' She scrabbled around among a collection of pot-plants and emerged brandishing a tarnished key. 'I knew that would be useful one day.' She unlocked the door and struggled inside with her belongings. The air had a strong musty smell of disuse.

Tweddle entered closely behind her and surveyed the dark interior. 'There's no one here,' he suggested again. 'I think—' He was interrupted by a muted shout and glanced anxiously at Laura. 'What was that?'

'I don't know. I think it came from the cellar.'

'We'd better call the police,' whispered Tweddle nervously.

'Don't be silly. Daniel has a workbench down there. He probably just hit his thumb with a hammer or something equally as stupid. Why don't you go and have a look?'

'Me?' He sounded horrified.

'You said you were going to check out the house for me,' Laura reminded him.

'I know, but there's no point taking foolish risks. We should get the police to check it out. That's what they're paid for.'

Further faint shouts reached their ears. 'That sounds like a woman's voice,' said Laura. 'You can stay here, but I'm going to take a look.'

At the sound of the woman's voice, Tweddle visibly straightened and puffed out his chest. 'No, no, it's all right, I was only thinking of your safety.' He pushed past Laura and flung open the cellar door.

～

Jordan endured a troubled sleep as he struggled to separate his dreams from reality. He occasionally checked on his prisoner, but Rathbone remained safely secured. Banks and Jane arrived with a supply of fresh milk shortly before breakfast, and they held a council of war over a bowl of cold cereal.

'Now you're certain he doesn't know where he is or who we are?' asked Banks.

'I've already told you, he doesn't have a clue,' replied Jordan with a touch of exasperation.

'It's an important point,' replied Banks. 'Previously the accusations against us were either false or defensible, but now we've committed a real crime.'

'It's only a problem if we're caught,' said Jordan. 'Come on. Let's get this over with.'

Rathbone turned to listen as they trooped down the stairs, and then he started pleading to the room in general. 'Please, I don't have much money, but if you let me go you're welcome to what I've got.'

Tracey turned to Kilpatrick and lowered her voice. 'Do we cut off his ear or a finger to show we're serious?' She was rewarded by a muffled grunt from beneath the hood.

Kilpatrick grabbed Rathbone's left hand and then elbowed him in the side of the head as he tried to snatch it away. 'Behave,' he said gruffly. 'Answer our questions, and you won't get hurt. Prevaricate, and we'll carve you up bit by bit.'

Jane blanched slightly and whispered to Banks. 'I don't like this.'

'It's just scare tactics. I'm sure he didn't show compassion for his victims, including Tracey's father.'

'I know, but it still doesn't feel right.'

'You could always leave.'

'No, we're in this together, and I need to carry my fair share. I'd feel even worse if I walked out.'

Rathbone finally pulled his manacled hands free from Kilpatrick's grasp and hugged them to his body. 'What the hell do you want with me? Is it money?'

Banks walked over to Rathbone. 'All we're after is a little information.'

'But why treat me like this? I think you've kidnapped the wrong person. I don't know anything important.'

'Is your name Richard Rathbone?'

There was a slight pause. 'Yes.'

'And you're a doctor at Mercy West?'

Rathbone cleared his throat. 'Yes.'

'Then there's no mistake,' said Banks in a cold voice.

'Who the hell are you people?' demanded Rathbone wildly. 'I have a right to know.'

'Wrong,' replied Banks. 'You have no rights. Either do as we ask or suffer the consequences. Now enough idle chatter. You've been brought here because of your relationship with Memtech. We want to know what that relationship is and the names of your contacts.'

'I don't know anything about Memtech,' protested Rathbone.

Banks flat handed him across the side of the face, the sound muffled by the balaclava. 'Wrong answer. We know you've been using your position at the hospital to help them, so start talking.'

Rathbone's hooded face sank to his chest. 'I can't tell you,' he whispered. 'They'll kill me if I talk.'

'And how are they going to find out? We're not going to tell them.'

Rathbone laughed mirthlessly. 'Believe me; no secret is safe from them. If I talk, they'll know about it one way or the other.'

'If you don't answer our questions, we'll spread the word that you did, and you'd be finished anyway,' threatened Banks.

Rathbone snorted derisively. 'Empty threats carry no weight with me. Memtech will know if I talked, so I'm telling you nothing.'

Banks signalled to the others, and they retreated to the kitchen and put the kettle on. 'He's more afraid of Memtech than us, so we need to change that around.'

'How?' asked Kilpatrick. 'We don't have any electrodes to attach to his nipples, and I can't see any of us bashing it out of him unless you have hidden talents in that direction.'

Banks studied their earnest faces. 'Rathbone doesn't seem particularly courageous so he needs to believe we really are capable of hurting him.' He paused and then added with a grimace, 'In order to do that, we'll need to rough him up.'

'I don't like that idea,' frowned Jane. 'It's not what I had in mind at all.'

Tracey looked at her scornfully. 'We've kidnapped him with the clear intention of making him talk. What else could we have had in mind?'

Jane dropped her eyes. 'I imagined that once we had him here he'd talk. I'm sure I would.'

'We're not really going to torture him,' Banks assured her. 'He'll only end up with a few cuts and bruises, which is a hell of a lot less than what they tried to do to you.'

'And Laura,' chimed in Jordan. 'I agree with Inspector Banks. We can't afford to pussyfoot about. If he suffers a black eye, so what. He certainly deserves it.'

Banks nodded. 'He must believe we pose a greater risk to his health than Memtech does.'

'That shouldn't be too hard.' Tracey grinned wickedly. 'We've got him. They haven't.'

'Perhaps he won't talk because Memtech is real to him, and we're not,' said Jane softly.

'This isn't real to him?' replied Tracey scathingly. 'The man is tied to a chair in a dark cellar; he's hungry, cold, and disorientated. He's probably got a thumping headache and is worried about going blind. Of course it's real.'

Kilpatrick gave her a consoling touch on the arm. 'Please, Tracey, let Jane finish.'

Tracey gave a rueful grin. 'Sorry, Jane. I'm a bit agitated at the moment.' She slowly clenched her fist in front of her face. 'I have all this nervous energy and no way to release it.'

'That's okay,' said Jane placidly. 'My editorial meetings are far more lively. Rathbone doesn't see us as real because he doesn't know who we are. We're merely disembodied voices inhabiting his dark world. This is just a bad dream to him, and he'll wake up soon and everything will return to normal.'

Kilpatrick shook his head dubiously. 'If Rathbone knows who we are, then he'll have us charged with kidnapping and assault. What's the point in freeing ourselves from Memtech's clutches if we end up in prison? It's a catch-22.'

'No, it isn't,' replied Jane swiftly. 'Rathbone will only talk if he thinks we're serious, and he will only believe that if he knows who we are and why we need the information. He needs to understand that if we can't expose Memtech, then we're dead; therefore, his only way out is to tell us what we want to know.'

Kilpatrick still looked uncertain. 'But he'll still go to the police once he's released. With our reputation, they'll believe anything he tells them.'

'Of course they will, but that's the last thing he'll do.'

'And why's that?' persisted Kilpatrick doggedly.

'It's simple really. The only reason we'd release him is if he talked, and if Memtech got wind of that, he'd be in deep trouble. So if he goes to the police, he effectively signs his own death warrant.'

'I think we should give it a go,' said Jordan. 'What do you say?'

Banks pushed himself to his feet. 'Let's do it. What's one more charge of kidnapping?'

Rathbone cocked his head to one side and listened uneasily as they walked down the stairs and gathered around his chair. Banks forced some warmth into his voice. 'How are you doing?'

'I've had better days,' replied Rathbone warily.

'You've been kept in the dark long enough,' continued Banks as took hold of the balaclava. 'It's time you understood who you're dealing with.'

'I don't mind remaining ignorant,' replied Rathbone nervously as he clutched at the balaclava with his free hand. 'I don't know if I can see anyway,' he added. 'My eyes need medical attention and shouldn't be exposed to the light.'

Tracey reached across and wrenched the hood off Rathbone's head, taking a handful of hair as she did so.

'Ouch!' grimaced Rathbone as he shut his eyes tightly.

'No point hiding,' muttered Banks as he forced Rathbone to face him. 'My name is Inspector Robert Banks. You may have heard of me. I'm wanted for killing two police officers, and I shan't lie to you, I did it. And do you know, it doesn't matter how many people you kill, the penalty doesn't change.'

Rathbone opened a tentative eye and squinted at him. His red-rimmed eyes had a thick crust of pus in each corner. 'I saw your picture on TV,' he confirmed gruffly. 'They say you kidnapped a girl.'

'Guilty again,' Banks admitted sadly. 'It's shocking when cops go bad, isn't it?'

Rathbone turned to look at the others. He stared at Tracey, trying to place her. 'I thought I knew your voice,' he said at last. 'I was supposed to have dinner with your mother.' His eyes opened slightly wider. 'Ah, now I understand.' Tracey merely nodded, not trusting herself to speak.

Rathbone peered at Kilpatrick. 'I haven't seen you before. Where do you fit in?'

Kilpatrick winked and made a trigger-pulling action with his right index finger. Rathbone blanched slightly and looked away. Jordan merely rolled his eyes.

'We're not here for polite introductions,' growled Banks. 'Your time has run out, so either give us the information or suffer the consequences.'

Rathbone looked at him beseechingly. 'I'm just a minnow. I don't know anything important.' He tugged at the handcuff. 'I need to go to the toilet.'

'Tough shit,' snarled Banks. 'Tell us what you do know. How did your relationship with Memtech begin? Who's your contact, and who does he report to?'

Rathbone shook his head. 'Don't you understand? If I tell you anything, I'm a dead man.' He pressed his lips together, virtually daring Banks to do his worst. Banks shrugged and glanced at Kilpatrick. 'I guess it's time to show us your skills, Killa. What's your preferred interrogation method?'

Kilpatrick was momentarily startled, the unexpected question catching him off guard. 'Oh, er … definitely knee capping.'

Tracey raised a questioning eyebrow. 'Knee capping? How does that work?'

Kilpatrick wandered over next to Rathbone. 'There are a couple of ways.' He touched the side of Rathbone's knee. 'If you're in a hurry, then a bullet here usually does the trick. It's quick, efficient, and extremely painful. Everybody spills their guts after that because they never want the other one done.'

'And the other way?' prompted Banks.

'Oh, that's more personal,' continued Kilpatrick as he warmed to his role. 'I hammer a nail through the front of the kneecap until it comes out the back. It takes more time but as I said, it's more personal.'

Tracey hurried over to Jordan's workbench and waved a hammer at Kilpatrick. 'Will this do?'

'I'm used to a bigger hammer, but it should do the job. See if you can find a couple of nails, the longer the better.'

'What about these?' asked Tracey as she held out several.

Kilpatrick peered at them through the gloom. 'No, they're too small. Twice that size if possible.'

Rathbone no longer contain himself. 'You can't be serious. There's no way you're going to do that.'

Kilpatrick leered at him. 'Hang around, and you'll find out just how serious we are.' He continued to stare at him. 'Are you religious?'

'What's it to you?' Rathbone replied sourly.

'Answer the question,' snarled Banks automatically.

Rathbone sniffed. 'I'm a Christian, if that's what you're asking.'

Kilpatrick clasped him on the shoulder. 'Excellent! You'll be pleased to know you're about to follow in the footsteps of Jesus Christ himself. I've decided to nail you through your feet.' He bent down so his face was only inches away from Rathbone's. 'It's much easier nailing somebody through the feet, and the pain is probably worse. Being a doctor, I'm sure you can tell us how many nerve endings there are in each foot.' He looked at him questioningly, but Rathbone remained silent. 'No?' continued Kilpatrick. 'It doesn't matter. This method's also easier for us with you being tied to a chair and all. It's very tricky nailing somebody's knees to the floor when they're sitting on a chair.'

Tracey held up several discoloured nails. 'Will these do? They're the longest I can find.'

Kilpatrick looked at them mournfully. 'It's a sad day when this is the best we can come up with.' He selected a nail and held it up for Rathbone to see. 'They're a bit rusty so they probably won't go in very smoothly. I hope you've had your tetanus shots because these are covered in all sorts of nasties. Okay, shoes and socks then,' he ordered imperiously. Tracey knelt down and ripped off Rathbone' footwear and placed a nail on top of his right foot.

Kilpatrick gestured to Tracey. 'No, not there, move it towards me so it's between those two bones.' He smiled at Rathbone. 'Well, last chance to talk.'

Rathbone smile bravely. 'You're bluffing, you'll never do it.'

Tracey pressed the point of the nail into his foot so that it drew a small drop of blood, and Rathbone winced and attempted to pull his leg back. The nail carved a thin line down his foot, and Banks casually forced it back into place with his boot.

'Hold still,' ordered Tracey. 'How can I hit the damned nail if you keep moving?' She peered up into Rathbone' pale face. 'Last chance to talk, you murdering bastard.'

'I didn't kill anybody,' protested Rathbone.

Tracey increased the pressure on the nail. 'Liar! What about my father?'

'Your father was in a terminal coma,' Rathbone replied hurriedly. 'He wasn't going to recover. That's the honest truth.'

'I didn't know there was any other truth,' muttered Kilpatrick.

Tracey didn't hear him. She was focused on Rathbone, her face a mask of cold fury. 'You didn't know that,' she said vehemently as tears trickled down her face. 'You never gave him a chance to fight back. Memtech needed a donor so you chose one. You murdered my father!'

'No I didn't,' retorted Rathbone loudly as he squirmed in his chair. 'You and your mother decided to turn off the machines, not me. It was your choice, not mine. If anybody killed him it was you.'

'You bastard!' screamed Tracey as she raised the hammer and drove the point of the nail deep into Rathbone' foot.

There was a blur of chaotic motion as everybody rushed towards Tracey, their movements punctuated by sobs, moans, and shouting. To add to the confusion, the door at the top of the stairs was flung open and two figures appeared on the landing. The leading figure dramatically pointed at the man bound in the chair and demanded to know what was going on. Then, just as suddenly, he was gone, and Jordan found himself staring at the remaining figure.

'Laura?' he called out questioningly. The figure turned to gape at him and began walking down the stairs, her steps stilted and uncertain. Jordan leapt forward to meet her. 'It is you. What are you doing here?'

'That's a question I should be asking you,' she said stiffly. 'It seems you've built a torture chamber, but that can't be right, can it?'

'First impressions can be misleading,' said Jordan as he looked around the cellar. Banks had managed to stuff the gag back into Rathbone's mouth although he was still thrashing around making a considerable amount of noise. Kilpatrick was struggling to extract the nail while Tracey was slumped at their feet crying hysterically as Jane attempted to comfort her. Jordan assumed an air of casual nonchalance and turned back to Laura. 'Was that Colin Tweddle I saw with you?'

'Yes. He mumbled something about getting the police.' She stared at Rathbone, her face very pale. 'Tell me what's going on?'

'That's Dr Rathbone. He was responsible for the death of James Chandler.'

'Rathbone? I know that name.' She frowned and shook her head. 'It'll come to me.'

Jordan quietly supplied the answer. 'He was the doctor in charge of your case when you were taken to Mercy West after the, you know'—he paused as he searched for the right word— 'incident.'

She nodded coldly. 'Oh yes. I'm not sure his own mother would recognize him now. What have you done to him?'

'Nothing much, it's just superficial.'

Laura suddenly looked at him. 'What do mean he was responsible for the death of James Chandler?'

'Not just Chandler,' said Jordan. 'Memtech also paid him to dispose of you,' added Jordan.

'Me?' Laura blanched at the news. 'Can you prove this?'

He smiled wryly. 'That's what we were trying to find out, except Tracey got a bit overwrought.'

'Ah, yes, Tracey? Who's she again?' asked Laura pointedly. 'I don't believe we've been introduced.'

Jordan's patience ran out. 'Can we go through the third degree later? If Tweddle's called the police, we don't have much time to sort out this mess.'

'Fine,' replied Laura icily. 'I'm sorry to be an inconvenience.' She folded her arms defiantly as Jordan joined the huddle around Rathbone.

Kilpatrick had Rathbone's foot in his hand and was explaining the problem to the others. 'The nail can't come out because it's bent at the bottom and I can't pull it all the way through because of the nail's head.'

'Hang on,' said Jordan. 'I've got the answer.' He hurried over to his workbench and returned with a large bolt cutter. 'I'll cut off the head and you pull it through from the bottom.' He looked over his shoulder at Laura, who was sulking by the stairs. 'Laura, can you fetch some antiseptic and bandages from the first aid kit in the bathroom?' She frowned in annoyance and then turned and disappeared up the stairs.

Rathbone gasped in pain as Kilpatrick tore the nail from his foot, and Banks grasped him by the hair and pulled the gag out of his mouth. 'Squeal again, and I'll stuff this thing so far down your throat you'll be able to use it as a pull-through when you wipe your arse, do you understand?'

Rathbone tried to nod but his head was held firmly in Bank's grasp. 'Yes,' he said finally.

He had gone extremely pale, and Banks slapped his face to help restore the flow of blood. 'Listen carefully,' he growled. 'Who's your contact at Memtech?'

'Isaac Borkov,' Rathbone replied miserably.

'That figures,' said Jordan, 'but we already know about him.'

Banks grunted in agreement. 'Who does Borkov work for?'

'I don't know, I swear to you, I don't know.' Rathbone's voice rose with each word.

Banks glanced at Kilpatrick. 'Massage his foot. We need to make sure there aren't any broken bones.' He stuffed the gag back into Rathbone's mouth and waited for the wave of pain to ebb before pulling it free. 'Now, let's try that again? Who does Borkov work for?'

'I told you, I don't know.' Rathbone' words were running together in a frantic bid to make them believe him. 'I only met Borkov once when we started the program. My only contact after that was over the phone. Borkov was always very secretive.' He finished in a rush and then cringed in fear as Banks stared at him.

Jordan took Banks by the arm and led him to one side. 'Colin Tweddle arrived here with Laura just as the situation went pear shaped. I think he's gone to call the police. If we have any further questions for Rathbone, we should ask them somewhere else.'

'I think he's told us all he knows.'

'Yeah, which is bugger all.' Jordan sighed. 'We should clean this up and get everybody out of here.'

'Worst-case scenario says we've got about fifteen minutes,' said Banks. 'With a bit of luck, they'll regard Tweddle as a crank caller.'

'So what do we do?' asked Jordan as Jane and an ashen-faced Tracey joined them. Kilpatrick was helping Laura to bandage Rathbone's foot.

'You and Laura should drop the doctor at the nearest hospital. Does Matt have his car here?'

'No,' said Jordan, 'he can take my car.'

Banks nodded. 'I'll stay behind and make sure we don't leave anything incriminating lying around. Jane and Tracey can go with Matt.'

'I'll stay and give you a hand,' said Jane as she gave him a brief smile.

'So where do we rendezvous?' asked Kilpatrick. 'I imagine we're not just going to drive off into the sunset.'

'A good point,' acknowledged Banks. 'Any suggestions?'

Tracey spoke up quietly. 'If we're sure that scum isn't going to talk, then my place is as good as any.'

'Great. Let's get moving then,' said Banks. Jordan pulled the hood over Rathbone's head, and they hustled him out of the house and into Laura's BMW.

Kilpatrick unlocked Jordan's car and then held the door open for Tracey. 'It's a bit battered, isn't it?' she remarked as she settled into the passenger seat and kicked several empty drink cans away from her feet.

'We drive what we can afford,' Kilpatrick replied philosophically. 'I'm a motorbike person myself but it gets so bloody cold in winter that I prefer to leave it in the garage. Now that it's warmer, I'll get it back on the road.' He glanced admiringly at an attractive woman herding a ragged line of school children along the footpath. As if aware of his attention, the teacher looked around and gave him a brief smile.

Tracey prodded him in the ribs. 'What are you doing? We don't have time to sit here while you ogle skinny women. In case you've forgotten, the police are on their way.'

'I was not ogling,' protested Kilpatrick. 'If you must know I was mentally censoring that young lady for wearing such a short dress.'

'Oh, now I've heard everything,' scoffed Tracey. 'Why can't you just admit that all you men think about is sex.'

'That's not true. We think about football and cricket as well.'

'It must be a comfort to be so simple minded,' muttered Tracey.

'It's the simple things in life that give the most pleasure.'

'Are you going to sit here all day talking rubbish?'

'Not at all.' He glanced once more at the teacher's long legs and then turned the ignition key.

Chapter 11

To tax and to please,
No more than to love and be wise,
Is not given to men.

Edmund Bourke

N othing happened.

'What now?' demanded Tracey. 'We'll never get there at this rate.'

'It's hardly my fault it won't start.'

'Try again,' ordered Tracey. 'Didn't you hear Daniel say it sometimes takes a while to start?'

'Yes, ma'am, I heard him.' He turned the key again but the engine was completely dead. Kilpatrick suddenly clicked his tongue in annoyance. 'Here's the problem. The idiot's left his parking lights on. No wonder the battery's dead. We'll have to catch a lift with the inspector.'

'You shouldn't ever assume,' said Tracey primly. 'Why don't you check the battery? The leads might be loose.'

He puffed his cheeks irritably and blew the air out between his teeth. 'This car's not going anywhere without a new battery, but if it'll make you happy ...' He released the bonnet catch and then ambled around to the front of the car. He glanced down the street hoping for another glimpse of the young teacher, but she had disappeared around the corner with her boisterous charges. 'It never rains but it pours,' he grumbled as he checked the battery terminals.

A brown wire coiled next to the base of the engine caught his attention. 'That shouldn't be there,' he muttered as he reached out and gave it a tug. He abruptly froze as he focused on the dark shape it protruded from. 'Oh, shit!' he hissed as he felt a rush of adrenalin course through his body. 'Tracey! Get out of the car,' he shouted.

'Did you say something?' she called back.

'Get out of the damned car. Now!'

'Why? What's the matter?'

'For God's sake, don't argue with me, just do it,' he barked, desperation tingeing his voice.

His tone chilled her, and she hastily joined him. 'What is it?'

He was still leaning over grasping the wire. 'I think it's a bomb.'

'A bomb!' She took an involuntary step backwards. 'If you're jerking me around, I'll kill you.'

'Take a number. Now please, move away before it explodes.'

'And what are you going to do? Disarm it?'

'Of course not. Do I look like a bomb disposal expert?'

'Then what the hell are you playing at?' she shouted. 'Leave the damn thing alone.'

'I'm afraid I can't move until you're safe,' said Kilpatrick with an air of quiet resignation.

'What are you talking about? Of course you can.'

'You don't understand. I loosened this wire before I realized it was a bomb. It's still connected but when I let go it'll spring free and anything could happen.'

'Let me have a look,' replied Tracey as she stuck her head next to his.

'Are you completely insane?' he muttered savagely. 'Get out of here while you can.'

Several strands of hair fell across her face, and she pushed them back behind her ear. 'I can't hear any ticking sounds,' she said reassuringly.

'Had a lot of experience with bombs?'

'No,' she replied tartly, 'but Inspector Banks may know something. Don't play with any other wires while I fetch him.' She ran off and quickly returned with Banks. He took one look at the bomb and ordered her back to the house. She patted Kilpatrick reassuringly on the head before hastily obeying.

'I wish I had that power,' said Kilpatrick wistfully.

'What power?' asked Banks absently as he peered under the bonnet.

'Nothing. How's it look?'

'Not good. Tracey said you pulled one of the wires out. Is this the one?' He touched the wire grasped between Kilpatrick's fingers.

Kilpatrick rolled his eyes. 'Yes,' he replied pointedly.

'Just making sure. In situations like this, it pays to ask the most basic questions. If I make an incorrect assumption, looking silly will be the least of my problems—and yours for that matter.'

'Yeah, sorry,' apologized Kilpatrick. 'I'm a little on edge.'

'That's understandable. Would you mind moving over and giving me a bit of room. I need to undo the battery terminal, and there's not enough room with us both stuck under here.'

'What about the loose wire?'

'Leave it where it is,' replied Banks matter-of-factly.

'What, just let go?'

'Yes,' said Banks as he gave the battery terminal a tug. 'Have a look in the boot for a toolbox. I need a small adjustable spanner.'

'So I just let go of this wire?' repeated Kilpatrick.

'If it isn't too much trouble. We don't have a much time, and a small adjustable spanner would be awfully handy right now.'

'Right,' said Kilpatrick as he shut his eyes and let go. Realising he was still alive, he quickly unlatched the boot, retrieved Jordan's tool kit, and hurried back to Banks.

Banks used a small spanner to undo the two bolts fastening the bomb to the engine and then eased it away and handed it to Kilpatrick. 'Hang onto this for me.'

Kilpatrick gingerly held the package, trying not to squeeze too hard in case the pressure set it off. 'What will happen if I drop it?' he asked breathlessly.

'Nothing much. The bomb's harmless without a power source,' replied Banks absently as he shut the bonnet with a clunk. 'Get your stuff out of the car and lock it up. You'll both have to come with me.'

'Yes, sir,' replied Kilpatrick as he gratefully handed over the bomb and retrieved Tracey's coat from the back seat.

~

Tweddle searched desperately for his keys as he scurried from the house, the image of the man standing behind the chair in the cellar nagging at his mind. As he scrambled into his car, he was surprised to find that Laura was no longer with him.

Realizing that he would be overpowered if he went back for her, he gunned the engine and drove recklessly for several blocks in a desperate search for assistance. A row of telephone cubicles outside the entrance to an underground station caught his eye, and he cut through the traffic and parked in a loading zone. A tall woman wearing a calf-length skirt was having a heated argument on the middle phone. A long yellow wig covered her neck and shoulders, capped off with a black beret. Tweddle picked up the nearest phone and waited for the dial tone but the phone remained dead. He cursed under his breath and hurried to the remaining phone. He gave a frustrated whimper as he saw that the receiver had been badly damaged and glared at the woman using the only working phone. She looked at him with amused indifference and then turned her back and unleashed a verbal barrage into the handset.

Tweddle carefully extracted several notes from his wallet, tapped on the Perspex surrounding the woman, and held up the notes when she glanced around.

The woman looked disdainfully at Tweddle. 'Listen, honey, I don't give the time of day for that piddling amount. A blow job will cost you at least five times as much.'

'What?' stammered Tweddle. 'No, it's nothing like that.'

'What then? A bit of bondage?' queried the prostitute. 'You look like the whip-and-punishment sort of person.'

Tweddle puffed out his chest. 'Listen here, I need your phone. It's a matter of life and death, and these others aren't working.'

'So you're offering me ten pounds for this phone.'

'Yes,' said Tweddle, relieved to be making headway at last.

'Well, I happen to have a customer on the other end of this phone who has already paid for my services, so you'll just have to wait.'

Tweddle was incredulous. 'You can't be serious?' He pulled out his wallet. 'How much is he paying you?' he demanded. 'I'll match it.'

The prostitute calmly weighed Tweddle's apparent affluence and his obvious desperation. 'Fifty pounds,' she said airily.

'Fifty pounds?' screeched Tweddle as stepped closer to the woman.

The woman shrank back against the side of the booth. 'All right, forty; but that's my final price.'

Tweddle sensed her fear. 'Take the ten pounds, bitch,' he snarled menacingly, 'or I'll take it for nothing.'

She raised the mouthpiece to her lips although her eyes didn't leave Tweddle. 'I'll call you back in five,' she murmured. She hung up, snatching the money from Tweddle in the same movement and was gone, her high heels clicking a staccato beat as she hurried away.

Tweddle shook his head in irritation as he called Scotland Yard.

PC Gibbons had strained his calf muscle chasing a petty thief through the docks at Millwall and had been transferred to 'customer service' while he recovered his mobility. He had just finished the last bite of his sandwich as his phone lit up.

'This is Colin Tweddle,' said a thin, reedy voice. 'I want to report a kidnapping and to inform you about a man being tortured.'

Gibbons sighed. 'You want to report a case of kidnapping and torture?'

'Yes, but they're not the same person.'

'Right. Can I have the name of the kidnap victim, please?'

'It's Laura Monroe. We've recently become involved and her ex-boyfriend isn't too happy about it. I'll give you the address so you can send a car around immediately.'

'Why do you believe she's been kidnapped, Mr Tweddle?'

'Her ex-boyfriend Daniel Jordan is a dangerous man. He's already assaulted me and killed another man.'

'The kidnapping, Mr Tweddle,' prompted Gibbons.

'Yes, of course. I took Laura back to her flat, and we heard a noise in the cellar. When we investigated we found several people torturing a man tied to a chair.'

Gibbons sighed inaudibly. 'We'll get to that in a moment. How do you know she has been kidnapped? Was there a struggle? Was she forcefully restrained?'

'I'm sure there was a struggle. When we saw what they were doing to that poor fellow, we decided to call the police. One minute she was right behind me, and the next moment she was gone. You need to send a car right away.'

'So you didn't see a struggle, Mr Tweddle?'

'No, but she wouldn't have stayed there by choice. I don't understand why you're wasting time asking me these questions. Laura's life is in danger so the sooner you get a car there the better.'

'We'll send the next available car, sir,' replied Gibbons soothingly. 'Tell me about the man in the cellar. Do you know who he is?'

Tweddle snapped his fingers in triumph. 'No, but I recognized one of the men with him.'

'Yes, sir?' asked Gibbons encouragingly.

'I don't remember his name,' continued Tweddle, 'but he's been in the news. He shot two policemen and kidnapped a woman.'

'Robert Banks?' asked Gibbons as he looked beseechingly at the operator working next to him. 'Is that the man?'

'Yes,' said Tweddle excitedly. 'That's him. You'd better send a couple of cars.'

'Let me review the facts, sir. Your girlfriend, Laura Monroe, has been kidnapped by her ex-boyfriend, Daniel Jordan. He also assaulted you previously and has killed another man.'

'That's right,' confirmed Tweddle. 'Bludgeoned him to death.'

Gibbons pressed on. 'You didn't see her being kidnapped, but the fact she didn't leave with you means she was forcibly restrained. Is that correct?'

'Exactly,' agreed Tweddle.

'And you left in a hurry because you saw a man being tortured in the basement by Robert Banks,' continued Gibbons in a dispassionate voice.

'Yes, yes,' said Tweddle impatiently.

Gibbons paused. 'Just for the record, sir, have you been drinking?'

'What!' spluttered Tweddle indignantly. 'How dare you fob me off as some drunken idiot? I demand to speak to your superior! If anything happens to Laura because of your incompetence ...' He let the threat dangle unfinished because he didn't know what he would do.

'Please, sir, calm down,' said Gibbons appeasingly. 'It's a standard question. There was no offence intended. I'm dispatching a car as we speak.'

'About damned time.' Tweddle took a deep breath. 'I know the whole thing seems fanciful, but I'm pleased we've finally got it sorted.'

'Yes, sir,' replied Gibbons formally. 'Thank you for your information. Leave this matter in our hands, and we'll be in touch if there are any further developments.' He hung up and considered his next step. He hadn't yet dispatched a car. In the past forty-eight hours he had received more than fifty calls from concerned citizens reporting sightings of Banks, although he had to admit that this was the most creative. He forwarded the report as a low priority with a routine check to be made by a local patrol car. His phone lit up once more, and he flexed his injured calf muscle and sighed.

~

Borkov completed his final diary note and leant back in his chair with a satisfied sigh. Once his memory was wiped, he would have no idea why he had taken these actions, hence the need for meticulous notes. Who to entrust with the discs was the key to the strategy. It had to be somebody he could rely upon, and yet somebody Memtech could never logically track down. His realized his list of names was too obvious. He needed to think outside the square.

He drew an empty pie chart and then began filling the sections with different periods in his life starting with his old school chums. He added sporting companions, colleagues, business associates, old friends, and neighbours, then he tore the list into sections, closed his eyes, and let them flutter onto the table. He gingerly felt around until he encountered a piece of paper. The scrap he'd chosen read 'old friends'. He smiled smugly as began writing names.

When his secretary announced Dr Ridgeway an hour later, Borkov had managed to write down thirty-seven names. Ridgeway sat down nervously and waited.

Borkov smiled reassuringly. 'I need to discuss several important matters with you.' Ridgeway remained silent. She was used to his tactics, but they still unsettled her. 'I'll start with Project Cocktail. When will we be ready to test our first group of subjects?'

Ridgeway relaxed slightly. 'The project on multi-implantation is progressing better than expected, and we'll begin human experimentation shortly.'

'That's excellent news. How soon then? A day? A week?'

Ridgeway thought for a moment. 'We'll be ready in two weeks, Dr Borkov.'

'What's stopping us from beginning tomorrow?'

'I need to repeat a couple of trials that were not entirely satisfactory and then run further verification tests.'

Borkov frowned. 'Are you telling me the implementation of this important project has been delayed because your team bungled some tests?'

Spots of red appeared on Ridgeway's cheeks. 'We're not delaying anything, Dr Borkov. My team has made excellent progress, and we are a month ahead of schedule. If we injected our first human subject in two weeks, we'd still be ahead of our target date.'

Borkov's eyes narrowed. 'Don't play semantics with me,' he growled, and Ridgeway blanched visibly at his tone. 'Could we begin tomorrow if we had to?'

Ridgeway refused to commit herself. 'Without the final tests and checks in place there is a possibility of memory confusion, particularly if there is more than one donor. This would then muddy the results and delay the next stage of our enhanced memory program.'

'And is that likely to occur?'

'It's a possibility, Dr Borkov. We should proceed cautiously.'

'If I followed your damned recommendations we'd still be fart-arsing round with Prototype One. Now answer my question. Could we begin tomorrow?'

'Yes, if it was necessary.'

'Fine. Make it happen.'

'Yes, Dr Borkov. Was that all you wanted?' asked Ridgeway stiffly.

'No, there is another small matter to discuss. I'm concerned our research is becoming too academic.'

'I don't understand.'

'We need to visit the coal face occasionally to appreciate what our subjects are going through. How can we deal with their problems when we haven't experienced them ourselves?' explained Borkov.

'I'm afraid you've lost me. A psychologist doesn't need to have suffered schizophrenia in order to understand it; the same way a doctor doesn't need to have had small pox in order to cure it.'

'This is a perfect example of why you will never amount to much,' sneered Borkov. 'You haven't learnt to think outside the square. Why shouldn't we also benefit from this groundbreaking technology?'

'But we are,' countered Ridgeway. 'Isn't that the reason you want to push through Project Cocktail?'

'Of course, but I was thinking of the reverse situation.'

'You'll have to explain that to me.'

'Do you have unpleasant memories that give you nightmares or cause you to cringe in embarrassment?' He smiled at her. 'I'm sure you do.'

Ridgeway nodded. 'I don't suffer from nightmares, but everybody has something in their past they're not proud of.'

'Exactly.' Borkov rewarded her with a small smile. 'How much do you think people would pay to have these memories eradicated? This is a gold mine waiting to be tapped.'

Ridgeway leant forward in her chair. 'Selected memory eradication? Yes, it could be done. We've already commenced work on short-term memory deletion with promising results. Once we made it an exact science, we could open clinics around the world. It would be legal and lucrative. We could even afford to wind back some of our less ethical activities.'

'That's not going to happen,' murmured Borkov. 'Those activities have grown legs and are off and running. The clinics, however, would be lucrative, and there's no reason why you couldn't run them.'

'Me?' replied Ridgeway in astonishment.

'Of course. You know more about memory deletion than anybody, including Dr Hauser. I'd have to sell it to the board, but that shouldn't be too difficult.'

'I don't know what to say.'

'There's no point in saying anything until we develop it further. To do that, we need to understand the effects of memory deletion. That's why somebody in the driving seat has to undergo the treatment.'

Ridgeway immediately protested. 'You ask too much, Dr Borkov.'

Borkov cut her short. 'Not you, my dear. Me. I will lead from the front by having my short-term memory erased.'

Despite her dislike for Borkov, Ridgeway was appalled. 'No, Doctor, it's too dangerous.'

'You just said that your results were promising,' snapped Borkov.

'Yes, but we still have too many cases where the eradication process fails to stop and long-term memory is affected. Until we understand the underlying cause, somebody like yourself, who is vital to the project, cannot be allowed to endanger himself in such a manner.'

Borkov smiled wryly. 'Your concern is touching, but I am determined to carry out this experiment, so I'll put this simply. Either agree to my request or forget about managing the memory-deletion clinics.'

Ridgeway shrugged her shoulders. 'I'm sure you know what is best, although I would require a signed request form.'

'Of course, I would have the same expectation if I was in your shoes.' He handed her an envelope. 'Here is your form signed, sealed, and now delivered. You see? I foresaw your need.'

Ridgeway took the envelope. 'Thank you, Doctor. Is that all?'

'I think so. I have been collecting newspapers for the past two weeks and will read them in sequence once the experiment is completed. It will be interesting to see if I have any sense of déjà vu. I want the experiment conducted in a week's time.'

'Very good, Doctor, I will pencil it into my diary.'

'Just remember one thing, in case you are dallying with the thought of turning me into a dribbling moron. These memory clinics are the ticket to your future, but without my endorsement, they will never happen.'

Ridgeway blushed. 'That is an unworthy thought, Dr Borkov. Please be assured that I will do my utmost to ensure the experiment is successful.'

Borkov inclined his head. 'Of course you will. The board members will also try to dissuade me if they hear about this, so please regard this as a confidential agreement.' He lowered his voice. 'I will be very angry if anybody else hears about this.'

'I understand perfectly, Dr Borkov.'

'Excellent. Keep me informed on Project Cocktail.' He dismissed her with a curt nod of his head and then took out his list of names. He cut them into squares, let the names drizzle onto his desk, and then selected the first piece his fingers encountered.

'Geoffrey Eastman. Perfect. I haven't seen him for years. If I can track him down, I've got myself the perfect safeguard.'

After he'd left work for the evening, he drove until he found a public phone. He flipped through the tattered phonebook, discovered there were only five Eastmans, and was rewarded on the third call with the sound of Eastman's voice.

'Hello, Geoffrey. This is Isaac Borkov. Long time, no see.'

There was a slight pause. 'Isaac, how wonderful to hear from you. It took me a moment to get my thoughts into gear. What's it been, twenty years?'

'Probably closer to twenty-five. What have you been up to?'

Eastman snorted loudly. 'How do you cover twenty-five years in a sentence? I've been working for Conway Mercantile for the past fifteen years as head of financial operations, so you could say I'm doing all right.'

'You could indeed,' replied Borkov with a touch of envy. 'What about life on the home front? Did you ever find a woman able to tame your wild streak and lull you into wedded bliss?'

'Of course. I've been married twice and divorced twice, so I've sampled the best of both worlds. Now what's this about, Isaac? You don't call somebody out of the blue after twenty-five years just to inquire about their marital status.'

'You're quite right. I have a business proposition that I think you'll find hard to refuse.'

'Oh, yes,' replied Eastman warily, 'and how much will it cost me?'

'Not a penny, my dear chap. All it will cost is an hour of your time.'

'It's not a networking scheme, is it? I don't have time to get involved in anything like that.'

Borkov laughed openly. 'Nothing of the sort, but it is very complicated. I was hoping to discuss it with you over a few drinks next week.'

'It's not illegal, is it?'

'Of course not,' replied Borkov firmly.

'Okay. It'll be good to catch up on the latest news. Where do we meet and when?'

'What about six o'clock next Monday at the Hilton? There's a small bar on the first floor that serves excellent martinis.'

'Sounds good, but I'll need to check my diary. Can I call you back in the morning and confirm?'

Borkov hesitated. 'Don't take this the wrong way,' he said finally, 'but my proposal is highly sensitive. If it fell into the wrong hands, it would make my life very awkward. I'll give you my work number, but you must call from a public phone, and you must not identify yourself.'

There was an awkward silence. 'This sounds very sinister. I really can't afford to get mixed up in anything that could harm my reputation or that of Conway Mercantile.'

Borkov decided it was time for a little honey. 'Do you know why I chose you out of the countless people I could have called upon?'

'I was wondering about that,' confessed Eastman.

'It's because you're absolutely dependable, steadfast, and reliable. You have all the qualities I need in an ally. Your role is completely safe but only if you maintain your anonymity.'

'That's all very flattering, Isaac, but what's in it for me? There's got to be some risk if I have to go through this cloak-and-dagger routine.'

'That's a fair question. I'm willing to pay you twenty thousand pounds for your assistance.'

'That's a lot of money, Isaac,' murmured Eastman. 'All right, I'll confirm my availability tomorrow from a public phone. Should I use a code name?'

'That won't be necessary, Geoffrey. Goodbye.'

∾

Tracey opened the door with a nervous smile when Laura and Jordan arrived at the rendezvous after dropping Rathbone off at the Mercy West hospital. Penny reluctantly stirred from her rug and gave them a perfunctory sniff. Jordan gave Laura's hand a reassuring squeeze. 'You've passed the Penny test anyway.'

'That's comforting to know,' she replied languidly as she glanced at the others in the room. 'Have you worked out what to do next?'

'We need to eat,' replied Kilpatrick. 'I'm starving.'

'How can you think of food at a time like this?' admonished Tracey.

Kilpatrick shrugged. 'Just lucky, I guess.'

Banks cut in before Tracey could reply. 'We'll eat when we've formulated our next steps. It's important to keep our strength up, but it's more important to have a clear plan of attack.'

'I trust your new plan is better than the last,' replied Laura scathingly. 'I refuse to indulge in mindless violence.'

'Laura, you don't know the full story,' said Jordan soothingly.

'You can dress it up any way you want, but violence is still violence,' replied Laura primly.

Tracey glared at her but said nothing. Strained silence settled over the group until Jane spoke in Tracey's defence. 'I know it looked bad, but it was only supposed to be a bluff. We were shocked when it happened the way it did.'

'I see,' replied Laura coldly. 'And the bruising on his face and damaged eyes, that was also unintentional?'

Jordan frowned. 'Laura, you can't take a couple of incidents in isolation. You really need to understand the full story.'

'Fine,' she said as she plumped down in a chair. 'I just wanted to make my thoughts clear.'

'We get the picture all right,' murmured Tracey belligerently.

Banks watched the exchange with concern. 'I know we're a bit upset, but the last thing we need is to fight among ourselves. Without a strong course of action we're bound to fail. We won't always agree, and we'll probably make mistakes, but we must remain loyal, otherwise our chance of success will be zero.' Laura made a half-hearted conciliatory gesture as he stared at her.

'Okay, so what's next?' asked Jane brightly as she attempted to lighten the mood.

'We need to unearth enough hard evidence to take to the authorities,' replied Banks.

'If we know who to trust,' interjected Jane.

Banks shrugged. 'Once we uncover the principal conspirators, we should know who to avoid. My next step is to contact my partner and see what he's found in the police database.'

'Won't that be dangerous?' Jane frowned. 'They'll be watching your partner like a hawk.'

'I won't do anything foolhardy, but we'll need to take a few calculated risks if we're going discover anything useful.'

'I see,' replied Jane. 'So what do you have in mind for me? Something as equally calculated, I hope.'

'Of course. Everybody will need to take their share of risks. When I was inspecting the Memtech facility, I noticed several vacant offices opposite the front gate that would make an ideal surveillance post. We could photograph everybody as they come and go and then get Evans to check them against the department files.'

'Photography is one of my specialties,' replied Jane. 'Finding the right camera won't be a problem if Tracey doesn't mind helping with the funding.'

'That's what the money's for,' agreed Tracey.

Banks turned to Laura. 'Jane will need a partner, so I thought you could work with her.'

'Me?' Laura blinked in surprise. 'I don't know anything about photography.'

'That doesn't matter. Jane's picture has been splashed across the news, so you'll need to rent the office and purchase the photographic equipment. Is that okay?'

Laura pulled a face. 'There's not much of a risk in any of that, is there?'

'Being that close to Memtech will be extremely risky. If you're spotted, your chances of surviving are remote, and remember, if you go, we all go.'

'I think we've got that message loud and clear,' retorted Laura. 'You don't need to keep harping on it.'

Banks stared at her in surprise. 'I was just making sure we understand the situation.'

Laura gestured around the table. 'Do we understand the danger we're in?'

There was a murmur of agreement, and Kilpatrick voiced what the others were thinking. 'We understood the first time it was mentioned.' He paused momentarily. 'And the second and the third.'

Banks raised his hands in surrender. 'Point taken. Overkill tends to be one of my more endearing traits. Speaking figuratively, of course,' he added quickly. 'Next on the list is finding somewhere to live. That'll be your job, Tracey.'

'What's wrong with here?' asked Tracey. 'We've got plenty of room, and my mum doesn't mind.'

'It's not safe. There are too many indicators pointing in this direction. It won't take a genius to eventually put two and two together. Scout around and find somewhere central that's quiet and discreet. It must have clear access from the front and rear.'

'Is that all?' asked Tracey despondently.

'Not quite,' replied Banks evenly. 'I'm afraid your mother will also need to find other accommodation.'

'My mother? But she's not involved in this.'

'We have no choice. Imagine if the people at Memtech got their hands on her. Even if they didn't utilize her memory, think of the leverage they'd gain by holding her hostage.'

Tracey had gone pale again. 'I hadn't thought of that. She can stay with one of her old school chums; somebody Memtech can't trace. I don't intend on losing both my parents to those sick bastards.'

'So that leaves Daniel,' said Banks.

Jordan shrugged apologetically. 'I'm sorry, I've been wracking my brain but ...'

'That's okay. I have something special for you.'

'Oh yes,' replied Jordan warily.

Banks gave him a pat on the shoulder. 'You are to beard the lion in its den.'

Jordan looked slightly taken aback. 'I am?'

'Fate has been kind to us for a change. You're going to tap Borkov's phone, and this is how you're going to do it.' Laura looked unhappy as Banks outlined his scheme but could think of no valid reason to veto it.

Banks and Jane then volunteered to cook dinner while Tracey went in search of her mother. The others settled down and watched the news with a degree of apprehension, but there was nothing further about Banks and no mention of Rathbone. The lead story centred on the latest scandal involving the Royal family. 'Well, that's something anyway,' said Kilpatrick once the sports report began. 'The less they focus on Robert, the easier it will be for him to move around.'

'Yeah,' replied Jordan uneasily. 'I wish we knew for certain that Rathbone hasn't gone to the police.'

'You should have thought of that before you kidnapped him,' replied Laura primly.

'We all agreed it was worth the risk,' explained Jordan. 'You would have as well if you hadn't run off with that Tweddle character.'

'I'm going to help Robert and Jane in the kitchen,' she announced disdainfully as she got to her feet.

'Oh God, I just remembered,' groaned Kilpatrick. 'I think I'm getting old.'

'Are you talking about what happened today?' asked Jordan. Kilpatrick nodded sadly. 'I think you're being too hard on yourself. Getting almost blown up would age anyone.'

'No, mate, you don't understand,' he said in a conspiratorial whisper. 'I saw the most beautiful girl in a short skirt today with legs that went all the way to heaven, and my first thought was that it was too cold to be wearing something like that.'

Jordan raised his eyebrows. 'You thought what?'

Kilpatrick shook his head mournfully. 'I need help.'

Jordan laughed. 'By the sound of it, you're past help.'

'I know. If there was a God he would have exploded that bomb as an act of mercy.'

Jordan sucked his lips thoughtfully. 'We could always replace the battery and try again. The car's insured for more than it's worth, so you'd be doing us both a favor.'

Kilpatrick shook his head. 'No, Robert isolated it and took it with him.'

'Robert?'

'Yeah, he asked me to call him Robert. That happens when you've been through a bonding experience.'

'And he took the bomb with him,' repeated Jordan.

'Well, he couldn't just leave it there, now could he?'

'No, I suppose not.'

Tracey wandered aimlessly into the room and sat down next to Kilpatrick. 'What a shit of a day,' she muttered. 'I feel totally washed out.'

'It hasn't been fun for anybody,' said Jordan agreeably. 'Imagine how Rathbone must be feeling.'

'That's right, rub it in,' cried Tracey. 'I don't know why you're feeling sorry for him. I'm the one who's going to have nightmares.'

Jordan scoffed. 'Nobody's feeling sorry for Rathbone. If anybody deserved to have his foot nailed to the floor, it was him. I'm just surprised you did it.'

'It was an accident,' she protested. 'I'm not that sort of person normally.'

Jordan looked at her over an imaginary pair of glasses as he spoke in his best judicial voice. 'Young lady, do you mean to tell me that the hammer just went off in your hand?'

'She didn't know it was loaded, your honour,' chimed in Kilpatrick.

Tracey suppressed a grimace. 'I didn't set out to deliberately drive a nail through his foot, so of course it was an accident.'

'What was I thinking?' said Kilpatrick as he gave himself an admonishing tap to the side of the head.

'Obvious, once it's explained,' agreed Jordan. 'Well, despite all the evidence to the contrary, this court has no alternative but to find the defendant'—he slammed an imaginary gavel against the palm of his hand—'not guilty.'

'Be careful, your honour,' warned Kilpatrick. 'That gavel isn't loaded, is it? We wouldn't want somebody getting hurt accidentally.'

Tracey looked at him disdainfully as she fought back her tears. 'You can be a real pig sometimes,' she said as she stalked from the room.

Jordan eyed him sadly. 'Always got to take it that one step too far.'

'Me? What did I do?' Kilpatrick asked plaintively. 'It was only a bit of fun among mates. You and I carry on like that all the time. It's not as though we're in a relationship or anything is it? We've only known each other for a couple of days.'

'So there's nothing going on between you two. You're not attracted to her in any way, shape, or form?'

'She's quite nice in a strange sort of way when she's not in one of her prickly moods or nailing people's feet to the floor.' He chuckled to himself. 'And she's got spirit. You have to admire her for that.'

'So it's the teeniest bit possible there's a relationship building between you.'

'I suppose,' Kilpatrick lamely conceded.

'Well, you've no choice then.' Jordan cocked his head towards the kitchen. 'Go on, off you go and apologize.'

'Do I really have to?'

'You're not scared, are you?'

'Of course not,' replied Kilpatrick firmly.

'I've been through this with Laura, and it can get damned ugly very quickly; so get moving, seconds count in this game.'

'Terrific,' grumbled Kilpatrick as he reluctantly followed Tracey's footsteps. 'Yet another case of the persecution of the innocent.'

Jordan smiled at his friend's departing back. 'Isn't love grand?'

Chapter 12

Not in the clamour of the crowded street,
Not in the shouts and plaudits of the throng,
But in ourselves, are triumph and defeat.
Henry Wadsworth Longfellow, The Poets

Kilpatrick awoke the next morning, drew back the curtain with a sharp tug, and was greeted with a muffled groan from Jordan. The sky was grey and overcast. 'You wouldn't know it was spring,' he muttered. 'I wonder if the girls are up yet.'

'They left an hour ago, and it's time I got going too,' replied Banks as he marched from the room without a backward glance.

'Single-minded character, isn't he?' said Kilpatrick.

Jordan tugged on his coat. 'Nothing wrong with that. I'll be late for work if I don't get a shuffle on. Without my car I have to rely on public transport.' He gave Kilpatrick a meaningful look as he headed out the door.

Kilpatrick gave a half-hearted wave and then picked up his phone. His call was answered after two rings. 'Memtech Industries. Lisa speaking. How can I help you?' She sounded young and vivacious, and he felt a sudden urge to impress her.

'Er, yes, my name is Matt. I'm completing my psychology degree, and I'm interested in becoming a past-life memory volunteer. I believe it will help my thesis.'

'Volunteers are always welcome, Matt. If you're suitable, we'll pay you for each session you attend. When can you come in for an assessment?'

'Anytime, although I'd prefer to start immediately.'

Kilpatrick heard the sound of pages being turned. 'Hmm, we have a group being assessed this evening but that's already full. The next assessment won't be for another month. Do you mind waiting that long?'

'Is there any chance of joining this evening's group? I'm already behind with my research, and if I'm late handing in my paper it will affect my marks.'

'I'm afraid that's not possible,' said Lisa hesitantly. 'We're very thorough with our assessments, and each one takes considerable time.'

'I don't mind going last if that helps.'

'First or last makes no difference. It's the total time taken that counts. It'll be a late night for the assessing team if I include you, and they won't thank me for it.'

'I'll thank you for it,' said Kilpatrick with a light-hearted laugh. There was a pause and he held his breath.

'Okay,' she said at last. 'I'll put you down as a reserve in case someone doesn't show up. That's the best I can do.'

'That's great, I appreciate your help.'

'I'm just doing my job,' replied Lisa sweetly. 'Please be here by six o'clock and report to Dr Ridgeway on the first floor. You may be lucky. One of the girls didn't sound too good over the phone, a touch of flu by the sound of it, so she may be a no show. Give me your details, and we'll have a pass ready for you at the gatehouse. Bring some ID, otherwise you won't be allowed in. Management is paranoid about industrial espionage. The company has its own internal security personnel stationed around the facility so don't be alarmed when see them.'

Kilpatrick happily gave her his details and then hung up.

He worked as a contract graphic designer with a group of advertising firms who farmed out contracts their own designers were unable to handle. After retrieving his motorbike from storage, he spent the rest of the day working on an advertisement for a new, improved shampoo.

Jordan arrived home just as he put the finishing touches to the fifth and final panel depicting Eve using one of the new shampoos with a strong apple fragrance.

'Nice work,' Jordon said as he studied the frames. 'Is this what you've been doing all day?'

'No. I spent the morning getting my motorbike started if you really must know. Besides, you can't hurry a creative intellect. You'd know that if you ever settled down and wrote something worthwhile.'

Jordan grimaced. 'Touché. How'd you do with Memtech?'

'It wasn't easy. I had to use my considerable charm just to get an appointment to be assessed.'

'Yeah? When's that?'

'Being such an exceptional specimen, they begged me to come in this evening.'

'Wow, I'm impressed. I'll have to get moving. I thought I'd have a couple of days to assemble my gear.'

'I don't imagine I'll achieve anything significant tonight,' said Kilpatrick. 'Once I'm accepted into their program, I'll be able to come and go on a regular basis, which will give me a greater opportunity to explore their facility.'

'Yeah, but what if you're rejected? Tonight might be your only chance.'

Banks arrived home as they discussed the problem, and Jordan asked for his opinion.

'The possibility of Matt finding anything incriminating lying on somebody's desk or in an unattended computer is negligible. We've agreed that the best chance of discovering anything is by tapping Borkov's telephone, so we should focus on that.'

Jordan nodded. 'Okay. A building the size of Memtech will have an environmentally controlled room to cater to their telephone and computer requirements. We need to locate the room, find the junction that Borkov's telephone feeds into, isolate his line, and then tap into his phone.'

'How does that work?' asked Kilpatrick.

'Fortunately for us it's fairly simple technology, and it's not difficult to get hold of the right equipment, especially if you work for a telephone company. Every time Borkov receives an incoming call or makes an outgoing call, my phone tap will automatically call a preprogrammed number. I know it's risky, but we can use the phone in our new location. I'll record his conversations, and we can review the tape each evening. It'll save time, and we won't have to worry about involving anybody else.'

'What are the chances of the tap being discovered?' asked Banks.

'They're undetectable over the phone. The only danger will be if there's a problem with one of the phones in that junction box. Even a second-rate technician would notice the tap.'

'That's just pot luck,' said Kilpatrick. 'The odds should be in our favour.'

'Let's say they did get lucky and find our tap,' continued Banks. 'Could they trace it back to this telephone?'

'Undoubtedly. It wouldn't take long to discover the number it was being diverted to.'

'Couldn't we rig it so it self-destructed if it was tampered with?' suggested Kilpatrick.

Jordan ignored him. 'The tap only works with external calls. Any internal calls, from Borkov to his secretary, for example, will not trigger the intercept.'

'Why not?' asked Kilpatrick.

'Because that's the way it is.'

'You don't know do you?'

'Of course I know,' retorted Jordan, 'but I can't be bothered explaining the complexities to a self-confessed technical nincompoop like you.'

'Fair enough,' sniffed Kilpatrick. 'What about a junction box? Do you think you could bring yourself to explain what one of those looks like?'

'That I can do.'

Once Jordan had finished, Banks handed Kilpatrick a black plastic card with bright yellow writing. 'Do you remember I mentioned my visit to Memtech?'

'How could we forget,' replied Jordan with a shudder.

'This is the card the doctor gave to me so I could exit the building. He looked important, so if the card still functions, it may help you gain wider access.'

'Terrific,' exclaimed Kilpatrick. 'This should make things easier.'

'Don't get too excited,' Banks cautioned. 'If they find that card on you it could be your death warrant. And never forget, if one of us goes, we're all gone.'

Kilpatrick picked up his scarf and wrapped it around his neck. 'It's time I was gone anyway. Memtech awaits. Wish me luck,' he said as he donned his leather jacket and headed for the door.

The office rental went without a hitch. Jane set up the camera next to a window overlooking the main gate and positioned it so the lens poked through a crack between the curtains. She cut a small hole for the viewfinder and then sent Laura into the street to see if there was anything that might give them away. They spent the remaining daylight hours taking photographs of the Memtech personnel as they came and went. Jane was wary about taking further shots once the day faded to dusk as the light spilling between the curtains could attract unwanted attention.

Jordan had left a text message on Laura's cell phone with the address of their new residence, and they arrived as dinner was being served. Everybody gratefully tucked into a hot steak and kidney pie while they took turns delivering a brief summary of their activities. It wasn't long before the discussion turned to Kilpatrick and his foray into the midst of the enemy.

~

As Kilpatrick parked his motorbike in front of the boom gate, an elderly guard opened the thick glass window and gave him a fierce look. 'Yes?'

'I'm Matt Kilpatrick. I have a six o'clock appointment to see Dr Ridgeway.'

The guard scanned a list of names on a battered clipboard and then gave a bored grunt. 'Identification?'

Kilpatrick handed over his driving license. The guard studied the photograph intently before looking up at Kilpatrick. 'You've had a haircut.' The guard's tone was an accusation.

'I've had several,' replied Kilpatrick cheerfully.

The guard's eyes narrowed slightly. 'I'll need corroborating ID.'

Kilpatrick flipped open his wallet. 'What would you like? I've got a library card, a credit card, my ambulance membership card, a couple of bank cards.' His voice tapered off as he waited for a reply. The guard glanced up as a limousine stopped behind Kilpatrick's bike.

'It doesn't matter.' He handed Kilpatrick a white plastic card. 'Use this for the front door and the elevator. Go to the first floor and sign in. Follow the sign posts and don't wander anywhere you're not supposed to.' He activated the boom gate. 'On your bike, Sunshine, you're holding up the traffic.'

Kilpatrick noticed a thickset guard watching him as entered the building and walked across to the elevator. He nervously inserted the white card into the elevator slot and pressed the button for the first floor, sighing with relief as the doors closed behind him.

Another sign directed him to a room down the hallway, which he entered, smiling anxiously at the other applicants as they muttered polite greetings. A lady in a white lab coat soon appeared from an adjoining office, introduced herself as Dr

Ridgeway, and asked for their names, informing Kilpatrick that he would be assessed as two other applicants had cancelled. She handed each of them a booklet and pen.

'Please fill out this simple questionnaire. It appraises your general strengths and weaknesses and will allow us to profile such areas as your language skills, deductive abilities, creative flair, sporting prowess, and so on. Answer the questions honestly. We want to know the truth about you, warts and all, as any undisclosed information could result in a flawed outcome. There's a kitchenette around to your right if you want a hot drink, and the toilets are to the left. Are there any questions?'

There were none, so Kilpatrick wrote his name on the first page and spent the next thirty minutes ticking boxes. Dr Ridgeway appeared a short time later and called for the first candidate. Kilpatrick pulled a book from his backpack and settled down to wait. The first candidate eventually reappeared and the next candidate was called. Kilpatrick decided it was time to explore his surroundings and walked along the passage trying several of the office doors, but they were locked. The toilets were at the end of the corridor and the passage continued around to the left as he walked past them. He finally found an unlocked door, but it led to a storeroom. He made a cup of coffee in the kitchen and wandered back to the waiting room. The second applicant walked out several minutes later and smiled at Kilpatrick as she retrieved her bag and quietly left. The procedure continued until it was finally Kilpatrick's turn.

Dr Ridgeway thanked him for his patience and directed him to a seat. 'I'm in charge of this project and therefore responsible for your wellbeing. We value your contribution and will not deliberately place you in jeopardy. Having said that, we're currently assessing new research and although each step is incremental to minimize any danger, not all risk can be eliminated. Will this be a problem for you?' She looked at Kilpatrick expectantly.

Kilpatrick cleared his throat. 'No, that's fine with me.'

'Good. If you're suitable for our research, you will need to sign a release form absolving Memtech of all responsibility for any future problems which may result from your association with us.'

'I see,' said Kilpatrick apprehensively. 'What sort of problems are you talking about?'

'I'll explain that as we go along.' Ridgeway smiled as she turned and indicated a third person in the room. 'My associate is Dr Cameron. He will be in charge of your case.'

Dr Cameron smiled warmly as he held out his hand. 'Call me Scotty.'

'Pleased to meet you,' mumbled Kilpatrick as he shook Cameron's hand.

'Now that the niceties are out of the way, let's get started,' said Ridgeway as she briskly rubbed her hands together. 'Can I see your questionnaire?'

Kilpatrick handed over the booklet, and she flicked through the pages, occasionally pausing to indicate a point of interest to Cameron before finally looking up at Kilpatrick with a smile of encouragement.

'You have an interesting profile, Matt, and will make an excellent subject if we choose to accept you.'

Kilpatrick smiled in return, not really sure what to say. 'I'll take that as a compliment.'

'I was merely stating a fact. All that remains now is to determine your susceptibility to hypnosis. Dr Cameron is the expert in this area, and he'll make the final decision.'

Cameron stared intently at Kilpatrick. 'Have you been hypnotized before?'

'No, it's not something I've ever considered.'

'That's not unusual,' replied Cameron as he leant across and shone a strong, narrow light in his eyes. 'Please stare at a point above my head.' He moved the torch slowly from side to side. 'You see that?' he murmured to Ridgeway.

'See what?' interjected Kilpatrick.

'Please hold your head still,' said Cameron firmly.

'Very promising,' replied Ridgeway. 'One of the best responses I've seen yet.'

Cameron shut off the torch with a snap. 'Congratulations, young man. I believe you'll make an excellent subject.'

'You can tell that by shining a torch in my eyes?'

Cameron gave him a tight grin. 'Hypnosis is a physical reaction to a set of well-defined external stimuli. We're taught to recognize compatible reactions, and yours are exceedingly high.'

'I see,' replied Kilpatrick, who had no idea what Cameron was talking about. 'How long will the program run?'

'It varies from subject to subject. We will need you here tomorrow evening and again five days after that. We'll then want to examine you on a weekly basis for the next month or two.'

'That's okay with me,' acknowledged Kilpatrick.

Ridgeway gathered her papers. 'Dr Cameron will give you a run down on the program while I look through your questionnaire. Before I forget, here is a card allowing you the same access as the one you received earlier and will be valid for the life of the experiment. Your current card will expire tonight so you may as well return it to me now.'

Kilpatrick reached into his pocket but stopped when he felt the second card given to him by Banks. The cards felt identical and he didn't want to make the mistake of pulling out the wrong card. 'I think I left it in my backpack,' he said slowly as he felt in his other pocket.

'No problem,' replied Ridgeway. 'Hand it in at the gatehouse when you leave.'

Cameron leant back in his chair as he studied Kilpatrick. 'Our research has shown that most people have at least three or four past-life memories, but what is the benefit of these memories, or experiences if you like, if we're unable to recall them?'

Kilpatrick shrugged. 'I'd have to say none. I can't recall having lived previously.'

'Exactly,' continued Cameron, 'nobody can, or at least they couldn't up until now. Your questionnaire indicates that you've already learnt many skills and gained a substantial amount of knowledge in a variety of areas. Imagine the skills and knowledge you would have acquired in your previous lives and think how enriched your current life would be if you could recall them.'

'It certainly is an interesting concept.'

Cameron laughed. 'Interesting? It would revolutionize our world.'

'Are you saying you can do this?'

Cameron paused. 'I'll let you be the judge of that. I'm sure you agree it's possible to access our past-life memories, yes?' Kilpatrick nodded as Cameron pressed on. 'It would appear that a mental block is put in place at birth, or before, that prevents us from remembering these lives. It is only through hypnosis that we can break down this barrier and remember these events.' He leaned forward to give his next words added emphasis. 'What if I told you we have developed a drug that bypasses this block and allows us to tap into these resources, these hidden treasures of our mind?'

'It sounds unbelievable,' replied Kilpatrick simply.

Cameron smiled smugly. 'We are on the verge of such a discovery, and all that remains is to test it on human volunteers. We have developed a drug that fosters the flow of past-life skills and knowledge into the present.'

'I'm amazed,' exclaimed Kilpatrick. 'Stunned actually. I'll have to buy shares in Memtech. If what you say is true, then your company will make an absolute fortune.' He was about to say killing but changed words without missing a beat.

'Unfortunately, we're not listed on the stock exchange.' Cameron glanced down at his notes. 'There is one other thing I need to mention before we finish. The drug has been extensively tested on laboratory animals and there have been no harmful side effects. However, it is a derivative of lysergic acid diethylamide, better known as LSD, and you may experience mild hallucinatory effects whereby you imagine things that are not part of this life. These may be whispers of past lives, but we have yet to determine this.'

'The whole thing sounds fascinating. This may explain why some LSD users experience attacks of schizophrenia.'

'Exactly,' confirmed Cameron. 'It may also explain why many people become more creative under the influence of the drug.' He handed Kilpatrick an envelope with his first payment. 'That covers everything, so unless you have any urgent questions, we'll see you again tomorrow at six o'clock.'

'You've certainly given me a great deal to think about,' said Kilpatrick as he tucked the envelope away, 'although I'm having difficulty understanding the role of hypnosis in this.'

'Hypnotism plays an important part in facilitating the flow of the drug, and if you're not susceptible to hypnosis, then you won't experience the full benefits.'

Kilpatrick stood up. 'Fair enough.' He shook hands with Cameron and gave Ridgeway a friendly wave.

Ridgeway gave a chuckle of appreciation once Kilpatrick had left. 'Your explanation gets better each time I hear it. That LSD touch was pure genius.'

Cameron smiled broadly. 'Thank you. I quite enjoyed it myself.'

Kilpatrick was feeling far less happy as he inserted the black card into the elevator slot. His palms were sweaty, and he wiped them on the side of his pants. This was one of those moments he had seen in films when, with ominous music playing in the background, the hero nervously made his life or death decision. If the card had been cancelled, the elevator would either sit there doing nothing or ear-splitting alarms would go off, the doors would be sealed shut, and his life would be over.

Kilpatrick held his breath as he pressed the button for the basement, and the doors slowly closed. The elevator made a smooth descent, and he retrieved the card with an audible sigh before stepping into the passageway. He could feel his stress level rising with each new challenge. The basement corridors were well lit, and apart from the absence of windows, he could have been on any floor in the building. He had expected it to be dank and gloomy, full of cobwebs and the sound of scurrying rats. The walls were painted a stark white and strong, recessed lights illuminated every corner. There was absolutely nowhere to hide.

As he cautiously tried the first door in the corridor, his shoulder blades itched as if somebody was staring at them, and he half expected to be challenged. He was not surprised to find the door locked and inserted the black card to see if it worked. A small green light by the door handle blinked twice, and he heard a faint click. He pushed the door open and felt around for a light switch even though his nose told him that he'd found another storeroom. Rows of cleaning chemicals were stacked neatly on shelves reaching to the ceiling along with boxes of toilet paper, hand towels, and containers of soap.

He crept along the corridor and found a stationery room, a room full of old office furniture, and finally what appeared to be an archive room. He wondered if there was anything incriminating hidden away among the many files. He randomly pulled out a folder and stuffed it under his shirt.

'You never know when dumb luck decides to play a hand,' he murmured. The room opposite proved to be more rewarding with two of its walls filled with tiers of computers. The soft hum and occasional beeps indicated they were operational and thick rows of black computer cords ran along the walls behind the machines, disappearing into a series of boxes in the far corner. These looked nothing like the junction boxes described by Jordan, but the five slim boxes attached to the third wall were a perfect match.

He drew a rough map of the area he had explored and then stepped back into the corridor. A rumbling noise to his right gave him a scare, and he darted back inside the computer room and pressed his body against the door. He peered warily into the brightly lit corridor but was unable to see anything and concentrated instead on the noise as it grew louder. There was something familiar about it, but he was unable to place it. The noise abruptly ceased, and he found himself holding his breath as he waited, but the corridor remained deserted. Whatever it was had stopped around the corner between him and the exit. He steeled his diminishing courage and ventured back into the corridor.

I'd make a hopeless cat burglar, he thought as he crept to the corner. He risked a quick glance around the corner and saw a grey cleaning trolley parked outside the storeroom.

Kilpatrick was undecided on whether to slip past while the cleaner was busy in the storeroom or wait until he had returned to his duties. The sound of a door slamming farther down the passage followed by indistinct voices moving in his direction made the decision for him. He glanced anxiously behind him and then darted around the corner and was halfway along the corridor when the cleaner emerged carrying an armful of paper towels. He was an elderly man with a painfully thin physique, and he looked up as Kilpatrick bore down on him.

Apart from the incident with Tweddle, Kilpatrick had never intentionally struck anybody in his life and he wondered if he had the mental strength to attack the old man. The cleaner watched as Kilpatrick strode towards him, and then he nodded a submissive greeting. Kilpatrick breathed a sigh of relief and nodded in return as he hurried past. He jabbed the elevator button several times and then stood back and watched the indicator arrow above the door. He could hear footsteps accompanying the voices and pressed the button once more to encourage the elevator to speed up. Two men turned the corner as the elevator doors finally opened and Kilpatrick raced in, hastily inserted the black card, and pressed the ground floor button.

The footsteps in the corridor suddenly quickened and a voice called out asking him to hold the elevator. He shrank back into the furthermost corner and willed the doors to close. He glimpsed an annoyed face as the doors slid shut and the elevator began its short journey. He tightened the straps of his backpack as the doors opened and hurried quickly from the building. A passing shower had left drops of beaded water on his motorbike seat but he ignored them and kicked the engine into life.

The guard at the gatehouse opened the window marginally and stared at Kilpatrick, who held out the white plastic card. 'I was told to give you this.'

The guard took the card as he continued looking at Kilpatrick. 'You're a bit late, aren't you?'

'It's my first session, and I was the last one to be tested. I think the excitement gave me a touch of diarrhoea.' He grinned weakly. 'I've been in the toilet for the past half hour, but I'm all right now.'

'Is that so,' replied the guard unsympathetically. The phone rang in the booth behind him, and he glanced at it in annoyance. 'If you've got a touch of the runs you'd best be off, hadn't you, otherwise you'll be in for an uncomfortable journey.'

'Indeed,' agreed Kilpatrick as he pulled on his gloves and opened the throttle.

By the time he arrived home, he was chilled to the bone. He stood in front of the heater demanding a hot cup of tea through chattering teeth. Once he thawed out sufficiently, he outlined the night's activities, briefly describing his assessment and showing them his map of the basement.

Banks gave him an encouraging pat on the back. 'That's exactly what we're after. Well done.'

Jane smiled warmly at Kilpatrick. 'It's nice to have some good luck for a change.'

'Oh, speaking of luck,' replied Kilpatrick as he unzipped his jacket and tugged out a manila file. 'I borrowed this from their archives. I have no idea what it contains, but I figured fate would direct me towards an incriminating file that will prove our innocence.'

Laura took the file and leafed through the pages as Jane and Tracey peered over her shoulder. 'It looks like an audit report,' said Jane.

Laura nodded. 'Jane's right. It's an audit on safe-working practices. Unfortunately, there's nothing in here to further our cause.'

'So much for the hand of fate,' replied Kilpatrick mournfully.

'We're still very proud of you,' said Tracey. 'I've been having kittens waiting for you to return.'

Kilpatrick gave a rueful smile. 'To be honest, I was scared silly most of the time. I don't have the courage to be a true hero.' He looked at Banks. 'The way you rescued Jane from those killers and Daniel fought off Laura's attackers, that took courage. When I heard that trolley coming down the corridor, I thought I'd have a heart attack.'

'I see,' murmured Banks. 'So even though you were wracked by fear, you still managed to complete your mission.'

'Well, yes, but I was worried the whole time,' replied Kilpatrick softly. 'At no time did I feel cool, calm, and collected.'

Tracey punched him lightly on the shoulder. 'What do you want? A medal? Of course you're a hero.'

'If you have no fear, you don't need any courage,' added Banks. 'I didn't have time to be afraid, and my reactions were instinctive. Daniel was probably the same.'

Jordan nodded. 'I was very angry at the time, but I began shaking like a leaf afterwards.'

Kilpatrick attempted a smile. 'Okay, now you're making me blush. So what's next?'

Banks turned to Jordan. 'Are you ready to tap Borkov's phone?'

'Nearly. I'll collect the last pieces of equipment from the supplies room tomorrow. I didn't want to take everything at once in case I aroused suspicion.'

'So you can do it tomorrow afternoon?'

'Sure. I'll arrange my schedule so I'll be working in the general vicinity from lunchtime onwards, although I'll need somebody to help me identify Borkov's phone line.'

'Can you get a pair of overalls for Matt?'

'Me? I don't know the first thing about tapping phone lines,' exclaimed Kilpatrick.

Jordan ignored him. 'There are plenty of overalls in the dirty laundry bin, so that shouldn't be a problem.'

'Hello, Earth to Fantasyland, did you hear what I said?' interjected Kilpatrick.

'Don't worry, you don't have to do anything technical,' replied Jordan

'Oh oh,' said Kilpatrick warily. 'I don't like the sound of that. Whenever you make something sound easy, it always turns out to be extremely hard.'

'Not at all,' promised Jordan. 'All you have to do is pick up Borkov's handset a couple of times so I can identify his phone line.'

'And that's it?' persisted Kilpatrick.

'That's it.' Jordan laughed at the dubious look on Kilpatrick's face and spread his arms in a gesture of innocence. 'Would I lie to you, baby?'

Banks cut off any further banter. 'Okay, gather 'round, everybody. Here's what I propose we do. If the gods are smiling, we should have a tap in place by this time tomorrow.'

∼

Jane took several photographs of an elderly man with a receding hairline and then turned to Laura. 'There's something I've been meaning to ask you. It's really none of my business, but in my line of work one develops an insatiable curiosity.'

Laura shrugged. 'Ask away.'

'How long have you been with Daniel?'

'We met about four years ago and moved in together a year later. I suppose we'll get married one day, that's if we ever get out of this mess.'

'Okay, so where does Colin Tweddle fit into the equation? When I first met you, I was under the impression you were with him.'

Laura's eyes lit up in surprise, and she threw back her head and laughed loudly. 'You thought Colin and I were ...' She couldn't complete the sentence and broke down into helpless laughter as tears streamed down her face. Jane found herself laughing with her, although she didn't quite know why.

Laura took a deep breath and held her hands against her stomach. 'Thanks, that's the first good laugh I've had for a while. I really needed that although I think I've strained my stomach muscles.' Laura explained the background to her convalescence at Tweddle's country residence and finished with a brief description of the final night. 'I really believed he was interested in my health and happiness. Talk about naive. Daniel didn't trust him from the start, but I thought it was jealousy. I suppose men have an instinct for this sort of thing.'

'You can't blame yourself,' said Jane soothingly. 'You weren't well at the time.'

'That makes it even worse, doesn't it? He deliberately took advantage of my weakened condition, and the only thing he wanted was to get me into his bed. Anyway, can you imagine being called Mrs Tweddle? I don't think so.'

Jane suddenly straightened up and peered through the telescopic lens as a car pulled up at the gatehouse. 'We've got another customer,' she muttered as she took several photographs of the driver. Shortly after four o'clock, a green Rover stopped at the gatehouse while the barrier was raised.

'Come and have a look,' yelled Jane as she squeezed off a photograph. 'I think that's our man.' She stepped to one side as Laura hurriedly bent down and peered through the lens. 'Am I right? Is that him?'

Laura straightened up, a strange expression on her face. 'That's him all right. Call the boys. The curtains have just opened on our window of opportunity.'

'Very poetic,' murmured Jane as she picked up the phone. Ten minutes later they watched as Kilpatrick drove Laura's BMW up to the gatehouse. 'That's your car, isn't it?' said Jane.

Laura nodded. 'Where's the damned sun when you need it?' she grumbled as she took off her jacket and undid the top buttons on her blouse. 'Wish me luck.'

Laura waited until Kilpatrick was waved past the barrier, and then she sauntered up to the guardhouse and rapped on the window. She thrust her breasts forward as the guard tugged back the window and peered out, his look of annoyance vanishing as he gazed down upon her.

'Can I help you, young lady?' He offered her his most disarming smile. He was well into his fifties and hadn't bothered shaving but still believed that if he charmed her he might have a chance.

'I surely hope so,' Laura replied as she batted her eyelids. 'I'm looking for Madam Madeline's School of Modelling and Deportment. I was told it was in this street, but I can't find it anywhere. I thought if anybody was to know where it was it would be somebody important like you.'

The guard struggled to maintain eye contact, his gaze slipping automatically to her blouse, and he took a moment to gather his thoughts. 'I'd love to help you, but unfortunately, I've never heard of Madam Madeline or her school.'

Laura smiled sadly. 'How disappointing. I would have been ever so grateful if you had known, but alas ...' She shook her head and then turned and walked seductively down the driveway. The guard watched her until she disappeared from view, and then he shut his window with a loud sigh.

Jane watched everything unfold from across the road. Kilpatrick had found a secluded parking bay next to the building, and once he saw that Laura had distracted the guard, he quickly opened the trunk. Jordan tossed out two bags, clambered out, and hurried into the shadows of the wall. Kilpatrick then entered the foyer with Jordan in close attendance.

Laura opened the door moments later and snatched her coat off the chair. 'It's freezing out there,' she muttered through chattering teeth.

'You did very well,' observed Jane. 'The guard couldn't take his eyes off you.'

'It was so cold I thought my nipples would burst through my bra and take his eyes out.'

'Your seductive allure was very effective; now it's up to the boys.'

'Waiting really is the worst part,' Laura complained. 'Not knowing what's happening and being powerless to help gnaws at your stomach.'

'I know the feeling, but we won't know how successful the boys have been until tonight. They won't be able to leave until Matt has completed his trials.'

Laura shuddered. 'Rather him than me. Fancy having a dead person's memory implanted into your mind. It makes me nauseous just thinking about it.'

Jane nodded vigorously. 'I know what you mean. Why don't I make us a nice cup of tea to take our minds off it?'

Banks had also made himself a cup of tea. He had also made the beds, done the dishes, swept the floor, and stripped down the Beretta and reassembled it twice. He wasn't due to contact Evans for another two hours and was thoroughly bored.

A welcome idea finally flashed through his mind. He hurried into the bedroom, pulled out a grey canvas bag from under the bed, and gingerly removed the bomb, peering at it from several angles. It contained enough high-grade Semtex to have blown out every window for a kilometre, and he could only guess at the size of the crater it would have left. Tracey and Kilpatrick would have been instantly vaporized. Their remaining body parts wouldn't have filled a matchbox.

He took out a small screwdriver and set about dismantling the bomb. The detonating system was very effective, and it was only the flat car battery that had foiled the bomber. He laid out the components and made several drawings. With a few electronic additions, he could easily make this bomb into an effective time-driven device. Just set the timer, activate the switch, and wait for the explosion. He jotted down his requirements and decided to risk dropping into an electronics shop on the way to contact Evans. He didn't think he'd need to use the bomb, but it gave him something useful to do, and he smiled cheerfully as he carefully packed the components back into the bag.

Chapter 13

And so from hour to hour we ripe and ripe,
And then from hour to hour we rot and rot,
And thereby hangs a tale.

William Shakespeare

Kilpatrick nudged Jordan as he stopped and looked around the foyer. 'Come on, no time for sightseeing.' He studied his watch as they took the elevator to the first floor. 'We've only got fifty minutes before my appointment with Cameron, so we need to keep moving.' There was a soft ping as the doors slid open, and they stared out into the empty hallway.'

'So far, so good,' murmured Jordan.

'Yeah. That covers the off chance one of the guards was interested enough to track our destination.' He inserted the black card into the scanner and pressed the button for the basement. 'This is the worst part. I'm not sure what we're going to find at the other end.' They waited apprehensively as the doors slid open, and then they made their way to the computer room.

When they were safely inside, Jordan handed him a pair of overalls, stuck a cap on his head, and began to unfasten the junction box covers.

'They must have their heaters turned on full bore. It's damned hot with these overalls on,' grumbled Kilpatrick as he tightened the buckles.

'Stop your moaning and take your sweater off. Who ties your shoelaces for you in the morning?' Kilpatrick gave him a sour look, and Jordan thrust a small toolbox into his hands. 'Take this; it'll help you look the part.'

Kilpatrick opened the lid and peered uncertainly at the contents. 'I wouldn't know where to begin using this stuff.'

'It's not for you to use,' replied Jordan as he pressed the lid firmly shut. 'It's your symbolic clipboard. Slip a couple into your pocket so they jingle a bit. Every tradesman worth his salt jingles when he walks. It's a sign of competence. Now off you go. We've got fewer than forty minutes if you're going to make your appointment on time.'

'Oh yes, that. I'm really looking forward to having someone else's memory pasted over the top of my own.'

'You don't need to keep the appointment you know. Once we've completed the phone tap, we can skedaddle. They won't be any the wiser.'

'Believe me, I'm tempted, but we need to make sure we've covered every base. If it was only my life in danger, I'd be out of here like a shot but ...' His words tapered off as he shrugged philosophically.

Jordan sniffed loudly into his handkerchief before noisily blowing his nose. 'Such bravery, such sacrifice, such gallantry.'

'Such an arsehole,' interjected Kilpatrick as he slipped out of the room. He used the black card to travel to the third floor; as the doors opened, he sauntered out into the foyer with an air of confidence he didn't feel.

A guard stationed near the elevator put down his magazine and stood up. 'Yes?' The single word conveyed both menace and helpful enquiry.

Kilpatrick pulled out the bogus work orders and held them out for the guard to inspect. 'I've come to fix Dr Brockhoff's phone.'

'Ain't nobody here by that name,' grunted the guard as he folded his arms.

Kilpatrick studied the work orders. 'Sorry, that should be Dr Borkov.'

'Right. Follow me.' The guard moved with an air of controlled aggression, and although he appeared to be walking slowly, Kilpatrick had to hurry to keep up. The guard stopped in front of an office occupying a prime corner position and indicated a woman in an adjoining cubicle. 'That's Dr Borkov's secretary. You'll need to discuss it with her.'

The secretary was probably closer to thirty than forty but had a pinched face that protruded threateningly from beneath a severe hairdo, adding years to her features. 'Good afternoon,' said Kilpatrick cheerfully as he walked over to her.

She looked up warily from her computer and ran an experienced eye over Kilpatrick's lean frame. 'How can I help you?' she asked with an air of forced enthusiasm.

'I'm looking for Dr Borkov's office.'

'I'm sorry but Dr Borkov is unavailable.' She paused as she wrestled with the next sentence. 'Perhaps I can be of assistance.'

'I'm not after Dr Borkov, just his office,' explained Kilpatrick. 'I've been sent to check his phone.'

'His telephone?'

'Yeah, according to the worksheet his line keeps dropping out. It sounds like a problem with the handset, so it shouldn't take long if that's the case.'

The secretary gave Kilpatrick an appraising look. 'That's strange. Dr Borkov hasn't mentioned any problems with his telephone.' Her tone attracted the guard's attention, and he moved closer.

'Yeah, well, you know how it goes,' replied Kilpatrick noncommittally. 'People like you and me are always the last to find out.' He looked around enquiringly. 'So which office belongs to this Borkov fellow?'

The secretary sprang to her feet, glancing at the guard as she did so. 'I'm sorry but I don't have the authority to let you into his office. He is a very important man and has many highly confidential documents stored in his room.'

Kilpatrick gave a shrug of indifference. 'That's fine with me. I've got plenty of other jobs to attend to. You've no idea how much this damp weather effects junction box circuitry.' He dropped the toolkit onto the floor with a jingling thump, pulled a sheet of paper from his overalls, and thrust it in front of the secretary. 'Sign this work order to say you don't want the work done, and I'll be out of here.'

She held up a conciliatory hand. 'You're placing me in a difficult situation. I'm not saying that Dr Borkov's phone isn't faulty, just that I haven't been informed. Why don't you come back later when Dr Borkov has finished his meeting?'

'Sorry, no can do. My next assignment is halfway across town. Tell Dr Borkov to send in another request if his phone continues to play up, and we'll deal with it in due course.'

'When will that be?' asked the secretary hesitatingly.

Kilpatrick made a sucking noise between his teeth. 'Who knows? His request will have to go to the end of the queue, so it could be a couple of weeks, a month, maybe longer. This weather plays merry hell with a lot of the older phone lines, and we're snowed under at the moment. Now if you'll sign the form, I'll be off.'

The secretary moistened her lips as she glanced at the guard, but he merely shrugged. She turned back to Kilpatrick and tried to make a decision. Dr Borkov was a tyrant, and if his phone really was faulty, he would be extremely annoyed with her. 'What do you have to do again?'

Kilpatrick emitted a heavy sigh. 'All I have to do is check the dial tone. If that's fine, then that's it. If the tone is faulty, I'll have to do a full diagnosis, which could take an hour or two.' He dropped his voice to a conspiratorial whisper. 'If it'll ease your mind, why don't you come with me and watch while I run my tests? It'll only take a few minutes, and if I need to make a full diagnosis, I'll schedule it for tomorrow, which will give you a chance to talk to the good doctor.'

'You can do that? What about your other jobs?'

'Once I pick up his phone, I've begun the work. It's not possible to carry every conceivable part with me, so it's normal to return to a job in order to complete it.'

The secretary smiled with relief, making her appear several years younger. 'That should be okay. I'm sure nobody could object if we watch while you do your test.'

Kilpatrick smiled reassuringly as he picked up his tools and followed her into the large corner office.

'Please don't touch anything unnecessarily, and whatever you do, try not to make a mess.' She said this as much for the guard's benefit as for Kilpatrick's.

'I only need to touch the telephone, and I'll even wipe it clean when I finish.' He gave her an encouraging wink as he dropped his toolbox next to the telephone. The décor was fashionably subdued but reeked of expensive taste, and it was apparent that Borkov had a liking for leather. Leather-bound publications filled an immense walnut-panelled bookcase on the far wall and a plush, leather swivel chair was situated behind a solid teak desk with a flat, black leather top. He pulled out his cell phone and called Jordan. 'Commencing dial tone check now,' he said loudly once Jordan answered. He picked up Borkov's phone, listened for a moment, and then replaced it in its cradle. 'Anything?' he asked.

'I don't think so,' replied Jordan. 'Do it again to make sure. There are a lot of other phones in use on this board, and I might have missed it.'

Kilpatrick repeated the exercise and waited for a moment. 'Test completed,' he said into the cell phone.

'It's definitely not that board. Give me a moment while I move to the next one.'

Kilpatrick smiled at the secretary. 'It's looking promising. My partner thinks it might have been moisture in the line causing a temporary local overload. We need to run another check to make sure. Starting test,' he said as he picked up the handset and waited a moment before replacing it.

'Bingo,' exclaimed Jordan. 'Do it again on my count of three to validate.'

Kilpatrick repeated the test on cue and grinned as Jordan confirmed success. 'It's definitely Borkov's line. Tidy up and join me down here, and I'll start work on the intercept. The sooner we get out of here, the happier I'll be.' Kilpatrick smiled at the secretary as he wiped down the phone. 'It's as I thought. The problem was caused by outside interference, but it was corrected during routine maintenance; I'm confident you won't have any further problems.'

'Very good,' replied the secretary. 'Would you like me to sign your work order now?'

Kilpatrick politely held out the paper and then returned to the basement, where he found Jordan already packed and waiting.

'I'm glad that's over,' said Kilpatrick. 'I had a guard follow me everywhere, and I had this eerie feeling he knew what I was up to.'

'That's just guilt playing with your mind. How long will you be with the memory doctors?'

'I have no idea.' He stepped out of the overalls and handed them to Jordan.

Jordan glanced around the room. 'I'd rather not stay here while you're gone. If somebody comes, there's absolutely nowhere to hide.'

'I'll take you to their archive room. You could hide a football team in there. Grab a couple of files while you're waiting, and we'll see if you're any luckier than me.'

Kilpatrick returned to the first floor in time for his appointment and met Dr Cameron, who inquired about his health. 'Mental or physical?' asked Kilpatrick.

Cameron laughed. 'Either or neither, it doesn't matter really. I was simply making polite talk to calm your nerves while I prepare this injection.' He took out a glass phial containing a pale, amber liquid and held it up to the light.

Kilpatrick watched apprehensively. 'Is this going to hurt?'

Cameron chuckled as he filled a syringe with the yellow liquid. 'You have no idea how many times I've been asked that question.'

'And ...' prompted Kilpatrick.

Cameron leaned across and swabbed the side of Kilpatrick's neck. 'I'll let you be the judge.' He deftly plunged the needle into Kilpatrick's neck and emptied its contents in one smooth action.

The pain was excruciating. 'For fuck's sake!' shouted Kilpatrick as he attempted to twist his body away.

Cameron had anticipated the reaction and expertly followed the movement. 'Apparently it does,' he muttered as he removed the needle and held a swab of cotton wool over the puncture mark. 'Now, that wasn't too bad, was it?'

Kilpatrick had tears in his eyes. 'You people aren't paying nearly enough.'

Cameron smiled apologetically. 'Unfortunately, the neck is very sensitive. Dr. Ridgeway has developed a new strain that can be injected into the upper arm but it's still in the testing phase. Fortunately this is the only injection you'll receive, and you should start reaping the benefits of your enhanced abilities by this time tomorrow.' He replaced the swab with a piece of sticking plaster and gave Kilpatrick a reassuring pat on the shoulder. 'Stand up and tell me if you feel dizzy.'

Kilpatrick felt momentarily light-headed, but the feeling quickly passed.

'I'm okay.'

'And the pain?'

'It stings a bit, but it's not too bad,' acknowledged Kilpatrick.

'Good. We'd like to see you again in five days to assess your new skills and abilities.'

'That won't be a problem,' replied Kilpatrick, who had no intention of returning.

'Do you feel well enough to drive or should we call a cab?'

'I told you, I'm okay.'

'Just making sure. That injection can be quite traumatic and affects some people more than others.'

'Now you tell me,' muttered Kilpatrick.

Cameron smiled. Kilpatrick's reaction was mild compared to some he'd experienced. 'All that remains is to escort you to your car, and then we're done.'

'Oh that won't be necessary,' said Kilpatrick hurriedly. 'I told you, I'm fine.'

'It's not open to discussion I'm afraid. One of our subjects collapsed in the elevator, so now we've made it part of our procedure.'

Kilpatrick couldn't see any way out of the dilemma and hoped Cameron wouldn't wait and watch him drive away. If he only accompanied him as far as the front door, then it would be possible to duck back inside and collect Jordan from the basement. He noticed Cameron patting his pockets with an air of annoyance as they stood in front of the elevator.

'Something the matter?'

'I left my card in my jacket,' replied Cameron. 'You'll have to use yours.'

'How will you get back up?'

'That won't be a problem. One of the guards can come with me. It'll give him something to do.'

The elevator doors opened and Kilpatrick pulled out his card and inserted it into the slot.

'Where'd you get that?' Cameron abruptly demanded.

Kilpatrick immediately realized his mistake. He had been so preoccupied with the change in plans that he had unwittingly used the wrong card. 'What?' he asked innocently.

'That black card. They're a restricted item. Where did you get it?'

'Oh, the card,' he said, realizing any excuse was going to sound feeble. 'The guard at the gatehouse must have given it to me by mistake. I wondered about that at the time but thought it must be a different colour for a different day.'

'Bullshit!' Cameron spat the word at him. 'The Gatehouse only issue white visitor cards. You'll have to do better than that.'

'Fine, then how about this?' Kilpatrick grabbed Cameron by the lapels of his jacket and drove his right knee firmly into his groin. He watched unsympathetically as Cameron sank gagging to the floor. 'I'll let you be the judge of whether that hurt or not.' He aimed a short kick into Cameron's ribs, eliciting a sharp grunt from his victim. 'Apparently it did.'

He pressed the button for the basement, peering out anxiously once it stopped, but the corridor was deserted. Cameron was still struggling for breath as Kilpatrick hauled him to his feet and half carried him to the archive room before propelling him inside. There was a muffled crash followed by a breathless curse as Cameron stumbled headlong into a shelving unit.

'Who the hell's this?' asked Jordan as he stepped into view.

'He's the doctor assigned to my case. Unfortunately he saw me using the black access card in the elevator.'

'That was rather careless.'

'Yeah, well, what's done is done. I was under a lot of pressure up there.'

'So what's the next part of your brilliant plan? We can't just leave him here. They're bound to wonder what we were doing in the basement.'

'We could always take him with us,' replied Kilpatrick lamely, hoping an idea would crystallize as he spoke.

'I don't think so. The place is crawling with guards, and even if we did get him out, what then? Our record in that area isn't encouraging.'

'We could start a fire and set off the alarms. There'd be people running everywhere, and we could whisk him out in the confusion.'

'The last thing we want right now is to destroy the evidence or delay the next part of our operation.' He turned and stared coldly at Cameron. 'We have no alternative I'm afraid. He has to stay here.' Cameron huddled back fearfully against the shelving.

'But he'll give us away,' protested Kilpatrick.

Jordan turned and picked up a handful of files. 'It won't matter. We've got the documents we came for. You tie him up, and I'll put the rest of the files in my bag. Once we're out of here, he can jump and shout all he likes.'

'Of course, the files,' exclaimed Kilpatrick. 'So the time and effort we've spent searching through here has paid off?'

'In spades,' replied Jordan, his eyes warning Kilpatrick not to overdo it. They secured Cameron's arms and legs with string torn from bundles of files but were unable to find anything suitable to use as a gag.

'Why don't we stuff his mouth full of paper,' suggested Kilpatrick.

Jordan shook his head. 'It won't take him long to chew it up and spit it out. I don't want him found for at least twenty-four hours.'

Cameron spoke for the first time since being thrown into the room. 'You can't leave me here to rot. If you let me go, I won't say anything. You've got my word on it.'

'I'm sure we all believe that,' snorted Jordan derisively.

'I've got it,' cried Kilpatrick as he began pulling off his shoes. 'We'll stuff his mouth with my socks and tie them in place with more of that string. They're about worn out anyhow.'

Jordan looked dubiously at Kilpatrick. 'I'm not sure the Geneva Convention would condone such barbaric behaviour.' His face relaxed into a grin. 'Still, beggars can't be choosers. The worst they can charge you with is cruel and unusual punishment.'

'Me? We're in this together.'

'I've still got my socks on. It's your DNA that's going to be all over the evidence.' He picked up one of the socks and grimaced. 'Jesus! How long since you washed your feet?'

'I've got active sweat glands if you must know. It's nothing that a liberal dose of Odour Eaters can't handle.'

Cameron pulled his head back in disgust as the socks were jammed into his mouth and tied firmly in place. They dragged him to the back of the room and left him slumped in the corner.

'You should be comfortable here for the next twenty-four hours,' said Jordan. 'Matt's socks should provide you with enough water and nourishment to keep you going. Toilet breaks are out of the question so keep your legs crossed.'

'Shouldn't we tie his feet to one of the shelving brackets so he can't wriggle up to the door and start kicking?'

'Good idea,' agreed Jordan. 'You do that, and I'll collect the rest of the files.' He bent down and patted Cameron on the head. 'You should get used to being confined, although at least in here you won't have to worry about fighting off unwelcome sexual advances.'

They stuffed Jordan's bag full of files and then gave the room a quick scan and turned off the light. 'Nighty night,' he murmured into the darkness.

'That was quick thinking,' whispered Kilpatrick as they hurried along the corridor. 'Let's hope it works.'

They returned to the car without incident, and it was sufficiently dark to allow Jordan to slip unobserved into the trunk. 'Let's hope I never have to return here again,' muttered Kilpatrick as he was waved through the open boom gate.

Toulemonde stared angrily at the board members; his face was a mask of fury, and he didn't care who saw how ill-tempered he was. He abruptly slapped the table with his open hand and pushed himself to his feet. 'Let us be in no doubt, this is a grave crisis. Our security has been breached and our project work compromised. I want answers, and I want them now. Any delay to Project Eternalism could prove fatal in more ways than one. I don't need to remind you that none of us is getting any younger. I have asked Michael Madison to provide an update.'

Madison looked uncertain as he stood to address the board. 'As you are aware there has been growing concern over our security arrangements, which is why I was instructed to report directly to Monsieur Toulemonde.'

'Yes, yes,' growled Toulemonde. 'Nobody's blaming you so don't worry about covering your backside. Just get on with it.'

Madison nodded. 'I received a call from the guardhouse two nights ago when Dr Cameron failed to log off duty. It's not unknown for members of the core team to work through the night but they usually notify security so we don't waste time looking for them. We received no such notification from Dr Cameron and so conducted an unsuccessful search of his building. We then received an anonymous call advising us to check our archive room in the basement.'

'Our archive room?' queried Jarvis.

'The caller was referring to the room we use as a repository for obsolete files.'

'Get on with it,' snapped Toulemonde, effectively curtailing any further questions.

'We found Dr Cameron trussed up in the corner of the room.' There was a muted gasp, and Madison waited until they settled down before continuing. 'Dr Cameron was unharmed, although he was in some discomfort. Being tied up for twenty-four hours can place undue duress on various parts of the anatomy.' He gave the group a tight grin and then hurried on when Toulemonde cleared his throat threateningly. 'He informed us that he'd been assaulted by one of his research volunteers.'

'Did Dr Cameron say why he was assaulted?' asked Jarvis.

'Yes, he did,' replied Madison, relieved to be moving forward again. His assailant's name is Matthew Kilpatrick. Dr Cameron was accompanying him to his car and as they entered the elevator, Kilpatrick pulled out a black master card to activate it. Dr Cameron naturally challenged Kilpatrick about the card and was subsequently assaulted.'

'So how did he get hold of a black card?' growled Toulemonde.

Madison swallowed nervously. 'We've checked our paperwork, and a black security card was logged as being lost several days ago by Dr Rathbone.'

'Why wasn't the card deactivated?'

Madison had been expecting the question. 'As you are well aware, we've been very shorthanded lately, and the paperwork that would have triggered the deactivation procedure was buried in the in-tray of one of my operatives. Naturally he has been severely reprimanded.'

'Naturally,' replied Toulemonde sourly. 'Please continue. I'm fascinated to know how this person ended up with the missing card.'

'During the past twelve hours we've used our contacts within the police department to mount extensive enquiries concerning Kilpatrick and have established a link with Daniel Jordan.'

'Jordan ...?' mused Jarvis as he let the word hang in the air. 'The name rings a bell, but I don't remember why.'

'Jordan was Laura Monroe's boyfriend and was responsible for killing one of the operatives sent by Dr Borkov to deal with her,' explained Madison.

'Remind me about the reason for that?' prompted Toulemonde.

'Monroe was asking too many questions about Prototype One. She was assigned to his case after he was arrested for breaking into James Chandler's house and harassing his wife. Borkov decided she was getting too close to the truth and arranged for her to be eliminated.'

'Ah, yes, James Chandler,' said Toulemonde quietly. 'Our first successful memory download, and now it appears he has come back to haunt us. Another version of life after death. This is quite a long thread you've unravelled, Madison, but it still doesn't explain the card being in Kilpatrick's possession.'

'There are a few splices in the thread,' replied Madison, his confidence growing. 'The officer investigating Monroe's attempted murder was none other than Inspector Robert Banks.'

Toulemonde's eyes narrowed. 'Banks? That's too much of a coincidence.'

'It gets better. Banks was lured into our facility so we could discover what he knew about our operations. Dr Rathbone was the surgeon called in to operate on him.'

'A fat lot of good it did for us,' snorted Jarvis. 'The man knew nothing about our affairs.'

'That's correct,' agreed Madison. 'His body was cremated next door and we believed that was the end of it.'

'Where is this leading?' asked Toulemonde impatiently.

'We now know that Banks didn't die on that table, that it was in fact one of my best agents who gave up his life. We believe Banks took Dr Rathbone's card and used it to escape. We're trying to confirm this with the doctor, but he's not returning our calls.'

'All right, so now we know how they got in. The next question is what were they up to? Tell me more about this filing room.'

'There's not a lot to tell,' replied Madison as he absently dispersed the sweat gathering on his brow. 'It's a repository for documents needed to satisfy statutory requirements. Cleanouts are occasionally scheduled but are seldom carried out. Our investigations confirmed that these documents are innocuous and cannot possibly damage or incriminate us.'

'So you say,' grunted Jarvis. 'I've read the initial report. Dr Cameron stated quite clearly that the assailants escaped with a large stack of files, and they seemed pretty damned pleased about what they'd found.'

Madison frowned. 'It does seem strange, but I assure you that they can't have found anything of value in that room.'

'Our security's an absolute joke,' continued Jarvis. 'How do we know you're not trying to cover up another disaster?'

Madison coloured at the insult, and Toulemonde interjected before he could respond. 'If Madison says there was nothing there, then we must trust him, unless you'd rather check for yourself.'

'No, no, it's all right,' muttered Jarvis. 'Why have a dog if you're going to bark yourself? But if Madison's correct, then we still don't know what they were up to. I have an uneasy feeling about this.'

'Rest assured that we will investigate this matter thoroughly, and it's only a matter of time before we'll have the answer for you,' Madison replied confidently.

'Eternity itself is a mere matter of time,' grumbled Jarvis contemptuously, 'and the way things are panning out, eternity in our lifetime will pass us by. I warned you about going public, and now we're paying the price.'

'Arguing among ourselves will not serve any purpose,' replied Toulemonde with a piercing glare. 'I suggest we think about finding a solution rather than searching for blame.' He held up a warning finger. 'We shouldn't underestimate these people. I believe the events in the basement were a red herring.' He turned to Madison. 'Tell Fenwick he must intensify his efforts to arrest Banks. Make him and his cohorts responsible for the next violent crime even if you have to carry it out yourself. I want their pictures splashed everywhere.'

'An excellent idea,' replied Madison. 'I'll get onto it immediately.' It was with some relief that he began to gather his papers together.

A timid knock on the door caused him to look up. His heart sank as the worried face of his assistant appeared in the opening and anxiously beckoned to him. 'What are you doing here?' asked Madison accusingly as he met him halfway.

His assistant leant towards Madison and whispered urgently.

'What?' Madison exclaimed loudly, the disbelief in his tone evident. His assistant repeated the message as the others strained to hear. 'All right, all right, I understand.' Madison waved him away and turned grim-faced towards the expectant board members. 'More bad news I'm sorry to say. Dr Rathbone has disappeared. He failed to turn up for work and isn't at home.'

Jarvis shook his head in disgust. 'Why am I not surprised?'

Toulemonde swore under his breath. 'Is Banks involved?'

'I doubt it. There could be any number of reasons for his disappearance. He could be simply spending a few dirty days with one of his nurses without telling anybody.'

'First Cameron disappears and now Rathbone,' said Toulemonde, his voice dangerously neutral. 'You think this could be a coincidence?'

Madison looked unhappy. 'It's quite possible, sir. We won't know until we've investigated further.'

'Then find out fast because, unlike you, I don't believe in coincidences,' snapped Toulemonde.

~

Jarvis was a worried man as he hurried from the meeting. The latest security developments smacked of amateurs being too cute, and he knew Northfield would be tempted to march into Memtech and seize the operation.

Northfield's response did not disappoint him. 'So the people at Memtech have lost control of their operations, is that your evaluation?'

'They're on the brink of disaster, certainly, but if they can eliminate these rogue elements, then I believe they will regain full control.'

'Ah, yes,' replied Northfield with a sigh as he handed Jarvis a photograph. 'Inspector Robert Banks. The report describes him as an excellent officer with a promising career. It's a pity he got himself mixed up in this business. The woman he rescued was that magazine editor, wasn't she?'

'Yes, she was invited to invest in Memtech Industries but got cold feet and tried to blow the whistle on the operation. Banks interfered with the attempt to silence her, and it was only through my quick intervention that we averted a complete disaster.'

'I know there's collateral damage in any operation,' replied Northfield pensively, 'but sometimes I wish there was a better way.'

'We all do, sir, but in order to win the war sometimes it's necessary to sacrifice pawns.'

'You don't need to patronize me,' replied Northfield stiffly. 'I'm quite capable of making hard decisions, but it doesn't mean I have to like it.'

'No, sir. I'm sure nobody thinks you do.'

'Do you think it's time to seize their facility?' he asked, his eyes glittering.

Jarvis shook his head. 'No, sir, such a move would be precipitant.'

Northfield snorted. 'You think so? You just told me that Memtech has lost control. What's to stop it making a quick profit by hawking this technology around the globe? Imagine the damage if our enemies got their hands on it. By controlling the technology, we would eliminate this significant risk.'

'Who's to say our department is completely secure?' replied Jarvis. 'There's always somebody out to make a quick buck or a bleeding heart hell bent on appeasement at any cost. Word could still leak out.'

'And treason's still capitol offence,' snapped Northfield. He leant back and folded his arms. 'So why would it be precipitant?'

Jarvis relaxed slightly. 'There are several reasons. Firstly, the procedure is still unstable, so we'd be acquiring a flawed process. Secondly, they're still a legitimate company, so locking them down and ensuring their silence would be extremely difficult. Too many people are already aware of the memory-transfer principle. There are the board members, scientists, researchers, guards, and probably even the accountants and secretaries. Thirdly, the cartel of investors is also involved. It would only be a matter of time before the media found out, and then it's game over.'

'Damn!' scowled Northfield as he peered at Jarvis. 'So how should we go about this?'

'I'm afraid there won't ever be a good time to take direct control.'

'And why is that?'

'There's no doubt this knowledge will eventually go public, and unless we've kept our distance we'll be crucified. The media would destroy the government, and we'd be the sacrificial pawns.'

Northfield stroked his chin pensively. 'A career-limiting move by the sound of it.'

'And possibly a life limiting move,' added Jarvis.

'A pity really,' said Northfield softly. 'So it's business as usual then. Oh well, keep me informed.'

∼

Eastman had called Borkov the following morning to confirm that Monday evening was suitable. The conversation was kept to a minimum, and no names were used. Borkov was starting to enjoy himself. He welcomed a challenge, and finding a solution to a seemingly insurmountable problem always provided the greatest exhilaration. Everything was in readiness for the next stage. He had made an extra copy of the disks and mailed them to himself. The originals would go to Eastman while the first set of copies was for the board to enjoy at their leisure.

He summoned Ridgeway and informed her that he wanted the memory-deletion procedure brought forward to Monday night. 'I'm sure you don't mind working late. As the process takes about twelve hours to run its full course, I'd rather be asleep while it happened.'

'That would definitely be more comfortable,' acknowledged Ridgeway.

'I will meet you in your office around eight o'clock. By the way, is there much pain?'

'Unfortunately there is some discomfort associated with the injection.'

'In that case, I expect you to be as gentle as possible.' Borkov chuckled mirthlessly. 'We are told to associate pain with gain, but in this case there can be no loss without pain.'

'A clever observation, Dr Borkov,' observed Ridgeway coldly. 'Do you mind if I use that? A touch of humour often settles a patient's nerves.'

'You might as well,' replied Borkov airily. 'By Tuesday morning, I won't even remember I said it.'

Borkov spent a restless weekend endlessly reviewing his strategy; his stress eventually degenerated into a dull headache. He was relieved when Monday morning finally arrived and withdrew the twenty thousand pounds for Eastman on the way to work. The building was abuzz with rumours of break-ins and industrial espionage, and he wondered how much blame would be deflected towards him. His mood became increasingly foul as the day wore on, and his assistants quickly made themselves scarce. His phone rang early in the afternoon, and he ignored it in the hope his secretary would answer but was finally forced to snatch it up.

'Yes?' he snapped.

'Hello, Isaac, old chap,' replied a melodic voice. 'Wonderful telephone manner you have.'

Borkov failed to recognize Eastman's voice. 'Who is this? How'd you get my number?'

Eastman sighed loudly. 'I told you I should have a code name. It would avoid this unnecessary confusion.'

'It's you,' replied Borkov in surprise. 'Why are you calling me? I thought I made it quite clear that any contact between us is dangerous and must be avoided at all costs.'

'You certainly did, dear fellow,' confirmed Eastman almost jovially, 'but please don't think I'm stupid or irresponsible. I'm calling from a public phone in Paris, so my anonymity is assured. Unfortunately two important points have arisen that I need to discuss urgently.'

Borkov's stomach lurched. Surely Memtech wasn't on to him already? 'What is it? What's happened?'

'Now, Isaac, don't get your knickers in a knot. It's nothing that can't be sorted out. My flight has been delayed by an hour, and I didn't want you waiting around, thinking I'd changed my mind. Will that be a problem?'

Borkov sank back into his chair as he felt the tension in his stomach ease. 'No, that's fine. Seven o'clock's okay with me, and don't worry if you're a bit late. You had me worried for a moment,' he grunted in relief. 'Now, you mentioned two things,' prompted Borkov, eager to end the call now he realized he wasn't in any danger.

'Ah, yes, the second point,' murmured Eastman. 'I have built a distinguished career determining what the market can or cannot bear, and now that I've had time to reflect, I've decided that your offer isn't sufficient.'

'What do you mean?' barked Borkov. 'We had an agreement.'

'I'm not a greedy person, Isaac,' replied Eastman soothingly. 'My company pays me an excellent wage, but my two divorces have crippled me financially, and I'm currently involved with several high maintenance women who can be very demanding. Twenty thousand pounds will certainly be beneficial but thirty will be even more so.'

'Thirty thousand pounds!' fumed Borkov. 'What makes you think I can lay my hands on an extra ten thousand at this late stage? If you're not careful, I'll find somebody else, and you'll end up with nothing.'

Eastman remained calm. 'As I said before, Isaac, I make my living judging what the market can bear, and I'm not often wrong. It appears to me that you're playing for very high stakes, and the extra money is probably insignificant in the overall scheme of things. You've obviously gone to a lot of time and trouble to single me out and keep my involvement confidential, and you're probably running to a tight timetable. If you decide to give the discs to someone else, I'll put my loss down to experience, but I don't think you're going to do that. So, do we have a deal?'

There was a prolonged silence as Borkov weighed up the situation. 'All right, it's a deal, but you'd better not keep me waiting because if you're not there on time, I'm walking out, and you can kiss your money goodbye.' He slammed the phone down in annoyance.

∼

Kilpatrick noticed the recording light blinking by the telephone, rewound the tape, and played it through. He then quickly summoned Banks and replayed the tape. 'What do you think?' he asked once it finished.

'I think we may have stumbled on to something,' he replied softly. 'Gather everybody together and meet me at the observation post. Oh, and bring your motorbike.'

Banks had already explained the situation to Jane and Laura by the time the others arrived, and they gathered excitedly around the recorder as Banks played it once more.

'It's fairly obvious something's going down,' said Banks. 'Borkov is paying somebody to babysit a couple of disks, and they've decided to up the ante.'

'Computer disks?' asked Tracey.

Banks smiled. 'That would be my bet.'

'Why would he do that?' asked Laura.

'Insurance,' replied Banks and Jane together. They looked at each other and smiled.

'I realize that,' replied Laura patiently. 'But what's the point?'

Banks shrugged. 'Who knows? Maybe Memtech's not happy with his performance, and they're applying a bit of pressure. It could be any of a dozen reasons.'

Laura sighed. 'But with the technology Memtech has, surely Borkov would realize that they only need to take possession of his memory to know who received the disks and then simply retrieve them. His insurance would be worthless.'

'Good point,' agreed Banks, 'and I don't know why he'd think otherwise, but fortunately for us he does. If these disks are

Borkov's insurance against Memtech, then they should provide all the proof we need.' He grinned broadly. 'I think our luck is changing.'

'That's if they contain something incriminating, and I should point out that we don't have them yet,' cautioned Jordan.

'No, and we don't have much time to formulate a plan,' replied Banks briskly. 'Borkov said he would be meeting this other fellow at seven o'clock tonight and presumably this is when he'll hand over the disks.'

'And the money,' added Kilpatrick with a grin.

'No. We focus on the disks,' Banks growled. 'The money will only distract us.'

Kilpatrick shrugged. 'It's your call.'

'I'll fetch my laptop from work so we can read the disks,' offered Laura. 'The sooner we know what's on them, the better.'

'You can take Jane with you once you've cleaned out the observation post,' replied Banks. 'Now we must assume that Borkov will be at work today, so we'll follow him when he leaves. Do you remember what sort of car he's driving?'

'Was it that green Rover?' asked Jane as she glanced at Laura.

'That's the one,' confirmed Laura. 'Remember the fat face with the piggy eyes and stupid goatee beard? We got him on the first day peering out of his car at the gatehouse. Remember I told you it was Borkov?'

Jane nodded enthusiastically. 'Oh yes, the piggy eyes, I remember him.'

'That's settled then,' confirmed Jordan, who was anxious to get on with it. 'All we need to do now is work out how to grab the disks.'

'With some ingenuity and a little acting I think we can do it,' said Banks. 'After tonight our troubles may be over.'

Chapter 14

Ye friends to truth, ye statesmen, who survey,
The rich man's joys increase, the poor's decay,
'Tis yours to judge, how wide the limits stand,
Between a splendid and a happy land.

Oliver Goldsmith

I t was late evening as Jane peered through the telescopic lens searching for her target. Laura struggled to keep her nerves under control as she watched her friend's face. 'Anything?' she asked as she glanced anxiously at her watch.

'No, nothing,' murmured Jane as she swung the camera in a slow half circle. 'I can't see any dark green cars although a lot of them are hidden. I'm worried that he left early to get the extra money.'

Laura peered through the gap in the curtains. 'No, he's here all right. I can feel it in my bones.'

'Psychic bones, eh. Interesting phenomenon, I must say. There could be a magazine article in that.'

Laura looked at her quizzically. 'You don't really think you can return to your old life, do you? Even if we can prove Memtech's guilt, we'll never be safe from the men in the shadows. If you return to your magazine, you'll just be a sitting duck.'

Jane sighed. 'You may be right, but my life is meaningless without my magazine. It's what I've always dreamed about and done. I've sacrificed everything to make it work. I think you could say it's who I am, and without the magazine I simply don't exist. I have a magazine, therefore I am.'

'Should I be congratulating or commiserating with you?'

'Neither. I'm quite happy with the choices I've made, and I'll face any new situations as they arise.'

'You mightn't have to do it alone,' suggested Laura playfully.

Jane looked up quickly. 'What are you talking about?'

'Don't play dumb. I've seen the looks you've been giving Robert, and it's obvious he feels the same about you.'

Jane's cheeks coloured. 'Don't talk rubbish. He doesn't even know I exist.' A succession of cars waiting to leave the facility stopped at the gate, and she peered at the first car.

'What can you see?' asked Laura.

'Nothing yet.' Jane adjusted the focus and then suddenly beckoned excitedly to Laura. 'Take a look. Is that him?'

Laura bent down and squinted through the viewfinder. 'That's him all right. Call the boys.'

Jordan answered immediately, and Jane quickly told him that Borkov was in the green Rover pulling out of the driveway.

'I can see him,' confirmed Jordan. 'Wish us luck.'

Laura watched as Borkov turned right and headed for the distant traffic lights with the brown Ford following behind. Kilpatrick emerged from a driveway further down the street and trailed after the two cars on his motorbike, the exhaust echoing off the buildings as he changed gears.

'Well, that's our part of the job done,' sighed Jane. 'Now it's up to the boys and Tracey.'

'Yes, and we're forced to wait again. It doesn't seem fair.'

'I hate waiting as much as you, but we all have our jobs to do.' Jane stood and stretched. 'Now we need to pack our gear, give this place a quick clean, and then collect your laptop.' She smiled encouragingly. 'I realise it's not very exciting, but it's got to be done.'

Laura watched absently as Jane unscrewed the camera from its tripod and then abruptly picked up her handbag and walked towards the door.

Jane noticed the movement. 'Going somewhere?'

Laura looked apologetic. 'I'm just in the way at the moment, so I thought I'd get my laptop while you're packing the gear. I won't be long, and I'll help you clean when I return.'

Jane looked doubtful. 'I'm not sure that's a good idea. Robert told us to pick up your computer together.'

'Robert's a worrywart. I don't need anybody holding my hand while I run a simple errand. I'll be back before you know it.' She hurried out the door and down the steps to the car park. Laura was sick of being treated like a china doll and didn't need a nursemaid while she carried out such a straightforward task. She slammed the car door and tossed her handbag on the seat next to her. Picking up the laptop might not be as much fun as following Borkov, but it was just as important.

~

Jordan was not having fun. Banks had been trained to drive pursuit cars and some of his last-minute lane changes had Jordan clutching desperately at the armrest for security. Tracey, on the other hand, was leaning forward in the back seat enjoying the ride. Jordan tugged his seat belt tighter and looked balefully at Banks. 'Shouldn't we drive more slowly? We don't want Borkov to know we're following him.'

'Tailing a car is a fine art,' grunted Banks as he checked the mirror and then abruptly changed lanes. 'The car in front uses natural gaps in the traffic whereas the following car has to force similar gaps that often don't exist if he's to stay within red-light distance.'

'Red-light distance? What's that?'

'If the lights change at an intersection as the first car goes through, the second car must be close enough to go through as well without the traffic in front stopping.' Banks suddenly changed lanes again and zoomed past Borkov's vehicle.

'Hey! What are you doing? We just passed him,' yelled Jordan as he turned and looked back at Borkov.

'Don't stare at him,' snapped Banks. 'You'll give the game away. Don't you know anything?'

'But now we're in front of him,' protested Jordan. 'How can we follow him if he's behind us?'

'Exactly the point. If he thinks he's being followed, he's hardly going to suspect a car that's already passed him, now is he?'

'But what if he turns off?' persisted Jordan. 'We'll lose him.'

'If you study the road ahead you will notice there is no major intersection for some distance, and by then he'll be in front of us again. In the unlikely case he did turn down a minor road, Matt would have to follow him to his destination.'

Banks slowed down and allowed the traffic on the inside lane to overtake him. He veered into the left lane and continued to follow Borkov, maintaining a constant buffer between the two cars. Kilpatrick moved up behind them and adjusted his speed so that the three vehicles manoeuvred through the heavy traffic in unison.

Borkov moved into the right-hand lane ahead of them, but Banks didn't follow.

Jordan watched anxiously as the gap increased between the two vehicles and was finally unable to control himself. 'He's getting away,' he blurted. 'Didn't you see him change lanes?'

'Do you mind not shouting at me?' requested Banks in annoyance. 'If he turns right at the next intersection, I'll still be able to follow him. In the meantime, I suggest you watch and learn.'

'What do you mean?'

'Just be patient and stop bothering me.'

Borkov abruptly swerved into the left hand lane, forcing a blue Austin to brake sharply. He allowed his momentum to carry him across the lane and then turned left with a squeal of tyres at the Bayswater Road intersection. The Austin blasted his horn in anger as he also turned left. Banks followed suit and glanced in his rear-view mirror to make sure Kilpatrick was keeping up.

'Why did he do that? Does he know he's being followed?' asked Tracey anxiously.

Banks shook his head. 'He's just being careful. That manoeuvre is standard evasive training. Anybody who had changed lanes to follow him would either have been stranded in the right-hand lane or stood out like a sore thumb if they attempted to barge their way through the traffic.' He gave Jordan a meaningful look but didn't say anything further.

'Won't he be watching to see who else turned at that corner?' continued Tracey.

'Most likely,' agreed Banks, 'but several cars turned with us, so we just need to drop back and look innocuous.' They were heading into the heart of London in heavy traffic, so it wasn't difficult to increase the gap and still keep Borkov comfortably in sight. The traffic began to crawl as they followed him into Baker Street and eventually ground to a halt.

'What the hell's going on?' muttered Jordan irritably as he tried to peer past the cars in front.

'Road work by the look of it,' murmured Banks.

The traffic began moving slowly once more and then abruptly picked up pace, opening up several gaps. A furniture van, waiting in a side street, immediately charged out and bullied its way in front of Banks, forcing him to stand on his brakes. The driver gave Banks an airy wave of apology and then proceeded to blow a thick cloud of black smoke over their car as he slowly accelerated.

'Bloody lunatic!' yelled Banks as he hurriedly wound up his window to avoid the choking fumes.

'Can you get around him?' implored Jordan.

Banks allowed the car to drift out from behind the truck. A car traveling in the opposite direction furiously flashed his lights as he hurtled past. A hurried glance at the long line of rapidly approaching traffic convinced Banks that any passing attempt would be futile. 'There's no way we can get past along this stretch of road,' he muttered angrily. 'It's a single lane for the next couple of blocks.' He gestured at the van. 'Our only hope is that this idiot turns off.'

'We've got to do something,' exclaimed Jordan in exasperation. 'We'll lose Borkov if this fat bastard doesn't move out of the way.' He leant over and gave the horn a blast and the lorry driver responded with a lazy gesture out his side window.

Banks glared at him. 'Feel better?'

'Not really.'

'Why don't you shoot out his tyres?' suggested Tracey.

'Neither of you are being helpful,' replied Banks as he allowed the car to drift out once more. 'Damn! There are traffic lights ahead. If Borkov goes through and we don't, we'll lose him for sure.' He wound down the window and gestured to Kilpatrick to overtake them. 'Our only hope is that Matt can get past the van, follow him to his destination, and give us a call.'

Kilpatrick had been wondering what to do ever since the van pushed into the line of traffic. He had considered several half opportunities to pass both Banks and the lorry but the oncoming traffic forced him to abort each time. Banks moved to the edge of the road to give him more space, and he eased the bike past with a squirt of the accelerator. The slipstream from the van buffeted him slightly and the diesel fumes filled his helmet as he steeled himself to shoot past.

'He's never going to make it,' said Tracey nervously as they watched Kilpatrick search for a break in the oncoming traffic. The lorry began to slow as it neared the intersection and Kilpatrick suddenly veered through an empty loading zone and up onto the footpath. Tracey let out a whoop of excitement as Kilpatrick roared along the footpath, his exhaust reverberating off the building. 'Go Matty!'

The pedestrians strolling along the footpath weren't as appreciative, yelling angrily as they hurriedly jumped out of the way. Kilpatrick jumped the bike over the gutter and back onto the road as the lights turned red, and then he opened the throttle and dashed between the converging traffic, nodding in acknowledgement to the blaring car horns.

Jordan watched Kilpatrick race out of sight along the footpath and shook his head as he turned anxiously towards Banks. 'It's up to Matt now. There's nothing more we can do until we hear from him.' He gestured angrily towards the lorry idling in front of them. 'Fucking useless hunk of shit! Bloody moron!'

'There are ladies present, you know,' Tracey reminded him primly.

'Yeah, sorry. I just get annoyed when things don't go right.'

'You must spend your whole life being perpetually pissed off,' observed Banks tartly.

'Don't you start,' muttered Jordan sourly.

The traffic began moving and the road eventually widened into two lanes allowing them to pass the lorry, but there was no sign of either Kilpatrick or Borkov. 'That's it then,' said Banks. 'We've lost them. Let's stop for a bite to eat while we wait for Matt to call us.'

'How can you even think about eating?' said Jordan. 'My stomach's just one big twisted knot.'

'It's important to keep your strength up,' replied Banks, his tone almost lecturing. 'Until Matt calls, we're out of the game, and as I'm hungry I intend to eat. What you do is up to you.'

'Do you think that's safe?' asked Tracey. 'What if somebody recognizes you?'

'I've changed my appearance, and besides, I'm old news now. I'm sure the public has new scandals to worry about.'

They ordered coffee and cake at a quiet restaurant and sat at a secluded corner table and chatted as they waited for their order to arrive. A television in the far corner was screening a news program, and Jordan glanced at it as he waited for the sports results. The sound had been turned down, making each story difficult to understand although the accompanying pictures offered occasional clues.

'This coffee's taking an eternity,' muttered Banks as he looked at his watch. 'It's not as though they're being rushed off their feet.'

'Hey!' exclaimed Jordan suddenly. 'That's me.'

'Keep your voice down,' snapped Banks as he looked around hurriedly. 'What are you talking about?'

Jordan gestured towards the television. An attractive reporter, her face showing grave concern, was talking to the camera. In the background was a recent picture of Jordan. The graphic suddenly switched to the more familiar photograph of Banks. As she continued talking, the picture changed to a scene showing several bodies covered in blankets being placed into the back of an ambulance.

'What's all that about?' whispered Tracey.

'Shh!' hissed Banks as he waved her to silence. 'I'm trying to listen.'

The camera returned to the studio presenter who was wrapping up the story. Jordan found it impossible to hear what she was saying but was able to lip-read her next words. 'Armed and dangerous,' he mouthed as he watched her. He turned to the others. 'She said we're armed and dangerous.'

'I know,' replied Banks as he scrambled to his feet. 'Come on, we've been sprung.'

'Sprung?' repeated Tracey as she grabbed her handbag.

'That's why our coffee's been taking so long. The cops will already be on their way. I think the waitress recognized Daniel when we gave our order.'

Inspector Kent had responded immediately to the tip-off from the restaurant and had marshalled his forces with impressive speed. He stood behind his car and peered into the restaurant, confident that all the exits were covered. He drew in a deep, satisfied breath before addressing his second-in-command. 'I'm tempted to throw in a couple of tear gas grenades, but I suppose we should give them a chance to surrender.'

Lieutenant Jackson studied the inspector for a moment and decided he wasn't joking. 'Yes, sir, tear gas is probably not the best option at this stage.' He reached into the back seat and handed Kent a megaphone. His men had already erected roadblocks to divert traffic away from the restaurant.

Kent's voice boomed across the street although the accompanying tinny echo diluted the full effect as his voice rebounded off the surrounding buildings. 'You in the restaurant, this is the police. Come out with your hands up, and you will not be harmed. There is no escape.'

'What if they decide to take hostages?' asked Jackson in the silence that greeted Kent's announcement.

'We'll cross that bridge when we come to it,' scowled Kent. 'They must be apprehended whatever the cost, so whether they have hostages or not, this is the end of the road for them.'

'Look!' exclaimed Jackson. 'Somebody's coming out.' A white towel was being waved from around the corner of the restaurant door.

'Very sensible,' muttered Kent. He raised the megaphone to his lips. 'Step out into the open where we can see you.' A figure emerged from the shadows, still waving the white towel vigorously.

'It looks like one of the waiters,' commented Jackson.

'It could be a trick,' snapped Kent. 'Banks is a psychotic killer capable of anything. That could be one of his men dressed up as a waiter with an Uzi hidden under his jacket.' He spoke into the megaphone. 'Lie face down in the street with your arms and legs apart.' The waiter glanced at the dusty ground and shouted something at Kent as he slowly complied. 'Did you hear what he said?' he asked Jackson.

'He said the people you're looking for have already gone.'

'Blast it,' snarled Kent. 'Search that man and then find out what the hell's going on.'

～

Borkov walked into the hotel and spotted Eastman seated at the bar, flirting with a young barmaid who was half-heartedly wiping the bench top as she waited for her next customer. Apart from aging, Eastman hadn't changed. He was still the ladies' man. The sunglasses perched carelessly atop his curly hair, the open shirt, and the gold chain along with the familiar roguish grin were clear evidence that he fancied his chances with the barmaid despite being twice her age.

Eastman flashed his teeth once more at the girl and then turned to face Borkov as he became aware of a shadow looming over him. 'Isaac, old chap, how are you? Please, have a seat.' He gestured to the barstool next to him and grinned at the girl. 'I'm sure Sarah would love to serve you, wouldn't you, Sarah? Order anything you want, it's on me. Somehow I feel lucky tonight.'

'Not here,' Borkov muttered tonelessly, his voice barely audible. 'We'll sit at a table and discuss business like civilized people.' He gestured to the maître d', who immediately hurried over.

'A discreet table for two, please,' Borkov commanded. The maître d' nodded politely and gestured for the two men to follow him. Eastman gave the barmaid a wink of future promise before following Borkov.

'I see you've been grazing in a lush paddock, Isaac,' said Eastman as he seated himself opposite the big man. 'Life has been kind to you.'

'And I see you haven't changed your adulterous ways,' grunted Borkov as he struggled to fit his ample backside into the confines of the chair.

Eastman laughed dismissively. 'You mean Sarah? I was just keeping myself amused while I waited for you. I'm too old for the likes of her.'

'Not from what I observed. If you want my considered opinion, that girl is very interested in you.'

'Do you really think so?' replied Eastman as he glanced over at the barmaid. He suddenly laughed. 'I get it. You want to see me make a fool of myself. You always did enjoy humiliating people, Isaac.'

Borkov shrugged. 'Have it your own way, Geoffrey.' He waved a hovering waiter away with an admonishing gesture before turning back to Eastman and dropping a thick envelope on the table. 'These are the disks I spoke about. I am trusting you with my life, so please guard them with your own.'

Eastman hefted the envelope in his hand before slipping it into his jacket. 'You know you can trust me, Isaac.' He treated Borkov to his famous grin, allowing the tip of his tongue to protrude between his teeth.

'I know I can, that's why I chose you from the hundreds of people available.'

'I'm honoured and flattered.'

'You should be, and you're also wealthier by thirty thousand pounds.' He pushed back his chair and grunted as he picked up the worn leather briefcase from between his feet. He was wheezing slightly as he placed it on the table. 'It's all there. You can count it if you wish.'

'There's no need for that, Isaac. I trust you completely, and you'd have nothing to gain by cheating me, now would you?' He glanced across at the girl behind the counter and gave her a brief smile. He wondered how she'd respond if he gave her a generous tip.

'Precisely, now please take your mind off the girl, and pay close attention to what I am about to say. I have enclosed a list of instructions, but I will go through them anyway to make absolutely sure you understand.'

'Sure,' replied Eastman, who was not offended by Borkov's tone.

'I find I'm repeating myself, but these disks are my life insurance; if anything were to happen to me, these must be made public.'

'I understand that, Isaac, I really do. It's not that hard to comprehend.'

'Oh you understand, do you? In that case, how would you make the information public?'

'Not knowing what's on the disks makes it difficult, but I'd probably send copies to the police. I'm sure they'd know how to use the information.'

Borkov frowned. 'I'm sorry, Geoffrey, but that's exactly what you don't do. Keep the police out of it. They cannot be trusted. If they discovered that you had this information, you'd be dead within twenty-four hours.'

Eastman sat back in his chair, distancing himself from Borkov. 'Isaac, if you're trying to scare me, you're succeeding. I'm a businessman, not a friggin' spy.'

'Good. It's healthy to be scared. It's important that you understand the seriousness of this matter. I have made absolutely certain that these disks cannot be traced to you. If nobody knows you've got them, then you cannot be in any danger. I have even made plans to ensure that I don't know you've got them.'

Eastman scoffed. 'Give me a break, Isaac, that's impossible. How are you going to do it? Hypnotize yourself?'

'How I do it is not your concern. Just believe me when I say it can be done. The point I'm making is that nobody will know you've got the disks unless you tell them. Remember, loose lips slit throats, mine included.'

Eastman turned pale. The thirty thousand pounds no longer seemed such a good deal. 'I think you've made your point, Isaac.'

Borkov nodded. 'Good. So we've agreed not to involve the police. Send copies of the disks to each of the major newspapers, along with a copy of the letter I have included. That should be sufficient. Once the newspapers have the information, your service to me will be completed and you will be safe, although it may be wise to carry out my instructions anonymously.'

'I'm sure I can handle that, although if I'd known how dangerous this was I would have asked for more money.'

'Don't push it. I'm already paying you too much. Finally, you must never contact me under any circumstances. If I know you've got these disks, then we're both dead. Is that clear?'

'No, of course it's not clear. You've just handed me these damned disks and now you tell me that I mustn't ever tell you I've got them because if you find out we're both dead? What sort of bullshit is that?'

Borkov remained calm. 'The more you know, the more dangerous it will be for you. Just trust me when I tell you that I have developed a process that can erase parts of a person's memory. Tomorrow morning when I wake up, I will have no knowledge of this meeting. That's why you're safe. I can be bribed, tortured, subjected to chemical inducements, and I will still not betray you. Why? Because I won't know. The only way I will know is if you tell me. Is it clear now?'

'It seems a bit fanciful, but it makes a vague sort of sense.' He paused. 'How will I know if you're dead? I can check the obituaries, but from the tone of this conversation it's quite possible that your death will be kept hush hush.'

Borkov fixed him with his cold grey eyes. 'It's a good question, and I have given the matter some thought. You will find a slip of paper in the envelope with two phone numbers and an address. Every six months you will follow a verification review to determine if I am alive. The fact that I am paying you an extra ten thousand pounds will cover this imposition.'

Eastman lowered his head as he hid a smile. The thirty thousand pounds might be easy money after all. If the task was too onerous, he simply wouldn't do it. Borkov would never know. 'It doesn't seem too difficult. I keep the disks securely tucked away, and as long as I keep quiet I'm safe. Once you're dead, I go to the newspapers and expose your enemies.' He held out his hand. 'Consider it a done deal.'

Borkov grasped Eastman's hand by the end of his fingers and gave it a brief shake. 'Excellent. I'm glad we've reached a satisfactory agreement.' He pushed back his chair and struggled to his feet. 'I have another appointment I must keep. Enjoy a long and prosperous life.' He gave Eastman a languid wave as he walked away.

Kilpatrick was sitting at the bar chatting to the barmaid as he watched Borkov leave. He had a theory that the best place to remain inconspicuous was out in the open. People in films always checked the dark recesses for lurking villains, never the most obvious. He saw the exchange take place between Borkov and the curly-haired man sitting by the window and so decided not to follow Borkov.

He wandered out into the lobby just as Tracey and Banks hurried around the corner. 'Where's Daniel?' he asked.

'I'll explain later,' replied Banks briskly. 'Where's Borkov?'

'You just missed him. He made the exchange and left a moment ago. I was worried that if you bumped into him on your way up he might recognize you.'

'We took the stairs because it was faster,' explained Tracey. 'I imagine Borkov would have taken the elevator as I can't see him doing any unnecessary exercise.'

'You're certain the exchange took place?' asked Banks as he peered at him closely.

'I'm positive.' Kilpatrick gestured with his head. 'You see that man sitting alone by the window?'

'The one with the sunglasses on his head?' asked Tracey.

'Yes. Borkov gave him an envelope and a briefcase. The envelope is in his jacket and the briefcase is on the floor between his feet.'

'Excellent,' murmured Banks. 'Now we have to lure him outside and relieve him of the disks. Did you notice anything else that might be helpful?'

'Not really. Borkov did most of the talking while the other fellow listened, although it didn't look as though he was paying much attention.'

'Why do you say that?'

'When I came in he was sitting at the bar chatting up the barmaid. After they moved to the table he kept winking at her, and Borkov got really annoyed. I couldn't hear what he was saying, but you could see it in his face.

Tracey smiled impishly and batted her eyelids. 'Perhaps I could wander over and dazzle him with my charm. It shouldn't take much to coax him to come outside with me.'

'It wouldn't work,' replied Banks bluntly. 'With the disparity in your ages, he'd think you were a hooker. The hotel would as

well. He'd either offer you money to take you upstairs, or hotel
security would throw you out.'

'A hooker!' exclaimed Tracey indignantly. 'Well, thank you
very much.'

'I'm just telling you like it is.' Banks suddenly smiled. 'Perhaps
if we tinker around the edges we might work something out.' He
briefly outlined his plan, and they nodded in agreement when
he finished.

'Right, here we go then,' murmured Tracey. 'Act two, scene
one. Tracey enters stage left. Wish me luck.' She rose lightly to
her feet and walked into the restaurant. A waiter directed her to
a table and took her order for a drink.

Kilpatrick waited for a moment and then followed her in.
He waved the waiter away and strode over to where Tracey was
seated. She looked up as his shadow fell over her and grimaced.
'Carl! What are you doing here? Have you been following me?'

'So you thought you could slink out and meet your new
fancy man did you, you cheating bitch. Where is he?' Kilpatrick
growled as he looked around the room. The other diners
studiously avoided his gaze, and he noticed one of the waiters
talking hurriedly into the phone. 'I'll teach the bastard to play
around with you behind my back.'

Tracey sighed loudly. 'I'm here by myself, Carl, and I told you
two weeks ago that we were finished.' She leaned forward and
glared at him. 'I'm going to powder my nose, and when I get back
you'd better be gone.' She pushed back her chair and flounced
away. Kilpatrick started after her and caught her roughly by the
arm as she was walking past Eastman. 'Let go of me, Carl. You're
hurting my arm,' she hissed vehemently between gritted teeth
as she tried to shake free. 'When are you going to get it through
your thick head that it's over between us?'

'I'm the one who says when it's over,' he sneered, 'not you.'
He tugged her arm as if to drag her towards the door. 'Come
on, you slut, we're going back to my place. It's time I taught you
some respect.'

Tracey looked desperately at Mr Sunglasses, but he refused to meet her eye. She turned back to Kilpatrick and tried to wrestle free. 'I'm not going anywhere with you.' She pulled back her free hand and slapped him savagely on his cheek, the noise echoing around the room. He looked at her, momentarily stunned, and then shoved her forcibly away so that she stumbled back against Eastman's table.

'Here, steady on,' muttered Eastman as he snatched up his wineglass to prevent it spilling onto the tablecloth.

'You keep out of this, fuck-knuckle,' snarled Kilpatrick. 'This ain't got nothin' to do with you.'

Everybody in the restaurant was now watching him, and Eastman reluctantly realized he would have to intervene. With a bit of luck, hotel security would arrive before the situation got out of hand. He could feel his pulse racing as he slowly stood up and faced Kilpatrick, ensuring that the table was between the two of them. 'I believe the lady has made it quite plain she doesn't want anything further to do with you. Now why don't you leave quietly and allow us to continue dining in peace.'

To Eastman's surprise, Kilpatrick made a vaguely threatening gesture and then did just that. He stopped at the door and glared back into the room. 'This ain't over, bitch, not by a long shot,' he yelled before disappearing down the stairs.

There was a slight smattering of applause followed by a buzz of conversation as the other diners resumed their meals. Tracey smiled gratefully at Mr Sunglasses. 'Thank you. I don't know what I would have done if you hadn't helped.' She staggered slightly and clutched at a nearby chair. 'Do you mind if I sit down? I'm feeling a little faint.'

Eastman was feeling quite the hero. 'Not at all.' He gave her a warm smile and gestured towards a spare chair. 'Can I get you a drink?'

Tracey smiled gratefully in return. 'That would be nice. I need something to settle my nerves. I'll have a scotch and Coke. My name's Heather, by the way.'

'Heather,' repeated Eastman as he signalled to one of the waiters. 'What a nice name. I'm Geoffrey.'

Tracey held out her hand. 'I'm pleased to meet you, Geoffrey. I should apologise for Carl's appalling behaviour. He's extremely jealous. I can't believe he followed me here. Thank goodness you stood up to him.'

'It was nothing, really,' replied Eastman as he waved a deprecating hand. 'I'm sure anybody else would have done the same thing.'

'No, that's where you're wrong,' replied Tracey as she touched him gently on the arm. 'Society has become far too insular, too selfish. My generation refuses to get involved in the plight of other people in case they're personally disadvantaged. That's why I prefer to spend my time with more mature men. They know how to treat a lady like a lady.'

Eastman sat up straighter and sucked in his stomach as he tested the water. 'I find it interesting that you prefer older men, but that Carl fellow wasn't very old.'

Tracey snorted derisively. 'He's just a boy. We were introduced by one of my so-called friends and look what a disaster that turned out to be. Never again,' she said emphatically. The waiter placed her drink in front of her, and she looked coyly at Eastman over the top of her glass as she took a dainty sip.

'Would you care to join me for dinner?' he asked carelessly.

'I'm sorry,' she replied with a pert shake of her head. 'You've been so kind and there's nothing I'd like better, but I dare not stay much longer.'

'Oh, are you meeting somebody else?' asked Eastman as he masked his disappointment. 'I should have realized that a pretty girl like you wouldn't be dining alone.'

'Oh no, it's nothing like that,' she laughed as she tossed her hair away from her eyes. 'It's Carl. He has a fierce temper when he's drunk, and right now I bet he's drowning his sorrows and moaning about his unfaithful bitch of a girlfriend to anybody who'll listen. It's a familiar story with him. Once he gets himself tanked up, he'll return to finish what he started. When that happens I don't want to be anywhere near this place.'

Eastman blanched. 'Do you think that's likely to happen? I thought he left quietly enough before.'

Tracey grimaced. 'It's the drink, you know. Once that gets into him he becomes a raging bull and there's absolutely no stopping him. He just goes berserk.' Eastman blanched further, and she pulled a face at him. 'Oh, poor Geoffrey, I can see I've ruined your evening—and after everything you've done for me.' She lowered her voice as she leaned closer. 'I've got an idea you may be interested in. There's an intimate restaurant not far from here where we could get to know each other better without having to worry about Carl.' She smiled at him teasingly as her shoe caressed his ankle. 'What do you say?'

Eastman smiled broadly and leaned forward in return. 'It sounds like an excellent idea.' As he moved his foot to return the caress, he touched the briefcase under the table and his smiled disappeared. Opportunities like this were rapidly diminishing from his life. Strike while the iron's hot had always been his motto, but he couldn't simply walk around carrying thirty thousand pounds in a worn black briefcase. Anything could happen.'

Tracey studied his face. 'Is something the matter?'

Eastman reluctantly sighed. 'I can't go with you after all.'

'Oh, that's a pity,' said Tracey wistfully. 'Is it something I've done?'

Eastman gave a rueful grunt. 'Hardly.' He stared at her as he considered his options and then reached for the briefcase. 'I've been entrusted with some valuable documents, and I can't risk losing them. It pains me grievously, but I fear I'll have to pass up your delightful company.'

Tracey looked crestfallen. 'Oh dear, and I had such wonderful plans in mind. Where are you taking the documents? Perhaps we can work something out.'

'I have to take them home tonight and place them in a security box first thing tomorrow.'

Tracey gave him an artful smile. 'How about we go back to your place, and I'll cook up a meal for the two of us?'

Eastman blinked in surprise. 'You'd do that?'

'Only if you want me to, but we really need to get our skates on because Carl could return at any moment.'

Eastman gave her a beaming smile as he picked up the briefcase. 'Okay, Heather.' He spoke her name tentatively as if trying it on for size. 'This promises to be the best home-cooked meal I've had in a long time.' He took her gently by the elbow, and after paying his bill, escorted her from the restaurant. As they left, he turned and gave Sarah a final suggestive wink. Experience had taught him that it always paid to keep your options open.

Banks followed them into the elevator and positioned himself so he was slightly behind Eastman. Tracey chattered constantly, distracting him so that he barely noticed the third person sharing the elevator.

They exited into the car park and stopped while Eastman sorted out his bearings. 'I always have trouble remembering where I parked my damned car.'

'I'm the same,' Tracey admitted with a giggle. 'I find if I start walking I soon work out where I left it. Come on, let's go this way.' She took his arm and gave it a playful tug.

Eastman looked doubtful as he pointed in the opposite direction. 'I think it might by this way.'

'Okay, let's go that way then, shall we?'

Banks had taken an interest in a Mercedes parked around the corner while Jordan was crouched patiently behind a white Saab waiting to see which direction they would take. As Eastman and Tracey started walking, he silently slipped between the rows of parked cars and followed behind. Jordan watched as Banks suddenly moved in on Eastman and curled a muscular arm around his neck, catching him in a vice-like grip, and then rammed his gun into Eastman's kidneys, causing him to arch his back in pain. Jordan leapt to assist as Banks propelled his victim further between two parked cars, kicked away his supporting leg, and turned him as he fell so that he ended up lying flat on his stomach on the dusty concrete floor. The briefcase jarred free from his outstretched hand and finished up against a car wheel.

'Don't even think about calling for help,' warned Banks gruffly as he stuck his knee in Eastman's back and secured his wrists firmly with a plastic tie. Jordan handed him a black ski mask and he tugged it on backwards over Eastman's head. 'Now I believe you have something we want?' He rolled Eastman over, tugged the envelope from his jacket pocket, and handed it to Jordan. 'Have a look and make sure we've got what we came for.'

Jordan ripped open the envelope and studied its contents under the dim light. There were three disks and several pieces of paper. 'Everything's here,' he replied softly.

'Right, take them to the car, and I'll join you shortly.' He gestured silently to Tracey, and she slipped away to catch up with Jordan. Banks grabbed Eastman by the ski mask and lifted his head off the ground. 'Right, pal, listen carefully. I'm going to loosen this plastic tie just enough so you can wiggle your hands free. You might lose a bit of skin but you should be free in about five minutes. We're taking your girlfriend with us, so don't call the cops. We'll let her go once we're safely away. Do you understand?'

Eastman grunted in reply.

Banks gave him a jovial slap on the side of the face. 'Good boy.' He pushed himself to his feet and hurried after Tracey and Jordan. Eastman listened to the sound of the footsteps fading into the distance and then rubbed his wrists together to test the strength of the plastic tie. As he struggled into a sitting position he heard a rustling noise as somebody stepped past him. 'Who's that?' he whispered. 'Who's there?'

Kilpatrick leaned across him and picked up the briefcase. 'Keep quiet, or I'll gut you like a fish,' he growled menacingly.

Eastman sank back to the concrete floor and remained completely motionless, recalling Borkov's strict orders not to contact him under any circumstances. He would comply.

～

Colin Tweddle locked his office and trudged listlessly towards the car park, still depressed by the events of the previous week. As he sauntered between the rows of parked cars, a familiar sight caught his attention and he stopped in mid-stride. The grey BMW parked in Laura's parking space had to be hers, and his heart skipped a beat as he recognised his opportunity. Jordan was now a wanted felon, his face leering out at everyone from the evening news. If he could pluck Laura to safety from under Jordan's nose, he could plead her case before the courts and have her released into his protective custody.

He hurried over and placed his hand on the car's hood, relieved to find it still felt warm. He had been fearful that the car had been sitting here for the past week and in his depressed mood he hadn't noticed. He pulled out his phone and rang the police.

A gruff male voice answered immediately. 'Scotland Yard, how can I help you?'

'I have urgent information concerning Robert Banks. I need to speak to somebody in charge immediately.'

'You can tell me, sir, and I'll make sure the information is passed on.'

'I don't have time to play games,' fumed Tweddle. 'Either put me through, or I'll hang up.'

'Hold the line, sir, and I'll check if anybody is available.' Kent was out of his office, and the officer hesitated before finally putting the call through to Fenwick.

'Chief Inspector Fenwick here. Who am I talking to?'

Tweddle cleared his throat nervously. 'My name's Colin Tweddle. I gave your department information on Inspector Banks and now I have information on Laura Monroe.'

'Why would we be interested in Laura Monroe?'

'She's innocently mixed up with Banks and has nothing to do with kidnapping and torturing people,' replied Tweddle.

'Mr Tweddle, I'm really busy, so please get to the point.'

'I've just seen her,' replied Tweddle hurriedly.

'You've just seen Laura Monroe? Might I ask where?'

'Well, not her exactly,' amended Tweddle. 'It's her car. It's here at work, and the engine is still warm. She must have dropped into her office to pick up some of her things.'

'Is anybody with her?'

'I don't know. All I've done is find her car. They could have blackmailed her into working for them, or they might have somebody with her; it's impossible to tell.'

'Give me the address, and we'll send a car immediately. You've been a great help, Mr Tweddle. If we had more community-minded people like you, this country would be a safer place.'

Tweddle felt emboldened by the compliment. 'I'm sure you realize that Laura has been an innocent victim in all of this, and I was hoping that once she's answered your questions you'd see fit to release her into my custody.'

Fenwick made no response, so Tweddle hastily continued. 'I'd put up the bail money, and speaking professionally, I believe Laura would suffer irreparable harm if she were held in police custody, particularly after the trauma she has recently endured.'

Fenwick smiled to himself. 'You put forward a most compelling case, Mr Tweddle, but before we can make the rabbit stew, we must first catch the rabbit.'

'Pardon?'

'We can't make any promises until we have Laura safely in custody. In the meantime, I want you to prevent her from leaving.'

Tweddle frowned. 'How do I do that? Even if she's by herself, she's quite a strong woman and any sort of struggle will attract attention.'

Fenwick sighed. 'I was thinking more along the lines of disabling her car, Mr Tweddle. Can you manage that?'

Tweddle felt a wave of panic wash over him as the words stumbled from his tongue. 'I'm not sure. The car's locked, and if I try to force any of the doors the alarm will go off.'

'That's okay, Mr Tweddle. Just let down one of her tyres and then wait until she returns. If she is alone, you can act the gallant gentleman and offer to change the tyre for her. Take your time, and we'll be there shortly. I'm sure you can manage that, and your cooperation will be a decisive factor in determining a favourable outcome when considering your request for custody.'

Tweddle was relieved as he ended the call. Life was finally starting to look sweet; all he had to do was let down a tyre. There was nobody in sight, so he bent down and removed the valve cap from the rear tyre and then pressed the end of his pen into the opening. The hiss of escaping air sounded impossibly loud, but there were no distant shouts and he nervously continued. He considered attacking another tyre but decided it would be too suspicious and retired gratefully into the shadows to await Laura's return.

He fidgeted anxiously every time the doors opened, and when Laura finally appeared, he was relieved to see she was alone. He smiled when he heard her indignant exclamation and readied himself for the next scene in the drama. A car appeared in the distance, and he scurried back behind a pillar until it had gone. He took deep breath, stepped out onto the roadway. Laura had opened the BMW's boot and was unfolding a jack as she crouched down by the flat tyre. She didn't notice Tweddle, and he was forced to speak first.

'Hello, Laura,' he said pleasantly. 'Having a spot of bother?'

She glanced up at him, her eyes narrowed in disdain. 'It's nothing I can't handle, thank you, Colin.'

'Changing a flat tyre is not a suitable task for a lady.' He gave her his most charming smile as he made a little bow. 'Please allow me to help.'

She stood up and placed her hands on her hips, oblivious to the dark smears her fingers made on her clothing. 'I think you've helped enough already. First you molest me in the back of a taxi, and then you squeal to the police about Daniel and Inspector Banks.'

'Aha! So it was Banks I saw in the cellar. I knew it.' He paused momentarily. 'How did you know I've been talking to the police?'

'It doesn't take a genius to figure that one out.'

'I did it for you,' he said earnestly. 'After what they did to that poor man in the cellar, I was afraid of what they'd do to you when you were captured.'

'Captured?' Laura scoffed as she held out her arms. 'Do I look as though I've been captured?'

Tweddle smiled weakly. 'What happened? How did you get away?'

Laura shook her head in annoyance. 'Nothing happened. Just because I didn't scurry away with you doesn't mean I was a prisoner.' She stared at him thoughtfully. 'And I have to say, you didn't sound very surprised when you saw me just now.'

'Well I was. Now are you going to let me help with that tyre or not?'

Her mouth curled in distaste. 'I've already told you I can handle this, so why don't you do me a favour and slink off home so I can get on with it.' She turned away dismissively and bent down to position the jack under the car.

Tweddle was aggrieved. 'One day you'll appreciate everything I've done for you.' He wasn't sure what to do next. If he wasn't here when the police came, he wouldn't get the credit for Laura being taken into custody.

'I thought I told you to go,' grunted Laura as she forced the jack handle to rotate through another complete circuit.

'Shouldn't you loosen the wheel nuts first?'

Laura dropped the handle on the ground with a metallic clatter and picked up the tyre lever. Her eyes were reduced to thin slits, and there was a look of menace and determination around her mouth that he hadn't seen before. She took a step towards him and waved the lever in his face.

'You are the most annoying and simplistic person I have ever known, and if you haven't disappeared by the time I count to three, I will take the utmost delight in loosening *your* wheel nuts.'

Tweddle's dilemma was solved by the appearance of a black Peugeot. The car pulled up behind the BMW, and a man and woman emerged. Laura turned to assure the couple that she wasn't in any danger but froze in horror when she recognized the swarthy man striding towards her. Before she could shout a warning, the man snatched the lever from her outstretched hand and put her in a headlock.

'Hey, take it easy,' cried Tweddle. 'You don't need to be so rough. She hasn't done anything wrong.'

As DeLuca propelled Laura towards the back door of the Peugeot, she turned and shouted at Tweddle. 'This is one of the men who tried to rape me. You've got to do something.'

To her amazement, Tweddle merely smiled and stepped out of the way. 'No, Laura, you've got it wrong. These people are with the police, and they've come to rescue you.'

She grabbed hold of the door as she fought to free herself. 'You told these people where to find me?' she gasped. 'How could you be so stupid?'

Her last words were a muffled jumble as DeLuca jabbed a pressure point on the inside of her elbow and her arm simply collapsed, allowing him to bundle her into the back seat. The driver leant across and injected a sedative into her upper arm while the woman pointed a gun at Tweddle. 'What about him?'

'He's a witness,' replied DeLuca. 'Kill him.'

'What?' cried Tweddle as he backed away in panic.

'He might still be useful,' replied the woman, although her voice lacked conviction.

'I doubt it,' said DeLuca dismissively. 'Shove him in the trunk, and we'll let Madison decide.'

The woman jerked her thumb at Tweddle. 'You heard the man. Get in and keep your fuckin' mouth shut.' Tweddle climbed in dejectedly and curled himself into a forlorn ball as the woman slammed the trunk shut.

The kidnapping of Laura had taken less than sixty seconds.

Chapter 15

I gave my life for freedom—This I know,
For those that bade me fight had told me so.

William Norman Ewer

Jane peered anxiously through the curtains for Laura's BMW. Even allowing for abnormally heavy traffic, Laura should have returned an hour ago. Although loath to disturb the others with foolish misgivings, she snatched up the phone and called Robert. She found the steady tone of his voice reassuring and was confident he would know what to do.

'It's Jane,' she said without preamble. 'I'm worried about Laura. She left to get her laptop two hours ago and hasn't returned.'

Banks didn't reply, and she knew he was thinking through the angles. She was quietly relieved he hadn't berated her for allowing Laura to go off alone. 'Have you packed up your gear?' he asked.

'Yes.'

'Sit tight and we'll pick you up. Let me know if Laura returns.' The call was disconnected. Jane gave a heavy sigh and seated herself on the edge of a chair next to the window. She felt better now the problem was shared.

Banks stopped the car in a side street and turned to Jordan. 'We have a problem. Laura's missing, and we need to presume the worst.'

'What do you mean she's missing?' Jordan demanded. 'She was with Jane. How could she be missing?'

'That was Jane on the phone. Laura went off to collect her laptop two hours ago and hasn't returned.'

'I still don't understand how she can be missing,' persisted Jordan. 'Why wasn't Jane with her?'

Banks raised his voice to talk over the top of Jordan. 'We can worry about how it happened later. What we need to do now is assume that Memtech people have snatched her, and we need to formulate a plan to get her back.'

'Her car may have broken down somewhere,' said Tracey quietly from the back seat. 'We could be worrying about nothing.'

'She has her phone with her,' replied Jordan, struggling to keep his voice calm and level. 'If she'd broken down she would have called me, so I'm afraid Robert is right. The thing is, what can we do about it?'

Banks gave him a tight grin. 'Fortunately, we still have our trump card.'

'The disks?' asked Jordan grimly.

'Precisely. If we play our hand correctly, we can use the disks to engineer her freedom.'

'We have to do it, but it means we're back to square one.'

Kilpatrick tapped on the window, and Banks wound it halfway down in an effort to keep the warm air in the car. 'What's going on?' Kilpatrick asked through chattering teeth.

'We think Laura's been kidnapped,' replied Jordan as he leant across.

'You're kidding,' gasped Kilpatrick. 'How did that happen? Nobody knows where we are.'

'It doesn't matter how it happened,' replied Banks, 'but we need to make sure she really has been taken before we do anything further. Do you know where she works?'

'Yes, I've been there a couple of times with Daniel.'

'Scout around and see if her car's in the car park. She may still be at work or perhaps her phone needs recharging. There could be a dozen reasons why she's late. Give us a call if you find anything.'

Kilpatrick stamped his feet and slapped his gloved hands against his body to induce a more active flow of blood. 'Anything else?'

'Just be careful. Somebody may be waiting around to see who else shows up.'

'I can take care of myself,' muttered Kilpatrick as he turned and stamped his way back to his bike.

'What do we do now?' asked Tracey.

Banks scratched his head while he thought, leaving his hair in an even untidier state than usual. He tossed his phone back to Tracey. 'Call Jane and tell her to sit tight. We'll pick her up shortly. We need to copy these disks, and we might not have much time.'

Jordan grimaced unhappily. 'How are you going to do that at this time of night?'

'Let me worry about that,' replied Banks calmly as Tracey handed the phone back to him. 'One more job for you,' he said. 'Call my partner. Look in the directory under Roger Evans.' Tracey waited until the phone started ringing and then passed it to Banks. 'Hello, Roger? I'm sure you remember the procedure of our previous conversation. Activate it again in twenty minutes. While you're waiting, gather up your Stalingrad memento along with the equipment we borrowed for the ecstasy bust.'

'The ecstasy bust,' repeated Evans uncertainly.

'You know the one. Everybody turned green with envy that night.'

Evans suddenly laughed. It was a sharp barking sound, clearly audible to the others. 'Gotcha.'

Banks tucked the phone back in his pocket. 'Now let's get these disks copied before the shit hits the fan.'

Jordan looked at him anxiously. 'You still haven't told us how you're going to do that.'

'I told you not to worry,' replied Banks as he accelerated through an intersection as the lights turned red. 'My Aunt Doris lives about fifteen minutes from here. I gave her my old PC last year, so I know it can do the job. I've been using her as my go-between with Roger. With a bit of luck, we'll have time for a cup of tea and a biscuit as well. All we can do now is hope Laura tells them about the disks. Once they know about them, they'll do everything possible to get them back. That should buy her some time, and the rest will be up to us.'

$$\sim$$

Laura dreamt she was lying under a blazing sun on the beach. She was naked, which surprised her, but when she made an effort to cover herself, she found she was unable to move. A large wave abruptly surged out of nowhere, splashing across her and shattering her dream. She was suddenly aware of people standing over her, watching her intently, and she instinctively moved to cover her nakedness. To her horror she discovered, as in the dream, she was unable to move any of her limbs and shuddered when she realized she was firmly bound by thick, leather straps.

The heat in her dream turned out to be a large lamp projecting a blinding light, and when something soft touched her arm, she gave a panicked scream and struggled once more against her restraints.

'Nobody can hear you, mam'selle,' said a disembodied voice laced with a strong French accent, 'so I suggest you save your energy for answering our questions. I find loud women most annoying, and if you persist in screaming, then I will be forced to inflict painful indignities on your lovely body.'

She had a monumental headache, and the strong light was causing her eyes to fill with tears. She closed them in an effort to gain some relief, but a hand slapped her roughly across the face. 'Open your fucking eyes, bitch. Nobody gave you permission to close them.' She tried to obey, but her tears immediately reformed and streamed down her face, and she found her eyes shutting of their own accord. The hand slapped her again, harder this time. 'I told you to open your fucking eyes.'

'I can't,' she whispered miserably. 'The light's too strong. They won't stay open.'

'Turn it off,' ordered the Frenchman.

The other voice protested. 'The light will encourage her to answer our questions.'

'Turn it off,' repeated the Frenchman. 'I think she will tell us what we need to know.'

The other voice laughed, almost a sneer. 'You're right of course. She'll tell us one way or the other.'

The light snapped off, and Laura felt the heat dissipate. She opened her eyes and watched as a blurred head moved into her line of sight. 'You know who I am?' It was the Frenchman. She blinked as she focused her eyes and the Frenchman leant over and wiped a soft cloth across face. 'Maybe that will help you,' he said kindly. His face did seem familiar, and she realized they'd taken photographs of him. Her eyes moved instinctively to the second man, and he smiled wickedly in return.

'I think I'm going to be sick,' she muttered as a wave of nausea washed over her. Her teeth felt thick and furry, and she had difficulty articulating the words.

'I'd prefer it if you didn't,' replied the Frenchman. 'Apart from the mess and smell, you'll probably choke to death lying as you are.'

'I think I'd feel better if I sat up.' Now that the warming effect of the light had disappeared, she began to feel cold and gave an involuntary shiver. 'And I'd really appreciate a blanket as well.'

The Frenchman snapped his fingers at the other man. 'Fetch a coat for Miss Monroe while I undo these straps. I believe she is ready to talk.'

The man didn't move immediately and instead ran his fingers down Laura's thigh. 'The old methods might take longer, Monsieur Toulemonde, but they're certainly more fun.'

Toulemonde chuckled softly. 'Be patient, Michael. If Miss Monroe is uncooperative, then you can try your old-fashioned ways. We can compare results after I tap into her memory.' He undid the leather straps and helped Laura sit up.

Madison returned with a white lab coat, and she nodded her thanks to the Frenchman as she put it on. He gave her an appraising look. 'I assume you're aware of our memory retrieval technology?'

'I know a little bit about it, yes.'

'Then I'm sure you understand that the best way to conceal information is by telling us everything we want to know.'

Laura blinked as she tried to make sense of the statement. 'I'm sorry; I didn't understand that. It's probably the effects of the drug.'

Toulemonde laughed. 'The drug has nothing to do with it, Laura. Our new technology has resulted in a paradigm shift. I'll explain it to you this way. If you answer our questions openly and honestly, we will find out everything we think to ask about. However, we will continue to remain ignorant of other pertinent knowledge simply because we failed to ask the appropriate question. Do you understand?'

Laura waved her hand feebly as her headache worsened. 'Go on.'

'If we made the effort to extract your total knowledge, nothing would remain hidden from us. Therefore, the best way to conceal information is to tell us everything, do you see?'

Laura's complexion paled further, giving her skin a wax-like sheen. Toulemonde smiled wolfishly. 'I know you're thinking why don't we simply kill you. Unfortunately, we're discovering problems with doing that. Disposing of your body isn't the issue,' he said dismissively. 'No, the problem is memory overload. In the early days, we transferred memories and knowledge holus-bolus. You've no idea the things my poor brain has had to assimilate, and I occasionally struggle to distinguish my real memories from the artificial. We've learnt that loading too much information over a short period can lead to a degree of mental incapacitation along with mild schizophrenia. We have almost solved this issue with the development of an enzyme that will self-activate after a defined period. We attach the enzyme to the memory chemicals as they are transferred, and then the enzyme activates at a later date and destroys the injected memory. Any temporary knowledge we required could be assimilated, acted upon, and then discarded.'

'Isn't there a danger the enzyme would also destroy your own memory?' asked Laura, who was curious despite her predicament.

'Absolutely, but we'll eventually iron out the bugs. So, if we are forced to download your knowledge, then we will certainly do it, but we'd rather avoid that unpleasantness. The choice is yours.'

'Some choice.'

'Yes but it's still a choice.'

'So what do you want to know?'

Toulemonde smiled encouragingly. 'I knew you'd understand. Please tell us the whereabouts of Inspector Banks and that woman he's with—Jane.' He glanced across at Madison, who shrugged his shoulders.

'Astbury,' prompted Laura.

'Yes, that's the one. So you obviously know where she is.'

'What do you want with them?'

'We just want to have a little talk, that's all,' replied Toulemonde with a comforting grin. 'Banks is in a lot of trouble, and we'd like to offer him an arrangement that will solve his problems and guarantee our continued secrecy. We're proposing a win-win solution.'

Laura snorted derisively. 'No doubt. How about I offer you an arrangement instead?'

Toulemonde's grin faded and his eyes narrowed threateningly. 'You're in no position to offer deals to anyone.'

'You should listen to what I have to say before you jump to conclusions.'

Madison stepped closer and held a knife to her throat. 'She's just stalling for time. If you don't want to drain her brain, give her to me, and I'll soon have her singing like a canary.'

Toulemonde studied the tips of his fingers for a moment before answering. 'I thought you were smarter than that, Laura, but you leave me no choice. I hope you enjoy Michael's persuasive ways.' He turned and began walking away.

The knife held to her throat brought back painful memories, and Laura couldn't help but feel her life had come full circle. 'You're making a serious mistake,' she whispered loudly. 'We have disks from Borkov that compromise your entire operation.'

Toulemonde swivelled gracefully on his heel and motioned to Madison, who reluctantly removed the knife from Laura's throat. 'What did you say?'

She shuddered as she ran her fingers down her throat. 'Dr Borkov made several disks outlining the full details of your operation. We collected them this evening. Once they're made public, you'll be finished, and your operation closed down permanently.'

'You've got to do better than that, Laura. Borkov would never jeopardize his own work, and he certainly wouldn't hand incriminating documents to someone like you.' He paused while he studied her face. 'Tell me what's on these alleged disks.'

Laura shook her head. 'I don't know. I was retrieving my laptop so we could read them when I was apprehended.'

Toulemonde glanced across at Madison. 'Is it possible? Could Borkov have done such a ridiculous thing?'

Madison scowled thoughtfully. 'He's been under a lot of pressure lately, but what's the point? He knows he could never threaten us with these disks. No, I don't believe it. It's too far-fetched.'

Toulemonde smiled sadly. 'I'm sorry, Laura. Your little scheme won't wash.'

'What if I could prove it was true? What then?'

'Then I would reconsider my position, but I don't see how you can prove it.'

'I can prove it, but before I do I want you to agree to my list of demands.'

Madison grabbed the front of Laura's coat and twisted it in his left fist. 'Fucking demands? I'll give you fucking demands.' He turned beseechingly to Toulemonde. 'Let me have this bitch for half an hour. She's absolutely begging for it.'

'You're too impetuous, Michael.' Toulemonde sounded tired. 'What if she is telling us the truth? How do we make a trade if you've damaged her?'

Madison looked surprised. 'We'll make her tell us where the disks are, of course.'

'Somehow I think the little birds will have flown the coop and taken the disks with them long before we arrive. Don't you agree, Laura?'

Laura nodded eagerly. She was breathing in shallow gasps. 'I can get the disks for you, but first you must agree to my conditions.' She sounded like she had asthma.

'Let's pretend these disks do exist,' replied Toulemonde calmly. 'I imagine one of your conditions would be your safe return to the welcoming bosoms of your friends. Is that not so?'

Laura looked at him hopefully. 'Yes.'

'How far away is your current base of operations?'

Laura considered the question but couldn't see any danger in answering. 'I'm not sure about the distance, but it usually takes an hour to get here.'

Toulemonde nodded thoughtfully. 'And what else would you require?'

'We're going to need money. The only way my friends and I will be safe is to start a new life in a different country and forget we ever heard about Memtech.'

'I see. How much will you need to feather your future?'

'I haven't really thought about it, but half a million pounds should be sufficient.'

'Half a million pounds?' sneered Madison. 'Pull the other one.'

'The disks are worth a hundred times that amount to you,' argued Laura. 'Half a million pounds is a bargain.'

'Assuming the disks actually exist,' murmured Toulemonde. 'I believe you said something about proving their existence?'

Laura glanced quickly around the room. 'Where's my bag?'

'You don't need to worry about your bag, Laura, it's quite safe,' replied Toulemonde impatiently.

'My phone is in the bag,' Laura explained patiently, 'and my boyfriend's number is in the phone. If you call him, he'll confirm the existence of the disks, and you can arrange a swap.'

Madison grunted in annoyance. 'I'm sure he'll say anything to gain your freedom. You probably cooked up this story in case you ended up in our hands.'

'Possible, but not probable,' replied Toulemonde. 'However, collusion is a risk I'm willing to take. Please fetch Miss Monroe's phone.'

Madison bristled at the order but did as he was told, thrusting the phone at her when he returned. 'Call your fucking boyfriend.' He snapped the words at her, and she knew what to expect if he ever got his hands on her.

'For your sake, I hope you're not bluffing,' warned Toulemonde. 'You call, but I'll do the talking.'

Laura rang Jordan's number and then handed the phone to Toulemonde. He stared intently at Laura as the phone continued to ring; then a muffled voice answered, shouting her name.

Toulemonde winked at Laura before answering. 'I'm afraid not,' he replied smoothly.

'Who are you?' demanded the voice belligerently. 'What have you done with Laura?'

'We'll get to that in a moment,' said Toulemonde as he continued to stare at Laura. 'First I need to know who you are.'

'What's it to you?' replied Jordan obstinately.

'Dear me, I'm afraid that wasn't the answer Miss Monroe was hoping for. Let's call that strike one. Now if you want to see your lovely Laura again, I advise you to answer my questions accurately, succinctly, and promptly. If we get to strike three,

I'm afraid Miss Monroe will only be a memory, if you follow my drift.'

There was silence as Jordan struggled to control his emotions. He didn't want to give the psychopath holding Laura any excuse to hurt her. 'My name is Daniel Jordan. How do I know Laura's okay? Let me speak to her.'

'You don't, and the answer's no,' said Toulemonde. 'That's strike two, because I don't recall giving you permission to ask any questions. Your impetuosity is placing Laura's life in grave jeopardy. I'm calling you as a favour to her, but it seems her faith in you has been sadly misplaced. Now do not risk her life by asking any more foolish questions. Just listen carefully and answer my questions truthfully. One more mistake and it's all over. Do you understand?'

'Yes,' replied Jordan sullenly. The others were crowded around him demanding to know what was happening, and he fiercely waved them to silence.

'Excellent,' replied Toulemonde. 'Did you collect something interesting tonight?'

'Yes.'

'Tell me what it was.'

Jordan hesitated, not sure how much to tell him. 'We picked up some computer disks,' he said finally.

'I'm afraid you haven't taken me seriously,' chided Toulemonde. 'While you may have told the truth, you chose not to answer immediately. This implies you were considering lying to me. You only have yourself to blame for Laura's fate. Goodbye.'

He disconnected the call and raised a questioning eyebrow at Laura. 'Is your boyfriend usually this dim-witted?'

Laura was staring at the phone. 'He was telling the truth,' she said desperately.

'Yes, but he was telling me the truth on his terms.' The phone began to ring, and he disconnected the call. 'Daniel must tell me the truth on my terms, so I'm conditioning him so he understands.' Toulemonde casually pressed the redial button.

Jordan answered immediately. 'Yes?' He sounded breathless.

'Laura has begged me to give you one more chance, and being a soft touch, I agreed. However, if we fail to reach agreement, I have promised her to some people who are looking forward to spending time with her. Is there anything you wish to say about that?'

'No.'

'Very good, now no more slip-ups. Who created the disks?'

'Dr Borkov,' replied Jordan quickly. 'To the best of our knowledge,' he added as an afterthought.

'That's the spirit,' replied Toulemonde encouragingly. 'How many disks are there?'

'Three.'

'Have you copied them?'

'No.'

'Don't lie to me, Daniel,' warned Toulemonde ominously.

'I'm not lying. We haven't copied them.'

'Why not?' persisted Toulemonde. 'Surely that would be the first thing to do.'

'We haven't even had a chance to look at them yet. Laura went to fetch her laptop, and that's as far as we've got.'

'Fortunately for you that agrees with what Laura has already told us,' conceded Toulemonde. 'How did you get them? I'm sure Dr Borkov didn't just leave them lying around.'

'We followed Borkov to a rendezvous he had arranged. We waited until he handed the disks to his colleague and then followed up with an offer his friend was unable to refuse.'

'Ah, humour in adversity, how very English. How did you know about the rendezvous?'

'We bugged the phone in his office.'

'Of course you did. That little episode in the basement suddenly makes sense.' Toulemonde glanced in annoyance at Madison. 'Cretin,' he muttered darkly.

'Pardon?' said Jordan, a touch of panic in his voice. 'I didn't catch that.'

'It was nothing,' replied Toulemonde smoothly. 'I should be thanking you for bringing these disks to light. How long will it take to bring them to our gatehouse?'

Daniel knew they needed time to copy the disks. 'Just under an hour, depending upon the traffic.'

'Once again your facts agree with Laura's. You have forty-five minutes, and the clock starts ticking once I hang up. I think a speeding ticket would be the least of your concerns, so don't be late,' warned Toulemonde as he terminated the connection.

Madison frowned thoughtfully. 'So the disks do exist.'

'It would appear that way.'

Madison shook his head. 'That stupid puffed-up old bastard. What the hell was he thinking? Do you want me to bring him in?'

'No, not yet, let's see what's on these disks first. They may contain nothing more than his favourite poetry. Borkov's still a valuable member of this organization, so there's no point upsetting him over nothing. Time is on our side, so we can afford to wait.' He turned back to Laura.

'It seems you have gained a temporary reprieve. I'll have somebody bring in your clothes, and we'll decide what to do next.'

'What about Colin?' asked Laura.

'The imbecile that turned you in?' snorted Madison. 'He's safe enough for the moment. We started to question him, and he passed out. He's worthless to us, so if you want him he's all yours.'

'Fetch him now,' said Toulemonde, 'and I'll come with you. There are several things I need to discuss, and we can talk on the way.' He smiled at Laura. 'Please make yourself comfortable, and somebody will bring you your belongings shortly.'

'Are you really going to let her go?' asked Madison as they strode down the corridor.

'If the disks are genuine, I'll have no choice.'

'I don't like it,' muttered Madison darkly. 'She knows too much.'

'You needn't worry. I have a little surprise for the lovely Laura.' They unlocked the door to the storeroom, where Tweddle had been unceremoniously dumped. He was slumped in the corner, oblivious to the world.

'What a wimp.' Madison prodded him with his boot. 'I didn't even touch him, and he passed out.' He bent down and slapped him roughly on the face. 'Come on, wake up!' Tweddle stirred slightly but his eyes remained firmly closed. Madison turned back to Toulemonde. 'What surprise do you have in mind for Laura?'

'Are you aware Dr Ridgeway has been working on an enzyme to destroy implanted memory?'

Madison shrugged. 'I heard you mention it before.'

'Her team has developed an enzyme that will lie dormant in the brain for twenty-four hours and then activate itself and start destroying strings of chemical memory.'

Madison looked closely at Toulemonde. 'That sounds very good, but I feel there's a "but" coming.'

Toulemonde nodded. 'Unfortunately, there are still significant flaws to be ironed out. The enzyme doesn't stop once it has destroyed the donated memory. It continues to search out and destroy any memory it finds. We've had to dispose of a few homeless guinea pigs because of it.'

'It's a clever solution,' observed Madison.

'I like it. We get the disks and they get Laura, but she'll never be a threat to us.'

'What about Banks?'

'I'll leave that up to you. Once we've got the disks, he's fair game. That goes for all of them so I want you to ensure they receive a warm welcome.' He gestured at Tweddle, who still hadn't stirred. 'This idiot may be harmless but he's a loose thread, so tell Dr. Ridgeway to inject him as well.'

'Leave it to me, boss. I'll arrange a special welcome they won't forget in a hurry.' He pulled a worn mop from a metal bucket and up-ended the bucket's dirty dregs over Tweddle, who spluttered awake. Madison kicked him savagely in the thigh and dragged him to his feet. 'Get moving, scumbag, I'm in a hurry.'

~

Banks was also in a hurry. He wanted to capitalize on the time Jordan had bought for them. Doris had hunted down several blank disks, and they made two copies of the originals and then backed them up on the hard drive. Evans had spoken to Banks and was hurrying to meet up with Jane. The office building roof would make an excellent observation point to oversee proceedings.

Doris had volunteered to drive Tracey around the East End and find a new residence for the group. Banks had politely refused her offer that they stay with her. She was a vital link in their chain of communication, and they couldn't run the risk of compromising her position.

Kilpatrick had confirmed that Laura was not at work. He had found her abandoned car in the underground car park and had suggested that she may have gone looking for assistance to replace a flat tyre. Banks had updated him with the latest news and instructed him to return home and pack as many items of value that he could squeeze into the saddle pack on his motorbike. He warned him to take care, as Laura might already have revealed their location to Memtech.

Jordan was anxious to be off and fidgeted incessantly as he waited for Banks to finish talking to Kilpatrick. 'If we don't get a move on we're going to be late,' he snapped as Banks ended the call.

Banks smiled reassuringly. 'Memtech's not far from here, so we have plenty of time. Being early will be worse than being late, as they'll know we've been less than truthful.'

Jordan slumped back into his chair and banged on the table in frustration. 'Fucking goddamn Memtech,' he swore savagely. 'At some point they're going to pay for this.'

Banks popped the Beretta's magazine clip, cast an expert eye over it, and then snapped it back in place with a satisfied grunt. 'Okay, let's fetch Laura.'

The traffic was surprisingly light, and they made excellent time. Jordan was lost in thought as they drove through the city. A passing shower of rain gave the streets a cold, reflective sheen as he stared absently at the passing traffic. He had never doubted that he would spend the rest of his life with Laura, but his mind was now filled with gloomy, depressing thoughts. Despite the numbing darkness invading his soul, he found he was still unable to offer up a prayer and ask for divine intervention. 'So be it,' he muttered resolutely. If he was unable to find faith during the darkest moment in his life, then he was destined to never believe.

The rain had cleared by the time they arrived, and Banks turned the car around and reversed up the driveway, leaving the engine running. 'Leave your door open when you get out,' he instructed Jordan. 'We might need to make a quick exit.'

They walked around the gentle curve in the driveway, and Banks tucked the Berretta into his waistband as they approached the gatehouse. Low, scudding clouds swept overhead, and Jordan was acutely aware of the cold wind whipping around his face. He felt disorientated, and the small stones crunching beneath his feet heightened the sense of surrealism.

A gruff voice commanded them to stop, and they were immediately illuminated by the harsh glare of a powerful spotlight. They instinctively shaded their eyes but were unable to see through the dazzling glare. 'Stay right there, Banks,' snarled the voice. 'The boyfriend can bring the disks by himself. He doesn't need you to hold his hand.'

Banks averted his gaze before the spotlight totally destroyed his night vision, and he pulled a disk from his pocket. 'Tell them they can have this as a show of good faith.' He thrust his face closer to Jordan's. 'But make it very clear that they don't get the other two until we have Laura. Very clear, you understand? This is non-negotiable.'

The disembodied voice floated out of the darkness, annoyed at the delay. 'Get a move on, lover boy. We ain't got all fucking night.'

'Non-negotiable,' repeated Banks.

Jordan began groping his way forward, squinting through slitted eyes to minimize the effects of the glare. He stopped momentarily, unsure of his next steps. 'Would you mind turning off the light?' he called. 'I can't see a damn thing.'

'Tough shit,' laughed the voice. 'Keep walking straight ahead. You're doing fine.'

Jordan took a tentative step and banged his knee painfully against the concrete post supporting the boom gate. He stepped beyond the spotlight's beam and stopped to refocus his eyes, but the bright light had rendered him virtually blind. A dim light shone through the gatehouse window, but he was unable to discern anything else. He heard a footstep next to him and rough hands suddenly frisked his body; he stood completely still until they had finished.

'Satisfied?' he asked as the hands finally withdrew.

A breath of malodorous air assaulted his nostrils and a voice hissed in his ear. 'Where are the disks?'

Jordan peered at the shadowy figure. 'Where's Laura?'

'You'll see her soon enough.'

Another dark figure was also watching him. DeLuca lay prone on the roof of the Memtech building, adjusting the sights on his rifle until they were centred on the chest of his target. The man looked familiar, but he couldn't place him. The stark shadows distorted the man's features, denying him immediate recognition, but DeLuca knew it would come to him. His orders were to wait until the exchange took place and then eliminate Banks. He could then pick off the others at his discretion. The girl, however, was not to be harmed as Madison had other plans for her.

He moved the sights up to the man's forehead and imagined himself squeezing the trigger. 'Bang, you're dead,' he whispered as he smiled thinly into the darkness. He returned the sights to Banks and readjusted the focus. Banks made a perfect target standing in the circle of light. He itched to pull the trigger but was powerless to do so until he received the signal from Madison. He was wearing a radio headset linked to Madison and could hear everything spoken in Madison's immediate vicinity. A low concrete sill ran around the perimeter of the roof, shielding DeLuca from the worst effects of the chilling wind. It also served as a rest for his rifle, ensuring he would not miss when the time came.

He was dressed completely in black with blacking smeared over his face and knew he would be invisible to an observer on the Memtech grounds. Banks and his buddies would never know what hit them. He smiled in anticipation as he patiently waited.

Evans had also found a comfortable position on the roof of the office block and was methodically scanning the windows of the building opposite for telltale signs of a sniper. The bright spotlight above the gatehouse had destroyed the effectiveness of his night-vision goggles, and the streetlight to his immediate right was under-lighting his position. He continued his slow search, but without the goggles he was unable to detect any signs of danger. Jane had been waiting for him when he arrived, and he instructed her to load her gear into his car and then meet him on the roof.

It took Jane several trips to complete her task. The bleak wind bit into her body when she finally emerged on the rooftop, and she crouched behind an air vent while she searched the roofline for Banks's partner. A low whistle attracted her attention, and she hurried over to join Evans, who was hunkered down behind the corner of an advertising billboard. He handed her a thick coat, and she put it on gratefully, surprised at the thoughtfulness of his planning. He watched her struggle into the coat and then handed her a radio scanner and a battered headset. 'Do you know how to use one of these?'

She shook her head. 'I don't even know what it is.'

'It's a scanner. If they're planning anything nasty over there, they'll need to keep in touch by short frequency radio. It's difficult enough coordinating an operation in broad daylight, but in the dark it's almost impossible without radio contact. All you need to do is put on these headphones, set the frequency to the first one on the dial, and then slowly twiddle this knob. You'll pick up all kinds of chatter, taxi cabs and such, but ignore them and keep tuning. Once you've exhausted that frequency, move on to the next. It's tedious but if we find them it could mean the difference between success and failure.'

She settled down next to him, a grim expression on her face, and began searching.

Jordan was oblivious to these events as he held out the disk, his night vision slowly returning. 'This is the first disk, and you'll get it when I see that Laura is safe.'

'I could kill you and just take it,' sneered Madison.

'That would be a mistake,' replied Jordan in an even voice. 'Can I talk to the person I discussed this with on the phone? He understood the importance of this exchange.'

'A smart arse. Hand over the disk or suffer the consequences,' warned Madison.

'No, I want to see that Laura's safe.'

'Oh for fuck's sake, of course she's safe,' snarled Madison. He raised his voice. 'Bring the bitch to the window so this arse-wipe can see she's alive.'

Laura's shocked and gaunt face was abruptly thrust against the glass and then withdrawn. The fleeting glimpse told him that she was alive but desperately afraid, and he could feel his blood boiling as he handed the disk to Madison.

Madison rapped his knuckles against the glass, the window opened briefly, and the disk was snatched from his outstretched hand. 'Now we wait.'

On the rooftop opposite, Jane stopped scanning. She had already picked up three cabs, an ambulance, and a truck driver but this one sounded much sharper and could hardly be classified as a conversation. 'I thought I heard something,' she said glancing up at Evans, 'but it was only a couple of words and now there's nothing.'

'What did you hear?'

'We wait.'

'Leave the dial where it is for the moment. It's probably nothing, but you never know. Give it a minute, and if there's no further conversation, write down the frequency and move on. You can always check it again later.'

Things were moving quickly in the gatehouse. Toulemonde had loaded the disk and was waiting with Jarvis as the first of the files opened.

'Holy hell,' swore Jarvis as he skimmed through the information. 'This stuff is dynamite. He's got names, dates, everything. If this got into the wrong hands, we'd be finished.' He jabbed an urgent finger at the screen. 'Open the next one.'

'This is even worse,' muttered Toulemonde. 'This traces our financial contributions. He has outlined the amounts, dates, and sources along with the relevant account numbers.'

'Let me see,' exclaimed Jarvis as he thrust his head closer to the screen, frantically searching for evidence that his department had been compromised. He abruptly froze in horror when he saw his name against several large sums of money. Any competent auditor would be able to follow the money trail through Jarvis to his department and then to the government. 'This is a disaster,' he moaned as he glanced at Toulemonde, his face looking distinctly pale in the muted lighting. 'These people cannot leave here,' he said urgently.

'Please calm yourself,' replied Toulemonde. 'Everything has been taken care of.'

'But they may have made copies. We need to deal with them while we have the chance. We may not get another opportunity.'

Toulemonde smiled complacently, his thin lips almost disappearing. 'There are no copies. I have already made sure of that. Once they hand over the originals, this threat will have passed.'

Jarvis gestured towards Laura and Tweddle, who were sitting silently by the far wall, thick black bags over their heads. 'What about them? They could identify us. They must be dealt with as well.'

Toulemonde clasped Jarvis on the shoulder. 'Don't distress yourself over minor matters, my friend. I assure you, everything has been taken care of. Borkov has done us a favour by flushing out these vermin.'

'Ah yes, Borkov,' spat Jarvis. 'What do you plan to do about him?'

'He's still an important asset, so we need to give the matter some thought.' He scratched his thinning hair. 'I'm looking forward to discovering how he intended to carry this out, but we need to finish this business first.' He tapped on the window and gave Madison the thumbs up.

Madison nodded and leered at Jordan. 'It looks like your information passed inspection. Too bad, I was hoping to spend some quality time with your stuck-up bitch. Still, the night is young, and who knows what might happen.' He grinned and licked his lips suggestively but Jordan refused to be baited, staring back impassively. Madison's grin turned into a snarl. 'So if you want your snotty bitch back you'd better hand over the other disks, otherwise I'll simply come and take them and you'll end up with bugger all.'

'Nothing doing. Hand over Laura, and then I'll give you the disks.'

Madison stared back and then shrugged dismissively. 'Fine, have it your way.' He tapped on the window and instructed his assistants to bring out the captives. Jordan waited patiently as a guard appeared, holding Laura firmly by the arm. She now had a bag tied over her head, and her hands were secured behind her. She stumbled slightly as the guard pushed her towards Jordan, and he caught her before she could fall. She was sobbing quietly, and he began to untie the bag but Madison ordered him to stop. 'You can untie her when we've got the disks. Anyway, we've got another present for you.' A heavyset guard rounded the corner with Tweddle in tow, the bag over his head disguising his features.

'What do you mean, somebody else?' queried Jordan, momentarily confused. His first thought was that they had captured Matt Kilpatrick but the figure being dragged towards him was too short.

'It's Colin,' replied Laura, her voice muffled by the bag. 'They picked him up when they kidnapped me.'

'Colin Tweddle? How did he get involved in this?' asked Jordan irritably.

Laura sighed. 'It's a long story.'

'I bet it is.' Jordan held out an arm to prevent Tweddle from lurching into Laura.

Madison interrupted them. 'You can save the lover's chitchat for later. We've delivered our end of the bargain, so now it's your turn.'

Jordan turned and waved to Banks, unaware that the glare from the lights prevented Banks from seeing him.

Madison didn't appreciate the gesture, suspecting it signalled the launch of an attack, and he thrust his pistol towards Jordan's suddenly anxious face. 'What the fuck do you think you're doing?'

DeLuca immediately zeroed his sights onto Jordan, his finger tightening on the trigger as he reacted to the tone of Madison's voice.

Jane picked up the conversation on the scanner and immediately handed the headphones to Evans. 'It's them,' she whispered.

Evans listened anxiously to Madison's angry voice but was unable to see anybody apart from Banks, who was silhouetted in the bright light. He considered shooting out the spotlight but decided to wait a little longer.

Jordan hurriedly took a step back to avoid being struck by Madison's gun. 'Hey, take it easy. Inspector Banks has the remaining disks, and I was signalling for him to bring them to you.'

Madison stared fiercely at Jordan before lowering his gun and swinging it in a small arc so that it pointed at Laura. 'That's not going to happen. Banks will stay right where he is. You can fetch them.'

Jordan glanced worriedly at Laura, not wanting to leave her. 'What are you waiting for, a written invitation?' barked Madison. 'These two will be safe until you return.'

Laura began shivering uncontrollably, and Jordan put his arm around her. 'I'll take Laura with me and leave Colin as collateral.'

'Nice try, dickwad,' jeered Madison as he held the gun to Laura's head. 'I wasn't born yesterday. You can take your useless buddy, but the girl stays here until I have the disks.'

It wasn't the concession Jordan was hoping for but it was a step in the right direction. 'I'll be right back,' he murmured encouragingly to Laura and marched a strangely silent Tweddle back through the bright light to Banks.

'That's not Laura!' exclaimed Banks as he peered at the dark figure coming towards him.

'It's our friend Tweddle,' commented Jordan derisively. 'Somehow he's managed to get himself mixed up in this, and we've had to save his sorry arse yet again.'

Banks turned Tweddle around and untied his hands. 'So where's Laura?'

'She's with one of their henchmen. She'll be free to leave when I hand over the disks.'

'Don't bet on it,' snorted Banks as he gave Jordan the remaining disks. 'There are no rules in this game. I have an ominous feeling they're planning something nasty. As they're holding the whip hand there's not much we can do about it, but if push comes to shove, don't hang about being heroic. Grab Laura and race for the car. Don't run in a straight line and don't wait for me. If I'm not there, just take off. I can look after myself.'

Jordan nodded automatically. 'Gotcha. Race for the car and take off. I can do that.'

He shielded his eyes from the light and retraced his steps, being careful not to bump into the boom gate. He stepped past the spotlight's beam and found Madison still holding his gun against Laura's head. 'There's no need for that,' Jordan said softly. 'I've got the remaining disks.'

'You can never be too careful,' replied Madison as he gestured for the disks. 'You know the routine. We'll verify the disks; then you can have the girl.'

'How do I know I can trust you?'

Madison laughed scornfully. 'A bit late to be asking that, isn't it? Just do what you're told, and everything will be fine. We're not going to start shooting people on our front doorstep and have the police and a bunch of nosy reporters asking awkward questions. Give us some credit for intelligence. You people are nothing without these disks, so hand them over so I can get out of this fucking cold.' He pushed Laura across to Jordan. 'Here, take her, and let's get on with it.'

Jordan wrapped a protective arm around Laura as she stumbled into him, and then he held out the disks. Madison snatched them and tapped against the window. 'You've got what you wanted,' said Jordan, trying to keep his voice firm, 'so now we're done. I'm taking Laura home.'

'You're not a quick learner, are you?' sneered Madison as he swung his gun onto Jordan. 'You're not going anywhere until these have been verified.'

Banks had eased himself out of the spotlight's glare and was now able to see Jordan, Laura, and Madison standing behind the boom gate. His eyes hadn't fully recovered, but the light spilling from the gatehouse illuminated the group sufficiently for Banks to understand what was happening. He had seen Jordan hand over the disks and had then watched in horror as the guard raised his weapon and pointed it at Jordan. He tugged the Berretta free from his waistband and flipped off the safety.

He could usually tell a person's intentions by watching their eyes but the darkness made it impossible. He took a couple of steps into the shadows and aimed the small gun at the guard, confident of hitting him but worried about the gun's stopping power. Jordan thrust Laura behind him, away from Madison's gun but the movement obscured Banks's line of fire, and he was forced to retrace his steps to improve the angle.

DeLuca had watched apprehensively as Banks drifted into the shadows. He still had him centred in his sights but was now aiming at his dark outline, and he was worried that if Madison didn't give the order soon, his target might disappear. Banks suddenly moved back into the light, but DeLuca's relieved smile was wiped from his face as saw the gun in Banks's outstretched hand. He instinctively squeezed off a shot and grunted in satisfaction as Banks was violently thrown back, the gun flying from his hand. An instant later the spotlight was extinguished, leaving the dull light from the gatehouse as the only source of illumination.

Jane heard the gunshot as the sound cracked across the parking lot and saw Banks thrown bodily to the ground. She instantly turned to Evans, anguish written over her features. Evans reacted by shooting out the spotlight and then snuffing out the streetlight below them, the silenced weapon sounding like a door slamming. The light spilling from the guardhouse was abruptly extinguished with the only remaining light coming from the interior of the car parked in the driveway. Jane gave a despairing cry as she leapt to her feet and ran back to the stairwell. Evans called out to her, but Jane ignored him as she hurried down the stairs and out into the street. Thoughts of her safety were the last thing on her mind. Banks had saved her life, and it was time to repay the debt.

Evans cursed softly and hastily tugged on his night vision goggles. A flare on the rooftop of the building opposite was immediately followed by another loud report. Evans toggled his gun to semi-automatic and replied with a hose of staccato fire.

DeLuca was instantly sprayed with a shower of concrete shards. He flattened himself against the floor as he heard several bullets whine harmlessly overhead. A powerful sledgehammer smacked into his left buttock and he cried out in agony as the pain coursed through his body. As suddenly as it started, the attack stopped, leaving DeLuca shaken and bleeding. He dared not raise his head in case the movement triggered another burst of fire. He could feel a warm pool of blood gathering around his body but wasn't sure how badly he was bleeding. Banks obviously had an accomplice on the building opposite, and it was short odds that the gunman was watching for further signs of movement.

He forced himself to relax and, as if in response, his brain suddenly supplied him with the information he had been seeking earlier. The man by the gatehouse was the same one who had killed Dawson, the same person he had vowed to destroy. He had expected the car bomb to do the trick, but now the means for revenge would be far more personal.

He decided to worm his way to a new position and give himself the chance of another shot. If he could get under cover, he could also stem the flow of blood and bandage his wound. He inched slowly around, steeling himself for another hail of bullets, and began crawling towards a nearby air vent. The pain in his buttocks as he pushed forward with his left leg was severe, with the exertion causing his wound to bleed more freely.

Beads of sweat broke out on his brow despite the cold, and the loss of blood was making him feel dizzy. He knew he had to staunch the flow soon if he was to survive the night. He slid his rifle across the rooftop and crawled quickly after it, taking a calculated chance that his enemy could no longer see him. As he reached the safety of the air vent, he took out his knife and began fashioning a makeshift bandage from strips of his shirt.

Both Jordan and Madison were momentarily stunned when the first shot had rung out, and Laura, fearing the worst, had emitted a muffled scream. Jordan reacted first, his karate training giving him a split second edge over Madison, who always used underlings for the close and personal work. Jordan chopped the inside of Madison's wrist so that his gun was no longer pointing in their direction and then followed with his favourite disabling technique, a savage upward kick to the groin, his foot flattened to maximize the impact area.

Madison was in good physical condition and responded quickly, instinctively pushing down with his hands to stop the impending impact. It made little difference. The explosive kick burst between his hands and crashed into his unprotected groin, the butt of his pistol striking Jordan a painful blow on the ankle as it was ripped from Madison's fingers. Madison made a faint gagging noise as he doubled over. Jordan stepped in and delivered a double-fisted blow to the back of his head, raising his knee into his opponent's face as he did so.

He didn't wait to see the result of his handiwork. He grabbed Laura around the waist and hurried her down the driveway, jerking the bag off her head as he did so. Her hands were still tied behind her back, making it difficult for her to run, but Jordan forced her on, acutely aware that either of them might receive a bullet in the back at any moment. As he reached the car, he desperately pushed Laura into the passenger seat and shut the door behind her, unaware that Banks had been shot.

Despite Banks's instructions to leave him behind if necessary, Jordan was loath to do so, particularly now events had gone amiss. He slid into the driver's seat and reached across and untied Laura's hands, telling her to scrunch down so she would not make an obvious target. Banks had still not turned up, and Jordan honked the horn in exasperation. A grey figure loomed out of the darkness, and Laura stifled an involuntary gasp, cut short when she recognized Jane's gaunt face.

'Robert's been hit,' Jane said breathlessly as she tugged the door open. 'I saw him go down. I'll need your help to get him back to the car.' She didn't wait for an answer and went running into the darkness calling Robert's name.

'Wait here,' commanded Jordan gruffly before hurrying after Jane, cursing Banks for having the temerity to be shot. A toneless grunting attracted his attention, and he slowed and cautiously approached the sound. He found Tweddle, dragging Banks by the armpits.

'Could you give me a hand?' gasped Tweddle. 'This chap weighs a tonne, and those goons will soon be all over us. One of them ran past a moment ago.'

'That was Jane,' replied Jordan as he bent down and hoisted Banks over his shoulder. He threw caution to the wind and loudly called Jane's name. Speed was of the essence. His voice carried on the night breeze, and Jane joined them as they hurried back to the car.

The sound also carried as far as DeLuca, and he nodded grimly as he recognized Jordan's voice. He hefted his rifle and edged his way around the corner of the air vent, focusing on the lights of the car and centring his sights on the figure sitting in the front passenger seat. 'That's probably Jordan's bitch,' he muttered as he considered splattering her brains over the inside of the windscreen. He took up the slack on the trigger and then checked his anger. Madison had given clear instructions that she wasn't to be harmed, and besides, it was the man he was after. She was obviously waiting for him, so it was just a matter of being patient. A movement at the rear of the car drew his attention. He struggled forward and swung the telescopic sight down to focus on the small cluster of people struggling to manoeuvre a limp figure onto the back seat. As Jordan straightened up, DeLuca crowed in triumph as he recognized his enemy and set the crosshairs directly between Jordan's eyes.

'This is for Dawson,' he whispered as he squeezed the trigger.

Chapter 16

The young have aspirations that never come to pass,
the old have reminiscences of what never happened.

Robert Burns

Evans watched the gunman's image edge out from the protection of the building. He had a reasonable shot but decided to wait a moment longer to see if his target became more presentable. He was aware of other images moving in the foreground but concentrated his attention on the gunman. His target suddenly moved forward, and Evans fired off two rapid shots. The first one found its target just as DeLuca squeezed his own trigger, the bullet drilling a neat hole in his forehead and jerking his rifle marginally off line. DeLuca was already dead when the second bullet crashed into his left eye.

Jordan jumped in fright as a bullet smashed through the window of the door he was holding. 'Bloody hell!' he shouted. 'Get in the car, quickly, we're under fire.' Jordan flung himself into the driver's seat and had the car screeching down the driveway before he bothered to pull his door shut. 'How are things in the back?' he yelled as he fishtailed onto the roadway, narrowly missing a parked car. He hurriedly signalled to Evans by flashing his lights before roaring off to the nearby intersection. Evans watched the car until it was out of sight before methodically repacking his equipment, ducking down the stairs, and disappearing into the night.

∾

Jane sat on the back seat of the car with Robert's head on her lap, oblivious to the blood seeping into her clothing. She had torn ragged strips off her dress and wadded them against the wound in an attempt to stop the bleeding. The bullet had smashed into his chest below the collarbone and exited under his armpit. Tweddle was slumped next to her, his eyes wide and staring. Jane shook her head despairingly. 'We've got to get Robert to a hospital. I've stemmed the bleeding, but he's already lost a lot of blood, and God only knows what internal damage he's suffered.'

Banks had been drifting in and out of consciousness and made an effort to sit up as Jane spoke. 'No hospitals,' he protested feebly, his voice thick with pain but quite coherent.

Jane pushed him gently down. 'Hush, Robert, lie still. We're doing what's best for you. Without proper care you could die.'

'I'll be dead either way. A lose-lose situation.' His brief laugh quickly turned into a coughing fit.

'What did he say?' asked Jordan. 'I couldn't hear the last bit.'

'He doesn't want to go to hospital,' repeated Laura. 'I think he shares your phobia.'

'We haven't got a choice,' replied Jordan loudly. 'We've got copies of the disks so that should clear the inspector's name, and Jane can vouch that she wasn't kidnapped.'

Laura swung around to face him. 'You've got copies of the disks?'

'I'll explain later,' he said softly.

'No hospital,' repeated Banks as he struggled to sit up once more.

'Please, Robert, lie still,' implored Jane. 'Hospital's the only option.'

'No, it isn't,' replied Banks doggedly. He could feel himself passing out again, and his ability to speak was rapidly diminishing. 'Take me to the White Stag Hotel. Frank will know what to do.' His words tailed off in a slur as he slumped down into Jane's lap.

'No!' Tweddle suddenly blurted. 'I must get to a hospital immediately; Laura too for that matter.'

'Me?' asked Laura in surprise. 'I'm a bit shaken up, but I'll be fine.'

'You don't understand,' replied Tweddle desperately. 'I overheard them talking when I was locked up. They thought I was unconscious, but I was only feigning so they wouldn't torture me anymore.' Jane gave a sympathetic gasp, but Tweddle ignored her and ploughed on. 'One of the men was concerned we'd be a threat if we were released, but the one with a French accent just laughed and said they've invented a drug that can erase memories and they intended to inject it into us so we'd become virtual vegetables.'

Jordan swung around and faced Laura, his face etched with lines of concern. 'Is this true?'

She nodded slowly, her eyes suddenly wide with fear. 'They told me it was only a mild sedative, so I wouldn't become hysterical during the exchange.' She started sobbing as her remaining defences crumbled. 'I'm just so sick and tired of this. Perhaps having my memories deleted is a good thing. Maybe then I'll be left in peace.'

Jordan slammed his fist against the steering wheel. 'Well that's not going to bloody happen.'

'That's why we have to get to a hospital,' insisted Tweddle. 'They'll know what to do. They can inject us with something to reverse the process.'

'It could be too late already,' replied Laura softly. 'Our memories are probably being eaten away while we speak.'

Tweddle shook his head. 'Oh no, that's not true. The Frenchman said the drug wouldn't activate for twenty-four hours. That's why I allowed them to inject me. I knew they'd kill me if I didn't, and I thought twenty-four hours was plenty of time to get to a hospital.'

'That doesn't make any sense,' said Jane. 'What's the point in waiting?'

'That's what he said,' replied Tweddle forcefully. 'I wasn't in a position to seek clarification.' He looked out the window at the passing buildings. 'There's a hospital not far from here if you turn right into Fulham Road.'

'I appreciate your concern,' replied Jordan, 'but I'm not taking Laura to a hospital.'

'How can you be so damned selfish?' cried Tweddle as he leant across and glared angrily at Jordan. 'Maybe you don't give a damn about me, but what about Laura? Concern for your own safety should be the last thing on your mind.'

Jane pushed Tweddle away from her. 'If you calm down you'll realize Daniel is correct. Taking you to a hospital is pointless. All they could do is care for you while the situation deteriorated. It would take months to develop an antidote. I'm afraid the only people who can reverse the process are the same people who injected you.' She leant forward and touched Laura. 'Sorry, but sometimes it's necessary to be blunt in order to reach a quick decision.'

'No, that's fine,' murmured Laura. 'I'm just numb at the moment. I don't know what to think.'

'Well, I do,' said Tweddle. 'If Jane's correct then we have to go back and insist that these people neutralize the drug.'

'And how are we going to do that, Einstein?' sneered Jordan. 'We barely escaped from that place alive. Going back would be tantamount to suicide.'

Tweddle frowned as he slumped back in his seat. 'So you're happy to let our memories rot away and do nothing about it.'

'Do you mind?' Laura interjected sharply. 'I'm scared enough as it is without you two scoring points off each other.' She twisted in her seat. 'Is Robert awake? He'll know what to do.'

'Yes, I'm still conscious,' muttered Banks. 'How can anybody sleep with that racket going on?' He put his hand on Jane's knee. 'Help me sit up.'

'Do you think it's wise?'

'God damn it! Of course it's not wise, but I can't think straight lying down, and by the sound of it, if somebody doesn't start thinking soon, I'll end up dead, and Laura will spend the rest of her life staring at blank walls. So please, just do it.'

'I was only asking,' replied Jane in a small voice as she helped him up.

The blood immediately drained from his face, and he remained still while he recovered his composure.

'Let me think for a minute,' he said tonelessly as he rested his head against Jane's shoulder. Just when Jane had thought he'd dozed off, he opened his eyes and struggled into an upright position. 'Are we heading for the White Stag?'

'Yes,' replied Jordan, 'but we're still undecided about taking you to a hospital. Jane's stemmed the bleeding, but you've lost a lot of blood, and you'll certainly require surgery.'

'Just do it,' ordered Banks, his voice reflecting the pain he was suffering. 'It's my life, if I'm wrong. Frank has friends who can look after me without the authorities knowing.' His voice faded to a whisper, and he coughed into his handkerchief. When he took the cloth away, Jane noticed in dismay that he had coughed up several large flecks of blood.

Banks momentarily closed his eyes while he waited for the pain to subside. 'We need to act fast if we're going to help Laura. Jane was correct. Memtech has the only people who can fix this, so you need to return and force them to help. Did anybody pick up my gun? I dropped it when I was shot.'

Tweddle shook his head. 'I didn't see it. I was too busy dragging you out of there. Sorry.'

'It's not your fault.' Banks coughed again. 'How much further to the White Stag?' His voice was decidedly weaker.

'About five minutes if the traffic stays the way it is,' replied Jordan.

'All right, listen carefully. I'm confident there's another entrance into the Memtech facility. There's a crematorium at the rear of the building, and I believe they're connected.' Jordan started to ask a question but Banks cut him short. 'Don't interrupt. If you have any questions you'll have to work them out for yourselves.'

Banks began coughing again, and Jane directed an abusive look at Jordan, her eyes furrowed into angry slits. 'Take your time, Robert, nobody will interrupt again.'

'Unfortunately, you can't coerce them with my gun,' he continued, his voice coming in gasps, 'but I have something just as good. Daniel, do you remember the bomb we took out of your car?'

'How could I forget,' replied Jordan as he drove into a side street and parked outside the White Stag.

Banks turned to Jane, and she noticed that his complexion was almost yellow. 'Please fetch Frank while I explain the rest of this.' She patted his hand encouragingly and then clambered out and ran into the hotel. Banks frowned as he gathered his thoughts. 'Where was I?'

'You mentioned a bomb,' replied Laura.

Banks nodded and wiped his mouth. 'I've rewired the bomb and attached an electronic timer. If you can isolate your doctor and wave the bomb under his nose, then he may feel inclined to cooperate.'

'It was a lady,' replied Laura absently.

The back door was wrenched open, and Frank began easing Banks from the car. 'Where's the bomb, and how do we arm it?' yelled Jordan hurriedly as Banks disappeared from view.

'It's with my belongings at the house,' replied Banks with a grimace as Frank dragged his left arm over his shoulder. 'It's very simple, I'm sure you'll work it out.' Jane grabbed his other arm, and they hustled him behind the car and into the hotel.

Jordan gave Laura a tentative smile. 'What do you think?'

Laura faced him, her eyes completely dry and with a look he'd never seen before. 'It's our only hope. If they refuse to help,

I'll blow them all to hell with me. I refuse to live my life as a vegetable.'

Tweddle wasn't impressed by the thought of exploding bombs. 'Are you sure a hospital can't help us?'

'Yes!' replied Laura sharply. 'If you insist on going to hospital, then we'll gladly drop you off, but I'm going back.'

'I was just making sure.' Tweddle did his best to sound aggrieved.

Jane hurried out of the hotel. 'Frank's summoned a doctor, and he'll be here shortly. Robert's going to need someone to change his dressings and look after him so I'm staying until he's over the worst of it.'

'That's very kind of you.' Laura smiled. 'We've decided to return and force the doctor to administer an antidote. Unfortunately the plan involves a great deal of hit and miss, so there's every chance I'll never see you again.' She gave a mirthless laugh. 'Even if I survive, I could still end up a dribbling idiot.'

'Don't even think that,' replied Jane as she bent forward and gave Laura an awkward hug through the window. 'I'm sure everything will turn out just right. Good luck!' She gave a brief wave and disappeared back into the hotel.

'Okay,' said Jordan. 'It's time for action.'

'Do you really think we should be using a bomb?' asked Tweddle. 'They're very unstable, and this one is homemade. What if it goes off prematurely? Some of us could be killed.'

Laura swung around in annoyance. 'If you have a better idea, Colin, then I'll gladly listen, otherwise please shut up. I've put up with your snivelling behaviour because that's what friends do, but your constant moaning is getting on my nerves, and quite frankly I've had enough. The only reason we're in this position is because of your selfish interference, so one more negative word and I'll ask Daniel to stop the car, and I will personally throw you out. I hope I've made myself clear.'

Tweddle sighed dejectedly and settled back in his seat. It was unfair of Laura to pick on him. They were both in the same predicament, so that surely counted for something. It was only because he cared about her that he had called the police. It wasn't his fault that the Memtech thugs had turned up instead. He suddenly leant forward excitedly. 'I know who the mole in the police department is!'

'What are you talking about?' snapped Jordan.

'The mole, I know who he is,' he repeated. 'I spoke to Chief Inspector Fenwick when I found Laura's BMW, and he said he'd send a car around immediately, only it wasn't the police who arrived, was it? Fenwick is the mole.'

'Or somebody connected with him.' Laura's eyes narrowed dangerously. 'You didn't have anything to do with my flat tyre, did you?'

Tweddle made a vague derisive snort. 'Of course not. You may remember, I offered to help you fix it.'

'The whole thing is very suspicious if you ask me,' growled Jordan. 'Every time you appear, things go wrong. You're a regular Jonah.'

Laura gave his thigh a gentle squeeze. 'Let it go. What's done is done, so let's focus on the future.'

'You're right,' agreed Jordan as handed her his phone. 'Call Killa and ask him to meet us at the house. We'll need his help if we're going to pull this off. He knows the layout of the facility better than any of us.'

Kilpatrick was lounging by the front door when they arrived, a pile of bags strewn about him on the front porch. He gave Tweddle a scornful look. 'What's he doing here?'

'It's a long story,' replied Jordan, 'although to be fair, he probably saved Robert's life tonight.'

'Really?' replied Kilpatrick. 'Who'd have believed that? Miracles do happen.' He gestured at the bags on the porch. 'I've packed everything I could find, although Laura should probably do a quick check because I suffer from severe domestic blindness.' Laura gave him a withering look and reappeared several minutes later with an armful of clothing. 'You didn't think to check inside the laundry room?' she asked caustically.

'We have a laundry room?' said Kilpatrick innocently.

'What have you done with the bomb?' Jordan asked cautiously.

Kilpatrick pointed to a grey bag at the end of the porch. 'That's it over there. Whoever's sitting in the back should nurse it so it doesn't get jolted around too much.'

'I guess that'll be you, Colin,' said Jordan. 'Do you think you can handle it?'

'You've underestimated me all along,' replied Tweddle stiffly as he gestured for the bomb. 'Besides, if it does explode, it won't matter where you're sitting, will it?' He gave Jordan a frosty smile as he climbed into the back seat. 'I'm ready when you are.'

'I'll be right with you once I've picked up a couple of things,' replied Jordan. 'If I lost Father O'Brien's book he'd never forgive me.'

They left Kilpatrick's motorbike at a twenty-four-hour car park, and it was after one o'clock in the morning when they arrived outside the crematorium. A light fog had settled over the streets, diffusing the streetlights and muffling the distant traffic noise. They stared around in silence as they contemplated the task ahead of them.

'It's rather dark, isn't it,' said Laura quietly. 'I've never broken into a building before.'

'Just one more crime to add to the charge sheet,' replied Kilpatrick nonchalantly as he flicked on a small torch. 'I'm discovering talents I never knew I had.'

Jordan took a tyre lever from the trunk and smacked it against the palm of his hand. 'I think we might need some assistance breaking into these buildings.'

Kilpatrick looked up and down the deserted street. 'Do you think it's wise leaving the car out the front like this? Shouldn't we park it further away so it doesn't advertise our presence?'

Jordan tossed him the keys. 'Okay, but don't park too far away. We may have to leave in a hurry, and I don't fancy having to sprint any distance with the hounds of hell after me.'

Kilpatrick stared anxiously at the silent building. 'Do you think they've got guard dogs?'

Jordan smiled. 'It's was just an expression. They probably just use a security company that drives around shining their lights everywhere and poking little cards into cracks to show they're on the job.'

Laura stood by the front gates and stared quietly into the crematorium grounds. A concrete birdbath and a worn statue of the Virgin Mary stood off to the left amid several low shrubs, but otherwise the grounds were bare. The front gate was a large wrought iron affair secured by a thick chain and stout padlock. Jordan gave the gate a perfunctory rattle and then stepped back and stared at the fence leading up to it. Kilpatrick appeared out of the shadows a minute later and also tested the gate.

'They don't make them like this anymore,' he observed cheerfully. 'Are you going to use your tyre lever on the chain?'

Jordan shook his head. 'Not much point really, is there? It looks far too strong. I brought the lever along for windows and wooden doors, not monstrosities like this.'

'We'll have to go over then,' said Kilpatrick as he stared at the fence. It was composed of a series of metal poles embedded into a low stone wall and held together by two horizontal metal bars that ran the length of the fence. They were too far apart to act as a step ladder. The top of the fence ended in a series of ornate spikes liberally coated in pigeon excrement.

'I'm not sure I'll be able to make it over the top,' said Laura.

'Of course you can,' replied Jordan encouragingly. 'Between the three of us we should be able to get you up and over.'

'Hang on a minute,' said Kilpatrick. 'I passed something before when I was parking the car. Don't go anywhere.'

He dashed off into the darkness and a minute later they heard a familiar metallic noise as he reappeared pushing a weather-beaten shopping trolley. 'These things turn up in the most unexpected places, although this one may have come here to die.' He tipped the trolley onto its end and leant it against the fence. Jordan quickly swarmed over the fence and jumped lightly to the ground, his feet making a dull sound as they landed on the gravel. Laura slowly followed, making a low grimacing noise as her hands encountered the bird dung. Jordan helped her down, and she walked across to the birdbath and rinsed her hands in the murky water. Kilpatrick took the grey bag from Tweddle and helped him over the fence; then he followed after him, the bag slung across his back.

'How are we going to get out again?' asked Tweddle.

Kilpatrick looked at him disdainfully. 'If we can't find anything to stand on I'll climb the fence and toss the trolley over for you. Okay?'

Tweddle shrugged dispassionately. 'Fine. It just seems to me a little forward planning wouldn't go astray.'

Jordan called from the shadows of the doorway. 'Are you two coming or what? We haven't got all night.' He inserted the tyre lever into the narrow space between the door and the doorjamb, and as he increased the pressure, the woodwork disintegrated, causing several splinters to fly from the edge of the timber. The door, however, refused to budge. 'This is never going to work,' muttered Jordan. 'It looks so easy in films.'

'They've probably got the right equipment,' said Laura. 'Why don't you try the window over there? It doesn't look as though it'll put up much resistance.'

A car drove slowly past as she spoke, and they flattened themselves against the building until it had gone.

'We need to get inside,' said Kilpatrick urgently. 'We'll be spotted if we stay out here much longer. Do what Laura says and give the window a try.'

Jordan crept along the side of the building and inserted the lever under the window and then pushed down, gradually applying more pressure. There was a harsh grating noise and the entire window collapsed in on itself and fell from the building with a resounding crash, spraying broken glass everywhere. They immediately froze, listening for signs that the noise had been overheard. A nearby dog began barking urgently, and there was an angry shout followed by a loud yelp.

'That worked well,' observed Kilpatrick as he stepped over the broken window frame and peered into the building.

Jordan scraped away the bits of broken glass and climbed cautiously inside and then helped Laura clamber through. The noise was quite loud, and Jordan was sure somebody would raise the alarm but the night remained undisturbed. Tweddle was the last to climb through, his feet grinding the shards of glass into smaller pieces as he stepped up to the window.

'Turn on your torch,' whispered Jordan. 'I can't see a damn thing in here.'

'What's that strange smell?' asked Laura.

'It's probably formaldehyde,' replied Tweddle. 'They use it to preserve bodies.'

'What's the point in that?' asked Kilpatrick as he shone his torch around the room. 'A crematorium is used for burning bodies, not preserving them.'

'It's usual for the bereaved family to take a final look at the dear departed before they're incinerated,' replied Jordan. 'Sometimes the body can't be cremated immediately due to legal requirements, hence the need to preserve it, now no more dumb questions. We need to find the door connecting this place to the Memtech building, and because you've got the torch, you need to lead the way, so get a move on.'

'Yes, sir,' replied Kilpatrick as he gave Jordan a mock salute.

The walls were lined with shelves holding various bottles of chemicals and substances, and there was a door immediately in front of them and another on the west wall.

Jordan tried both doors without any luck. 'They're locked. Bloody security conscious, aren't they. Who in their right mind is going to break into a crematorium?'

'Apart from us, you mean?' said Kilpatrick.

Tweddle laughed nervously. 'We've been pretty damned lucky so far. I think the simplest burglar alarm would have thwarted us.'

Jordan ignored him. 'Okay, which door do we tackle first? We don't have time to pry open every door in this building.'

'The door on the left,' replied Laura firmly. 'It should lead into the main foyer, and once we're in there we can orientate ourselves and find the door into the Memtech building.'

'Sounds good to me,' replied Jordan. He attacked the door, but it also refused to budge, providing only a few superficial splinters as encouragement.

'That lever isn't the best implement for housebreaking, is it?' commented Kilpatrick as he allowed his frustrations to surface.

'I'm doing the best I can,' replied Jordan through gritted teeth. 'These doors are solid timber, and the old locks don't give way easily.'

'Why don't you pry the hinges loose instead?' suggested Tweddle. 'They look rather old, and the wood surrounding them appears a bit rotten.'

'Yeah, that might work,' replied Jordan as he stuck the metal bar under the bottom hinge and heaved. There was a soft splintering sound. The hinge flopped away from the woodwork and remained hanging at an awkward angle.

'Well done!' exclaimed Laura delightedly. 'I was starting to think we'd never make any progress.'

Jordan pried the remaining hinge free and then pushed bodily against the edge of the door so that it pivoted out, forcing the lock away from the doorjamb. It resisted stoutly before giving a rasping groan and crashing noisily into the foyer.

'We're not the most subtle intruders, are we?' murmured Kilpatrick. 'I think we can forget about tidying up when we leave.' He held out his hands as a thought struck him. 'Shouldn't we be wearing gloves? Our fingerprints must be all over the place.'

Laura stepped daintily past him and into the foyer. 'I think that's a minor matter in the overall scheme of things, don't you?' The others stepped out behind her, and Jordan swung the torch beam around as they studied their surroundings. Several decorative glass windows mounted in two polished oak doors across the room reflected the light back to them.

Jordan hurried over and opened one of the doors. 'It's the chapel,' he said after a moment.

'We need to be heading in the opposite direction,' observed Laura as she walked towards a hallway on her right. 'Bring the torch, it's this way,' she called as she hurried down the passage. They passed several doors as they scampered along but they were locked.

The passage finished at a T-intersection with three doors set against the far wall. The first two led to a staff kitchen and a toilet but the third was locked, and Jordan set about the door with the lever.

It took several minutes to pry away the hinges, but when Tweddle and Kilpatrick leant their weight against the door and pushed, it swivelled and fell in. The room appeared quite large, and Jordan shone the torch past them, illuminating several rows of coffins stacked along the far wall. They stepped carefully across the broken door and ventured into the room while Jordan shone the torch along the walls looking for an exit.

'There's somebody here,' whispered Kilpatrick as he peered carefully around. 'I can sense it.'

'Nonsense,' replied Jordan. 'If somebody was here they would have raised the alarm. We've made enough noise to wake the dead.'

'A poor choice of words,' said Tweddle softly as he pointed into the shadows. 'Shine your torch towards that table next to Laura.'

Laura screamed and stepped back as the torch beam illuminated a dark figure with a very white face lying silently on the table.

'I think we've found the embalming room,' said Tweddle. 'They prepare the bodies in here before arranging them in their coffins.'

'There's another one over here,' said Jordan as he walked further into the room. The thought occurred to him that if things had gone differently, it could have been him and his friends lying on similar tables.

'This must be the room connecting the crematorium with the Memtech building,' said Laura, who had recovered from her fright. 'If they wanted to dispose of a body, then they'd just wheel it in here, load it into a coffin, and send it into the furnace. Nobody would be any the wiser.'

Jordan slowly trained the beam of the torch around the walls. 'It sounds good in theory, but the only door leading into this room is the one we came through.'

'I think it's safe to turn on the lights and have a good look,' said Kilpatrick.

Tweddle looked uncertain. 'Do you think it's wise? A security patrol may see the glow from the street.'

Jordan snapped on the light switch, bathing the room in a soft glow. 'If you don't like the idea, that's a good reason to do it.'

'It's a pity we can't shut the door,' said Kilpatrick pensively. 'That way we know we'd be safe.'

'Listen up, everybody,' said Laura firmly. 'I've something to say, and I want you to listen carefully because it's my mind that's going to be destroyed in fewer than eighteen hours.'

'And mine,' prompted Tweddle.

Laura glared at him before continuing. 'We're a team, whether we like it or not, and the only way we're going to succeed is if we all pull together. I've suffered more than anyone because of Colin's interference, and if I can move on, then so can you—so do me a favour and grow up.'

Tweddle smirked at Jordan's discomfort, causing Laura to scowl. 'Take that stupid look off your face, Colin. You need to grow up more than anyone. I believe the time for caution is over. We don't have time to discuss the pros and cons of every decision. We need to show faith in each other and just go for it. Now this is the obvious room for the connecting doorway, so don't stand there asking foolish questions and making snide comments. Get cracking and start looking for it.'

Kilpatrick considered throwing a mock salute but wisely decided against it and peered at a large bookcase instead.

Jordan stopped in front of a full-length mirror set into the wall. 'This is rather strange. Why would they have a large mirror in a room like this? It's not as though the bodies need to see the effects of the makeup, is it?'

'You're right,' agreed Tweddle. 'It doesn't serve any purpose apart from making the room look bigger.'

'So you think this mirror is covering the exit into Memtech,' said Kilpatrick as he felt around the frame for a hidden button. 'Why would they worry about disguising it?'

'I'm sure most of the people working here aren't involved with Memtech, and a door leading to another building would excite unwanted curiosity,' replied Laura.

'Well, if it is camouflaging the Memtech entrance, it's doing a good job,' said Kilpatrick. 'It just seems to be an ordinary mirror to me.'

'Well, we'll see about that,' said Jordan as he picked up a heavy porcelain vase and heaved it into the mirror. The mirror and vase both shattered on impact, and shards of glass and porcelain cascaded to the floor, revealing a solid metal door.

'Voila!' said Jordan with a sweeping wave of his hand and a slight bow. They others crowded forward to inspect their discovery, but their excitement quickly turned to dismay.

'You're not going to open that with a tyre lever,' said Tweddle as he ran his hands over the metal surface.

Laura felt her heart sinking. 'What are we going to do now?'

Kilpatrick sensed the need to keep a positive outlook. 'Perhaps we should forget about the door and scout around and see if Memtech personnel have left a window unlocked. They wouldn't be expecting us to return, so our chances should be good.'

Jordan shook his head. 'I'm sorry, but what you're suggesting is extremely high-risk with little chance of success. They're very security conscious, and I can't see them leaving any windows unsecured for the likes of you and me to get in. Unfortunately, the only safe way into that building is through this door.'

'And how do you propose to do that?' asked Tweddle. 'Use a table as a battering ram? Matt's idea may be risky but at least it gives us a fighting chance.'

Jordan waited until he had finished, conscious of Laura's words. 'This door can be opened with the right expertise. Unfortunately, none of us have the necessary skills, but I know somebody who should be able to help.'

'And that person would be?' prompted Laura.

'Robert's friend Frank, the old man who runs the hotel,' continued Jordan. 'Robert mentioned that he's got shady connections so he should be able to find somebody at short notice.' He checked his watch. 'It's quarter past two now and it's about twenty minutes from here to the hotel, so even if it takes Frank an hour to find a burglar, I should be back by four o'clock. That still gives us time to open this door and lie in wait for Dr Ridgeway.' He spread his hands in front of himself. 'So what do you think?'

'I don't see what else we can do,' replied Laura hesitantly.

'Okay,' conceded Kilpatrick, 'but if you're not back by four o'clock, we start checking windows.'

～

Frank was lounging in a chair with his feet perched on the front desk when Jordan walked into the lobby. A half-empty glass of whisky sat on the desk near his elbow. Frank casually glanced up and cast a professional eye over Jordan. 'You looking for a nice clean girl?' he asked with a smile as he swung his feet off the desk. He drained his glass in one easy swallow and wiped his mouth with the back of his sleeve. 'I've got a couple out back you might be interested in. Seeing as it's getting late you can have them both if you're willing to pay a bit extra.'

Jordan gave a wry grin as he shook his head. 'No, thanks. I've come to see Frank about some business. Is that you?'

Frank's smile faded, and he leant forward in his chair. 'Who wants to know?'

Jordan held out his hand. 'My name's Daniel Jordan. I'm a friend of Robert Banks.'

'Is that so?' He ignored Jordan's outstretched hand. 'So what brings you here?'

Jordan dropped his hand to his side. 'I'm the person who brought the inspector here tonight. His blood's all over the back seat of my car if you want to have a look.'

'I see,' said Frank slowly. 'And what's the name of the lass with him?'

'Jane.'

Frank nodded to himself. 'The inspector's been heavily sedated, but the prognosis is good. I suppose you want to see him?'

'I'd like to,' replied Jordan 'but I don't have time. As I said before, it's you I've come to see.'

'So you said. What business is so urgent it can't wait until the morning?'

'I'm going to be completely honest with you because I don't want any misunderstanding.'

'Now I am worried. Just spit it out, and I'll see if I can help.'

'Fine.' Jordan was having trouble forming the appropriate words and took a determined breath. 'I need the services of an experienced burglar.'

'What's the job?' Frank was unfazed by the request.

Jordan felt his cheeks redden. 'Uh, we're breaking into a crematorium.'

'I see,' replied Frank slowly. 'A crematorium. How much is the job paying?'

'I don't know. I hadn't thought about that. What's the going rate?'

'For a crematorium? Does it have any security alarms?'

'Not that we know of.'

'Okay, a crematorium, no alarms, short notice, hmm, all up I'd say five hundred pounds.'

'Five hundred pounds?' echoed Jordan.

'Plus travelling expenses, of course.'

'How much would that be?'

'Depends on how far I have to travel.'

'You?' asked Jordan in astonishment.

Frank scowled at him. 'You think I'm not up to it? Is that it? I'm just an old man who's no good for anything?'

'Not at all,' stammered Jordan, surprised by the verbal onslaught.

'I've forgotten more about breaking and entering than any of these young whippersnappers will ever know. In my day, it was a skilful craft handed down from father to son. We'd be in and out like a gentle breeze, silently wafting from room to room but now, with all these half-dead druggies trying to feed their habits, it's a case of slam-bam-thank-you-ma'am with no finesse at all. Now, do you want my services or not?'

'I'd be grateful for your help,' said Jordan diplomatically.

'In that case, I'm your man,' replied Frank emphatically. 'Now I normally expect payment in advance, but I'm guessing you don't have the money on you. Am I right?'

'We're definitely good for it,' replied Jordan quickly, 'and I'll make sure you get paid.'

'The inspector keeps an open account with me. I'll just put it on his tab, and you can pay him. Is that okay?'

'Fine, so I guess we have a deal,' replied Jordan, wondering what services Frank provided for the inspector.

'I'll meet you out the front.' Frank grabbed a tattered coat from a hook behind the desk. 'Don't drive too fast, and don't run any red lights, otherwise I'll lose you,' he said as he walked towards the rear of the lobby.

'Will I lock the front door behind me?' Jordan called out to him.

Frank kept walking. 'People know better than to knock over old Frank.'

Jordan checked his watch as he returned to his car. It was almost three in the morning, and he was feeling the first effects of sleep deprivation. He stifled a yawn as he started the engine. A nondescript delivery van pulled up next to him, and Frank gestured for him to get going. He drove sedately to the crematorium and parked in the same space he had occupied previously.

Frank had pulled up next to the main gates and was inspecting the padlock and chain when Jordan joined him. He noticed Frank had pulled on a pair of thin latex gloves and was wearing a balaclava as a hat. 'We used the shopping trolley to climb over the fence,' Jordan explained helpfully.

Frank glanced up at the spikes on top of the fence and gave Jordan a look of disgust. 'Well I'm going through the gate. If I try climbing that fucking fence, I'll either tear the arse out of my trousers or do my knee jumping down the other side, so do us both a favour and take that bloody thing away. You may as well have hung up a sign saying intruders on premises. Bloody amateurs,' he muttered as took a set of heavy bolt cutters from the back of his van and thrust them at Jordan. 'Make yourself useful and cut through that padlock.'

Jordan was surprised by their weight. 'The chain or the padlock itself?' he asked cautiously.

'Didn't I say the padlock?' replied Frank grumpily.

'Sorry, I was just making sure.' Jordan positioned the jaws of the bolt cutter against the padlock and slowly squeezed the handles together. He was surprised at how easily the jaws sliced through the hardened steel of the lock. 'That was easy,' he murmured as he replaced the cutters in the van.

'Padlocks are meant to deter casual trespassers,' replied Frank as he pulled his balaclava down over his face then pushed the gates open. 'They're not designed to keep out a seasoned burglar. There are more sophisticated devices for that.' He shut the gates behind him, arranging the chain and padlock to look as though they were still in place.

'I noticed you left your van parked out the front,' said Jordan as they crunched their way down the gravel path.

'Have you also noticed that I'm an old man who can't move very fast?' sneered Frank. He had a slight limp that he did his best to disguise. 'It's a matter of weighing up one risk against another. The chances of this place being on a security guard's round are remote. Who in his right mind would want to break into a crematorium?' He glanced quizzically at Jordan, who remained silent. 'Whoever runs this place still has to make a profit so they're not going to throw away money on a service that's of no benefit, are they?'

'I suppose not.'

'Jesus bloody Mother Mary!' exclaimed Frank as he noticed the broken window lying on the ground. 'Is that the best you could do? Don't you have any class? I thought druggies were bad enough.' He took out a small flashlight and inspected the front door. 'This is such a simple lock even a child could have opened it.'

'Well we couldn't find any children at this time of night so we had to make the best of our limited resources. This is a new experience for us.'

Frank inserted two metal picks into the lock and turned the bottom one until he heard a faint click. He opened the door with a grunt and moved into the foyer, looking around for a light switch. As the lights came on his attention was attracted to the broken door lying across the floor. He tugged the balaclava from his head and gave Jordan a look of disappointment as he stepped gingerly across the broken panelling.

'No class,' he muttered.

'Isn't it dangerous with the lights on?'

'It's much safer than having the beam of a flashlight announcing that you shouldn't be in here. If people see a light on, they assume somebody is either working late or the cleaners are on the job. If they see a torch flashing around, they call the cops. Now let me do what you're paying me to do, and stop asking bloody stupid questions. Judging by the evidence at hand, I'd say you've already managed to break into this building, so what is it you want me to do exactly?'

'There's a door further around we've been unable to open,' explained Jordan.

'I find that surprising,' Frank chuckled in a guttural growl. 'A door you couldn't open, well fancy that. Where is this super door that has you baffled?'

'It's around here,' said Jordan as he took the lead. They walked silently along the passage, the only noise being a gentle wheezing as Frank hurried to keep up. 'It's in here,' whispered Jordan as he indicated the room. The door hung drunkenly off its hinges, and Frank shook his head once more before shuffling into the room where Jordan started to introduce him to the rest of the group.

'Forget that,' grunted Frank as he peered at the bodies lying around the room. 'Where's this door? It's getting past my bedtime.'

Jordan pointed silently to the far wall, and Frank picked his way through the shattered glass and porcelain and studied the door. 'Where does this lead to?'

'There's a building on the other side we're trying to get into. The only safe access is through this crematorium,' explained Jordan.

'Although I'm relieved to hear that, the question that springs to mind is why the crematorium and your building have a hidden connecting doorway.'

'We figure that it's a convenient way for them to dispose of inconvenient dead bodies,' continued Jordan.

'Dead bodies,' repeated Frank sotto voce. 'That explains the inspector's condition.' He indicated the broken frame surrounding the doorway. 'I gather there was a large mirror in this frame. Am I right?' The others nodded silently as they sensed his disapproval. 'Did any of you realise that the mirror actually slides out of the way?'

'We figured that,' said Kilpatrick helpfully, 'but we couldn't work out how to move it so we resorted to brute force.'

'Neanderthals,' muttered Frank as he peered closely at the wooden frame still containing the jagged remains of the broken mirror. 'It may be best if we move this out of the way.' He knelt down among the broken glass and traced his fingers along the skirting board. 'This has been well engineered,' he muttered as he straightened up with a groan. 'Now where would they hide the switches?'

'Maybe it's activated on the other side of that door,' suggested Tweddle.

Frank gave him a pitying look. 'The whole idea behind having the damned mirror is to preserve the secrecy of this door. How would it look if the wrong people were in this room when the mirror started moving? The other side of the door,' he scoffed. 'Give me a break.' He looked around the room and then wandered over to the solid timber bookcase and ran his fingers up the side before giving another grunt of satisfaction. There was a faint click and the false section of skirting board slid smoothly away from the wall, revealing a well-lubricated metal rail. The wooden frame surrounding the doorway shuddered momentarily and began gliding away from the door. 'Simple deduction,' said Frank triumphantly. He walked stiffly over to the door and inserted two small metal probes into the lock.

Kilpatrick watched with interest as Frank moved the probes in opposing directions, stopped for a moment, and then withdrew them. 'A difficult lock?'

'Not at all,' replied Frank. 'Do me a favour and turn off the light. We don't want it shining into the other building and announcing our presence.'

He waited for Kilpatrick to obey and then opened the door. It was pitch black on the other side. He took out a torch and shone it briefly into the darkness. 'It's a short passageway leading to another door.'

'We really appreciate your help,' said Laura warmly. 'You've no idea how much this means to us.'

'You'd better save your thanks until I've got this other door open,' Frank said gruffly.

'I have every faith in you, Mr um …' replied Laura as she stumbled over his name.

'Just call me Frank.' He shone his torch around the door and thought for a moment before gesturing to Kilpatrick to come forward.

Kilpatrick squeezed his way between the others and stood next to Frank, an expectant smile on his face. 'Yes?'

'It's good that you're a big lump of a lad because your assistance is going to be vital,' said Frank in a serious voice.

'Yes?' repeated Kilpatrick happily.

'I want you to get down on all fours and move up really close to the door. Do you think you can do that?'

'I suppose,' replied Kilpatrick looking puzzled. He knelt down and moved slightly forward. 'Like this?'

'Perfect, nobody could have done it better, now don't move.' He held out his arms to Tweddle and Jordan. 'Give me a hand up and then hold me steady while I take a look at this.' He clambered up onto Kilpatrick's back and swayed there for a moment while he got his balance. 'This is a delicate procedure,' he said to Kilpatrick, 'so don't collapse on me.' He popped a piece of chewing gum into his mouth and handed his torch to Laura. 'Shine the beam on those wires in the corner.'

'Is that an alarm?' asked Laura as she illuminated the wires protruding from a gap above the door.

'It's a very simple burglar alarm,' replied Frank as he took a knife from his pocket and gently cut away a section of plastic coating from one of the wires. 'It's a contact alarm that's set off when this door is opened.'

'Isn't that rather unnecessary?' asked Tweddle. 'The passageway is hidden and both the doors are locked.'

'Jesus Christ, how would I know?' growled Frank. 'Bugger off with your fucking questions and leave me in peace.' He unwound the small wire coil and ran it across the top of the door until he couldn't reach any further. 'Hey, you on the ground,' he called out gruffly.

Kilpatrick was feeling slightly humiliated. 'Yes?'

'Move slowly to your left will you?' He waited until Kilpatrick had finished shuffling before resuming his work with the wire.

Kilpatrick's muffled voice floated up to them. 'I don't like complaining but your shoes are digging into my back. Are you wearing high heels or something?'

'I'll just be a moment longer,' said Frank as he took the gum from his mouth and stuck it on the doorframe. He then trailed the wire down the side and pushed it firmly against the gum so that the exposed end rested against the contact panel. 'You can help me down now,' he instructed Jordan. 'The alarm should be neutralised.'

'You are wearing high heels,' exclaimed Kilpatrick as Frank stepped from his back and stood next to his lowered head.

'I am not wearing fucking high heels,' snapped Frank. 'Do I look like a bloody girl? They're Cuban boots if you really must know.'

Kilpatrick eased himself up to his full height and gingerly massaged his back. 'No offence, mate; it's just that they were digging holes in my back.'

Frank sniffed loudly and stuck his picks into the lock. 'Wish me luck,' he whispered as he turned off the torch and opened the door.

Everybody froze in anticipation, but the only sound they could hear was their own breathing. The fresh air blowing into the passage was a strong indication that they had found the entrance to the Memtech building and Frank gently closed the door and flicked his torch on. 'You're in, so if you no longer need me, I'll be off.'

'Thanks for everything,' said Laura as she reached across and gave him a kiss on his stubbly cheek. 'There's no way we could have done this by ourselves.'

'Humph,' muttered Frank. 'Only did what you paid me to do, nothing more, nothing less.' He sidled past the group and disappeared down the dark passage.

Kilpatrick suddenly grabbed hold of Jordan's arm. 'We can't let him go yet. How are we going to open the door to Ridgeway's office?'

'You're right,' replied Jordan. He hurried back down the passageway and caught up with Frank in the embalming room. 'Frank!' he called urgently, trying to keep his voice low.

'For fuck's sake,' cried the old man as he jumped in fright. 'What the hell do you think you're playing at? I thought one of these bodies had come back to life.'

'Sorry,' apologised Jordan, 'but we need you for one more door.'

'In that other building, I suppose?'

'I'm afraid so.'

'That's the building with the inconvenient dead bodies you were talking about earlier.'

'Yes, sir, that's the one,' confirmed Jordan.

'All right,' Frank agreed begrudgingly, 'but it's going to cost you extra.'

'Great,' said Jordan as he thrust out his hand. 'I'm glad we've got a deal.'

'No need for that rubbish. Let's just get on with it, otherwise I'll never get to bed.'

Kilpatrick walked out of the passage and picked up the grey canvas bag. 'Mustn't forget the bomb,' he said cheerily.

'You have a bomb in that bag?' Frank asked ominously.

Kilpatrick had heard that particular tone before, usually when he had done something stupid and his first instinct was to lie. 'It's not a real bomb, Frank,' he hurriedly replied. 'We just need the people at Memtech to believe that it's real so they'll do as we want.'

'Wouldn't a gun have been better?' Frank limped over and looked at the bag.

'We thought of that but Inspector Banks lost his gun when he got shot.'

'If you wanted a gun you only had to ask. My prices are very reasonable.'

'You don't happen to have a gun with you now?' asked Tweddle, who was still concerned about the bomb.

'Do I look stupid enough to walk around carrying a loaded piece, especially when I'm in the process of breaking the law? I might be getting old, but I'm certainly not going senile.' He continued to stare at the bag. 'Let me see your bomb. If you want to deceive people, then it needs to be convincing.'

Kilpatrick gave Jordan an unhappy look as he unzipped the bag and laid the bomb gently on the table. 'It looks real enough doesn't it?' said Frank as he bent down and studied it closely.

'Yes, it does,' replied Kilpatrick with a weak grin.

'What happens if I press this button right here?' He jabbed his finger towards the timer switch.

'Don't do that,' yelled Kilpatrick as he pushed Frank's hand away.

'I thought so,' growled Frank angrily. 'You lied to me, and I never do business with people I can't trust. Good luck with your fucking door.' He turned and stomped angrily towards the exit.

Kilpatrick looked anxiously at Jordan and then hurried after the old man. 'Wait. I'm sorry I lied, but I didn't want to worry you, and I said it without thinking.'

Frank stopped and glared at him. 'So you make a habit of telling lies, do you, boy?'

'No,' replied Kilpatrick miserably. He felt like a small child again.

Jordan watched helplessly. 'We'll pay you double,' he suddenly blurted.

Frank's eyes narrowed. 'Okay, but that's it. One more door and then I'm out of here. We've already been in this place too long.' He gave Kilpatrick a final look of disgust and then stomped back down the passage. 'Can somebody show me where this office is located?'

'I can, Frank,' replied Kilpatrick as he slid the bomb carefully back into the bag and hurried after him. Frank turned off his torch as he motioned for Kilpatrick to lead the way. The building was bathed in a muted light, allowing Kilpatrick to move cautiously towards the stairs. The others warily followed, their nerves stretched tight.

It took Frank fewer than thirty seconds to open the stairwell door, and they filed silently past as he held it open. The door at the top was not locked. After carefully checking that nobody was working late, Kilpatrick led the way to Dr Ridgeway's office. Frank applied his deft touch, opened the door, and gestured for them to enter. 'Are we done?'

'Yes, Frank,' replied Laura sweetly. 'We really appreciate your time and effort.'

Frank scowled in acknowledgement. 'Fine. I don't know what you're up to, but don't wait too long. Once the police are called to the crematorium you'll be snookered.' He pulled the balaclava over his face and stepped into the passage.

Laura eased herself into Ridgeway's chair and put her feet up on the desk. 'We should try and get some sleep before the doctor turns up. I'll take the first watch. I don't think I'll be able to sleep anyway. If I've only a few hours of memories left, I want to make the most of it.'

'Me too,' said Tweddle softly as he slumped down against the wall. 'I've been thinking of all the things I'll miss, all the memories giving meaning to my life that will just disappear. I don't mind admitting that I'm scared to go to sleep because when I wake up I might not be me anymore.'

Jordan stood behind Laura and gently massaged her neck. 'I'll stay awake with you.'

'No,' replied Laura firmly. 'We'll have to be alert if we're going to pull this off, so you need to rest. I'll wake you in two hours' time. I might be tired enough to get some sleep by then.'

Kilpatrick had already commandeered Ridgeway's small sofa, so Jordan yanked the cushion from beneath his head. 'You can't have all the comforts,' he grumbled as he stretched out on the floor.

Jordan had only just dozed off when he was gently nudged awake. 'What is it?' he asked thickly.

'Shh,' cautioned Laura softly as she placed a warm finger against his lips. 'Some of the office workers are starting to arrive. I heard footsteps and voices in the passage.'

'At this hour?' asked Jordan incredulously as he peered at his watch. It was still dark in Ridgeway's office, and he had difficulty making out the time.

'Oi! Sleeping Beauty, it's almost nine o'clock,' laughed Kilpatrick, who was still lounging back on the sofa. 'You've been asleep for nearly four hours.'

'You're kidding.' He gave Laura a reproachful look. 'You were going to wake me after two hours.'

She ran a playful hand through his ruffled hair. 'You looked so peaceful; I didn't have the heart to wake you. Besides, I told you I was going to make the most of my remaining hours.'

The sound of a woman's laughter accompanied by a key scraping in the lock halted any further conversation. They hurriedly flung themselves behind the desk while Kilpatrick positioned himself by the door.

Chapter 17

All of humanity's problems stem from man's
inability to sit quietly in a room alone..

Blaise Pascal

D r Ridgeway was still laughing as she stepped into her office and turned on the light. Dr Cameron followed behind carrying a box of files, and she directed him to dump them onto the sofa. As Ridgeway pulled the door shut, Kilpatrick stepped forward and shoved her forcefully against her colleague, sending them both sprawling. He planted himself in front of the door, arms akimbo. 'Remember me?' he growled.

Dr Ridgeway blinked rapidly as she pushed herself to her feet, the laughter wiped from her face. 'Yes, I do, although your name escapes me,' she replied coldly.

Cameron struggled angrily to his feet. 'You're the bastard who tried to choke me with those wretched socks. Now you burst in here and attack Dr Ridgeway. What the hell's wrong with you?'

Kilpatrick waggled a finger at them. 'There's nothing wrong with me that a little cooperation won't cure. If you do as I ask, you won't be harmed.'

'Harmed?' asked Ridgeway questioningly. 'Why would you want to harm us?'

'Because he's a dangerous maniac, that's why,' yelled Cameron. 'The man's clearly unhinged.'

'Keep your voice down, or I'll be forced to gag you again,' warned Kilpatrick. 'You may understand better once you've met my partners in crime.'

Laura and Jordan emerged from behind the desk followed closely by Tweddle. 'Do you recognise me?' Laura demanded tonelessly.

'And me?' Tweddle chimed in as he angrily thrust his face forward.

'Yes, of course' replied Ridgeway nervously. 'I saw you last night.'

'That's right,' continued Laura ominously. 'We were brought to you trussed up like chickens, and you injected us with an enzyme designed to destroy our memories, isn't that right?'

Cameron was confused. 'What are they talking about, Moira? What's going on?'

'Hush, Scotty,' replied Ridgeway curtly. 'It's a simple misunderstanding, that's all.'

'There's no misunderstanding,' retorted Jordan. 'You injected a drug into these two, and now we want you to inject the antidote. Do that and you'll be allowed to live. Is that simple enough for you?'

'Hey, this has got nothing to do with me,' replied Cameron as he edged away from Ridgeway. 'I don't even know what's going on.'

'Stay where you are, buddy,' warned Kilpatrick. He took out the bomb and held it in front of him. 'Do you know what this little beauty is?'

'It looks like a bomb,' replied Cameron warily. He turned to Ridgeway. 'I told you he was crazy.'

'Give the man a cigar,' said Kilpatrick cheerfully, 'although I'm not too happy about the crazy part.' He took a step closer. 'There's enough explosive in this little baby to blow you all to kingdom come, so if I was you, I'd give us the antidote and be damned quick about it.'

Cameron didn't know how to react. Ridgeway was his colleague, but the bomb clearly overrode any thoughts of loyalty. His chance to escape came as Kilpatrick turned to place the bomb on a table by the sofa. He leapt for the door and grabbed the doorknob. A savage kick smashed into his midriff driving the breath completely from his body, and he ended up sprawled at Ridgeway's feet.

'Remember that little injection you gave me?' said Kilpatrick. 'Thanks to you I now have some unbelievable karate moves, so your treatment was very effective.'

Ridgeway glanced dispassionately at Cameron before addressing Laura. 'I'm afraid you're mistaken. You don't have anything to worry about, so you're wasting your time by making empty threats.'

Ridgeway's calm manner caused Laura's temper to snap, and her face contorted with fury as she savagely jabbed a finger at her. 'No! You're the one who's mistaken. Colin and I would rather be dead than spend the rest of our lives as drooling vegetables, and we'll do whatever it takes to acquire the antidote.'

Ridgeway paled slightly under Laura's furious onslaught. 'You can make all the threats you like, but as I've already said, you're wasting your time. Our attempts to formulate a drug to neutralise that particular enzyme have failed completely.'

Cameron struggled onto the sofa and put his hand on Ridgeway's thigh. 'What about Batch 25? We've had some promising results with that formulation.' If he could have winked at Ridgeway, he would have.

Ridgeway cocked her head to one side. 'Batch 25? I don't remember that particular one.'

'Of course you do,' replied Cameron insistently as he tightened his grip on her thigh. 'Dr Hauser discovered a flaw in the enzyme design and came up with a new formulation. The testing has been incredibly successful. Do you remember now?'

Ridgeway pushed her colleague's hand away. 'I know you mean well, Scotty, but you're not helping.' She gave Laura a wry smile. 'I'm afraid no such antidote exists, so you can force slivers of bamboo under my fingernails or set off your precious bomb, but I still won't be able to help you.'

'You're lying,' said Jordan angrily. 'You're both playing fucking games. If you think we're bluffing, you've made a serious error of judgement. Matt,' he said in a cold voice, 'set the timer for ten minutes.'

'Right,' said Kilpatrick as he bent over and studied the bomb's electronic system, his hands visibly shaking. He hadn't given the control system any thought, believing the doctors would do as they were told. He studied the back of the control panel and then flicked a switch. The display lit up immediately and he turned a small dial at the side until the number ten was illuminated.

'Are you sure you've set the timer in minutes and not seconds?' asked Tweddle nervously.

Kilpatrick studied the display. 'Fairly certain, yes.' He looked up at Jordan. 'Should I activate it?'

'Yes. We need to show these two we're serious.'

'Okay, here goes.' Kilpatrick flinched as he pressed a green button on top of the panel. The numbers in the dial began counting down towards zero. Kilpatrick opened his eyes and smiled at Jordan. 'There you go—a piece of cake. We have nine and a half minutes before we're all blasted to hell.'

'Do you mind if I sit down?' asked Ridgeway with a sigh. 'If you're determined to blow me up, then I'd like to make my last moments as comfortable as possible.'

'I suppose you'd like to send out for pizza as well,' said Kilpatrick sarcastically.

Laura glanced at the timer steadily winding down. 'It's your choice whether these are your last moments. I can't understand what you have to gain by denying us access to the antidote.'

Ridgeway sighed again. 'I suppose it's my fault. I've never been a great communicator. In my mind I believe I've made the situation quite clear, and yet my audience, you in this case, behave as if I haven't spoken. If I was trying to deceive you, I could have simply done as my colleague was suggesting and given you a placebo. I'm sure you wouldn't have known the difference.'

'All right,' said Laura as calmly as she watched the counter tick past the eight-minute mark. 'Why don't you explain it again?'

'I'm not sure I can put this any other way. As far as the enzyme is concerned, neither you nor your friend has anything to worry about. I've already said this yet you continue to threaten me.'

'I think that's because you haven't actually explained why they don't have anything to worry about,' said Jordan. 'Just saying it doesn't make it so.'

'That's right,' said Laura. 'Colin overheard the Frenchman saying we'd be given a drug to destroy our memory, and you injected the drug into us. How can there be any misunderstanding?'

'Oh, I see,' replied Ridgeway as she removed her glasses and gave them a quick polish. 'It's true I was asked to inject the enzyme into your bodies, but I didn't do it for two reasons.'

'Can we hurry this up?' said Kilpatrick. 'The bomb is ticking as we speak, and I don't mean this in any figurative sense.'

'Just put it on pause for a moment,' said Jordan. 'We can reactivate it if we're not happy with Dr Ridgeway's explanation.'

'Okay, put the bomb on pause,' mumbled Kilpatrick as he studied the panel once again.

'You were saying you didn't do it for two reasons,' Jordan prompted Ridgeway.

'That's right.'

'And those reasons were …?'

'Firstly, I have strong ethical standards and could never intentionally do such a thing to a fellow being. I know that not everything here is entirely above board but that's the case with most innovative industries.'

'So we weren't injected with that enzyme after all?' interjected Tweddle, desperately hoping he'd heard correctly.

'That's what I just said. The other reason I didn't do it was because I didn't have any on hand. I had a small batch, but I modified it for a project my boss was working on, and I haven't had time to prepare any more. These things take considerable time and effort.'

'So even though you were told to inject the enzyme into us, you didn't do it,' said Laura, who also wanted confirmation.

'Er, guys,' said Kilpatrick loudly. 'I hate to interrupt your little tête-à-tête, but I can't find a pause button on this thing, and we're down to fewer than six minutes.'

'Well, just turn it off then,' suggested Jordan.

'I've already tried, but it's not responding.'

'Let me have a look,' said Jordan as he hurried across the room.

'But you injected something into us,' persisted Laura as she ignored the mini-drama.

'Well, I had to, otherwise Madison would have known something was wrong. It never occurred to him that I would disobey a direct order from Monsieur Toulemonde.'

'So what did we receive?' asked Laura.

'Oh, it was a language enzyme I was working on. I'm confident it can be artificially duplicated. I intended to inject into myself as I've always wanted to learn Japanese.'

'If that were the case I should be able to speak Japanese and I can't, so obviously you're lying to us,' snarled Tweddle furiously.

Ridgeway looked thoughtful as she put her glasses back on. 'It's been more than twelve hours, so you should be able to. Have you tried?'

'Of course I haven't tried,' said Tweddle incredulously. 'Why the hell would I even think of trying to speak Japanese? I haven't tried to speak Urdu or Russian either.'

'So try now,' replied Ridgeway simply. 'If you remember that you can speak Japanese, you should be able to do so.'

Jordan interrupted them again. 'We've been pressing buttons all over the place, and we can't shut this thing down so we've got about five minutes before it goes off. If the doctor is telling the truth, you should be able to say something in Japanese, so get a move on so we can get the hell out of here.'

Tweddle screwed up his face as if constipated and then shrugged his shoulders helplessly.

'Laura,' prompted Jordan. 'What about you? Say something, anything at all.'

'*Eigo shika shirimasen*,' she said almost tearfully. '*Watashi wa Nihongo hanishimasen*.'

'What did you say?' asked Jordan, his eyes wide with hope.

'She said she can't speak bloody Japanese, that she only speaks English,' replied Tweddle irritably. 'Are you deaf?'

Ridgeway smiled in satisfaction, while Laura and Tweddle turned to each other in astonishment. 'I believe you have your proof.'

'I think we do,' agreed Jordan with a wry grin, verging on embarrassment.

'So now you can tell me the truth, is that bomb real?'

'It's real all right,' confirmed Jordan. 'I'm not sure how powerful it is, but it'll do some serious damage to your office when it explodes.'

'How serious?'

Jordan shrugged. 'Probably blow out your windows and damage your furniture. It might even start a fire.'

'Then I suggest you take it outside and allow it to explode harmlessly' replied Ridgeway. 'I have irreplaceable research in this office.'

'Uh, guys,' interjected Kilpatrick. 'A red light has started flashing. I'm not sure what it means but it can't be good. This thing could go off at any moment.'

'In that case the bomb's staying here, and it's time we left,' replied Jordan firmly.

'We must evacuate the building,' said Ridgeway briskly. 'We can use the fire alarm in the passage.'

'I noticed a cleaner's cupboard next door,' added Kilpatrick. 'If we stick the bomb in there it might muffle the blast and minimise the damage.' He grabbed the bomb and rushed out the door. Jordan followed behind in search of the fire alarm.

Ridgeway opened a filing cabinet and hurriedly rifled through her files, placing the important ones in a pile on her desk.

'We don't have time for that,' protested Cameron as he grabbed her arm and pulled her towards the door.

'I'm not leaving behind years of valuable research,' she cried as she dragged her arm clear of his grasp and scooped out several more files. 'If you really want to help, then take these with you.'

The strident tones of the fire alarm abruptly echoed through the building, and Ridgeway grabbed an armful of files and ran after Cameron. Tweddle and Laura were already waiting for them by the elevators.

'Forget the elevators,' yelled Ridgeway. 'The alarm overrides the elevator system and sends them all to the ground floor. We'll have to use the stairs.' There was a steady swirl of people flowing noisily along the passage, chatting excitedly. Kilpatrick appeared moments later, and they joined the throng clambering down the stairs and out into the front gardens. The Memtech personnel were assembling at a rally point near the far end of the car park. Ridgeway and Cameron hurried off in that direction. Jordan led the others on a circular route that appeared to be heading towards the rally point but actually brought them closer to the front driveway.

A fire siren sounded in the distance. A guard emerged from the gatehouse and shouted at them to join the groups already assembled in the car park. Jordan stopped and looked at his watch. 'How much longer do you make it, Matt?'

'Within the next ten seconds I'd say.'

'Okay. Let's head towards those people but not too quickly. We can make our escape once the bomb explodes.'

'Do you think it will be noticeable from down here?' asked Laura.

'One can only hope,' replied Jordan.

'Maybe we shouldn't have stuck it in the cupboard,' said Kilpatrick as he did his best moonwalk impression.

'Do you want to go back and drag it out?'

'Not particularly.'

Jordan stopped and looked at his friend. 'Have you got a stone in your shoe?'

'I'm moon walking.' Kilpatrick sounded aggrieved. 'I'm giving the impression of walking forward while actually moving backwards.'

'Just walk normally,' grunted Jordan, 'otherwise somebody will think you're having an epileptic fit and try and jam a peg on your tongue.' He glanced at his watch again. 'It should have gone off by now.'

'Perhaps it already has and we didn't hear it.'

'It might have been a squib,' added Tweddle. 'After all, it was homemade.'

The sirens were sounding much nearer, and Jordan could see the lights reflecting in the distance as the trucks roared through the nearby intersection. He had just opened his mouth to speak when the top of the building erupted in a ball of flames, and his ears were brutally assaulted by the noise of the explosion. He stood there stunned as chunks of concrete thumped into the ground nearby, and he was showered with small shards of glass. The deluge abruptly stopped, and he turned and stared at the others. Kilpatrick was pointing at the building, and Jordan was aware of a woman screaming in the distance. A pall of dark smoke hung over the building, and smoke billowed from several of the windows. He noticed that every window on this side of the facility had been shattered.

Two fire engines screeched to a halt next to the building, and they watched in guilty silence as the firemen unwound their hoses and began directing jets of water and foam onto the leaping tongues of flame.

'Wow,' muttered Jordan as he surveyed the damage. 'For a little bomb it sure had a powerful kick.'

'You're not wrong. It's a good thing I placed it in the cupboard,' observed Kilpatrick.

Jordan was not in the mood for levity. 'I just hope nobody's been seriously hurt.' He watched as another fire engine roared up the circular driveway. 'If we weren't in serious trouble before, we certainly are now. I think it's best if we leave before any questions are asked.'

$\sim$

Borkov awoke feeling out of sorts. Troublesome dreams had tormented his sleep, although in the cold light of dawn he was unable to recall any of them. The clear sky viewed through the gap in the curtains cheered him briefly as he remembered that winter was drawing to a close. He struggled out of bed, pushing his feet into his worn slippers and shrugged on his dressing gown. He had an uneasy feeling he'd forgotten something important. A bright yellow envelope stuck to the mirror attracted his attention as he stepped into the bathroom.

'That's strange,' he thought as he noticed the words 'Open me now—Urgent!' written in his own handwriting. He ripped the envelope open and extracted three A4 pages covered in his small, precise writing.

He scratched the stubble on his chin as he ponderously lowered himself onto the edge of the bath and began reading. The first thing he noticed was the date, and he wondered why he would write a letter to himself and date it two months in the future. His notes began by telling him to check the date on the newspaper he would find draped over the towel rack. He heaved himself to his feet with a grunt and retrieved it. To his astonishment, the newspaper bore the same date as the letter.

'What the fuck?' he muttered aloud as he lowered himself back onto the edge of the bath. The raised rim dug painfully into his fleshy buttocks, but he didn't notice. As he read the pages outlining Memtech's duplicity, the subsequent danger that this placed him in, and his own response to the threat, he realized he had cleverly neutralized the menace. It would be in

Toulemonde's best interest to ensure that Borkov lived a long and healthy life. He congratulated himself as he opened the newspaper and began catching up with events of the past two months.

He was smiling contentedly when, upon his arrival at work, he received an urgent summons to appear before a hastily convened meeting of the board. He dropped his briefcase on his table and, whistling happily, strode confidently past his secretary, causing her to look up in astonishment.

Borkov was slightly out of breath by the time he reached the boardroom. The subdued buzz of conversation ceased as he stepped into the room. They obviously understood the shift in power.

'My dear Isaac,' murmured Toulemonde solicitously. 'Thank you for favouring us with your presence at such short notice. Something important occurred last night that we need to discuss with you, but I'm forgetting my manners.' He clapped his hands imperiously. 'Please, Michael, a chair for our guest and be quick about it. Poor Isaac looks as though he's about to collapse. Really, Isaac, you should take better care of your health. We wouldn't want you to have a heart attack, now would we?'

Borkov smiled wolfishly as Madison struggled from his chair and walked carefully from the room. He looked as though he was nursing a lower back injury and his gait, when he returned, was almost crablike. He gave Borkov a venomous look as he dropped the chair in front of him. Borkov lowered himself into the chair and then turned towards Toulemonde with a look of immense pleasure. 'I see you appreciate the importance of my letter.'

The solicitous expression faded slowly from Toulemonde's face as he fixed Borkov with his pale eyes. 'And what letter would that be, Isaac?' He glanced theatrically around the room. 'Is it an apology for your boorish behaviour the other day?'

'It's got nothing to do with any damned apology,' grunted Borkov, 'quite the opposite in fact.'

'Well, never mind,' continued Toulemonde suavely. 'We can sort it out later. We have several serious questions concerning the disturbing events of last night, and your help would be greatly appreciated.'

'I have no knowledge of any disturbance,' replied Borkov haughtily, ignoring the frown spreading across Toulemonde's face. 'Whatever happened can wait, as we have more pressing matters to discuss. Several days ago I was treated most shabbily by this board for daring to take a few calculated risks. I'm sure you remember the blatant threats made against me.' He laughed scornfully. 'It appears you misjudged me badly because now the worm has turned.'

Several board members began muttering angrily, and Toulemonde gestured for silence. 'Please pay Dr Borkov the courtesy of listening with an unprejudiced mind, otherwise we will never reach a mutually satisfactory conclusion. I'm sorry for the interruption, Isaac, please continue; I'd like to hear more about this turning worm of yours. It sounds fascinating.'

Borkov laughed harshly. 'There will be no mutually satisfactory conclusion, Jean-Paul,' he said, mimicking Toulemonde's French accent. 'I now hold the whip hand, and you either do things my way or you're finished.'

Toulemonde smiled benignly. 'Dear me, Isaac, that sounds rather dire.' He gestured impatiently. 'Well, go on then, spit out your demands, don't keep us all in suspense.'

Borkov peered at Toulemonde curiously. That wasn't the reaction he had expected. The other board members—apart from Jarvis, who wore a derisive smile on his narrow face—were also staring intently at Toulemonde. The summons to the early morning meeting had been unusual enough, but Toulemonde's calm reaction to Borkov's ponderous provocation was out of character.

Borkov decided that Toulemonde was trying to unsettle him and went on the attack. 'Being a man of strong principles, I refused to meekly succumb to this outrageous slur upon my character and decided to redress the situation in my favour. Naturally, the issue of memory transfer appeared to be insurmountable.' Several board members nodded sagely. 'I pondered the dilemma for several days and finally formulated a foolproof plan that even you'll appreciate.'

'You have our undivided attention, Dr Borkov,' Toulemonde encouraged. 'This is an unexpected treat for all of us, and I, for one, eagerly await your next revelation.' A thought occurred to him. 'The Borkov revelations. A clever witticism, is it not?'

Jarvis laughed softly, and Borkov turned towards him in anger. 'Dismiss me for a fool at your own peril.' He scanned the room, fixing the board members with an angry glare before returning to Toulemonde. Why was Toulemonde treating him in such a cavalier fashion? He decided to press ahead with his ultimatum, but as he opened his mouth Toulemonde curtly cut him off.

'Enough!' barked Toulemonde. 'I've grown tired of this game just as I've grown tired of you. You're nothing but a pompous blowhard. You're not even fit to lick my boots.'

'You will regret those words,' promised Borkov, his eyes veiled in fury. 'I'll show you I'm not playing bloody games.'

'Such theatrics are an embarrassment to you, Isaac, so keep quiet and listen. It will save us a lot of time.' He turned and addressed the room at large. 'Dr Borkov's ingenious solution was to gather sufficient documentation on our operation to guarantee lifetime sentences for all of us if the authorities ever got their hands on it.' This news was greeted by muted gasps, and Borkov sat back in his chair and smiled smugly. Obviously Toulemonde had read his letter.

'I don't understand why you are looking so smug, Isaac,' Jarvis sneered. 'You've just signed your own death warrant.'

'Killing me will destroy this operation,' replied Borkov, who was filled with egotistical pride. 'You're only safe while I'm alive.'

'But we only have to transfer your memory to find out what you've done with the information,' cried Jarvis, who was still bemused by Borkov's stupidly.

'You'd think so, wouldn't you?' purred Borkov. 'However, if I don't remember what I did with the information, then transferring my memory won't be of much help, will it?'

'What do you mean, you don't know?' asked Jarvis. 'You're not making any sense.'

'I told Dr Ridgeway to erase my short-term memory,' explained Borkov. 'After making comprehensive notes for myself, of course.'

'This information you compiled, would you recognise it if you saw it?' asked Toulemonde innocently.

'I doubt it. If you're trying to trap me, then you're wasting your time because I have no memory of anything that occurred in the last two months.'

'Let's put it to the test then, shall we?' continued Toulemonde smoothly as he pointed to an image on the screen at the front of the room. 'Do you recognise this document, Isaac?'

Borkov studied it for a moment. 'The information is familiar, but the document isn't. Why are you showing me this?'

'Be patient, Isaac. What about this document?'

Borkov gestured disinterestedly. 'Again the information is familiar to me, as I'm sure it is to everybody else, but that's all.'

Toulemonde addressed his fellow board members. 'You've all heard Dr Borkov's sad attempts to blackmail us into compliance. However, I'm pleased to inform you that Michael Madison and his team have successfully thwarted Dr Borkov's bungling attempt.'

'What?' shouted Borkov as he struggled from his chair. 'That's impossible! My scheme is foolproof. There's no way you could have foiled it, especially in such a short time.'

Toulemonde gestured to the guards by the door. 'Take Dr Borkov down to the surgery. If he starts rampaging around in here he could damage the furniture.'

Borkov used his immense bulk to momentarily prevent the guards from propelling him out the door. As he struggled, he turned his head back towards Toulemonde. 'You're bluffing,' he shouted desperately as another guard joined the throng. 'You're only safe while I'm alive.'

Toulemonde smiled sadly as the guards slapped a pair of handcuffs on Borkov and hustled him away. 'I'm afraid not, Isaac. You gambled and lost.'

The strident tones of the fire alarm interrupted his next pronouncement, and he turned to Madison in annoyance. 'We had a fire drill less than two weeks ago. Why have you scheduled another one so soon?'

Madison swallowed nervously and stared at the doorway. 'We haven't scheduled any drills. Perhaps it's real.'

'Poppycock,' snapped Toulemonde. 'First the break-in, followed by that unfortunate episode last night, then Dr Borkov and his foolish antics, and now an unscheduled fire drill. I told you before that I don't believe in coincidences, so get off your backside and find out what the hell is going on.'

'Shouldn't we evacuate just to be on the safe side?' asked Jarvis.

'Let Michael investigate first. I'm sure it's nothing. In the meantime, we need to decide what to do with Borkov. Nobody in our company knows more about our operations, and his knowledge and expertise are crucial if we are to achieve our goals on time. Unfortunately, he has also become our greatest threat.'

'Exactly,' agreed Jarvis. 'We cannot allow him to walk around like a loose cannon waiting to destroy us all.'

Toulemonde nodded. 'Clearly his memory must be transferred, and the question we need to resolve is who will be the recipient. As we cannot transfer memory between sexes, his assistant Dr Ridgeway is ruled out. I have a few suggestions, but I would like to hear your ideas first.'

The bomb exploded at that precise moment, effectively quashing any ideas from the other members. The blast knocked Toulemonde off his feet and up-ended several others from their chairs. The ensuing concussion blew out every window in the room. Toulemonde lay on the floor, momentarily stunned as chunks of plaster rained down on his head.

Borkov was faring better than Toulemonde. His trek to the holding cell had taken him down one floor and fifty metres further away from the site of the blast. He had become docile once he left the boardroom, and the additional guard called in to help had remained at his station by the boardroom door. The two remaining guards chivvied Borkov along at a steady pace, keeping him apart from the stream of workers hurrying towards the exit. He was being taken past the staff canteen when the bomb ripped through the interior of the building. The blast caused a heavy fluorescent light fitting to fall from the roof and crash onto the unprotected head of one of the guards, who crumpled to the floor. The other guard stopped in his tracks, staring wide-eyed at his partner, and then bent down to help him as dust and flecks of plaster dropped from the ceiling.

Overcoming his astonishment, Borkov doubled his fists and crashed them onto the back of the guard's head. He followed up with two further hammer blows and then hurriedly searched the guard for the key to the handcuffs. It took him several frustrating minutes to unlock his restraints, his bloated wrists allowing only limited flexibility. He used the handcuffs to secure the guards together, passing the cuffs through a loop in the leg of a nearby table. He relieved the guards of their weapons, throwing one through a shattered window and stuffing the other into his pocket, and then hurried down the corridor towards the exit. He wasn't sure what was happening, but he knew he had to disappear quickly.

Toulemonde climbed gingerly to his feet and dusted off his expensive suit. Clouds of dust swirled through the room and several people were coughing as they fought to clear their lungs. Madison had hurried back to the room and he helped Toulemonde steady himself.

'Get your people together and find Hauser, Ridgeway, and their staff,' said Toulemonde in a low voice. 'Tell them to collect their key documents and any other important files and then get them out of here. Round up Borkov while you're at it. We'll deal with him later.'

Madison nodded. 'Where should I take them?'

'I don't care, anywhere, a hotel, a deserted warehouse, you work it out. Our new facility near Paris is almost completed, so once we get them out of here, we'll ship them over to France.'

'Some of them might not want to move to France,' replied Madison, thinking of his girlfriend. 'Most of the staff have family and friends here.'

'This is not a debate. Just do as you're told.'

Jarvis spoke up as Toulemonde watched Madison disappear from sight. 'Do you really mean to move our operations to France?'

'Yes, it is no longer safe here. This explosion will bring all sorts of people sniffing around.'

'I'm not sure if it's a good idea,' replied Jarvis knowing his influence would diminish if Memtech left England. 'Some of our key staff might not want to go.'

'So you want to debate this too,' replied Toulemonde fiercely. 'Well, I've already decided. It's clearly time for a change and not just in our location. Our new facility will be a lockdown operation with all employees confined to the site. Their well-being will depend upon the quality of their work. As far as their families are concerned, their loved ones died in the explosion today. We're not moving quickly enough, and our security is full of holes, so if you can't see that it's time for a change, perhaps you're not meant to be part of our future.'

'No, no,' replied Jarvis hurriedly. 'I was merely pointing out a perceived minor weakness, but I see you've already got it covered. So how can I help?'

'We'll need to move these people across the channel discretely, so use your contacts to expedite it. I want these people in France tomorrow.'

Jarvis raised his eyebrows. 'That doesn't give me much time.'

'Then I suggest you start immediately.'

Jarvis fought his way through the bustle of firemen as he hurried from the building and pulled out his phone. 'We've got a Code Red situation at Memtech,' he informed Northfield without any preamble. 'There's been an explosion and the place is already crawling with firemen. We'll soon have the police and the media joining them. We need to step in and secure the site immediately.'

'What sort of explosion?' asked Northfield.

'I have no idea. It could have been a gas leak, but I'm only guessing.'

'Let me make a couple of calls, and I'll get back to you.'

Jarvis's phone rang five minutes later.

'I've contacted Harrison, and he'll have a team with you shortly,' said Northfield. 'I also spoke to Fenwick, and he informed me he already has two officers investigating a break-in at a nearby crematorium so he's getting them to set up a road block.'

'Forget the roadblock. I need them here. Toulemonde has given instructions for his key people and their documents to be taken to a safe location. They may be gone before Harrison arrives.'

'We can't allow that to happen.' Northfield sighed as he stewed over the situation. 'I'll tell Fenwick to prevent anybody from leaving until Harrison gives the all clear. In the meantime, make sure everybody stays put until the police are in place; rendezvous with Harrison when he arrives.'

'I'll do what I can. Do you have an ETA for Harrison?'

'They scrambled five minutes ago so they'll be there in ten minutes.'

'What are you going to do with Toulemonde's people?'

'I don't think it's appropriate to discuss this over an unsecured telephone line, do you?'

'No, sorry, boss, I just want to make sure all the loose ends are tied up.'

'Don't worry. I've got all the loose ends covered.' Northfield hung up the phone.

Jarvis studied his surroundings as he thought about a plan of action. The crowd milling at the far end of the car park were dispersing now that the fire was under control. Many of them were heading towards their cars while others straggled towards the entrance in small, animated groups. Jarvis hurried over to the fireman directing operations. 'Are you in charge here?'

The fire chief gave him a withering look designed to discourage fools and reporters. 'And you would be ...?'

Jarvis held his Memtech identification card in front of the fireman's face. 'My name is Dermot Jarvis, and I'm a director here at Memtech.'

The fireman held out his hand in greeting. 'Pleased to meet you, Dermot, I'm Chief Mitchell. What can I do for you?'

'We believe the explosion may have been a deliberate act of sabotage. The police have orders to detain and question everybody but they're somewhat tardy in arriving.'

Mitchell shrugged. 'The cops are always last to arrive.'

Jarvis smiled apologetically and gestured towards the car park. 'The employees are about to leave, and I'm afraid there won't be anybody left to question, so I was wondering if you could do me a small favour?'

'Oh yes, and what would that be?' asked Mitchell warily.

'Now that you've got the fire under control, do you think you could move one of your trucks so that it blocks the driveway? If anybody complains I'll talk to them.'

Mitchell shrugged. 'Sure, why not.' He whistled towards a group of men rolling up a hose and instructed them to move their truck. 'Will that do?' he asked once it was in position.

Jarvis nodded. 'It will probably help if you undo the engine covering and have one of your people play with the ignition leads.' He walked over to the first car waiting in line and explained that the truck was experiencing a minor ignition problem and would soon be fixed. He watched as the news was relayed down the line of cars and then wandered away to await Harrison's arrival. The traffic jam around the truck was chaotic enough to prevent anybody from leaving, including the scientists, and he watched with satisfaction as the police arrived several minutes later in a blaze of flashing lights and sirens and herded the employees back towards the car park.

The helicopters arrived a minute later, swooping in low over a group of elm trees on the western boundary. There were three machines in a staggered formation. As the first one touched down, a group of dark figures sprang lightly from it and jogged across to Jarvis.

'Commander Harrison?' called Jarvis as he addressed the group of men. They weren't wearing any insignia, and he wasn't sure who was in charge.

'Are you Jarvis?' replied a lean, wiry individual. Jarvis nodded, and Harrison took him firmly by the arm as he steered him towards the building. 'Our orders are to secure the key people. We have a list of names, but it will save time if you can identify them for us, okay?' Harrison's tone indicated that no was not an option.

Tiny shards of glass crunched beneath Jordan's feet as he urged the others past the patrol car parked outside the crematorium. Residents from the nearby houses were gathered in the street, looking anxiously at the pall of black smoke drifting across from the Memtech building. Their car was covered with a light coating of ash and dust and as they hurriedly piled inside, the patrol car suddenly took off with a screech of tyres and roared up the street behind them, its siren blaring. Jordan's heart skipped a beat as he frantically inserted the key in the ignition but the patrol car roared past and screeched to a halt at the end of the street. Two policemen leapt from the car and pulled out a heavy set of spiked chains from the trunk and strung them across the road.

'They're setting up a roadblock,' said Jordan. 'We'll have to go back past the Memtech building.'

Tweddle wasn't happy. 'But the police will have already blocked off that road. We'll be driving into a trap.'

Laura frowned at him. 'There are only two ways back to the main road, and we can't use this one, so we have no choice. If the other road's blocked, we can hide in our office until the dust settles.'

'But we don't have food,' persisted Tweddle. 'What if they keep the roadblocks in place for a week?'

Laura scowled impatiently. 'There's plenty of water in the tap, and you can always hunt for rats in the basement. Why do you always focus on the negatives?'

'That's unfair,' mumbled Tweddle. 'I was only being practical. It's important that one of us keeps his feet on the ground.'

'There's not much activity in this street,' commented Kilpatrick as they drove past the Memtech entrance.

'There's a fire truck blocking the entrance,' replied Tweddle. 'It doesn't look as though anybody can get in or out at the moment.'

'Watch out,' called Laura. 'There's a policeman ordering us to stop.'

'Right,' murmured Jordan as he stopped the car and wound down the window. 'Leave the talking to me.' He smiled at the young policeman as he approached the car. 'Good morning, officer. Do you know what caused the explosion?'

'Probably a gas leak. Please show me your licence.'

'Certainly.' Jordan fished in his wallet and handed over the card.

'What's your business here, Mr Jordan?'

'We run a film studio in an office across the road,' explained Jordan. 'This is Laura, my secretary, and the two gentlemen in the back are technicians.' Laura gave the officer a sweet smile while Kilpatrick and Tweddle merely nodded in acknowledgement. 'We'd just arrived at work when the fire alarm across the road went off followed by the explosion which blew in all our windows. We watched the fire trucks arrive and began cleaning up the glass, but then we decided it might be safer to leave until we were sure the danger had passed.'

'I see, sir,' replied the officer as he peered closely at Jordan. 'Those cuts on your face look to be very recent. Would you mind explaining how you got them?'

Jordan smiled kindly. 'I was standing by the window when the blast occurred. I was very lucky the curtains were still drawn as they took the brunt of the flying glass.' He touched the abrasions on his face. 'Unfortunately, some of the shards still got through.'

'Do you have any proof to confirm your story?' asked the officer, a hint of suspicion creeping into his voice.

'We have business cards in the office if that will be sufficient proof?'

The officer stepped back and gestured for Jordan to get out of the vehicle. 'Come along, Laura,' said Jordan in his best managerial tone. 'Let's not keep the young man waiting.' He whispered to the pair sitting in the back, 'Follow me once we've gone inside.' Another policeman emerged from the shadows and trailed behind the small group as they walked along the footpath.

'That makes it a bit tougher,' muttered Kilpatrick as he eased his door open. He saw the policeman suddenly speak into his radio and then curtly gesture for Jordan and Laura to return to their car. Kilpatrick waited until they turned the corner at the end of the road before asking what had happened.

'The policeman got a message on his radio and told us we could go.'

'Did you hear the message?' asked Kilpatrick.

'It sounded like they were concerned about terrorists still in the grounds and were told to prevent anybody from leaving the facility. He lost interest in us once he heard that.'

'So what do we do next?' asked Tweddle.

'We need to find out how Robert's faring,' replied Laura primly. 'Without him, none of this would have been possible.'

~

Jarvis was also thinking about what to do next as he surveyed the glowering and confused figures of his former allies huddled together in the damaged boardroom. Harrison had herded the scientists and section heads into the room while Madison and his guards were lying on the floor, their hands firmly taped behind their backs.

Harrison's men menaced the group with automatic weapons, and anybody who even shifted his weight received a stinging rebuke. Toulemonde was sporting a wicked red lump beneath his right eye. He had learnt the hard way that silence meant exactly that.

Jarvis glanced around the room, mentally ticking each person off against the list he had hurriedly prepared. The only significant name still missing was Dr Borkov. He should have been locked in the surgery but had somehow disappeared.

Colonel Harrison looked at him expectantly, prompting Jarvis to reach a decision. 'Everybody's here apart from Dr Borkov. If you like, I can wait by the front gate and scrutinise people as they leave. Borkov is critical to the overall operation.'

'That won't be necessary,' replied Harrison. 'My guards at the gate have a description of all key personnel so he won't get far.' He signalled to one of his men standing by the door. 'Inform the other employees that this facility will be closed indefinitely due to the structural damage, and then you can dismiss them.' The man offered a crisp salute as he marched from the room.

Harrison stood on a chair and addressed the remaining personnel. 'Listen carefully, because what I'm about to tell you is for your own protection. We have strong evidence linking today's explosion with a well-known terrorist group and believe some of you have been targeted for kidnap or assassination. Until we know more, we cannot take any chances. You will therefore be taken to a safe place until this threat has been fully assessed and neutralised. Your families will be protected in your absence, and once we have the situation under control you will be allowed to return home.'

He glared at them, his voice becoming more ominous. 'Unfortunately, our information indicates the presence of a terrorist mole among you, and until we discover who this person is, you will all be treated with due caution and suspicion. I advise you not to do anything stupid as it could have dire consequences.'

The sullen group glared back at him, confused and disorientated. Harrison pressed on. 'You will be debriefed upon arrival at your new base, and we will then answer your questions. Until then you must maintain your silence. That's all.'

The sergeant and his men immediately harried the prisoners out the door.

'Excellent job,' said Jarvis. 'I'll conduct a quick sweep through the building and see if I can find anything of value.'

Harrison shook his head. 'No need, sir. Mr Northfield has already arranged for the files to be secured and forwarded to the new facility.'

'In that case, I'll head back to the ministry.'

'That won't be necessary, sir,' replied Harrison. 'I have orders from Mr Northfield giving you temporary command of the memory enhancement program. Your knowledge of the people and their skills makes you're the logical person to successfully transplant the program. He said to regard it as a promotion.'

Jarvis screwed his eyes up uncertainly. 'I suppose that's true, but I wonder why he didn't discuss it with me personally.'

Harrison smiled encouragingly. 'I'm sure you'll agree there wasn't much time for social niceties. Now I'm sorry, sir, but we have to get going.'

'Now? You want me to go with you now?'

'Yes, sir. The others are waiting.'

'Okay, I'll just give my wife a call, otherwise she'll be worried.'

'There's no time, sir. Mr Northfield will notify your wife,' replied Harrison steadily. 'It's only a temporary appointment, so you won't be apart for more than a few weeks. Now I must insist that we get moving.'

Jarvis's eyes strayed to the large pistol Harrison was wearing and decided not to argue. After all, he would be in command of the facility; it was only temporary, and it was a promotion to boot. A couple of weeks without his wife and daughter wouldn't be that much of a hardship. There were some very attractive women among the prisoners who might be happy to earn a few extra privileges.

'Just where are we going?' he asked as they strolled briskly across the empty parking lot.

'I'm sorry, sir, that's confidential. If I tell you, I'll have to kill you.'

Jarvis's nervous laugh was cut short as he caught the cold gleam in Harrison's eyes. *My God,* he thought as he repressed a shudder, *I think he means it.*

'You're kidding, right?' Jarvis injected a note of cheerfulness into his voice.

'Only one way to find out, sir,' replied Harrison bluntly.

'It's not that important. I'm sure I can wait until we get there.'

'Suit yourself, sir,' replied Harrison as he helped Jarvis climb into the helicopter. The prisoners wore restrainers to prevent them causing a disturbance, and Jarvis smiled pleasantly as Toulemonde spat a savage scowl in his direction.

Jarvis braced his knees and arched his back against the thin metal wall of the helicopter as it took off with a stomach-churning swoop and then headed west over the boundary fence.

Harrison ducked low against the wash of air, swirling dust and engine noise as he watched the helicopters lift off. His task now was to secure the files, apprehend any of the missing personnel, and dissuade nosy investigative journalists from setting foot inside the facility. He had clear authority over the police on-site, and they had strict orders not to enter any of the buildings. His signalman jogged over and handed him a phone.

'Harrison,' he barked.

'It's Northfield. Is this line secure?'

Harrison activated a tiny scrambler on the hand piece. 'Secure at this end, sir.'

'Excellent. Give me an update.'

'Everything has gone according to plan. The key personnel have been apprehended and shipped off to our Dartmoor facility. The only exception is Dr Borkov.'

'Borkov!' exclaimed Northfield. 'He's extremely important. It's imperative you find him post haste.'

'It's just a matter of time,' replied Harrison calmly. 'He's probably cowering in a bolt hole somewhere. My men are searching the building, and if he's there, then we'll find him.'

'And if he's not?'

'We'll cross that bridge when we come to it.'

'All right, I'm sure you know what you're doing. How did Jarvis respond to his promotion?'

Harrison gave a snorting laugh. 'He wasn't sure how to take it, although he really had no choice. He's on the chopper with the others.'

'Good work. He was useful to have around, but he knows too much. I'll make sure his family receives a good pension. Do your men at Dartmoor understand their duties?'

'Yes, sir.'

'Okay. Once we've pumped the information out of Toulemonde and his cronies, they can quietly disappear. However the scientists must be encouraged to continue their work, and if that means bringing in their families, then so be it.'

Harrison laughed again. 'That facility was built as a safe haven for the government during the sixties when nuclear war was likely. Believe me, once you're down on level seven, the only way out, without the correct authorisation, is in a wooden box.' He gave his snorting laugh again. 'Even that won't be necessary because they installed high-temperature incinerators to manage their waste.'

'Okay. Let me know when you apprehend Borkov.' Northfield hung up and called the MI6 Operations Liaison Officer into his office.

'What's the latest news on the two extremists we captured in Grimsby last week?' he asked once the man arrived.

'They're still being softened up, so we haven't got much out of them yet.'

'Softened up? How?'

'We're blasting them with the Sex Pistols and depriving them of sleep. We'll commence our hard-core interrogation next week.'

Northfield smiled thinly. 'That won't be necessary. Who's our best agent to understand and act upon the terrorists' information?'

'Agent Lewis.'

'Okay, turn off the music and allow the prisoners to get some sleep. Have Lewis report to me first thing in the morning. They're all going on a little field trip.'

Northfield dismissed the officer and instructed his secretary to arrange an immediate meeting with Dean Aubrey, the Minister for Internal Affairs. Half an hour later he was seated in front of Aubrey, outlining the situation for him. The minister, however, wasn't enjoying the encounter. He paled visibly as visions of political annihilation arose in his mind.

'My God,' whispered Aubrey as he stared glassy-eyed at Northfield. 'If this ever got out, we'd all be finished. You, me, the Prime Minister, everybody. The opposition would flay our hides. Surely the sensible course of action is to expose the culprits while we still have a modicum of innocence to hide behind. This technology must be destroyed.'

'That certainly sounds like the correct decision,' replied Northfield. 'If we become embroiled in this, we'd destroy our careers and probably end up behind bars.'

Aubrey was visibly sweating. 'So we agree then.'

'The thing is, minister,' continued Northfield, 'such thinking represents a very narrow and selfish view. Memtech was about to open a similar facility in France. We don't know the exact location, but it's only a matter of time before we find out.'

'You mean through this ... er.' The minister was unable to complete the sentence.

'Exactly,' confirmed Northfield. 'If Toulemonde doesn't willingly supply the information, we'll extract it. Either way, we'll know everything within the next twenty-four hours. We can then send a crack team to neutralise the personnel and destroy their files.'

'But they're our allies,' Aubrey protested. 'Surely a phone call to your counterpart in Paris would resolve the situation without placing the alliance in jeopardy.'

'That's the normal course of action, but we don't believe the French authorities are yet aware of this technology, and we'd like to keep it that way.'

'What about mutual cooperation and all that?'

Northfield laughed pleasantly. 'It's a myth that both sides are happy to perpetuate. The unwritten rule is that you always tell your allies what they can find out for themselves.'

'But this technology would be valuable to all our allies. I'm sure the Americans would welcome it.'

'I'm sure they would, but there are two points we need to consider. Have you heard the line about women and secrets?'

Aubrey shook his head.

Northfield leaned forward conspiratorially. 'Do you know that women can keep a secret as well as men? It just takes more of them.' He laughed briefly and then became serious once more. 'How secure would you feel knowing that this information was being passed around among an increasing number of foreign agencies? Once you tell one agency, they would feel obliged to pass it on to their own close allies.'

'I understand,' replied Aubrey soberly. 'What was your second point?'

'This knowledge gives us a huge advantage over our enemies, but only if we have sole access. We have concerns that the French have been infiltrated by high-level moles linked to the Islamic fundamentalist cause.'

Aubrey frowned. 'Our government isn't entirely free from suspicion. Sensitive material has been surfacing in the Middle East for years.'

'Exactly my point! The only way we can secure this knowledge is by limiting the number of people with access.'

'How many people know now?'

'That's a good question. Not counting the prisoners isolated at Dartmoor, there are at least another half a dozen. Apart from Borkov, there is Inspector Banks and his misguided friends.'

'The rogue cop? What the hell is he doing mixed up in this?'

'He accidentally stumbled across the Memtech operation. We couldn't afford to have him blowing the whistle so we doctored the official report and made him a persona non grata. I must admit it worked a treat.'

'Well, I certainly believed it. What's the current situation with them?'

'They have no credibility and no evidence, so they're not a serious threat.'

'How much do they know?' persisted Aubrey.

'Probably as much as we do.'

'Then they're still a threat and must be apprehended.'

'They've been rather fortunate so far, but when their luck runs out we'll send them to Dartmoor and discover how much they really know. Banks may already have been dealt with, although it hasn't been confirmed.'

'So, officially, how many people know about this?'

'Just the two of us, Minister, and my confidentiality is guaranteed. Once we've rounded up the dissidents, you'll be the only person who can threaten your security, and I'm sure that isn't going to happen.'

Northfield smiled at the thought. 'I'll keep you abreast of developments, but in the meantime, you may want to give some thought to the personal benefits of this technology.'

'I don't follow you.'

'I'm sure there are many state enemies under lock and key who continue to withhold valuable information. Your political stocks would undoubtedly soar if you pulled off the occasional coup as a result of disclosing this information. Who knows where it could lead? Prime minister perhaps? Are we on the same wavelength now?'

'It's not something that appeals to me personally,' replied Aubrey primly, 'but the country would undoubtedly benefit from unmasking our enemies.'

'Exactly, so why don't you compile a list of these people and the information you're after, and we'll make sure it happens, no questions asked.' Northfield retrieved his briefcase from the table. 'It's been a pleasure talking to you, Minister.' He held out a card with the name and address of a quiet, backstreet coffee shop written on it. 'This is the address of our next meeting. Don't leave it lying around.'

He gave Aubrey's hand a perfunctory shake and strode from the office, pleased the discussion had proven favourable.

~

Things were not looking so favourable for Banks.

Jane met the others outside the front of the hotel, looking distressed as she hurried across to Laura's window. 'Robert's taken a turn for the worse,' she said tearfully. 'The doctor insists that he be hospitalised immediately. I didn't know what to do because Robert has been so insistent about avoiding hospitals.'

'Is Robert conscious?' asked Jordan.

'He's fallen into a coma. I'm afraid I had no choice, so I called an ambulance. That's why I was waiting out here when you turned up. Please tell me I did the right thing.'

'Of course you did,' Laura assured her.

'Why don't you all go inside, and I'll wait for the ambulance?' suggested Kilpatrick. 'There's no need to draw attention to ourselves.'

'That's a good idea,' agreed Laura as she draped an arm around Jane's shoulders. 'It'll give me a chance to tell you what happened at Memtech.'

Kilpatrick leant back against the pitted granite wall and gazed absently down the street. He hoped he would live long enough to get married and have children as the recent events were definitely worth telling his grandchildren.

Jane insisted on going with Banks once the ambulance arrived, even though her own life would be in danger. 'Hopefully I can convince the authorities that Robert is innocent,' she said as she climbed in the back with Banks. She looked frail and worn as her wan face peered out anxiously from the tinted side window. The ambulance drove away, leaving the others feeling surprisingly empty.

'What do we do now?' asked Laura dispiritedly.

Jordan looked equally forlorn. 'Frank wants to discuss something that Robert asked him to do. After that we need to track down Tracey and recuperate while we plan our next move.'

'Shouldn't we take the disks to the police?' asked Tweddle. 'Once they have the information, they'll know we're innocent.'

'Let's see,' replied Kilpatrick. 'So far I make it five counts of kidnapping, six of assault, one of grievous bodily harm bordering on torture, two counts of breaking and entering, one count of blowing up a building, plus numerous counts of property damage and theft. Just where exactly does the innocent part come into it?'

'Let's not forget that there were a few bullets flying around last night,' added Jordan. 'There's a good chance Robert wasn't the only casualty.'

'I know you mean well, Colin,' replied Laura 'but until we know who we can trust we're not going to do anything rash.

Now let's find Tracey because I'm really looking forward to relaxing in a nice, hot bath and soaking my troubles away.'

'I can scrub your back if you like,' suggested Jordan.

'Thanks, but I'm sure I can manage by myself.'

'Whatever happened to "you scrub my back, and I'll scrub yours"?'

Chapter 18

They flee from me, that sometime did me seek,
With naked foot, stalking in my chamber.

Sir Thomas Wyatt

orkov slipped quietly out the main gate when the guard was distracted by a fire truck stalled across the driveway. He cautiously headed towards the main road, evading scrutiny by skulking in the shadows of the abandoned warehouses. He had almost reached the main road when he noticed a police car cruising up the road behind him. He nervously pressed back into the shadows and hoped he hadn't been seen. The car slammed on its brakes several metres from Borkov's hiding place, and an officer leapt out and ran towards him. Borkov could feel his legs trembling as he pulled out the weapon he'd taken from the guard and eased off the safety catch. The officer promptly stopped and noisily relieved himself in a doorway.

Borkov's nerves were shredded by the time he hailed a passing cab.

'Where to, guv?' the driver asked as Borkov scrambled into the back seat.

Borkov stared at him, confused. He couldn't remember. The concussion from the explosion must have affected his memory. 'The station,' he said finally. 'Drop me off at the station.'

'Any particular one?' asked the driver.

'I don't care. The nearest station. Just get moving,' replied Borkov in exasperation. Try as he might, he couldn't remember the name of his station either. He settled back and closed his eyes. His memory would return once the concussion wore off.

After the driver had dropped him off at the station, Borkov drifted down the street, unsure where to go next. He felt dizzy and disorientated. He paused uncertainly at an alleyway and studied the surrounding buildings. He felt desperately tired and wandered further into the alley, looking for somewhere to rest.

To Borkov's horror, a dishevelled figure jumped out from behind a rusty dump bin and rushed at him, screeching that the alley belonged to him. Borkov fell back in fright, clutching at the automatic in his pocket. He pulled it free and fired a wild shot at the capering figure. The derelict stopped in mid-screech and abruptly vanished back up the alley. The crowd on the street instantly melted away and Borkov was left standing alone, confused, and bewildered, his gun emitting gentle wisps of smoke.

~

Northfield received the news an hour later. Toulemonde had already told them everything he knew about the French operation, and a small team was preparing for a low-level night flight across the channel. The facility would be infiltrated and destroyed during the early hours of the morning.

Northfield rang Aubrey. 'We need to meet,' said Northfield when Aubrey answered. 'Be there in fifteen minutes. I'll order the coffee while I wait.'

Aubrey was five minutes late. He peered anxiously through the gloomy interior of the little shop for Northfield, who attracted his attention by waving a copy of *The Times*.

'Nice place,' muttered Aubrey as he pulled out a chair. 'Do you come here often?'

'Never been here before, but their croissants have an excellent reputation. Now I have some good news and some not-so-good news. We've taken Dr Borkov into custody, although the circumstances were a bit bizarre. He was found wandering the streets and shooting at people.'

'Was anybody injured?'

Northfield waited until the waitress set down two cups of black coffee and a plate of croissants in front of them. 'The police apprehended him before any real harm was done, although it no longer matters.'

'I thought Borkov was the program's architect,' replied Aubrey.

'Dr Borkov is part of the not-so-good news. Apparently he carried out an experiment on himself using a short-term memory deletion enzyme. Unfortunately, the enzyme also erased large chunks of the doctor's long-term memory. To put it succinctly, Borkov is of no use to anybody. We'll ship him off to Dartmoor, but I doubt there'll be anything useful to salvage. There's also the added risk that whoever receives his remaining memory could also pick up the enzyme.'

'Not a pretty thought,' commented Aubrey.

'Undeniably, but I do have some good news. Inspector Banks is out of the picture. He was shot by Toulemonde's thugs and is in intensive care at London Hospital. Fenwick has a small team guarding him.'

'What if he talks?'

'He's barely alive and heavily sedated, so he won't be talking for some time. The woman he was accused of kidnapping is with him so we have to handle this carefully.'

'But she wasn't really kidnapped. Banks saved her life, in fact.'

'Yes, but the media don't know that, and the public believes what the media tells them. We have circulated a statement that

Banks has been captured following a shoot-out with police and that he is badly injured and not expected to live.'

'What about the girl? The current affairs programs will be wetting themselves at the thought of getting their hands on her.'

'We've only made a vague mention of her, hinting that she may already have come to a sticky end. We can't allow her to talk, so we'll send her to Dartmoor with Banks. If word does leak out, then we'll follow the Patty Hearst line about Stockholm Syndrome and come up with a more creative solution. She's been asking to speak to the authorities, so I've arranged to see her in the morning. If we use her intelligently, we may entice the rest of the gang into our hands.'

'Why don't you extract the information from his brain now? What's the point in waiting? Banks is sure to know the whereabouts of his colleagues, and you can snap them up before they realise what's happened.'

'Just be patient and everything will fall into place,' admonished Northfield lightly. 'These people shouldn't be underestimated. Guess what caused the explosion at the facility?'

'I thought it was a gas leak.'

'Banks's people detonated a bomb. A fucking bomb, if you don't mind! God knows what this world is coming to.'

'What were they hoping to achieve?'

'It's a long story, and time is short.' He handed over a white card. 'This is the location of our next meeting. Pay the bill on the way out, will you? There's a good chap.' Northfield stood up, offered a limp handshake, and departed. Aubrey was left patting his pockets to see if he'd remembered to bring any money with him.

∾

Tracey and Doris had found rooms at an old inn backing onto the Thames. The rooms had a damp feel about them, and the smell of the river flats was pervasive. At least they were able to watch the riverboats plying their trade.

Tracey gave Laura directions to the inn, and she stopped on the way and bought an assortment of groceries and toiletries. Jordan outlined the recent events, playing down the severity of Banks's wound for Doris's benefit. Doris looked tired and drawn, and she reluctantly agreed to return home. They thanked her for her help and promised to keep her apprised of Robert's progress.

With that in mind, Laura and Jordan sought out a public telephone and rang Jane. She told them that Banks had shown considerable improvement and was resting much easier. She added that she was meeting with a government official in the morning to discuss her situation.

Laura glanced at Jordan. 'Perhaps we can entrust him with the disks.'

'Perhaps,' replied Jane. 'We need to trust somebody. I'll check him out and give you my opinion.' He voice became more solemn. 'Have you seen the news?'

'I haven't had time,' said Laura. 'We've only just settled into our new home. Are there any reports on the explosion?'

'The news is full of it,' replied Jane softly. 'They're saying there are five confirmed deaths, while a number of people are still missing.'

'What? That can't be correct. Everybody had plenty of time to evacuate.'

'Not according to the reporters. They're saying the explosion was caused by a powerful bomb, and that a terrorist group has already claimed responsibility.' Jane paused and lowered her voice even further. 'I can't say too much because the police are loitering around the doorway. I'm sort of under house arrest. A female officer accompanies me everywhere, and I'm not allowed to go too far.'

Laura relayed the news to Jordan, who shook his head in disbelief. 'Moira Ridgeway knows we set off that bomb. I'm surprised she hasn't informed the police already. Five people dead.' He shook his head again. 'Maybe we should just give ourselves up.'

'We can decide that after Jane has met with the official. Everybody's tired and dispirited, and a good night's sleep will help us to think more clearly.'

When they returned to the apartment, it was obvious that the others had already seen the news flashes.

Kilpatrick was visibly shaking as he sat slumped on the sofa, his eyes glued to the set in the corner of the room. He occasionally muttered in disbelief as a female reporter stood in front of the shattered building, repeating the news in a grave voice.

'Have you seen the news?' asked Tracey, with a sideways glance at Kilpatrick.

'Jane told us,' confirmed Laura.

'Just because it's on television doesn't mean it's true,' remarked Tweddle in a loud voice. 'The media often get their facts wrong.'

'It's a bit hard to get something like this wrong,' replied Kilpatrick fiercely. 'They're saying we're cold-blooded killers, and there was a fellow on a moment ago who was advocating the death penalty.'

'If anybody was hurt, it was unintentional,' said Jordan softly.

'Tell that to their families,' spat Kilpatrick. 'I'm sure it'll make them feel much better.'

'So what do we do now?' asked Tracey. 'Matt was talking about giving ourselves up.'

'I had the same thought, but Laura suggested that we hear what the official has to say first.'

'Which official?' asked Tweddle.

Laura related her conversation with Jane, and the others lapsed into silence once she finished. She studied their drawn faces, wishing that Robert was still part of their group. His presence was always a comfort. 'I feel awful about this because you only went there to help me, but the thing that keeps me going is the thought that none of this is our fault. Everything that's happened has been forced upon us by Memtech personnel, and I believe we have a moral duty to survive so we can expose them for the murderers they are. Collateral damage is always unfortunate, but I'm not about to roll over and give up just because somebody else happened to be on the receiving end for a change. I'll probably have nightmares over this, but I intend to press on.'

'You're right,' said Jordan. 'We haven't come this far to fall at the last hurdle, but if we really have killed five people, the public will be baying for our blood.'

'You could always throw yourselves on the mercy of the court,' observed Tweddle. 'As Laura said, there are mitigating circumstances with your case.'

Laura looked at him. 'Our case? You've got blood on your hands too.'

'Me? I'm just an innocent bystander. I've been the voice of reason all along. I've done nothing to worry about.'

'So where were you when the bomb blew up?' replied Laura coldly. 'You're as guilty as the rest of us,' she added dismissively.

'They're going to really turn up the heat on us,' said Kilpatrick suddenly. 'It's only a matter of time before they catch us, and when they do ...' He drew his finger across his throat. 'Somebody in this building might already have recognised us and tipped off the police.'

Jordan suddenly clicked his fingers. 'That reminds me, Frank wants to take a picture of each of us.'

'He wants to take our picture at a time like this? What on earth for?' asked Laura.

Jordan smiled. 'Robert arranged for him to provide a change of identity and a new passport for each of us. Killa's right. If we stay in England, we'll be caught for sure. Our best chance is to quietly disappear overseas.'

The gloomy atmosphere in the room suddenly brightened.

'Where would we go?' asked Tracey.

'I hear Australia's very nice, and it's a long way away,' said Kilpatrick.

'What about Robert and Jane?' asked Tracey. 'We can't just leave them behind.'

'Sometimes an individual has to be sacrificed for the good of the group,' said Tweddle piously.

'What makes you think you're coming?' asked Kilpatrick pointedly.

'Well, I can't stay here, not after everything that's happened. It's your fault I got involved in this mess, so you have a moral obligation to include me.'

'Don't we have the same obligation to include Robert?' asked Kilpatrick.

'It's not the same thing,' replied Tweddle defensively. 'His ill health clearly makes him a liability.'

'This discussion is over,' replied Laura firmly. 'We're not leaving Robert behind.'

'And what about me?' asked Tweddle. 'Am I included or not?'

'If it was up to me, I'd leave you here to rot,' replied Jordan as he glanced at Laura, 'but I guess we have no choice.' The satisfied look on Tweddle's face immediately caused Jordan to regret his generosity, although he knew Laura would have overturned any other decision.

'Now that we've settled that issue,' said Kilpatrick, a little stony-faced, 'how do we rescue Robert once he's sufficiently recovered?'

'I have an idea,' replied Jordan, 'but I need to talk to Frank first.'

'I think we should get our mug shots taken immediately,' said Tracey. Once we're linked to the Memtech bombing, it won't be safe for us to leave this room.'

'Good point,' said Laura. 'We should also stock up on food, because we'll have to lie low for a few weeks until Robert is well enough to travel.'

'Why don't some of us go on ahead and set up a base in the new country, and the others can follow later?' asked Tweddle hopefully.

'No, Colin,' replied Laura sharply. 'We're in this together. We will all succeed, or we'll all fail. Please try and understand that concept.'

'It was only a suggestion,' replied Tweddle defensively.

'I should contact my mother,' said Tracey. 'She'll be really upset over this.'

'All of our families must be wondering what's going on,' said Laura.

Jordan picked up roughly wrapped brown-paper parcel from the table. 'And I need to return this to Father O'Brien before we go anywhere.'

Tracey looked at him curiously. 'Who's Father O'Brien?'

Jordan explained briefly about the exorcism and O'Brien's assessment of Stephen Kimpton. 'He lent me this book to help me with my newspaper article, although I've only had time to glance at a few pages. I promised him I'd return it as soon as I finished.'

'It's unsafe to travel at the moment,' cautioned Kilpatrick. 'Why don't you post it to him?'

'No,' replied Jordan. 'It's extremely valuable and might get damaged or lost in the post. I wouldn't feel right unless I handed it to him personally. Besides, it'll give me a chance to explain our side of the story to him. I'm sure he's been wondering about our involvement in all of this.'

'You have enough to do,' said Laura. 'I'll return it to him. My picture hasn't been in the news, so I'll be safe enough. He might even have a few suggestions.'

'I'll come with you,' said Tracey. 'We shouldn't go anywhere on our own.'

Jordan reluctantly agreed, and the girls decided to return the book early the following morning.

The entire group left to have their photos taken shortly after. Jordan waited until everybody had smiled for the camera before taking Frank aside and discussing his plan to release Banks. Frank listened intently and then shook hands on the deal once he realized money wouldn't be an issue.

The group spent a sleepless night surrounded by strange noises drifting fitfully in from the river, imagining that every small noise heralded the rush of deadly SAS troops.

Laura and Tracey were understandably tired when they arrived outside the church the following morning. The trees in the surrounding park showed a profusion of buds against the cloud-flecked sky, and there was even a hint of warmth in the air as they climbed the worn steps

It took a moment for their eyes to adjust to the dim interior as they walked down the central aisle in search of the priest. They found him preparing a cluster of candles at the front of the church.

'Excuse me, Father, do you remember me?' asked Laura softly. The priest nodded curtly but remained silent. 'This is my friend Tracey,' continued Laura hesitantly. 'We've come to return the book that Daniel borrowed from you."

Father O'Brien looked at her grimly as he took the book from her. 'Daniel seems to be in serious trouble. The news reports are linking his name with the bombing.'

'It was an error of judgement,' replied Laura contritely. 'We didn't realise the bomb was so powerful. We never intended to hurt anybody.'

'I don't have any experience with bombs,' replied O'Brien stiffly, 'but my basic understanding is that bombs are designed to destroy. You don't hear of too many bombs creating anything other than a mess.'

'It probably doesn't help, but we were devastated when we heard that five people had been killed.'

'Eleven people according to the latest news report,' corrected O'Brien coldly. 'Whether it was intentional or not, I cannot condone such an act.'

Laura's eyes widened at the news. 'Eleven people dead? That can't possibly be true. We set off the fire alarm and gave people plenty of time to evacuate.' She turned to Tracey. 'This is horrible. With eleven people dead, just imagine how many have been injured.'

Tracey shook her head. 'There's been no mention of injuries.'

O'Brien looked thoughtful. 'That's true, yet when the IRA was blowing up half of London, it was normal to read that five to six people had been seriously hurt for each person killed. With eleven people dead you would expect to find at least fifty to sixty people badly injured but, according to the papers, there were none. I do find that strange.'

'I hadn't thought about it,' confessed Tracey. 'Once people start dying, you tend to forget about injuries.'

'There does seem to be more to this than meets the eye,' replied O'Brien slowly. 'Come back to my study, and tell me what happened. I think I'm only getting half the story from the papers.'

Father O'Brien made a pot of tea as Laura brought him up to date, and he appeared satisfied when she finished. 'Daniel wanted you to understand the true facts,' she said. 'He was worried that you may have regretted helping us.'

'I admit I was concerned, although, to tell you the truth, I've been too busy planning my trip to St Kitts to worry about much else,' replied O'Brien.

'St Kitts?' replied Tracey. 'Where's that, in Wales?'

'Dear me no, child,' replied O'Brien, amusement plainly written across his fierce features. 'It's in the West Indies. You have heard of the West Indies?'

'Of course I have. I just hadn't heard of that place you mentioned.'

'St Kitts,' repeated O'Brien. 'Let me show you.' He tugged out a map from among a pile of papers on his desk and spread it across the table. O'Brien jabbed the paper with a well-manicured finger. 'These two islands are called St Kitts and Nevis and are well known for their beauty. I believe Lord Nelson met his wife there when he was a dashing sea captain.'

'I can't really picture you lying on a tropical beach in your colourful swimwear surrounded by a bevy of dusky beauties,' replied Laura slowly.

O'Brien grunted. 'The trip is completely work related. I'm in charge of a delegation attending an important conference there.'

'It's rather an exotic place for a conference, isn't it?' said Laura, who was happy they were no longer discussing bombs.

'The church has been struggling to formulate acceptable policies on contraception and abortion. With the population rapidly increasing in many African, Asian, and South American countries, and with AIDS spiralling out of control, it's important that we remain a relevant contributor to a workable solution. We have groups attending from all over the world, and it was decided that the West Indies was a central and, more importantly, a neutral location.'

'When are you going?'

'Next Tuesday morning.'

Tracey trailed her fingers idly over the islands on the map. 'I've heard of most of these places, Jamaica, Barbados, Trinidad. I wish we were going with you.' She suddenly jumped from her chair and placed her hand on O'Brien's forearm. 'That's it! Why don't we come with you? We were just talking about the need to get out of the country, and they'll never think of looking for us among a group of priests and nuns. There are nuns going with you?'

'No, I'm afraid it's impossible,' replied O'Brien brusquely. 'Everything has already been organised: the flights, accommodation, everything.'

'Oh, you don't need to worry about accommodation,' replied Tracey. 'We won't be staying with you. It's just a safe method for us to leave the country.' She turned to Laura. 'What do you think?'

Laura was dubious. 'I'd need to give it some thought.'

O'Brien was having none of it. 'I'm sorry, it won't work. Even if seats are still available on the flight to Caracas, the authorities would smell a rat as soon as I submitted your names, and then we'd all be for the high jump.'

'Why are you going to Caracas?'

'We couldn't get a direct flight from London, so we're travelling via Venezuela.'

'That's even better,' said Tracey. 'We could travel anywhere from there.'

'Is this what it's like being married?' asked O'Brien. 'My mouth is supplying a steady stream of words that apparently aren't reaching your ears.'

'Oh I heard you, but you don't need to worry because it won't be our names on the passenger list.'

'You still need a passport to leave this country,' replied O'Brien doggedly, 'so booking seats under bogus names won't work. I just don't see how it can be done, particularly at such short notice.'

'I appreciate your dilemma,' replied Tracey soothingly. 'You'd like to help, but you're unable to do so because of the circumstances.'

'Exactly. I don't like letting anybody down, but my hands are tied. I'm sorry.'

'What if we weren't wanted by the police? Would you be able to help us then?'

'Possibly, if sufficient seats were still available. What are you trying to tell me?'

'We're having alternative identities arranged for us, and if they're ready before next Tuesday, then we can go with you as part of your delegation.'

'False identities,' said O'Brien grimly. 'I assume that means false passports?'

Tracey nodded silently.

'You appear to have your fingers in many different pies,' muttered O'Brien. 'I wouldn't know where to begin to obtain such a thing.' He sighed theatrically. 'Well, a promise is a promise, but I'll need your names and the passport numbers immediately, otherwise forget it.'

'So we can come?' said Tracey gleefully as she hugged O'Brien, dancing a little jig as she did so.

'Steady on, child,' rumbled O'Brien as he disengaged Tracey's hands from around his waist. 'I haven't done anything yet. There's any one of a dozen things that could go wrong before we have you winging over the Atlantic. Just get me that information, and I'll see what I can do.'

'I wouldn't get too excited just yet,' cautioned Laura. 'We do have another slight problem.'

O'Brien raised an eyebrow. 'How surprising. Come on then, what is it?'

'Inspector Banks will probably be in a wheelchair.'

'I thought you said he was close to death and under police guard. He won't be going anywhere, let alone overseas.'

'He was very weak from loss of blood, that was all,' said Tracey. 'The bullet wound was nasty, but there was no damage to his vital organs. I'm sure they've given him enough transfusions to fill him up again, and he has five days to recover.'

'Five days counting today,' reminded O'Brien.

'If he's fit enough to travel, he'll be there,' promised Tracey.

'All right, all right, I'll see what I can do,' replied O'Brien irritably. 'That's the trouble with today's generation, you do them one good turn, and they end up milking you dry. I'm going to need your clothing sizes, and you'll require haircuts. It doesn't have to look too flash, just make sure you cut it short. Get that information to me by this afternoon, or you can kiss Caracas goodbye. Now if you don't mind, I have some real work to do. Goodbye to you now.'

Laura stepped forward and gave him a kiss on the cheek. 'You don't fool me for one minute, you old softy.'

They stopped at a travel agency on the way home and picked up a handful of brochures. The return journey seemed to take forever, and Tracey was bursting with excitement by the time they reached their lodgings. They knocked twice, and Kilpatrick greeted them with the news that eleven people were now reported dead and another five were still missing.

The girls dismissed the report and asked everybody to assemble in the lounge room. Laura outlined O'Brien's suspicions concerning the lack of badly injured people and then handed over the lead to Tracey, who was unable to hide a huge grin as she outlined the plans they had discussed with O'Brien. After a round of high fives in which even Tweddle was included, Jordan called Frank on the phone and asked him to track down the required information. Frank wasn't sure if the information was available, but once Jordan offered him a further fifty pounds he agreed to look into it.

Tracey tossed the travel brochures onto the coffee table and watched happily as the others excitedly poured through them. 'I think the Bahamas will make a good home, but there are more than seven hundred islands, so we'll need to agree on a specific island,' she remarked authoritatively, having read the brochures on the way home.

'Grand Bahama has a wonderful subtropical climate, with sparkling turquoise waters and powder-white beaches stretching for miles,' said Laura as she read through her brochure.

'That's bit different to the stony beaches and polluted water at Torquay,' said Kilpatrick.

'I don't like it.' Jordan frowned. 'It's too close to the states. I'd feel more relaxed with some distance between us and our enemies.'

'What about Cat Island?' said Tweddle. 'I've always enjoyed cats.'

Kilpatrick opened his mouth to speak, but Tracey cut him off with a warning waggle of her finger. 'Don't even think about saying it.'

Jordan dropped his brochure onto the table. 'We have plenty of time to make a decision. The most pressing issue is what to do about Robert and Jane. We need a workable plan by Monday night, which doesn't give us much time.'

Laura nodded. 'Still, if Jane can make a deal with that government fellow, then all this is unnecessary.'

~

Jane's interview with Northfield began promisingly. She was delighted when he informed her that, as a result of her information, all charges against Banks would be dropped. Once he was fully recovered, he would be free to resume his official duties. Northfield even hinted that Banks could be in line for a decoration.

'That's wonderful news,' said Jane tearfully. 'This has been such a harrowing experience that I despaired it would ever turn out okay. I can't wait to tell Robert.'

'The truth always comes out in the end,' replied Northfield reassuringly. 'It's a pity your friends took matters into their own hands. If they allowed the authorities to sort things out they wouldn't be in so much trouble.'

'Oh no, you're quite wrong there,' Jane protested mildly. 'They were only acting in self-defence. They're innocent of any real crimes.'

'Innocent acts do not result in the deaths of eleven people,' replied Northfield haughtily.'

'Eleven people dead?' repeated Jane as she blinked back her surprise.

'We have irrefutable evidence that your friends planted a bomb that killed at least eleven people.'

Jane shook her head. 'It must have been an accident. They would never intentionally hurt anybody.'

Northfield smiled. 'There may be mitigating circumstances. If they were to give themselves up, the courts would undoubtedly view their actions in a more favourable light.'

'And if they decide not to?'

'Then the consequences could be quite tragic indeed.'

'But that's not fair. Memtech is responsible for everything that's happened, and we can prove it.'

'How?' asked Northfield sharply.

'We have computer files detailing their operations and the names of those responsible. Everything needed to prove Memtech's guilt is there.'

Northfield blanched slightly. Jarvis had mentioned the existence of these disks, but he had been adamant that only one set existed. 'So why haven't you taken this evidence to the authorities?'

'We only received the information last night,' replied Jane as she studied Northfield's face. Her news had appeared to briefly unnerve him. 'We weren't sure who to approach with it.'

'I understand. It would be in your friends' best interests if they handed these files to me personally. If they contain everything you say, I'm sure they'll be exonerated.'

'Including the bombing?'

Northfield hesitated. 'So many deaths cannot be dismissed with a simple slap on the wrist, but there may be a solution. There are currently three terrorist groups claiming responsibility so it shouldn't be too difficult to redirect public perception in that direction, thereby exonerating your friends.'

'You could do that?'

'If your friends were to fully cooperate, we'd overlook any crimes committed in the course of obtaining this information. Of course, they'd need to sign a confidentiality agreement. Would they be open to such a deal?'

Jane smiled warmly. 'I'm sure they would jump at such an opportunity.'

'Excellent.' Northfield paused. 'So how will you contact them?'

Jane frowned. 'They're paranoid about calls being traced back to their location, so I'll send a text message and get them to call me from a public telephone.'

'You must impress upon them the urgency of this matter.' He gave her an encouraging pat on the arm as he stood up. 'I'll be in touch again shortly.'

Jane hurried back to talk to Banks but he was still asleep, so she fired off a text message to Laura and then patiently waited for a reply.

Laura received the message while giving Jordan's hair a severe trim. She read the message and then handed it to Jordan. 'It's from Jane. Apparently we've been offered a deal.'

Jordan raised his eyebrows as he scanned the text. 'Okay, take Tracey and call Jane from a public phone, and I'll contact Frank and find out where he is with the passport information.'

Laura and Tracey were waiting when Jordan returned from his meeting with Frank, and they sat down and discussed Northfield's deal.

'I think we should take it,' said Tweddle. 'Instead of being hunted like vermin, we'll end up being treated like heroes.'

'I'm afraid your vote doesn't count,' said Jordan waspishly.

'Oh, I see,' sneered Tweddle. 'When things are tough and you need my help, then I'm an important team member, but when you think you're home free, I'm simply discarded. Well, I have my thriving counselling practice to think of, and I don't intend to throw it away lightly.'

'Colin is entitled to have a say in the final decision,' Laura replied. 'How can we make an informed decision if we don't listen to all sides of the argument?'

Jordan glowered at Tweddle but grumpily bowed to Laura's judgement.

Kilpatrick broke the moment of sullen silence. 'My only worry is whether we can trust the government to keep their end of the bargain.'

Tracey answered quietly. 'If we have a chance to stay, I agree with Colin. My mother has been through a lot, and I feel terrible about leaving her in the lurch. We've always been a close family, and at the very time when she needs my support and encouragement, I disappear from her life. I understand Matt's concern about the government, but we have one of the most stable and transparent democracies in the world. Surely they'll deal with us in a fair and impartial manner.'

'I don't agree,' said Kilpatrick. 'Our system of government is one thing, but what about the shadowy individuals in the background. Silencing us would be a small price to pay if it meant keeping this technology secret. I vote for the Bahamas.'

'I'm with Matt,' said Jordan simply. 'It's too dangerous to stay here.'

'That makes it two all,' said Tweddle. 'I guess you've got the casting vote, Laura.'

Laura smiled weakly. 'I feel responsible for all this. None of this would have happened if I hadn't got involved with Stephen Kimpton.'

'That's nonsense,' said Jordan stiffly.

'Maybe so, but I can't help the way I feel, and as I've suffered more than anyone, it's probably poetic justice that I cast the deciding vote.'

'I'm sure you'll make the right decision,' said Tweddle smoothly.

'I'm fed up with skulking around in second-rate housing with only the bare necessities to sustain me. I'm tired of living in perpetual fear that the police might burst through the door and drag us off to prison. I want to live a normal life again so I can make plans that extend beyond surviving for the next twenty-four hours. I never appreciated the value of living a normal existence until I found myself deprived of it. Events such as this put your life into perspective. I now realize that it's the basic things in life that matter the most. I want a safe and secure future, and I want my children to have a safe and secure future, so I also vote for the Bahamas.'

Jordan gave Laura a quick hug. 'I guess we're leaving after all.'

Tweddle struggled to hide his disappointment. 'I think we're making the wrong decision.'

'You can stay if you want to,' said Kilpatrick. 'You'll probably be eligible for parole in thirty years, and then you can resume your thriving business.'

'No, no,' replied Tweddle hurriedly. 'I'll abide by Laura's decision. I'm sure she knows what's best.'

'What do we tell Jane?' asked Jordan. 'I think she was hoping we'd turn ourselves in.'

'I'll call Jane and tell her,' said Tracey. 'We have to give Father O'Brien our passport information, so I'll call her from a public phone on the way.'

'We've also got passports for them,' said Jordan, 'but if they've decided to stay, then that's final. We need to book the flights today.'

'I'll explain that to her,' said Tracey.

'Don't tell her about the Bahamas,' warned Jordan. 'You never know who is listening.'

'Speaking of the Bahamas,' added Tracey. 'Now that I've got my new identity, I can open an account there and transfer our money.'

'That's a good idea. Frank has organised two identities for each of us so use the second one,' said Jordan. 'Even if they trace us as far as Caracas they'll hit a dead end and won't be able to trace us to our final destination.' He handed the list to Tracey and then stood back as everybody crowded around, clutching at the sheet of paper to see what their new names were. There was a deal of good-natured teasing before Tracey managed to retrieve the list and head out the door.

Jane's conversation with Tracey was deliberately ambiguous. Banks had already warned her that Northfield was not to be trusted, and their only chance of survival depended upon him getting fit enough to escape from the hospital. As she returned to the ward with her escort, she thought about the best way to handle Northfield.

Fortunately for Jane, Northfield had other pressing matters to deal with. He had received a sealed bag from Jarvis containing the original disks taken from Toulemonde along with a synopsis of the technology's capability. Jarvis had added a brief note asking when he would be allowed to contact his wife and daughter.

Northfield grimaced as he lobbed the note into his waste paper basket. His department had already informed Jarvis's wife that he had been sent overseas on an urgent matter. He planned to wait several days before personally informing her, with his deepest condolences, that her husband was dead. His badly mutilated body had been discovered in a river and been immediately cremated once his identity had been confirmed. Due to the sensitive nature of his mission, his death would not be recognised through official channels. She would receive an adequate pension from a grateful government, and Jarvis would no longer exist.

Northfield flicked slowly through the report, underlining the key phrases in red and highlighting other sections of interest. He then rang Aubrey and instructed him to arrange an immediate confidential meeting with the Prime Minister. Aubrey baulked, arguing that such meetings were impossible to arrange. The Prime Minister was never bothered with the micro-details of dodgy projects so he could truthfully claim innocence if the shit hit the fan.

Northfield refused to be deterred and threatened to cut Aubrey out of the loop if he didn't cooperate. Aubrey rang back an hour later with the news that he had pulled a few strings and a meeting had been arranged for late that afternoon.

Northfield had attended social events at Downing Street, but this was his first formal meeting. He hurried past a reporter lurking by the front door and was shown into the waiting room.

The Prime Minister looked tired and irritable as Northfield and Aubrey were ushered into his presence. 'What's this all about? I don't like meetings held off the record. It's invariably bad news, and I usually end up regretting my involvement.'

Northfield nodded sagely. 'I understand, Prime Minister, but in this case it's a precautionary measure for your own safety. If you agree to any future discussions, you can make your own decision about secretaries, minutes, and recording devices.'

'How very cloak and dagger,' remarked the Prime Minister as he studied his watch. 'My driver's picking me up in ten minutes, so please be brief. I have a dinner engagement with the

German ambassador. If I'm late, my wife will make my life quite miserable. She's been looking forward to this for some time.'

Northfield smiled agreeably and began his measured discourse on the memory technology, aware that somebody as astute as the Prime Minister would quickly realise the personal and public benefits. An hour later, having answered a multitude of questions, Northfield reached the end of his presentation.

The Prime Minister sat quite still as he studied Northfield's face. He wanted to believe that the cup being offered was not a poisoned chalice. He finally turned to Aubrey. 'You can vouch for this, Dean? This technology exists? It's not just scientific fantasy?'

'It's real, Prime Minister,' confirmed Aubrey. 'Just as articles about man walking on the moon prior to 1969 weren't science fiction. It's just scientific fact awaiting development.'

'And we have access to it right now?'

'Yes, Prime Minister. We've already processed several enemies of the state and have used the information to arrest twenty-four terrorists working undercover in our country.'

The Prime Minister pressed a button on his telephone and a voice crackled from the speaker. 'Yes, sir?'

'Bring in a pot of tea with cups and biscuits for three, please, William.' He smiled wryly at his guests. 'I'm afraid I've missed my dinner engagement, and all this talk has made me peckish. My dear wife will never forgive me but from what you've been telling me, I may soon have the option of erasing selective parts of her memory, which will be a boon to husbands everywhere. How much is this going to cost me?'

Aubrey smiled. 'My department will need a significant budget increase, but more importantly I'm going to need a range of new sweeping powers.'

'The money I can understand, but why do you need to upgrade your powers?'

Northfield took over the discussion. 'We're the only people outside the Dartmoor facility who have any extensive knowledge of this program, so the information is tightly controlled. Quite clearly, you will need to expand your circle of confidantes at some stage. The problem is that some members of this inner circle may be tempted to create their own power base. In order to combat this we may need to occasionally breach the constitution.'

The Prime Minister held up his hand. 'You don't need to explain any further. It goes against my nature, but for the good of the country, it's sometimes necessary to make decisions that one personally regards as abhorrent.'

'I understand,' said Aubrey solemnly. 'With great power comes great responsibility.'

The Prime Minister gave a wry smile. 'The recent explosion at the Memtech facility should give parliament sufficient impetus to allow me to push through a series of antiterrorist laws that should suit your purpose. Now I have one final question for you, Mr Northfield: what is it that you want?'

'An excellent question, Prime Minister. My requirements however, are confidential.' He looked meaningfully at Aubrey, who coughed nervously, turned slightly red, and politely excused himself. 'Dean's a good man,' said Northfield as he watched the door close. 'He's solid and reliable but lacks the ruthless streak your new order will certainly demand.'

'You're telling me he's expendable,' said the Prime Minister.

'Eventually, yes.'

'And by the same token, you're not.'

Northfield spread his hands wide in a gesture of innocence. 'I don't harbour any ambitions to take your place, and you'll need somebody you can trust to run the program. If it isn't me, it'll have to be somebody else, so the issue of trust will always be a constant.'

'I see. So what are your requirements?'

Northfield took a sip from his cup before answering. 'I would like a personal fortune. I've thought about it and decided not to be greedy. Fifty million pounds should be sufficient.'

'Fifty million pounds,' laughed the Prime Minister.

'You know what you're getting is worth infinitely more than that.'

'It's still a lot of money,' grumbled the Prime Minister. 'It won't be easy siphoning off such a large amount without leaving an audit trail.'

'You can pay it to me over five years, I don't mind.'

'Okay, that should work. Are we finished?'

'Yes, unless you have any further questions.'

The Prime Minister closed his eyes in thought. 'This artificial memory you mentioned, how far away is that?'

Northfield shrugged. 'They've already had some success, but it's still in its infancy.'

'How long would it take to create an artificial memory?'

'It depends on the memory's complexity.'

The Prime Minister looked uncomfortable as he grappled with his next words. 'What if I wanted people to believe I was infallible, a figure of reverence. How hard would that be?'

Northfield laughed pleasantly. 'The hardest part would be finding the original memory to duplicate.'

'It was a serious question,' snapped the Prime Minister.

'Sorry, it's been a long day.' Northfield slowly smiled. 'What if we modified the memory of a religious zealot so that it was you they revered? It would take a bit of tinkering but it should be possible. Anybody who received that memory would think you were a god. You could even start your own religion.'

'I'm not too comfortable about the worshipping aspect, but if you can do it, I'll double your fee.'

'I'll talk to my people at Dartmoor immediately, Prime Minister.' Northfield rose and shook hands. 'I'll be in touch.'

Aubrey was waiting for him in the outer vestibule as he left the Prime Minister's office. 'That appeared to go well,' he said.

'I thought so,' replied Northfield blandly.

'I noticed you didn't mention Inspector Banks and his accomplices.'

'No and I would appreciate it if you didn't either. That situation will be resolved within the next twenty-four hours, and talking about it will only serve to muddy what is really very clear water.'

Northfield arrived at the hospital early the next morning and immediately sent for Jane. He inquired about Banks, and Jane told him that although he was still extremely weak, the doctors were hopeful of a full recovery, which wasn't quite true. Banks was actually feeling much better and had started a program of gentle calisthenics in the privacy of the toilet cubicle.

'I'm glad to hear that,' replied Northfield. 'Did you convince your friends to turn themselves in?'

'I believe so, although Daniel's still dubious and is insisting on a firm guarantee that they won't go to prison; but overall they're receptive. I think they're tired of living in constant fear.'

'Excellent. Tell them my word is their guarantee.' Northfield smiled ruefully as he left. He was a body language expert and knew Jane had been lying. Her friends had no intention of surrendering. After consulting with the doctor, he arranged for Jane and Banks to be transported to Dartmoor the following Monday. Between the two of them, they should possess enough information to sweep the fugitives into his net.

'I'll download the damned data into my own head if I have to,' he muttered.

Chapter 19

If you will only take the trouble always to do the perfectly correct thing,
and to say the perfectly correct thing, you can do just what you like.

George Bernard Shaw

ordan spent an hour with Doris making extra copies of
the disks. He then wrote a detailed account of the recent
events while Doris cheerfully fluttered around with
constant offers of tea and slightly stale chocolate cake. After
printing six copies of the statement, he drove to the White Stag
and picked up hospital uniforms from Frank. The remainder of
the weekend had been spent ensuring that all loose ends had
been tied up.

They picked up Frank early on Monday morning and drove
to the hospital while Tweddle followed behind in Laura's BMW.
As they skirted the road leading to the public car park, Jordan
absently watched a pair of window cleaners operating on the
fourth floor. They continued around to the rear of the hospital
and parked next to an unloading bay bordered by a cluster of
rusting dump bins.

Frank was sitting happily in the back, tightly flanked by
Tracey and Laura, and he frowned as the car rolled to a stop. 'I
think we should reconnoitre some more to get our bearings. You
can never be too cautious.'

'And you're a dirty old man who should know better,' snorted Jordan.

Tracey absently pushed Frank's hand away as she leaned forward to speak to Jordan. 'What if they don't want to come with us? We could be exposing ourselves for nothing.'

'You sound like Colin,' replied Kilpatrick dismissively.

'Calling me names doesn't diminish my concern,' said Tracey coldly.

'We owe them the opportunity to say no,' said Jordan. 'The fact that Jane hasn't responded to your text messages is significant.'

'You folks go right on talking,' said Frank as he leant back and put his arms around the girls' shoulders. 'I can sit here all day if necessary.'

'Talking is over,' said Jordan abruptly as he opened his door. 'It's time for you to earn your keep.' He walked back to the BMW and told Tweddle to stay with the cars. 'We should be back shortly and we'll need to leave in a hurry. If anybody tells you to move the cars just tell them to bugger off.' He vaulted onto the loading bay and ran his hands over a pair of solid metal doors before giving them a sharp tug. 'They're locked,' he called softly.

'I don't know what else you expected,' muttered Frank as he inserted his picks in the lock.

A short narrow passage led into the hospital, and Jordan scouted ahead to make sure it was safe. Both he and Kilpatrick were dressed as orderlies while the girls were wearing crisp, freshly laundered nurse's uniforms. Frank's contact had assured him that the uniforms were indistinguishable from the real thing, which was a reasonable statement given that they were stolen from the hospital the previous day.

Frank was dressed as a janitor. He pulled a rag from his back pocket and wiped the door clean of fingerprints as he waited for Jordan to give the all clear. Jordan whistled down the corridor, and Frank stepped back to allow the girls to pass, admiring their trim legs as they squeezed by.

'Where do we go now?' asked Tracey.

'Good question,' replied Jordan. 'I have no idea.'

Frank shook his head in disgust. 'Haven't you heard of planning? How you've got this far is a complete mystery to me.'

'It's not a problem,' said Jordan. 'We'll simply ask somebody.'

'Ask somebody,' repeated Kilpatrick, who felt Frank had a valid point. 'Just like that?'

'It's all a matter of innocent confidence,' replied Jordan testily. 'We'll need to find a busy area, and then you can watch me work my magic.'

The passage ended at an old wooden door with a thick opaque window. The dull sound of footsteps and barely audible voices indicated that they had reached a main thoroughfare. Jordan gave a cheery thumbs-up as he strolled out the door. He walked unhurriedly, setting his pace to that of the people around him. He was gratified to see that nobody gave him a second glance. He stopped and beckoned to Kilpatrick. 'I've got an idea, but we'll need a wheelchair.'

'Why am I not surprised?' groaned Kilpatrick. 'Hospitals and wheelchairs seem to go hand in hand where you're concerned.'

'I've been looking around but I can't see any.'

Kilpatrick pointed across the corridor. 'There's one right there.'

'Yes, but there's an old man sitting in it. I need an empty one.'

'We can soon make it empty.'

'I don't think so. We don't want to attract attention by dumping elderly patients onto the floor. Something tells me he won't take it quietly.'

'We won't attract any attention if we do it right,' retorted Kilpatrick. 'Give me some credit for intelligence.' He turned and stared down the corridor, stepping aside as he did so to allow a family group to pass. 'We passed an empty trolley a moment ago so give me a hand to fetch it.'

'No,' said Jordan. 'A trolley's too big. I need a wheelchair.'

'I know you do, and I'm going to get you one, ye of little faith.' Kilpatrick grabbed his arm, and they walked back past the girls, who looked at them curiously.

'What's going on?' asked Laura.

'They're lost,' muttered Frank scathingly. 'If you fail to plan, then you plan to fail.'

'We're not lost,' replied Kilpatrick. 'We're devising a plan of action and you can help by finding me a clipboard.'

Tracey gave him a small curtsey and then commandeered one from a nearby nurse's station, handing it to Kilpatrick as he returned with the trolley bed in tow.

'Absolute confidence backed up by a uniform is the key to success,' Kilpatrick said grandly as weaved the trolley carefully along the crowded corridor. They parked it next to the elderly man who was sitting placidly watching the passing parade. It was a welcome break from being cooped up in the ward.

Kilpatrick bustled over, smiling benignly as he stooped down and peered in his face. 'Good news, sir, we've finally found a trolley bed for you. Just relax, and we'll have you on board in no time.'

'Eh? A trolley bed?' repeated the elderly gentleman as he cupped a hand to his ear. 'For me? I'm afraid you're mistaken young man, I don't need no damned trolley bed.'

Kilpatrick's smile became even more condescending as he gently picked up the man's wrist and read his name on the plastic tag. 'No, Mr Mortimer, there's no mistake.' He held out the clipboard momentarily before snatching it away. 'It's important your leg gets sufficient elevation, otherwise there could be serious complications.' With Jordan's help he lifted Mortimer effortlessly onto the trolley and arranged a pillow under his left leg. 'There you go, mate,' he said encouragingly. 'You'll be fine now.'

'What sort of complications?' asked Mortimer in a tremulous voice. 'What does this have to do with my acute angina?'

'Ask your doctor,' Kilpatrick called over his shoulder as Jordan pushed the wheelchair down the corridor before stopping at the main nurses' station.

'My turn,' muttered Jordan as he plucked the clipboard from Kilpatrick's grasp and approached the duty sister. 'Excuse me,' he said with a worried frown.

The duty sister looked up from the staffing roster she'd been reviewing. 'Yes?'

'I'm sorry to trouble you, but I have to make a pickup for physio, and I can't locate my patient. I'm new here, and I still get confused.'

'It can be confusing,' agreed the sister amiably. 'What's your patient's name?'

Jordan consulted his clipboard. 'Robert Banks.'

'That name does sound familiar,' said the sister as she glanced at the computer screen. 'Is he a new arrival?'

'I have no idea.'

'Hmm,' she muttered as she scrolled down the list of names. 'We've got a Barnes and a Braithwaite but no Banks. Are you sure he was on this floor?'

'Fairly positive,' Jordan replied uncertainly. He brightened as a thought occurred to him. 'My supervisor mentioned something about a police guard. Does that help?'

The sister's kind smile tightened into a poorly disguised grimace. 'I believe you want the security ward on the fifth floor. Did your supervisor give you a pass?'

'No,' replied Jordan in a small voice. 'Should he have?'

'They won't let you in without a pass, so I suggest you go back to your supervisor and ask him for one.'

'You don't happen to have a spare one, do you?'

'Heavens, no, what would be the point of having a secured area if we lent passes willy-nilly? Go and talk to your supervisor,' she repeated in a voice that indicated the conversation was over.

Jordan thanked her and pushed the wheelchair back to where Kilpatrick and the others were waiting.

'Well?' asked Kilpatrick.

'He's on the fifth floor but we need a pass to gain access to his ward.'

'That shouldn't be a problem,' said Tracey brightly. 'I'm sure Frank can get us in.'

'Sorry,' said Frank. 'If they're using electronic swipe cards, then I don't have the equipment to override the security system.'

'What do we do then?' Jordan asked, fighting back an unexpected panic attack.

'Let's go up to the fifth floor and have a look. Something may occur to us,' replied Frank.

'And what if it doesn't?'

'Don't worry,' replied Frank firmly. 'I will not let the inspector rot in jail. We'll get him out one way or the other.'

They rode the elevator to the fifth floor in silence, and Jordan asked a passing nurse for the location of the security ward. They noticed that there were fewer people around as they walked briskly in the direction indicated by the nurse. A wall of metal bars extending across the corridor showed that they had arrived at their destination. An overweight policeman was lounging on a wooden chair on the far side of the bars reading a magazine, and he glanced up as they rounded the corner. Jordan noticed his scrutiny and led the others off into a side ward.

A young nurse was struggling to help an old man sit up in his bed, and Kilpatrick hurried over to assist. She thanked him with a smile and Kilpatrick explained that they were new to the hospital and were visiting the various wards as part of their orientation program.

'That must be a recent change,' remarked the nurse. 'They didn't do that when I started here. This is the DAD's ward,' she added in way of explanation is if it was now expected of her. 'We look after those suffering from dementia, Alzheimer's, and delusions.'

'It must be interesting work,' acknowledged Laura.

'Oh, it's a thousand laughs every day,' replied the nurse sardonically. 'One more month of this and then I'm off to maternity, thank goodness. Is there anything in particular you want to see?'

'No,' replied Jordan evasively. 'We're just looking around in the general sense. What's that place with the bars across it?'

'That's the security wing. It's used to treat criminals who have been injured or become ill.' Her voice became a conspiratorial whisper. 'They've got that policeman in there who murdered those people and kidnapped the magazine editor.' Her whisper became even softer, and they had to lean closer to hear her words. 'The strange thing is that the woman he kidnapped is in there with him. Isn't that weird?'

'The world's a strange place,' agreed Jordan. 'Have you ever been in there?'

'Oh no, you need a special pass to work in that section.'

'What sort of pass?' asked Jordan.

'My friend Delores is rostered in there, and she showed me her pass last week when they gave it to her. It's just a plastic card with your photograph on it. You hold it over a little red light and the door unlocks.'

'Do the nurses ever leave that area once they've started their shift?' asked Tracey.

'No, they've got everything they need in there.' She looked at them appraisingly. 'You certainly ask a lot of questions.'

'We have to do a test when we get back,' replied Kilpatrick apologetically. 'Our supervisor mentioned the security section as a point of particular interest.'

'Who's in charge of this program?'

'Why do you ask?' replied Jordan, hoping to sidetrack the question.

The nurse snorted indignantly. 'Well it doesn't sound as if there's much structure to it, and I should have been notified that you'd be turning up. Fortunately, I'm not very busy at the moment, but what if I'd been flat out? So who is the bright spark in charge?'

'We'd rather not say,' admitted Jordan. 'We're still on probation, and we'd be in trouble if he heard we were criticizing him.'

'Suit yourself.' The nurse shrugged. 'Is there anything else you want to know?'

'Is it possible to talk to your friend Delores?' asked Laura. 'Are you able to communicate with her?'

The nurse unclipped a small telephone receiver from a metal loop sewn to the waist of her uniform. 'They haven't given you one of these yet?' she asked as she held it up, and they shook their heads in reply. 'If somebody wants to contact you, he or she calls your number and the phone vibrates. However, I'd rather not disturb Delores, as the phones are only meant to be used if we need assistance.'

'But she'd come here if you asked her to?' persisted Laura.

The nurse frowned. 'I've already told you, I'm not willing to do that.' A patient began making intermittent beeping noises and the nurse walked over, picked up the television remote control, and changed the channel. The beeping became more insistent, and she flicked it onto another station and the noise immediately stopped. 'If there's nothing else, then I'd like to get on with my work,' she called from across the room.

'Uh no, you've been very helpful.' Kilpatrick smiled.

'Where's Frank?' muttered Jordan as they gathered by the door.

'He's cleaning in the corridor,' said Tracey.

Jordan motioned for Frank to join them and quickly explained the situation with the security cards. Frank grinned wolfishly as he listened. 'The problem's solved then. Leave this to me.'

The nurse was staring at them. 'Is something the matter?'

'Nothing's the matter, Missy,' replied Frank as he headed towards her. 'We'd like you to call your friend Delores and ask her to come and assist you.'

'What are you talking about?' she asked indignantly. 'Who are you anyway?'

'I'm somebody your mother used to warn you about when you were a little girl,' replied Frank with a leer.

'Listen, whoever you are,' cried the nurse angrily as she placed her hands on her hips and threw out her chest. 'There's a policeman just down the passage, so I suggest you play your pranks somewhere else before you get into real trouble.'

'That's one solution I suppose, but I'd prefer to do things my way.' Frank pulled a pistol from under his jacket and clapped a hand over her mouth. 'Now do as you're told, and don't even think about being cute or a lot of people are going to get hurt, including some of these patients.' He waved his gun around the room to emphasize his point, but none of the patients paid the slightest attention. 'Call your friend, now!'

She stared at him with wide eyes as she reluctantly activated her radio. 'Delores? It's Robyn. Do you have time to give me a hand for a few minutes? Okay, I'll see you shortly.' She ended the call and looked defiantly at Frank. 'I've kept my end of the bargain, so make sure you keep yours.'

'Don't worry about me,' grunted Frank. He directed Kilpatrick and Jordan to gather sashes from the dressing gowns hanging up around the room and then bound the nurse's hands and feet.

'Do you want us to gag her?' asked Kilpatrick enthusiastically. 'I'm an old hand at it.'

'Do we need to gag you?' asked Frank as he looked down at the slim figure lying on the floor between two of the beds.

'No,' she replied meekly. 'I'll be quiet.'

'That's what I thought,' replied Frank as he straightened up. 'Yes, gag her, but don't make it too tight.' The nurse gave an indignant shriek as Kilpatrick stuffed a gag in her mouth and tied it in place. 'Women,' muttered Frank as he walked across to the doorway. 'They say they're going to be quiet, but they rarely are.'

A soft metallic noise carried into the room, and Frank motioned for silence. A nurse hurried into the room and looked quickly around. 'Where's Robyn?'

'Are you Delores?' asked Frank as he blocked her exit.

She looked slightly surprised at being addressed by one of the cleaning staff. 'Yes, I'm Delores. Where's Robyn?'

'Robyn's tied up at the moment, but you've got something we need.'

'What? Who are you people?'

Frank smiled amiably. 'We're not going to hurt you, but I must insist that you move away from the door.'

The nurse backed away warily. As she turned to run, Kilpatrick grabbed her from behind, clamped his hand firmly over her mouth, and gently propelled her across the room to where Jordan helped tie her up. They applied a firm gag and removed the plastic security card she was carrying on a chain around her neck.

'Here's the card,' announced Kilpatrick as he held it up.

'Good work,' replied Frank. 'Now one of you girls will have to stay here and watch these people. We don't want them wriggling free and raising the alarm, and it might look strange if there isn't a nurse on duty.' He looked questioningly at the two women.

Before anyone could reply, they were interrupted by a firm voice. 'What's going on here? Where's Nurse Taylor?' A large woman in senior nurse's uniform stood unblinking in the doorway.

Kilpatrick was the first to react, walking quickly up to the ward sister and taking her by the arm. 'Thank goodness you came so promptly. Robyn's over here. I'm afraid she fainted.'

'What? Fainted? Where is she? What's the matter with her?' She continued firing questions as Kilpatrick led her across the room. Faint, muffled noises greeted her as she looked down in amazement at the two nurses lying on the floor. Kilpatrick slapped his hand across her mouth as Jordan and Frank bound her up and lowered her onto the floor.

'The silly cow tried to bite me,' muttered Kilpatrick as he carefully examined his fingers.

'We've got to get moving,' said Frank. 'It'll be standing room only if anyone else comes.' He stared at the elderly patients lying quietly in their beds. 'Fortunately this lot are off with the fairies.' He turned his attention back to the girls. 'Right, who's staying?'

'Laura's already done enough,' said Tracey, 'so she can stay.'

Laura opened her mouth to argue, but Frank cut her off. 'It won't be a picnic staying here. You'll have to deal with any other busybodies by yourself. Check the captives regularly to make sure they're not wriggling free, and don't get conned into taking off their gags.' He turned to Tracey. 'Your part is crucial. Once you've got the gate open, you must distract the guard until we can arrive and overpower him. It'll only take a few seconds, but a lot can go wrong in that time. Wait for me to start my cleaning routine; then make your entrance. You boys can follow behind with the wheelchair.' He gave them a look of encouragement and then disappeared out the door. Tracey waited a moment, gave a brief shrug, and then followed.

The guard slowly lowered his magazine as Tracey held the plastic card over the sensor. 'You're not the regular nurse.'

'I'm afraid Delores is indisposed at the moment,' replied Tracey sweetly as she stepped through the door. 'I'm her replacement.'

'Is that so?' He held out his hand. 'Show me your pass.' Tracey handed it over and watched as the guard studied the photograph. 'This belongs to the other nurse,' he declared irritably.

Tracey looked unconcerned. 'I told you, she's indisposed; if I don't look after the patients in here, who's going to do it?'

'I'm sorry, but I can't let you in without a proper pass,' insisted the policeman as he climbed to his feet. He suddenly jerked upright as Frank drifted in behind Tracey and thrust a gun in his ribs. Frank had one of his cleaning rags tied around his face.

'Will this do instead of a proper pass?' he asked pleasantly. The policeman nodded slowly as Frank pushed him back onto his chair. 'How many of your buddies are there in the room?'

'Two,' gasped the policeman as he held up two fingers to reinforce his words.

Frank whispered savagely in the man's ear. 'If you're lying, I guarantee it'll be the last lie you ever tell.'

'There's only two, I swear it.' The policeman was gasping for air.

Frank pulled the guard's gun from his holster and handed it to Jordan. 'Have you ever handled one of these?'

'Not really.'

'Well just wave it around and look fierce, and whatever you do, try not to shoot me.'

Frank gestured for them to move on ahead with the wheelchair and then told the guard to walk forward. As he moved into the passage, Frank clubbed him over the head and dragged him into the shadows along the far wall. 'Okay,' he whispered. 'Let's see if the inspector wants to check out.'

Tracey walked nervously down the passage and into the ward, catching Jane's eye as she entered the room. After the first astonished look, Jane hastily buried her head in the book she was reading. A female officer standing by the window gave Tracey a cursory glance before returning her attention to the scene outside.

Tracey held a finger to her lips as she took the inspector's pulse and made a few encouraging remarks about his progress. Without changing her tone, she asked if he wanted to leave and Banks solemnly nodded his head.

'You're doing very well, Mr Banks,' she replied in a louder voice. 'Keep this up, and you'll be out of here in no time.' She unhooked his chart and wrote a few comments for the benefit of the officer who had turned to watch her.

Frank walked nonchalantly into the room and picked up the rubbish bin. 'Don't mind me,' he said cheerfully. The officer's eyes narrowed warily as she watched him wipe down the bench next to the bed. Her instincts were aroused, and she straightened up as Frank walked around the bed towards her. He had slipped his gun into the bin and now pulled it out and waved it in her face.

'Nothing silly,' he murmured as he watched her body tense. 'Where's your buddy?'

Jane answered for her. 'He's in the kitchenette making a cup of tea. He should be back at any moment.'

'Tell Matt and Daniel to come in here,' he ordered. 'They're waiting in the corridor.' She hurried to comply while Frank hustled the officer towards the bathroom. He demanded the keys to her handcuffs and then chained her to the safety rail next to the bath. 'One word out of you and your buddy is dead.' He returned to the ward and directed the boys to huddle behind the bed.

They didn't have long to wait. As the officer walked into the room carrying two large mugs, Frank stuck his gun in his back and then quickly hustled him into the bathroom and secured him next to his companion.

Tracey and Kilpatrick slid Banks out of his bed and helped him into the wheelchair while Jane wrapped a blanket around him. 'Is he fit to travel?' asked Jordan.

'Probably not,' replied Jane, 'but he'll recover. He's as tough as an ox.'

'What doesn't kill you only makes you stronger,' observed Kilpatrick. He thought for a moment. 'That probably wasn't the most sensitive remark, was it?'

A muted voice in the corridor followed by a soft dragging noise stifled any further comments, and the group silently looked at each other as they strained to hear. Kilpatrick mouthed the words 'have a look' to Jordan, who nodded and held out his gun as he peered cautiously out into the corridor.

The shattering sound of a gunshot echoed savagely around the room, and Jordan felt something pluck at his sleeve.

'Jesus Christ!' shouted Frank as he burst out of the bathroom and spotted Jordan, who had hastily retreated but was still holding his gun in front of himself. 'Are you a fucking moron? Give that to me before you finish us all off.'

'It wasn't me,' stammered Jordan, his face extremely pallid. He crouched down against the wall. 'It was a man in a black uniform. He was creeping along the corridor, and when I peered around the corner, he took a shot at me. Here, look at this.' He poked his finger through a hole in his sleeve and wiggled it at Frank. 'I'm lucky to be alive.'

'A man in a black uniform took a shot at you? What the hell are you talking about?'

As if to confirm Jordan's story, a commanding voice called out from the far end of the corridor. 'Attention in the room. My colleagues and I are Special Service operatives. Your only way out is down this passage, and we have it covered with automatic weapons. Toss out your guns and come out with your hands up.'

'Where the hell did they come from?' snarled Frank. He looked at Jane. 'Is he correct? Are there any other ways out of here?'

'Not unless you can fly,' replied Jane.

'That's an idea,' replied Kilpatrick as he crept across to the window and looked out. 'I saw some window cleaners before, so perhaps we can hitch a ride with them.'

'I noticed them too, but I'm afraid they were on the other side of the building,' said Jordan.

Kilpatrick forced the window open and peered out. 'There's a narrow ledge just below the window. Maybe we could use it to find a fire escape.'

'Is there enough room for a wheelchair on your ledge?' asked Tracey sardonically.

'Oh yeah, I forgot about that small detail. Does anybody else have any ideas?'

Frank crawled across the room to Jordan. 'Sorry about yelling at you before. Do you think the man in the black uniform took a shot at you because he saw the gun in your hand?'

'I can't think of any other reason why he'd do it.'

'He might know you personally,' suggested Kilpatrick.

Frank smiled at Jordan. 'Okay, in that case you're the leader of this little terrorist group.'

'Me?' queried Jordan. 'Do I look like a terrorist?'

'They obviously think so, or they wouldn't have taken a shot at you.'

The voice called out again. 'What's it to be? Are you coming out or do we lob in a couple of tear gas grenades?'

'Tell them you've got hostages,' whispered Frank.

'Good idea.' Jordan raised his voice. 'Hey, fuck-knuckle, we've got hostages in here. Keep your distance or they're dead meat.'

'How do I know you've got hostages?'

'I can soon fix that,' replied Jordan with a laugh. 'Do you want me to shoot one of them and toss their body out into the corridor or throw one out the window and see if your buddies on the ground are any good at catching? You choose.'

'Okay, I believe you,' said the voice hurriedly. 'It seems we've got a stalemate, but you can't stay in there forever.'

'Who says it's a stalemate? We've got the hostages.'

'So you keep saying. Why don't you release one so we can confirm your story?'

'Do you think I'm a fucking idiot?' growled Jordan. 'The hostages are my ticket out of here.'

'It'll be an act of good faith on your part. Once we know you can be trusted, we can start negotiating.'

Frank leant closer to Jordan. 'Do it.'

Jordan nodded in sudden understanding. 'Okay, I'll release a hostage, but if I don't get some benefit out of this. I'll kill the other three.'

'You have four hostages?'

'You got that right. I've got two of your precious police officers, a nurse and a cleaner.'

There was a murmur at the other end of the corridor, and then the voice called out. 'Send out the nurse.' Frank quickly shook his head and pointed at himself.

Jordan gave a derisive laugh. 'It's not your call, fuck-knuckle. I'll decide who goes and who stays, and I fancy I'll keep the nurse with me a little longer. It could be a long night, and I'll need something to keep my pecker up, if you get my drift. I'll send you the cleaner. He's an ugly old bastard, so you're welcome to him.' Frank slipped his automatic into his waistband so it was snug against the small of his back. 'Get moving, old man,' snarled Jordan and shoved him into the passage.

'Don't shoot!' shouted Frank, his voice quavering as he peered around anxiously. He took a tentative step and then stood transfixed with his hands in the air. 'Don't shoot,' he repeated, more softly this time.

There were two men in dark uniforms at the end of the passage, and they both frantically beckoned to him. 'You're safe now, old timer,' said the taller of the two men as Frank hurriedly joined them.

Frank swallowed hard and took a deep breath as if to recover his composure. 'Who are you?'

'Special Services operatives. We were sent to pick up Banks and his girlfriend, and by the look of it, we got here in the nick of time. I'm Sergeant Harmes and this is Private Conner. How many of them are cornered in there?'

Frank gave them the details, describing Jordan and Kilpatrick as desperate men. He eyed them curiously as he finished. 'Are there just the two of you?'

'It was just a simple pickup, but we've called for backup,' replied Harmes.

'What happened to the policeman who usually guards this gate? Is he dead?'

'He was knocked unconscious, so we stuck him on a bed in the ward back there,' Harmes said as he pointed over his shoulder.'

'Do you mind if I go and check on him? He's an old friend of mine.'

'Why don't you do that,' replied Harmes absently as he peered down the corridor.

Frank hurried into the ward and found Laura waiting impatiently. 'What's going on?' she asked frantically. 'I heard a gunshot. Is everybody okay?'

'They're all fine,' Frank replied calmly.

'Who are those men? Where did they come from?'

Frank ignored her questions. 'Where's the policeman?'

Laura gestured to the bed. 'I've handcuffed him to bed and tied his feet, but I didn't like to gag him as he was having trouble breathing. I threw a dressing gown over the nurses so they wouldn't be spotted.'

'You've done well.' He looked around the room seeking inspiration. 'I need to overpower the two men guarding the passage. I'll have the element of surprise, but they're highly trained professionals, so I'll need an edge.' He took the gun from his pocket and slipped the safety catch off.

'You're not going to shoot them are you?' Laura sounded horrified.

'I'm not,' he replied as he handed the gun to her. 'You are.'

'Me? I can't shoot somebody. I can't even step on a spider.'

'Yes, but they don't know that. Can you clobber somebody over the head with a blunt object?'

'No, of course not.'

'That's what I thought. I want you to come with me and give them an update on the injured policeman. Once they're watching you, I'll knock out one of them, and you stick the gun in the other one's ribs and tell him not to move or you'll shoot him. Can you do that?'

'I suppose so, but what if he doesn't listen?'

'Then you shoot him,' Frank said simply. He left her with her mouth agape and walked around the room. He selected a heavy glass vase and after dropping the flowers on the floor, hefted it in his hands to get a feel for its balance. 'Right,' he said. 'Let's get this over with.'

Tracey walked nervously to where the men were crouched in the passage, the gun feeling huge and alien in her hand. Harmes was yelling something down the corridor, and Frank called out as he approached, to avoid startling them. 'The nurse has some urgent information about the injured policeman,' he said breathlessly.

'What is it?' asked Harmes as he swivelled around.

Frank watched Conner's eyes move from him to Laura, and then he brought the heavy vase from behind his back and bludgeoned him over the head. Conner made a soft hissing sound as he slumped forward against the bars of the gate. Harmes reacted immediately, reaching out and grasping Frank's wrist in a vice-like grip.

Laura jammed the gun painfully into his ear. 'One more move, and I'll blow your brains out.' Her voice sounded harsh, and she barely recognized it as her own. Harmes froze as he felt the cold metal press against his head. She could feel the tension coiled within his lean frame and knew he could explode into action at any moment.

Frank unwrapped Harmes's hand from his wrist. 'I knew you could do it,' he said gently.

'What do we do with him?'

'Same as the other one.' Frank struck him over the head. Harmes slumped forward onto all fours, shook his head and turned to face his tormentors, his eyes glittering in pale fury. A thin line of blood ran through his closely cropped hair and dripped onto the floor. 'This one must have a concrete skull,' Frank grunted as he pushed him back against the wall with his foot. 'Give me the gun, and I'll watch him while you fetch the others. I don't have the heart to hit him again.'

'Listen,' said Laura with a gasp, 'police sirens.'

'Well, don't stand there gawking at me. Get moving.'

Laura slipped through the gate and hurried down the corridor calling Jordan's name. He met her in the doorway and gave her a quick hug. 'We've got to get out of here now,' she said breathlessly. 'The police are on their way.'

'Too late,' replied Kilpatrick as he stared out the window. 'They're already here. Five cars just pulled up at the front door.'

'It might not be too late,' replied Jordan. 'There must be some degree of pandemonium and confusion on the lower floors so if we can get down there and mingle with the crowd we should be able to slip out unnoticed.'

'Then get moving,' croaked Banks. 'Every second counts.'

They pushed Banks out the door and dashed down the corridor, collecting Frank as they went.

Kilpatrick eyed the slumped bodies on the floor as he hurried past. 'What happened to them?'

'Frank hit them with a vase,' said Laura.

'A vase? Wow, really? I am impressed.'

'Flower power,' replied Laura, her face impassive.

'The lift or the stairs?' yelled Jordan as he hopped from one foot to the other, undecided.

'We'll be trapped in the lift if they cut the power,' replied Frank. 'We'll take the stairs.'

'What about Robert?' asked Jane. 'How's he going to walk down five flights of stairs?'

'I'll carry him,' said Jordan. 'Killa can bring the wheelchair.' He bent down and picked Banks up in a fireman's grip and slung him across his shoulder.

'Watch out for his stitches,' shrieked Jane as Banks gave an involuntary grunt.

'Don't concern yourself about minor matters,' interjected Frank. 'Robert won't mind losing a little blood if it means getting out of here.' He called Laura and Tracey over and directed them to go on ahead. 'Find out what's happening down there. We need to know if they've sealed the stairs off.' The girls nodded and scampered off while the others followed at a slower rate, keeping pace with Jordan's progress.

The girls reached the fourth floor without incident and continued down towards the third, frightened faces peering out at them from the rooms as they rushed past. Evacuating a hospital took time and the authorities didn't have that luxury. No announcements had been made but everybody knew something was going on. The third floor was also clear and they hurried on to the next. They heard voices at the bottom of the next stairwell and Tracey took a quick peep down the side of the stairs. 'There's an army of policemen down there,' she whispered. 'I think they're going to make a charge up the stairs.'

Laura looked grim. 'All right, you go back and warn the others and I'll try and bluff my way past them.'

'No,' said Tracey. 'They'll catch you for sure.'

'They're not looking for me. I'm just another nurse fleeing the scene. If I get through, I'll bring Colin and the cars around to the front and meet you there.'

'How will we get out?' asked Tracey plaintively. 'Everything's blocked off.'

'Not everything,' said Laura with an encouraging smile. 'Matt mentioned it before. Hitch a ride with the window cleaners.' She gave Tracey a quick hug and then dashed off down the stairs, shrieking loudly and pointing back over her shoulder. A burly policeman caught her as she ran blindly into him. He gratefully passed her on to a female colleague, and Laura allowed herself to be helped to the rear of the assembled men. She gave the officer an apologetic smile and assured her that she was okay. The officer let her go after telling her to report back later so she could be formally interviewed.

Laura stumbled away down the stairs before resuming her previous hectic pace. Tweddle was standing nervously by the cars as Laura burst through the door and hurried to his side.

'What's happening?' he blurted. 'There are police sirens everywhere, and an army helicopter turned up about twenty minutes ago.'

'There's no time to explain,' panted Laura as she slid into the driver's seat of the Ford. 'Get in my car and follow me. The police will be on their way to seal off the back entrance, and if we're still here, then we're all dead.' She gunned the engine, and Tweddle hurried across to the BMW.

Tracey smiled as she listened to Laura's desperate cries receding down the stairwell and then scooted back up the stairs. She met the others as they arrived on the third floor and hurried across to them. 'The police have blocked off the stairs,' she announced breathlessly.

'Where's Laura?' asked Jordan. 'Why isn't she with you?'

'She's trying to bluff her way through so she can bring the cars around to front of the hospital.'

Jordan motioned for Kilpatrick to bring the wheelchair to him and then bent down and carefully dropped Banks into it.

'What's the point of that?' groaned Banks as he stretched his back. 'With the stairs blocked off, we're pretty much stuffed.'

'Not quite,' replied Tracey as she glanced nervously down the stairs. 'If the window cleaners are still on the job, we can go down with them.' She turned around to gather her bearings and then pointed to a doorway. 'Follow me,' she ordered, and then she walked into the ward.

Heavily pregnant women occupied the beds. Several of them glanced up but most of their attention was focussed on two nurses busily helping a woman experiencing a series of strong contractions.

Tracey pushed against the window, forcing it open wide enough to press her face through the gap. 'There they are!' she exclaimed. 'They're right next door. Come on, we have to hurry.'

They spilled out of the room and crowded into the one next door. It too was filled with women, although none of them appeared to be pregnant. Several indignant voices followed them as they hurried to the window.

Frank spun around and held up his pistol. The noise ceased immediately. 'That's better,' he snarled. 'Anybody would think you were selling fish at the local market. Now just keep your bloody traps shut, and nobody will get hurt.' He turned his attention back to the window and saw it had been forced open far enough for a person to squeeze through. Two thick ropes hung down against the window and Kilpatrick was leaning out talking to somebody. 'They're refusing to come up,' he said as he straightened up.

'We'll see about that,' muttered Frank as he squeezed past Kilpatrick. 'I'm sure I can change their minds.' Two cleaners in white overalls were dangling between the second and third floors and as he watched, one of them moved towards the ropes controlling the platform's movement.

'Hey, you!' called Frank as he pointed his gun out of the window. The men looked up at him and Frank grinned encouragingly. 'Bring that contraption up here or I'll shoot you full of holes. If you think I'm bluffing it'll be the last thought you ever have.' The two men looked at each other and then hauled on the ropes until the platform was level with the window. 'Very good,' said Frank. 'Now I want you take me and my buddies down to the ground.'

'Have you considered taking the elevator?' asked the nearer of the two cleaners.

'Don't be a smart-arse,' growled Frank.

'How many of you are there?' asked the other cleaner.

'There are six of us,' answered Jordan.

'And a wheelchair,' added Kilpatrick.

'That's far too many,' the cleaner replied. 'This rig is only meant for two people.'

They heard the distant sound of heavy boots on the stairs, and Frank shouldered the window open wider. 'This is not a fucking discussion. Move your fat arse out of the way, I'm coming on board.' He grabbed hold of the ropes and stepped onto the platform, which creaked as it swung away from the building before bumping back against it. 'So now we know it takes three people. Come on, who's next?'

Jordan helped Tracey climb out the window. She squeezed past Frank and stood next to the cleaner at the far end of the platform.

'Nice day,' she said nervously. 'Do you have any safety belts?' The cleaner looked at her and then took a firm hold on his ropes.

The sound of hurrying feet gradually faded. 'They've gone up to the top floor,' said Jordan. He told Kilpatrick to fold the wheelchair while he helped Jane out the window. The platform groaned ominously as she settled her weight onto it.

'It'll never hold everyone,' shouted one of the cleaners. 'I'm taking us down and I don't care if you shoot me. If we load any more people on to the rig we'll all die anyway.' His mate had become quite pale, his knuckles showing white as he strengthened his grip on the ropes.

Frank shoved his gun against the cleaner's forehead. 'We're not going anywhere until we have everybody on board.'

The cleaner's eyes were wide with fear. 'And I'm telling you we can't hold any more.'

'Okay,' replied Frank as he came to a decision. 'You can get off.'

'What?'

'Climb back through the window and be quick about it. If you squeal to the cops your mate will be the first to suffer.'

Jordan helped the man back into the building and then took hold of Banks and stepped out onto the platform. The cleaning rig shuddered and suddenly plunged several inches before stopping.

'Whoa,' cried Jane. 'This is fun—I don't think.'

'I know what you mean,' murmured Banks from his head-down position. 'If I wasn't already half dead I'd be feeling a little apprehensive myself.'

Jordan smiled grimly at her. 'Let me edge past with Robert. It'll be a better balance if we're in the middle.'

Kilpatrick propped the wheelchair against the window, climbed through, and stepped gingerly onto the platform. The ropes groaned softly under the strain as Kilpatrick hurriedly pulled the chair onto the platform next to him.

'Let's get this thing moving,' ordered Frank.

'What do I do?' called Kilpatrick, who was standing next to the far set of ropes.

'Have you done any abseiling?' asked the remaining cleaner, who was clearly nervous.

'Once.'

'It's the same principle. Let the ropes out gradually to move and pull them down to stop.'

'Like this?' asked Kilpatrick as he disengaged his set of ropes. His end of the rig immediately began descending, throwing everybody off balance and causing them to spill towards him. The cleaner immediately reacted with practiced skill, steadying the platform as it sped towards the ground.

'We're going too fast,' yelled Jordan as he struggled to keep Banks upright.

'Okay,' replied Kilpatrick as he pulled down on the ropes and engaged the braking system. His end of the platform jerked to a sudden halt throwing everybody in the opposite direction. The cleaner frantically compensated by applying the brakes on his own ropes but Kilpatrick had realised his error and released his own side again. The see-sawing motion of the overloaded platform proved too much for the ropes securing it to the roof, and the cleaner's side gave away with a dull twang. Kilpatrick immediately applied his brakes, and the platform stopped its downward journey and swung in a rapid arc across the face of the building.

Jordan tumbled down the steep incline of the broken platform and grabbed hold of the metal safety rail to avoid falling any further. Banks also grabbed hold, and they were able to arrest their fall and prevent Jane from pitching over the edge at the same time. Kilpatrick had kept a firm hold on the rope and managed to pull himself up so that he was now standing on the safety railing.

The window cleaner and Frank weren't so lucky. The cleaner had lost his grip when his rope broke and toppled straight over the top of the railing and plunged head first into a mass of thick shrubbery. The bushes softened the impact and flipped him over so that he landed flat on his back as he hit the ground. He had a split second to appreciate his fortunate escape when Frank landed on top of him, driving the wind completely from his body.

'That was a bit of luck,' Frank acknowledged as he patted the writhing cleaner on the face. 'Much appreciated.' He climbed to his feet and saw Tracey hanging precariously from the end of the platform. He grabbed her by the ankles. 'Let go, and I'll catch you,' he called out. 'You're only a few metres off the ground. You'll be safe enough.'

'Are you sure?' she asked as she twisted her body around in an effort to look down. 'It looks a lot higher from up here.'

'I'm happy looking up your dress if you want to hang there a bit longer,' Frank cheerfully replied. Tracey gave a scream as she let go and landed on top of him. Frank caught most of her weight, but they still ended up in a heap lying on top of the window cleaner. 'There you go,' said Frank amiably. 'Safe and sound.'

She looked down at the cleaner, who was tucked up into a tight ball. 'Is he all right?'

'He's a little winded, but he's doing a grand job.'

They helped the others off the platform, and it became increasingly easier with more and more hands to catch the descending bodies. The wheelchair had fallen into a clump of bushes to their left, and Kilpatrick anxiously unfolded it, making sure it was still functional. Several onlookers appeared on the scene, and Tracey pointed them in the direction of the injured cleaner.

They dashed clear of the building, expecting to hear a challenge at any moment, and hurried towards the car park. A red patch of blood began seeping through the back of the Banks's pyjamas but Frank tersely refused when Jane asked if they could stop while she examined him.

A blaring car horn attracted their attention as Laura screeched to a halt next to them. They pushed Banks into the back seat and Jane climbed after him to act as his pillow. Kilpatrick folded the wheelchair and slung it into the trunk before joining Tracey and Frank in the BMW. The two cars then joined the stream of traffic flowing through the main gates of the hospital.

'I always seem to be fleeing from hospitals,' mused Kilpatrick absently.

'Only this time I'm not lying on the floor while somebody tap dances on my head,' replied Tweddle sourly.

'Yeah, sorry about,' said Kilpatrick. 'I was a bit of a tearaway in my younger days.'

Their progress was slowed by the congested traffic waiting to enter the street running past the hospital. Kilpatrick saw an officer lean out a hospital window and point at the broken platform. 'Get a move on,' he urged loudly. 'They're coming after us.'

'I can't,' replied Tweddle unhappily. 'The traffic's barely moving. We've just got to be patient and wait our turn.'

'We can't afford to be patient,' cried Kilpatrick as he watched several officers spill through the front doors and start running towards them. 'Drive up on the footpath.'

'What? There's not enough room. It's full of people, and Laura will kill me if I damage the paintwork.'

'I'll kill you if you don't get moving,' replied Frank as he leant over and wrenched the wheel, sending the car over the gutter and onto the footpath. Several people yelled obscenities, and an old lady beat the side of the car with her umbrella. 'Keep going,' urged Frank.

Tweddle gave the horn a blast and shouldered his way through the crowd, causing several people to leap into the ornamental rose bushes.

They drove past Laura, who scowled furiously as she watched people aiming kicks and blows at her car. 'What's that idiot playing at?' she muttered angrily.

Kilpatrick pointed back towards the hospital. 'Get moving!' he shouted. Laura glanced in the mirror and then immediately followed Tweddle onto the footpath. Several following cars joined in and the two lanes suddenly became three as pedestrians spilled onto the roadway to escape the advancing vehicles.

'There's only a narrow gate at the end of the path,' warned Tweddle. 'There's no way I can fit through there.'

'Then get back on the fucking road,' growled Frank.

'There's no room. They'll never let me back in.'

'Then bloody well make room,' declared Frank bluntly. "What are you? A mummy's boy? Use force if you have to. They'll give way if they see you're not going to stop.'

'What about Laura's car?' wailed Tweddle. 'It's already badly scratched.'

'Listen, Laura doesn't give a shit about her car,' said Kilpatrick harshly. 'It's not as though she's taking it to the Bahamas.'

'Of course,' replied Tweddle as he brightened considerably. 'What was I worried about? Talley ho!' He gave the horn a long blast and launched the car off the footpath. The car next to them foolishly refused to concede ground. Tweddle hit the car in front of the driver's door and then proceeded to scrape up against it until the horrified driver applied his brakes. Kilpatrick gave them a cheery wave of thanks as Tweddle gunned the motor and drove out onto the main road.

Laura also scraped along the side of the stalled car as she followed immediately behind. The driver wound down his window and yelled a string of obscenities at her. Jordan lazily pointed his gun at the man as they edged past. 'Watch your language,' he lectured. 'Haven't you ever seen a lady driver before?' Laura gave him a cursory frown as she roared down the road after Tweddle.

They parked their cars in a supermarket parking lot several blocks from O'Brien's church and walked back carrying their meagre belongings.

'What a day!' exclaimed Laura. 'I'd hate to go through that again.'

'It's been a hectic month as far as I'm concerned,' replied Jordan. 'I've done things I never thought I could do.'

'That reminds me,' said Tracey curtly as she turned and gave him a smack across the ears. 'Keep your pecker up indeed,' she said disgustedly.

'Hey! Do you mind?' winced Jordan. 'I was playing a role.'

'It's a good thing Laura wasn't there to hear it. She would have been absolutely disgusted.' She turned around and gave Frank a smack as well.

'Ow, what was that for?' he exclaimed.

'For looking up my dress, you dirty old pervert.'

'It wasn't as though I had a choice. You were dangling right on top of me. Besides, I don't care for black lacy underwear.' He winked at her suggestively with a cackle.

Chapter 20

An oppressive government is more to be feared than a tiger.
                                                        Confucius

O'Brien greeted them warmly when they arrived at the church and whisked them into his study. They updated him on the events at the hospital, and he laughed loudly as Tracey gave an indignant account of their antics on the cleaning platform.

'I don't condone the violence,' he said, 'but apart from the odd headache, it doesn't look as though anybody was seriously hurt.'

Frank announced it was time for him to go and shook hands all 'round. He gave each of the girls a hug, although Tracey was forced to slap his hand away from her backside.

'Now don't go thinking the wrong thing,' he said reproachfully. 'I noticed your underwear was slightly crooked before, and I was just straightening it for you.' He bent down and shook hands with Banks. 'It's been nice knowing you, Inspector. I'll send somebody to repair your stitches and stop the bleeding. Don't worry, mate,' he said to O'Brien, 'the doctor's discreet. Now if it's okay with you,' he said addressing the group at large, 'I'll dispose of your cars and keep the money as payment for my outstanding bills.' They nodded in agreement, and he gave them a final cheery wave as he walked out of the study.

'An interesting character,' observed O'Brien.

'An invaluable character,' amended Jordan. 'Without him, we'd be in a huge mess.' He took out a letter and handed it to Banks.

'What's this?' Banks eyed it curiously.

'It's our parting gift to everybody connected with the Memtech operation. It identifies the guilty parties and should clear your name. I'll post them tomorrow along with a copy of Borkov's disks. If this doesn't do the trick, then nothing will.'

'Who are you sending them to?'

'The major newspapers, the Labour Party and the Conservatives. With the elections only six weeks away, this is going to be a significant issue,' chuckled Jordan as he considered the mayhem he was about to unleash.

'They'll be looking for us everywhere,' observed Banks.

'They seek us here, they seek us there,' replied Kilpatrick carelessly.

O'Brien organized lunch and then handed out their clothing. 'The sizes aren't perfect, but they should do the job. Please start wearing them now so you look as natural as possible tomorrow. The nun's habits in particular can be difficult to get used to. No jokes, please,' he said, holding up his hand. 'I've heard them all.'

He ushered the girls into the vestry. Their giggles could be heard through the solid oak door as they helped each other into their new clothing. Banks was the odd one out as he had decided not to get changed until the doctor had repaired his stitches.

'I have one last thing to tell you before I attend to my other duties,' said O'Brien once they were together again. 'I have observed over time that my colleagues have a certain way of walking that you need to learn if you want to blend in with the rest of the party tomorrow.'

'Like this?' asked Kilpatrick as he minced up and down the room.

'I'm sorry, Father,' Jordan apologized. 'He's been watching too many gay and lesbian parades.'

'Don't make me leave you behind,' threatened O'Brien coldly.

'Sorry, Father,' mumbled Kilpatrick.

O'Brien glared at him before continuing. 'I was making the point that nuns and priests saunter. Our normal pace is slow and thoughtful, as if we have all the time in the world. The only other pace we have is the purposeful saunter. We use this to look as if we have urgent business to attend to, although it usually means we're late for morning tea. Practice both forms during the afternoon, and I'll test you when I get back. Anybody who fails will be given homework.'

~

Fenwick received the news that Banks had escaped within minutes of it happening and immediately sent for Kent. Fenwick's glowering countenance indicated that something was amiss, although Kent wasn't sure if it affected him or not.

'Reporting as requested, sir,' he said smartly as he approached Fenwick's desk.

'What do make of the news?' barked Fenwick angrily.

'Which news would that be?' replied Kent nervously. It was difficult to defend your position when you weren't sure which direction the missiles were coming from.

'Banks, of course,' spat Fenwick as he rose to his feet. 'He's escaped from the hospital and taken his fancy girl with him.'

'Are you sure the news is correct?' Kent swallowed nervously. 'I inspected the ward myself. There's no way he could slip past three of my best officers, especially in the condition he was in.'

'Oh, so you think they've merely misplaced him, do you? If they look under the bed they'll discover he was hiding there all along? Even my ninety-year-old grandmother couldn't have cocked this one up.'

'I'm as shocked as you are, sir. The officers involved will be severely admonished.'

Fenwick glared at him. 'You've got twenty-four hours to find Banks, otherwise I'll bust you down to constable, and you'll spend the rest of your career writing parking tickets in Upper Trentham. Understand?'

'Yes, sir,' replied Kent miserably.

'I want all the airports, the tunnel, and the seaports locked up tighter than a fish's arsehole. My instincts tell me he's going to do a runner, and when he does I want to make sure we have sufficient personnel to catch him. Cancel all leave and arrange for everybody to work double shifts. I'm getting flak right from the top on this, so don't stuff up.'

Kent hurried from the office, grateful that the tongue-lashing had been brief. His own people must have known about the escape, but they hadn't bothered to inform him. Double shifts be damned, he'd have them working triple shifts, and they could whistle for the overtime. He stormed into his office and began making arrangements to seal off every exit out of Great Britain.

~

O'Brien carefully inspected his novice nuns and priests the next morning, and after making several adjustments, he declared them ready. 'However,' he growled as he stared directly at Kilpatrick, 'I don't want to see anybody blessing people.'

They loaded their scant luggage into the taxis and headed off towards Heathrow Airport. O'Brien introduced them to the other clerics, and they shook hands, murmuring in low voices as the introductions were made.

They filled out the customs documentation, handed over their passports, and stood impassively as the desk clerk asked them the same routine questions. Everything went without a hitch, although the clerk did stare at Kilpatrick for an unusual amount of time before returning his passport.

'There seems to be a lot of police officers around,' observed Jordan as they sauntered towards customs. 'Is that usual?'

'I've noticed it as well,' replied Banks as Jane pushed him along in the middle of the group. 'I know security was beefed up after the recent terrorist scares, but this seems excessive. I think they're looking for somebody.'

'Do you think they're looking for us?' asked Jane.

'It's possible, particularly after the mayhem we caused at the hospital.'

'Do you think we can get this group to move a bit quicker?' asked Jordan anxiously. 'I'd hate to get caught when we're so close to victory.'

'Just saunter along with the rest and do nothing that marks us as different,' replied Banks.

'That's all very well, but I have this overwhelming urge to hurry everything along, to make time move faster.'

'My advice to you is to enjoy the moment. It's incidents like these that define your life. You either look back and regret your lack of fortitude or rejoice in your strength of character.'

'Thanks for the lecture,' replied Jordan sardonically, 'but I think I've already had my fair share of character-defining moments.'

Banks was no longer listening. His attention had been caught by a figure in a plain grey suit lounging in the doorway of a gift shop. Two police officers were standing next to him scanning the crowd as it drifted by.

'That's Kent,' hissed Banks.

'Who?' asked Jane.

'Yeah, I know him,' replied Jordan. 'He's the idiot who tried to arrest me for assaulting Laura.'

'That's the one,' murmured Banks. 'We can't go past him; he'll recognise me for sure.'

'There's no other way,' replied Jane as she desperately looked around. 'This is the only way to the departure gate.'

The group of clergy continued to move forwards, bringing Banks and his wheelchair closer to discovery. 'Quick, into that bookshop,' snapped Jordan as he grabbed Jane and pointed.

'Father O'Brien!' he called loudly. 'I think we should all buy a book for the plane trip. It will help pass the time.'

'I already have enough to do on the plane,' replied the priest. 'However, if you want to buy one, then we'll wait for you.'

'No, Father, I think it would be a really good idea if we all went in and looked for a book; a really good idea.' O'Brien caught the urgent inflection in Jordan's voice and calmly ushered his charges towards the small shop.

One of the officers standing next to Kent suddenly noticed the wheelchair as Jane stepped back to allow a woman and her young daughter to exit the bookstore. 'Sir,' he said excitedly. 'Do you see that wheelchair being pushed into the bookstore across the road?'

'Yes, what about it?' replied Kent as he listlessly turned and watched the group of clergy walk into the shop.

'What was the name of the hospital Banks escaped from?'

'London Central, why?' Kent sounded bored. It had already been a long day for him, and he had personally inspected the occupants of over a dozen wheelchairs.

'That wheelchair had London Central Hospital stencilled on the back of it.'

Kent snapped out of his lethargy. 'Are you sure?'

'I'm positive.'

'That's him then,' gloated Kent. 'It's got to be, and we've got him trapped in the store.' He turned to the other officer. 'Call for backup and then follow us in. Come on.' He pulled his gun free and sprinted across to the bookstore, narrowly missing a group of Japanese tourists. He shouldered his way through the clerics and strode purposefully after the wheelchair. A nun was slowly pushing it past the crowded bookcases, its occupant perusing the books. Kent manhandled her out of the way and savagely spun the wheelchair around so that it was facing him. 'I've got you, you bastard!' he cried loudly as he pointed his gun triumphantly at the dark figure sitting in front of him.

The man's face was hidden by the rim of a hat pulled down low across his forehead, and Kent twitched it off his head and twirled it halfway across the room. 'No point hiding now, you scum,' he crowed happily.

The figure in the wheelchair slowly raised his head and glared at Kent with a pair of pale brown eyes. 'I hope you have an excellent reason for subjecting me to this barrage of abuse,' the man said coldly. Kent felt his heart drop through his stomach. The man was a stranger.

Father O'Brien pushed his way through and jabbed an angry finger at Kent. 'What's the meaning of this?' he demanded. 'Why are you pointing a gun at Father Sampson? Have you lost your mind?'

He spotted the officer standing in the doorway and targeted him with his finger. 'You there, this man is threatening us with a gun. I demand that you arrest him immediately.'

'I'm sorry, Father,' said Kent sheepishly. 'We're hunting a dangerous felon, and we thought we'd found him. Obviously we were mistaken.'

'You thought Father Sampson was a dangerous felon?' asked O'Brien incredulously.

Tweddle, who had hurriedly slipped into the chair once they had entered the bookshop, glowered disdainfully at Kent. 'I've often read about police brutality and incompetence in the papers but until now I'd always given you the benefit of the doubt. However, after witnessing this shameful episode ...' His voice trailed off as he shook his head disgustedly.

'Now, hang on a minute,' Kent replied. 'I can understand you're slightly peeved, but in all fairness it was an honest mistake.'

Tweddle watched in quiet satisfaction as Kilpatrick and Jordan helped Banks walk out of the store. 'Rest assured that we will be carefully considering whether or not to lodge a formal complaint. When innocent citizens are verbally harassed and have their hats knocked off and flung away by the police in what can only be described as wanton vandalism, I believe questions should be asked in parliament.'

'Now, now,' said Father O'Brien appeasingly. 'The officer has admitted it was an honest mistake, so I think we should let it go at that.'

Tweddle was enjoying himself and in no hurry to bring it to a close. 'It was certainly a mistake, but I fail to see the role that honesty played in it.'

'Well, that's the strange thing,' replied Kent as his confidence slowly returned. 'The felon we're after escaped from London Central Hospital in a wheelchair, and naturally, when we saw you being pushed around in a similar wheelchair, we decided to investigate.' He stared at Tweddle thoughtfully. 'This of course leads to an interesting question. How is it that you happen to be using a wheelchair from London Central Hospital?'

'Are you trying to justify your wretched behaviour by implying that I'm guilty of some vague crime involving a hospital wheelchair?' blustered Tweddle.

'Not at all,' replied Kent, who had the vague feeling he was on to something. 'I simply want to know why you're using a wheelchair with London Central Hospital written on the back.'

Father O'Brien moved in between the two men. 'I'm afraid Father Sampson is still distressed, and he tends to become testy when he's upset, so I'll answer your question. We have many elderly parishioners in our community, and the local government donates several of these obsolete hospital wheelchairs to us every year. This particular one is from London Central, but we have others from St Vincent and Queen Anne. Father Sampson slipped in the bath the other morning and injured his knee, hence the need for a wheelchair. Do you have any other questions?'

'Uh no, I think you've explained everything,' muttered Kent. 'I shan't trouble you further.'

Tweddle coughed loudly. 'I don't believe I have received an adequate apology, and I certainly haven't received my hat.'

'Now, Father,' replied O'Brien as he patted Tweddle firmly on the hand. 'Let's be generous and allow these men to get about their business. After all, they still have a dangerous felon to catch.'

Kent glared at Tweddle and then turned on his heel and stalked out of the store. 'I thought these people were into turning the other cheek. What happened to the meek inheriting the earth?' he muttered as he hurried away.

~

The flight to Venezuela passed as if in a dream. They finally relaxed once the wheels of the Boeing 747 left the tarmac at Heathrow. Even after the doors were shut and the cabin crew had performed their locking and cross checking ritual, they still half expected to hear a last minute announcement that the flight had been unexpectedly delayed. It was agonizing to being so close to freedom and know that their plans could still come unstuck.

Laura took a deep, satisfied breath and placed her hand on top of Jordan's. 'I love you,' she whispered.

Jordan put down his book and rolled his eyes at her. 'I don't think it's appropriate for nuns to talk like that. You're supposed to be married to Christ. If you keep this up, I'll start having impure thoughts and that would never do.'

'What about this then?' she said impishly as she leant across and kissed him on the lips.

'You'll blow our cover if you keep this up,' he whispered fiercely. 'The folks across the aisle are already starting to stare.'

She turned and waved saucily at Tracey and Kilpatrick, who were deep in their own private conversation. 'No, they're not,' she said as she punched him on the shoulder. 'They've only got eyes for each other.'

She continued to stare happily at Jordan, who became increasingly uncomfortable with the attention. 'What?' he said at last. 'Why are you looking at me like that?'

'My hero,' she said softly. 'Do you want to know something?'

'I know you'll tell me anyway whether I want to or not.'

She slipped her arm under his and rested her head on his shoulder. 'Sometimes you need to experience the worst in order to appreciate the best. Our thoughts are often clouded by personal ambition and material desires, but when you've been through something like this, you realise that some of your supposedly important values are in fact quite inconsequential.'

'This sounds deep and meaningful.'

'That's because it is.' She paused as she looked at him. 'Do you remember asking me a certain question a short time ago?'

'I'm always asking you a certain question.'

Laura punched him on the arm. 'Not that one. Anyway, I now realise my answer was incorrect.'

'I see,' he said as he felt his heart rate quicken.

'So is the question still on the table?' she asked as she pulled back and stared at him.

'Well, it was some time ago,' he said slowly, 'and a lot has happened since then to change both of us, and I do have it on good authority that there are many other fish in the sea ...' She whacked him again. 'Ow!' he exclaimed as he rubbed his arm. 'Okay, if you're going to beat me into submission, then the answer is yes.'

'And so is mine,' she replied with an open smile.

He detected signs of tears in her eyes and put a finger to her lips. 'If we're going to do this, then we should do it properly.' He rummaged in his bag, took out a bunch of keys, and then proceeded to take them off the key ring.

'What are you doing?' she asked impatiently.

'Hush,' he said softly. 'All will become clear.' He took out his handkerchief and wrapped the empty key ring in it.

'Okay, I'm ready,' he said as he gave a small cough to clear his throat. He picked up her hand and stared in her eyes. 'Laura?'

'Yes?' she replied hesitatingly.

'I've got something to ask you.'

'Yes?'

He unfolded the handkerchief and displayed the key ring. 'Will you marry me?'

'Oh, I don't know,' she replied with a giggle. 'This is so unexpected. Let me see, you're a wanted criminal on the run and unemployed with no future job prospects.' She looked thoughtful. 'When do you want my answer?'

'Anytime in the next five seconds will do.'

Laura looked at the key ring. 'What girl could possibly refuse such an elegant engagement ring? All right, the answer's yes, I will marry you.' She leant over, kissed him again, and then held out her right hand. 'A perfect fit,' she said as he slipped the ring on her finger.

Tracey's female antennae picked up the signals from the newly engaged couple, and she leaned forward to see what was going on. 'What are you two up to?' she asked curiously. Laura proudly held out her right hand. 'No way,' Tracey gasped. 'That's great news.'

'What's great news?' asked Kilpatrick curiously as he glanced across at Jordan and Laura.

'They've just got engaged, silly,' said Tracey. 'Look at Laura's hand.'

'And that's the ring?' said Kilpatrick in amazement. 'Well done, buddy. How'd you get away with that?'

Jordan winked in reply. 'It's all a matter of timing.'

~

The hot and oppressive weather in Caracas did little to dampen their spirits, although they were happy to change into more suitable clothing in the airport's toilet cubicles. After gathering their borrowed clerical garments, they made their way to Father O'Brien. Jordan spoke first, apologising for the trouble they had caused.

'There's no need for apologies,' he replied. 'I make my own choices in life. Drop me a line when you're settled, and let me know how you're getting on.'

'I'm afraid not, Father,' said Jordan regretfully. 'This truly is goodbye. The less you know about us, the safer you'll be.'

'You're right, of course,' said O'Brien. 'I was just being diplomatic. It's the sort of thing people say to each other when they're saying goodbye. It helps to ease the pain.'

'Oh, sorry,' replied Jordan. 'In that case we'll be sure to write.' He handed over the suitcase containing their discarded clothing, and they watched pensively as O'Brien and his group sauntered towards their departure lounge.

Jane patted Banks lightly on the shoulder. 'There are some warm-hearted people around.'

He reached back and put his hand on top of hers. 'There certainly are.'

～

The Prime Minister angrily waved his newspaper in Northfield's face. 'You lied to me! You said everything was under control. The opposition are calling for my resignation, my ministers are plotting behind my back, and the media are demanding my head.' He threw the paper onto his desk. 'It'll take a fucking miracle to get out of this.'

'I can understand why you're annoyed ...' began Northfield.

'Annoyed? I'm not fucking annoyed, I'm fucking furious!' shouted the Prime Minister.

'There's still nothing to directly link you to this scandal,' replied Northfield soothingly. 'Aubrey's unfortunate suicide has severed any connection between Memtech and you.'

'Yes, poor Dean,' replied the Prime Minister softly. 'Who'd have thought he'd have done that?'

'Who indeed,' murmured Northfield. 'The fact remains that with Aubrey's death there is nothing to link you to the smoking gun. The opposition can bluster all they like, but that's all it is.'

'Even if that is true, my political standing is at rock bottom. The party sees me as a liability, and my popularity has sunk to an all-time low. The elections are just around the corner, and I'm expecting a leadership spill any day.'

'Then you need to act quickly, Prime Minister.'

'Eh? By doing what? Declaring martial law?'

Northfield smiled thinly. 'Nothing as drastic as that. I was thinking more about the latest avian flu alert.'

'What are you talking about? We have nothing to fear. That's just a media beat-up.'

'I beg to differ. I think you should announce that a pandemic is imminent, and that a national vaccination program will be carried out immediately.'

'I doubt that a campaign of distraction will work. The Opposition are too astute for that.'

'Politicians should be inoculated first,' declared Northfield. 'That will give us more time.'

'What does this have to do with my political future?' demanded the Prime Minister impatiently.

'Do you remember the request you made at our last meeting?'

'Remind me.'

'You wanted to be revered.'

The Prime Minister looked slightly sheepish. 'Oh, yes, that.'

Northfield smiled. 'We've done it. It wasn't as difficult as we first thought.'

'You've manufactured the artificial memory?' asked the Prime Minister eagerly as he desperately searched for a glimmer of hope.

'Yes sir, and it's been successfully tested. There are three people at Dartmoor who regard you as a deity.'

'Fancy that,' muttered the Prime Minister, his eyes gleaming. 'So where is this leading?'

'I think you already know. We've made enough trial batches to vaccinate the members of both houses, so any questions about your competency will soon disappear. After that, we can start mass production and can roll it out through the country. You'll be Prime Minister for life.'

'And that could be an eternity,' mused the Prime Minister. 'I'll notify the Minister for Health immediately. The public must be warned about this impending pandemic.' He suddenly chuckled.

'The French president is seeing me tomorrow to discuss our trade agreements. Do you think he would be agreeable to a free vaccination?'